P9-DGM-260

TELL ME NO LIES

ANNIE SOLOMON

WARNER
FOREVER

NEW YORK   BOSTON

If you purchase this book without a cover you should be aware that this book may have been stolen property and reported as "unsold and destroyed" to the publisher. In such case neither the author nor the publisher has received any payment for this "stripped book."

WARNER BOOKS EDITION

Copyright © 2004 by Wylann Solomon
Excerpt from *Blind Curve* © 2004 by Wylann Solomon

All rights reserved. No part of this book may be reproduced in any form or by any electronic or mechanical means, including information storage and retrieval systems, without permission in writing from the publisher, except by a reviewer who may quote brief passages in a review.

Cover design and art by Tom Tafuri
Hand lettering by David Gatti
Book design by Giorgetta Bell McRee

Warner Books

Time Warner Book Group
1271 Avenue of the Americas
New York, NY 10020
Visit our Web site at www.twbookmark.com.

Printed in the United States of America

First Paperback Printing: April 2004

10 9 8 7 6 5 4 3 2 1

To Mom, *who taught me to love books*,
and to Dad, who couldn't be prouder that I do.

Acknowledgments

Thanks to Nadya Geneizer for all her help with my many bizarre requests for Russian phrases and cultural hints. The book would have been far less rich without her.

For information on apple growing in the Hudson Valley, I'm indebted to David Fraleigh of Rose Hill Farm, who took time out of his busy schedule to talk with me, and to Erin Millus of Hardeman Orchards, who patiently answered all my questions.

I also owe a debt to Detective/Lieutenant William Siegrist, head of the Detective Division of the Poughkeepsie Police Department for giving me insight into homicide investigations in a small city. And to Special Agent Jason Locke of the Tennessee Bureau of Investigations for answering all the questions I put before him; and to Detective Patricia Hamblin of the Wilson County Sheriff's Department, whose encouragement and support—not to mention her willingness to share information—is once again greatly appreciated.

For points of legal process, I received help from Professor Susan Bandes, Professor Joshua Dressler, and attorney Austin Campriello.

To my editor Beth de Guzman and my agent Pam Ahearn, for helping to make all my books as good as possible.

Finally, I must once again say thanks to my wonderful writer pals—Jo Boehm, GayNelle Doll, Linda Kearney, Trish Milburn, and Beth Pattillo—who stuck with me and my words no matter how cranky I got. And to everyone at Music City Romance Writers. You guys are the best.

TELL ME NO LIES

1

The eyes of the dead held secrets. Detective Hank Bonner knew that just as he knew his job was to uncover them. He looked down at the body of Luka Kole.

What secrets did your eyes hold, old man?

Hank didn't want to find out. He had a little over a week left as a cop, and he wanted to spend the time writing reports, cleaning up old cases, and shutting down what had been a major part of his thirty-six years.

But two hours ago, Parnell, head of the Sokanan Police Department's detective division, had other ideas. "Dead body on Rossvelt." He'd handed Hank a scrawled address, the expression in his face daring Hank to object.

Hank knew what Parnell was doing. He could have given that DB to anyone. But he was using it to hook Hank, paying out the line, trying to reel him back with one last case.

Hank buried himself in a box of assorted memorabilia—a cracked coffee cup that had been a Christmas present years ago, a faded picture of himself just out of the academy, papers he still needed to sort through. "Let Klimet handle it."

"Klimet couldn't handle a cat stuck in a tree. Not yet anyway. I got your butt 'til the end of the month, Bonner. Get going."

So here Hank was, haunted by another pair of dead eyes.

He scanned the crime scene inside the Gas-Up on Rossvelt Avenue, the latest in a string of convenience store robberies that had plagued the Hudson Valley for the last month. Luka Kole, who owned the place, lay behind the counter, a squat, gray-haired man with a hole in his barrel chest. The open cash drawer stood empty, the overturned candy bin lay on its side. Lindt truffles wrapped in shiny blue, green, and red paper were strewn on the counter and floor, along with Slim Jims, cigarette lighters, and Van Dekker County souvenir pens.

The mess was a sure sign of struggle. Whoever he was, Luka Kole hadn't gone down easy.

The only thing detracting from the obvious was the bank bag. Hidden beneath the cash drawer, it contained over a thousand dollars, fat and ready for deposit. Why would the robber leave it behind?

"Because he's a mope, not a rocket scientist." Joe Klimet stared down at Luka Kole's sightless brown eyes as though he expected them to confirm his conclusion.

Hank studied the younger man. He wore a sharp black suit, silver-gray shirt, and patterned tie in yellow and gray. Slick and flashy with a grin to match. But Hank forgave him. Or tried to. He remembered what it was like to be cocky.

"So he leaves the money because he's stupid," Hank said.

Joe shrugged: why not?

Hank bent to get a closer look at the body. He'd already scouted the scene, starting with a careful walk around the outside perimeter and gradually moving closer to the victim, who was always the last thing he examined.

"Seems to me a guy who's managed to get away with four of these jobs right under our noses is no dummy."

Klimet frowned. The detective division's newest addition, he didn't like being challenged. "Something scared him off before he could check below the drawer."

Hank looked at him calmly, ignoring the irritation in the younger man's eyes. "What?"

"How the hell should I know? A customer, a car pulling in. Something."

"Maybe he wasn't after the money."

Klimet rolled his eyes. "You know, you're nuts, Bonner. The scene is clear—the cash drawer's empty. If the scumbag wasn't after money, what was he after?"

"Who knows? Revenge maybe. The clerk said Kole argued with someone earlier in the day." Hank flipped through a small notebook. "Adulous McTeer, also known as Big Mac. Maybe this Big Mac wanted the last word."

"Then why take anything?"

"To make it look like a robbery."

"It was a robbery." Klimet crossed his arms, not hiding his annoyance. "Just like all the others."

Hank was silent. "Looks like. But I want to talk to Mr. Big. We got someone rounding him up?"

"Already on it." Klimet ducked under the yellow crime scene tape to confer with the patrolman who'd been the first to arrive.

Hank called to Greenlaw, one of an elite cadre of patrol officers trained as crime scene technicians. "Still no brass?"

"No, sir," Greenlaw said.

No shell casings could mean a revolver. Or a smarter than average creep. "Keep looking."

Someone handed Hank the victim's wallet. Hands gloved, he examined it, hoping for something that would give him insight into Luka Kole. The clerk—who'd found the body after returning from his dinner break—hadn't been very helpful; Kole owned the store, but the clerk had worked there only a few weeks and didn't know much about his boss. The wallet didn't give away much either, except that Kole was no spendthrift. The case was old and thin, the outline of credit cards imprinted on the worn leather in front. The guy must have been sitting on the thing for years.

Inside, Hank found the usual: credit cards, driver's license, plus fifty dollars in cash the robber had been good enough to leave behind. Behind the bills he found a newspaper clipping, the headline half-torn but still readable: JOINT US RUSSIA ECONOMIC VENTURE BRINGS JOBS TO VAN DEKKER COUNTY.

Quickly, Hank scanned the print. Normal press release stuff. Quotes from Mikail "Miki" Petrov, the businessman who was bankrolling the Russian end of the deal, and from A. J. Baker, the American consultant who'd set the whole thing up. Mr. Petrov was a big shot in Manhattan and Washington, and not easily accessible. A. J. Baker, on the other hand, apparently lived right here in the Hudson Valley.

Hank replaced the clipping and slipped the wallet into an evidence bag. So, like everyone else in town, Luka Kole was looking forward to the deal with Renaissance Oil. But how many people carried around articles about it?

Hank ducked under the yellow tape. "Klimet." He handed the younger detective the bagged wallet. "Subpoena the phone records. Here and at the vic's apartment. Take Finelli with you to canvass the area. Maybe we'll get lucky and someone heard or saw something. And see if you can track down a home address. We got keys, but the driver's license is pegged to the store address. I'll see you back at the station."

"Where are you going?"

But Hank had already walked off and pretended he hadn't heard.

Outside, he ignored the small crowd milling around in uneasy formation at the edge of the parking lot. He understood their fascination and their horror. When murder hit close to home the two things melded together. It could have been me. Thank God it wasn't.

He got in his car, backed out, and called in to the station, waiting for the dispatcher to hunt down an address on Baker.

Then he turned down Route 9, Klimet's question circling inside his head. What had the shooter been after?

Dead man's secrets.

Ten minutes later, he turned off the highway and slowed down to peer into the wooded roadside for addresses. The house was somewhere along this road.

At least Luka Kole was dead. And dead men were a lot more predictable than live ones. They didn't turn crazy, eyes wild and maniacal. They didn't come at you with guns or knives or . . . A chill shivered through Hank. Or screwdrivers. Instinctively, he pressed a fist to his chest. Still there. Still beating.

As if he'd never felt that death blow and then, somehow, lived.

"That's one strong breastbone," the emergency room doctor had said. "Deflected the blade. A little to the left or right and we'd be saying prayers over you. Count yourself lucky."

Oh, he did. Damn lucky.

But the problem with luck was sooner or later it ran out.

A wave of sick certainty rippled over his skin. It welled up inside him as he found the address and turned the car into a long, gravel drive. Woods lined the road, thick, green, and impenetrable. His heart started that upward chase, his hands gripped the steering wheel. This was crazy. No one was hiding back there. No one waited for him with murderous intent.

He swallowed, forced the runaway train inside his chest to slow down. He was there to do his job. Gather information. Find out what he could about Luka Kole.

Concentrate on the dead man, he'd be fine.

When the house came into view it was easier to remember the drill. He braked, paused to gape. The place was a sculpture of glass, stone, and wood, but nearly overwhelmed by the natural forest overlooking the Hudson. Undergrowth tangled around it, thick as the briars surrounding Sleeping Beauty's castle in the book he read to his niece. A lair or a hideout, even a retreat. Hank sympathized. He understood the wish to submerge, to bury yourself. Did Mr. Baker? Or was he just too cheap to hire a crew to cut back the growth?

He pulled up to the house and noticed the tail end of a green van parked around the side. Out of the car, he walked around to investigate. Edie's Flowers, the van said. In front of it were two more vans. Caterers. A flurry of people swarmed in and out of the house.

Someone was throwing a party tonight. By the looks of it, a big one.

And then Hank remembered what day it was.

Alex Baker's reflection stared back at her from the large, gilt-framed mirror that hung above her dresser. She was all angles tonight, cheekbones like razor blades. Once, she might have cringed at the sharp edge in her eyes, but she was glad of it now. She felt well honed, a killing blade.

And if her stomach fluttered, she ignored it. If that queasy awareness that she was alone, and always would be, haunted her thoughts, she pushed it away.

Stuffed it deep down where it couldn't rise up and make her weak. Defenseless.

She concentrated on the way her silvery slip dress clung to her body, the way the barely there straps blended with and exposed her skin. Her body was a tool, a smoke screen. It would compel and distract, and slowly, slowly open the door of the trap she was setting.

And it all began tonight.

She checked her watch. Nearly seven. She had a good hour or more before guests arrived; plenty of time to get ready. And yet, here she was, dressed and perfumed, hair perfect, makeup perfect. Only one small detail to add. She caressed the blue velvet case on her dresser. Inside was the necklace her father had given her on her sixteenth birthday. She would wear it tonight, in honor of him.

She smiled at herself, a tight, deadly smile, and opened the case.

A knock sounded.

Her head swiveled in the direction of the sound. "Yes?"

The door opened to reveal Sonya, the shapeless brown dress over her short fat legs making her appear like a wrinkled mushroom. A worried mushroom, if her expression was any indication. Immediately, Alex crossed to the old woman and drew her into the room. She'd been fretful all day, not used to strangers in the house.

"Why aren't you in your room?" Alex spoke softly. "Let me bring you a plate of goodies. We're having blinis tonight. With caviar and sour cream. You love that. It's been a long time since you had real blinis."

Sonya shook her head. "Too much . . . noise," she said. "And now—" Her hands twisted together and a word burst out from her. A word in Russian. Police.

Alex stilled. "What are you talking about?"

Sonya emitted another torrent of Russian and instinctively Alex put a hand over the older woman's mouth, looking around as though the room held spies. "English, dear one. English. Slow down. Tell me."

The old woman bit her lip. Tears formed in her eyes. "Sorry, so very sorry." But the words came out in Russian. "He frightened me so."

"All right," Alex soothed. "Take a breath. Here." She went into her bathroom and filled a cup with water. "Drink this."

Sonya drank and handed back the cup with trembling hands.

"Now tell me, what is this about the police?"

"They are here."

"Where—at the house?" Alex smiled. "Of course they are. We have a security detail."

Sonya shook her head. *"Nyet.* Not . . . party. To talk. Questions. He said, questions."

A small alarm went off inside Alex, but she quickly silenced it. Sonya's English had never been very good; she often got things mixed up. "It's all right, darling. I'm sure it's nothing." She settled the woman into a large upholstered armchair. "Stay here and rest. I'll be right back. And don't worry."

Swiftly, Alex closed the door and made her way toward the front of the house. Preparations for the party were rapidly coming to a close. The house sparkled with lights and flowers. Silver trays and goblets, crystal bowls for candies and tidbits. As the sun set, fairy lights outside would turn the woods and garden into a magic kingdom seen through glass. A kingdom aglow with the rich, silky flush of oil. Russian oil.

She stopped just short of the entrance, where two workers from the florists were putting the finishing touches on the man-sized centerpiece—a wire structure in the shape of an oil rig and entirely covered in thick golden mums.

"Quite an eye-catcher," said a deep male voice. The owner of the voice stepped from behind the structure and gave her a crooked smile. A big man with wide shoulders under a rumpled sport coat, he had fair hair and sun-kissed skin. A surfer stranded on land. A man out of place somehow. She met his eyes. Nothing out of place here. They were green. Sharp. Evaluating. Was this what had frightened Sonya?

His greeting replayed itself in her mind; had he been referring to something other than the decorations? To her?

She stiffened, a wall of ice rising like a protective shell around her. "May I help you?"

He flashed a badge. "Detective Bonner from Sokanan PD. I'm looking for A. J. Baker."

"I'm A. J. Baker."

His eyes widened, giving her a moment of satisfaction. She liked surprising people.

"You're . . . " A jolt shook Hank. The shimmer of femininity in front of him looked no more capable of putting together an international business deal than he was. But perception wasn't always reality, as he knew only too well.

Quickly, he reassessed. Her ice blond hair glistened and fell to her shoulders in a straight, silky waterfall, a perfect foil to the silvery dress, which swirled around her curves like mercury. Not beautiful in the classic sense, but in an outrageously exotic way, with high, angled cheekbones, and eyes the color of sky before it rained. A pulse quickened inside him, and he saw the look of recognition come over her. The look that said, I know what you're thinking pal, and forget it.

Yeah, he'd bet she did know. He'd bet A. J. Baker was used to men drooling over her. And he wasn't going to get in line. Ignoring his purely chemical reaction, he let out a breath to cover his initial surprise. "So what does the A. J. stand for?"

"Alexandra Jane. Alex."

He noted the drawn-out *a*. Alexaaandra. Some kind of British thing. Or New England. Boston maybe.

"As you can see," she said, "we're preparing for a big event tonight. Is this about the security detail? I hope there's no problem." She gave him an impersonal smile, and he saw hardness congeal behind those cloudy eyes. Not a streetwise toughness, but the cool confidence that only money and years of private schools could instill.

"Security detail? You mean for the big wingding half the department will be at? No, it's not about the security."

"Detective, I'm busy. How can I help you?"

Polite but impatient. Eager to get rid of him. Because he was a cop, or something else? He glanced at the team of floral workers. On ladders and on the ground they hovered over the huge structure that probably cost more than his car. "Is there some place we can talk privately?"

"What is this about?"

Again, he glanced at the workers, and she let out a small sigh of irritation. "This way."

She led him through the glass terrace doors and into a garden courtyard. The forest was even thicker here. Trees huddled over the house, enclosing it in a suffocating embrace as though hiding it from the rest of the world.

He nodded toward them. "I can recommend a gardener."

She looked in the direction he'd pointed, eyes narrowed in puzzlement. Then, as though she saw what he'd seen, "I like a lot of foliage."

Short, crisp, and by the aloofness in her voice, all the explanation he was going to get.

"I don't mean to be rude, but I'm expecting a lot of people. What can I do for you?"

He leaned against the edge of the garden wall, a low brick structure that framed the patio. The air smelled earthy and green and reminded him of the orchards of Apple House, the Bonner farm. But that memory brought up others, leading always to two orphaned children and his own part in their fate. A bleakness descended, and he had to force himself to focus on the woman in front of him.

"I'm looking for information about a guy called Luka Kole. Ever heard of him?"

Her expression shifted, but quickly as the change came, her features composed themselves into disinterested lines. "Lu—Luka who?"

"Kole. Luka Kole. Know him?"

Did her shoulders tense? She frowned, looked down and then over at the woods beyond the garden as though trying to remember. "The name isn't familiar. Why? Who is he? Has he done something?"

Hank watched her closely. "Got himself killed today."

Her head snapped around. "Killed? You mean in an accident? Look, Detective, tonight is a very important—"

"Definitely not an accident. He was shot."

"I see." She sank into one of the wrought-iron chairs. Her silver dress shivered against the black metal, and the neckline drooped to reveal a dip of cleavage. "And what does that have to do with me?"

Hank tore his eyes away from her breasts. "I don't know." He cleared his throat. "Probably nothing. It was a long shot. We found an article about your Russian business deal in his wallet. Thought I'd see if there was any connection."

She smiled, a dismissive, lady-of-the-manor curve of her lips, but something else lurked behind it. What? "As I don't know him, I can assure you there isn't." She rose. "I'm sorry I can't help you. And I am busy." She indicated the door back into the house and escorted him inside. "Will we see you tonight?"

He shook his head, dreading the evening ahead. "Got a previous engagement."

"Well, enjoy your evening."

Alex saw him out, closed the door behind her, then wilted against it, her legs suddenly gone.

Luka. My God.

One of the floral workers noticed her. "Are you all right, Miss Baker?" He started toward her, and she drew a steadying breath. She could not draw attention to herself. Not now. Not when she was on the brink of everything she'd worked so hard for.

She straightened, brushing her dress as if nothing had happened. "It's all right. I'm fine. I haven't had much to eat today. Too much excitement."

The man nodded understanding, and Alex thanked him, then swept past, shoulders back, head high, though it cost her.

Get to the phone. She must get to the phone.

She was halfway to her room when she remembered Sonya. Oh, God, she couldn't face the old woman now. Not with this catastrophe. But she couldn't avoid all contact with her either. Sonya would only worry.

Retracing her steps, Alex forced her pace into a casual stroll and walked into the sunroom, where a white-coated bartender was setting up a portable bar.

Take a breath. Smile.

She introduced herself. "Opening night jitters," she confided. "I don't suppose you could spare a little vodka."

The bartender laughed. "We've got so much Stoli we could swim in it. There's plenty to spare." He found a bottle and upturned a glass. "Ice?"

She shook her head. "Never."

He handed her the drink and she thanked him, but didn't take a sip. *Luka, what happened?* She carried the glass into the kitchen, where the rich fragrance of Stroganoff nearly turned her stomach. A platoon of cooks and servers made the place look like a staging area for a major battle. They stirred pots, checked ovens, and plated canapés. Several were setting silver and glassware on huge trays to take to the buffet area. She filched a plate and spooned some of the thick beef-and-cream concoction on it, added blinis and Russian black caviar, herring salad, and mushrooms in sour cream. Two finger-shaped *saikas* with jam for dessert, then up the small flight of stairs at the back of the house.

Luka. Luka. The name echoed with every step.

Outside her bedroom door, she closed her eyes and breathed. In and out. Steady. Sure. She could do this. She'd been hiding her feelings for years.

With a smile on her face, she pushed the door open and strode into the room.

Sonya dozed in the chair, her chin sunk to her wide, fleshy chest. Alex laid the food and the vodka on the small table next to the chair, knelt, and shook Sonya gently. "Dearest, look what I've brought you."

Sonya woke slowly, gasped when she saw Alex, and gripped her hand, the hold shaky with fright. "Everything is all right?"

"Yes, it's fine. Didn't I tell you it would be? The policeman was only here to double-check the security arrangement."

Sonya brought a hand to her chest. "Oh, so glad. I thought—"

Alex stroked the old woman's white head. "I know, I know. But there is nothing to worry about."

Tears formed in the older woman's eyes and she stroked a gnarled hand down Alex's cheek. "Sashenka, you are such a good girl." She spoke in Russian. "God watch over you."

Alex squeezed Sonya's hand. She didn't have the heart to argue with her about speaking Russian again. And she didn't know about God, but if anyone was watching over them it would be Alex herself. "Do you want to stay here for a while?"

The old woman shook her head and rose with a grunt. "I go to my room."

Carrying the plate and the vodka, Alex followed the older woman down the spacious hall and settled her into an upholstered rocker. She handed her the food and the drink and kissed the top of her head. "I'll see you in the morning."

"*Spokoynoy nochi, rodnaya moya.*" Good night, dear girl. For once, Alex replied in kind. "*Spokoynoy nochi.*"

Then she raced back to her room, closed the door, and scrambled in her purse for her cell phone. Glancing wildly around, she saw the broad windows that usually gave her such comfort with their view of the solid, protective tree line. Now, the windows seemed to unmask and expose her, and though it was irrational, she dashed into the bathroom, closed the door and the curtain over the window. Huddled on the toilet, she punched in a series of numbers with shaky fingers.

Luka. What did you do? What did they do to you?

A man's voice came on the line. Alex opened her mouth

to speak, then realized the voice was recorded. A message. The man wasn't there. A wail sounded deep in her head.

What should she do?

Outside, someone knocked on the bedroom door. *Not now, please, not now.* Alex checked her watch. Past seven. No time to think. Too dangerous to leave a message. She ended the call and bolted from her hiding place to open the door.

A woman in a black maid's uniform stood there. "Your guests are beginning to arrive."

Alex nodded. "Thank you."

The maid left, and Alex closed the door. It was time. Luka Kholodov was dead, and if she wasn't careful, she could join him.

But first, she would clear her father's name. And have her revenge.

Grimly, she marched to the dresser, where she'd left the jewelry box open. A brightly colored necklace sparkled up at her from its blue velvet nest. She lifted it and fingered the tiny cloisonné locket. Designed in the round shape of a jolly peasant woman, it was a matryoshka, a replica in silver and jewel tones of the wooden nesting dolls so famous in Russian folk art. This one had been designed to hold two even tinier women, one inside the other. Three smiling sisters, her father had said as he'd placed the necklace around her.

She closed her eyes briefly, remembering, and tried not to let the sadness clog her throat.

She sealed the clasp around her, and if her hands shook, she pretended otherwise. Just as she pretended that the happy colors of the little sister shimmering against her skin meant everything would be all right.

Without warning tears prickled, and for an instant she felt

lost, brittle with loneliness. It was all up to her now. Her alone.

Quickly, she forced the tears back before she ruined her makeup. She couldn't show up downstairs with red, swollen eyes.

She sat deadly still until she'd regained control. Then rising, shoulders back, she glided to the door. Lightly, she brushed the locket.

For you, Papa. You and Luka. For you both.

Then she swept into the hallway and made her way toward her guests.

2

Hank pulled out of the Baker drive, turned left and followed the road to Route 9 and home. Not to his own home, the house he'd bought in downtown Sokanan, but to Apple House, the Bonner farm. He'd promised himself a few rounds of basketball with his twelve-year-old nephew, Trey. A sop, Hank knew, but one in an ongoing campaign for forgiveness—from himself as well as the boy. A campaign they both knew wasn't going well.

Trey's face rose in Hank's mind, the angry set to the mouth, the sullen look in the eyes—and, as always, that sinking feeling settled in the pit of Hank's stomach. Better to think about Alexandra Jane Baker.

Not that she would be any easier to handle. The world she inhabited—of wealth and connection—was a world away from Hank's tiny neck of the woods. Odd that they should collide today of all days, on the eve of the party that was supposed to kick off a better future for his hometown and the surrounding county.

The highway took him past the gated entrance to the old General Electric plant. A fenced-in ghost town, the place was gloomy and deserted and had been for years. A. J. Baker's deal with the Russians could change all that.

A lot was riding on the shindig tonight. Is that what was going on behind Alexandra Jane's cool gray eyes? Was she annoyed or upset that he'd brought murder into the picture on her big night?

He turned on to Route 30, the familiar road that had once been the only throughway in Van Dekker County. Now there were any number of choices to zip you through, the Taconic, two Interstates. But the two-lane highway was tree-lined and quiet, an oasis in a desert of concrete overpasses and car exhaust. When he and his sister Maureen were kids, they used to go on long walks down the highway, him tugging his little sister behind and protecting her from the cars.

Lot of good it did.

He focused on the road, staring hard at the stripe separating the two lanes.

Fifteen minutes later, the Apple House Farm sign appeared around a bend. Hank pulled into the winding orchard drive, passing the roadside farm stand and gift shop, which were closed for the day. He could have taken the route that led directly to the house, but that would have meant passing the white clapboard cape cod that Maureen and her husband Tom Stiller used to own. A quarter mile away from the farmhouse, it had been built by his parents as a wedding present. Hank still couldn't drive by without remorse shifting inside him like sand.

Besides, he liked the orchard road for its own sake. It cut through acres of ancient apple trees, all planted by generations of Bonners. It was too dim to see clearly, but he knew the trees were blossoming. He rolled down the window and inhaled the sweet fragrance. A stab of something went through him, pride or ownership, or maybe just belonging. All undercut by an uneasy shimmer. Maureen had inherited the Bonner green thumb, but now carrying on the tradition would be up to him. He pushed the thought away. Ten more days until he had to face that.

Pulling up to the house, he saw Trey in his usual place—outside dribbling and shooting by the glow of the light over the garage. The boy looked up as Hank's car approached, his long narrow face so like the face in all of Hank's nightmares. Thank God the hair was Bonner blond and the eyes his mother's cornflower blue.

Hank got out of the car and held his hands chest high for Trey to pass the ball. Today was the first day in two weeks that he hadn't received a call from Trey's principal about the boy's behavior. "How about a game of Horse?"

Instead of throwing the ball, Trey dribbled and shot. The ball hit the rim and bounced off. "No thanks."

Trey went after the ball, but Hank got there first. "Afraid I'll beat you?"

A thin smile crossed his nephew's face. "Afraid you'll think it's another 'bonding' opportunity." The adult phrase sounded funny coming out of the kid's mouth, and Hank might have laughed except he knew Trey wouldn't appreciate it.

And as if Hank needed further persuasion, Trey said, "I like my game question-free."

Hank nodded. "Fair enough. No questions. Just dribble and shoot."

Trey sighed and shrugged. "Whatever."

Hank passed the ball back to Trey, then took off his sport coat and tossed it onto the car's hood. He loosened his tie. Trey eyed him, one leg thrust forward in a surly stance. Bony legs stuck out of the oversized basketball shorts, and the arms holding the ball were long and thin, with knobby elbows and shoulders that hadn't filled out yet. Christ, the kid was skinny.

"Did you have dinner?"

A grimace flashed across Trey's face. "You can't stop even for thirty seconds, can you?"

"Stop what?"

"Being a cop. Interrogating people. Yeah, I had dinner." With a brutal jerk, he slammed the ball in Hank's direction, pivoted, and walked away.

Hank sighed; he never seemed to get it right with Trey. Christ, he remembered *giving* Trey that basketball two years ago. The kid had been so excited, not even birthday cake had kept him from running outside to try it out.

The memory came back, sharp and painful. How they'd all watched through the window, and how Mo had joked bitterly. "I have two men—an alcoholic and a balloholic."

Hank had put an arm around her shoulders and given her a squeeze.

Gone. All gone now.

He looked toward the house. Trey had disappeared inside. Well, at least the kid was eating again. Unlike the first few weeks, when he'd barely touched a thing.

Hank swerved his thoughts away from that time, and from that awful day that had defined all their lives since, as though it were a great chasm with before on one side and after on the other. Automatically, his hand went to his chest again. His heart was still there, strong and healthy.

He found his mother in the kitchen, wearing an apron with Apple House Farms stenciled on it. Her shoulder-length hair, once honey brown but now dulled and stippled with gray, was caught by a rubber band in the no-nonsense ponytail she usually wore around the farm. The girlish style, which hadn't changed since he was a boy, emphasized the strong planes of her face, scraped clean of makeup and artifice.

She smiled when she saw him, but the lines around her mouth were deep, and her eyes looked tired.

"Saw you out there with the boy. Good of you to pay him attention. He needs it."

Hank kissed her cheek, warmed by her support even if it was misplaced. "Try telling him that."

She clucked her tongue. "He's angry and confused. He wants to blame someone, and you're it. Doesn't mean it's your fault, Henry."

Doesn't mean it wasn't either. "Boy's got no parents. Somebody's got to take the blame for that." He grabbed a piece of tomato from the leftover salad sitting in a bowl on the counter. It tasted like sawdust.

"Tom Stiller's to blame for that, and you know it."

Hank blew out a breath. His chest felt as though it were filled with lead. "Look, can we talk about something else?"

"Sure. How about your decision to quit your job and become a farmer?"

Jesus. "How about warming up some of whatever you made for dinner while I change? I'm starving."

He headed down the hallway toward his room. His mother's voice followed him. "You just want a free meal ticket, Henry Bonner."

He grinned. Rose Bonner always did know how to break the tension. And God, she was so good at letting him off the hook.

Truth was, unloading his job would probably be a relief. Who in his right mind wanted to be a cop anyway? All that stress, the crazy hours, the things you see.

The things you do.

He cut down the hallway and peeked into what his grandmother had called the back parlor. Nine-year-old Amanda was exactly where she usually was, in front of the television. "Hey, Uncle Hank." She had Tom Stiller's dark hair and eyes, but they were alleviated enough by the square-jawed Bonner face that somehow she never reminded him of Tom.

"Hey, Mandy." He stopped to rub her head. "How was school today?"

"Okay." She fixed on the flickering pictures on the tube in front of her. "We made a lanyard." From a pocket, she fished out a two-inch piece of leatherette braid. "Want it? You can put your keys on it."

Hank's heart squeezed. "Sure. That'd be great. I needed a new key chain. How'd you know?"

She grinned at him. "I'm psychic."

"Oh. Well, that explains it."

"Uh-huh."

"Well, thanks."

She went back to watching her show, a sitcom about twin sisters where everyone loved everyone and all problems came complete with happy endings.

He backed out and proceeded up the stairs to his room, knowing Mandy's was far from assured. But he'd do what he could to mend the hole he'd made in the lives of his sister's two kids. Leaving the force was the first step.

He'd been divorced for far longer than he'd been married, so there was no wife to pick up the slack when call-outs came at two in the morning or when he couldn't make it home for days at a time. Now that Tom and Maureen were gone, his mother's load at the farm was three times what it used to be. Oh, she'd jump in, no questions asked, but he saw the weariness etched into her face. He couldn't ask her to take on more.

That left him to do the parent-teacher meetings, pick up the kids, go to basketball games. School would be over in a month, then the long, slow summer stretched in front of them. Amanda would go to camp, but Trey . . . Hank didn't know what he was going to do about Trey. For the thousandth time, regret seared him. He and Trey used to be such good friends.

Inside his room, he flipped on the portable TV he'd brought over last week along with half his clothes. The room made him feel awkward, a giant in a place built for a dwarf. His mother had never gotten around to throwing away his trophies, so they still stood on a shelf, all his high school achievements displayed as though they were the pinnacle of his success.

Maybe they were. Maybe he should have done what his father had always wanted. Stayed here, grown apples, run the fruit stand. If he'd done that, maybe things would have turned out differently for everyone.

His hand shook as he pulled off the tie and unbuttoned the white shirt. The local newscaster was foaming at the mouth about the Renaissance Oil party that night, and Hank turned up the volume, glad for the distraction. Looked like Alexandra Jane was throwing quite a bash. The governor was expected, and some State Department hack from DC was supposed to be there, too. A picture of the Renaissance Oil logo, a huge "R" with a long, sweeping descender, filled the screen, then Sokanan mayor Benton Bonner was talking.

"This is an exciting moment for our city and for the world." Hank's older brother had that officious look on his face, as if he himself had made the deal with Miki Petrov. "Economic cooperation is the way to peace among nations. Sokanan is proud to be part of this historic agreement between the United States and Russia."

Proud was an understatement. Sokanan was desperate. After GE closed its plant, the town began a long, slow downward spiral. The Russian deal would bring the boom back. Petrov had bought the plant and was retrofitting it to become the new headquarters of Renaissance Oil. It would provide distribution, administration, marketing, and sales for what everyone hoped would become a global company.

His brother the mayor included.

He turned the sound down as a live shot of the Baker home replaced his brother's overeager face. Limousines had begun to arrive. Hank saw Joe Klimet in the background, checking invitations. Two guys from patrol were standing at attention on the sidelines, faces sober, gazes moving over the incoming throng dressed in suits, sequins, and silk.

What was Alexandra Jane Baker doing at this moment? Something about that woman wasn't right.

Then she was there in the picture, leading a local news crew through the house. She wasn't wearing that body-hugging sliver of a dress, so he gathered this had been taped earlier.

Sound off, he watched her in pantomime. Her high cheekbones and wide, generous mouth looked good on TV, but there was something cold about her. Something stiff and held back. As though she were hiding the most important part.

His eyes narrowed. Secrets were something he knew all about. What secrets was Alexandra Jane hiding?

And did they have anything to do with Luka Kole?

The camera panned a room, some kind of den, even though it seemed big enough to fit two of his bedrooms into it.

He blinked, peered closely into the TV, but whatever he'd seen was gone, and the broadcast returned to the live shot of the Baker house and arriving guests.

His stomach growled, and he thought longingly of the

supper Rose was warming in the kitchen. Maybe he hadn't seen anything. Maybe he'd imagined it.

Silently he cursed Parnell for suckering him in with this case, opened the closet, and found a clean shirt and another tie. Dinner would have to wait.

Whether she liked it or not, A. J. Baker was about to see him again.

Mikail Petrov turned off the television in the back of the limo. The little report on tonight's opening event had been carried by ABC's national newscast, which pleased him. Soon the whole country would be buying his Renaissance Oil.

"Big night tonight, Mr. Petrov." Jeffrey Greer, the assistant to the assistant undersecretary for Economic Affairs at the State Department gave him an ingratiating smile.

"Oh, yes," Miki Petrov said. "Big night for everyone." He settled back against the leather seat, satisfied that everything was off to a good start. Not bad for a kid from the Moscow ghetto.

But he had always been smart, always done what had to be done, no looking back. And now that he'd taken care of every loose end, he could relax. Nothing stood in his way. After all, money talked in the new Russia, and the man who brought Russian oil to America would have a lot to say. People would listen. Rich, influential people. In the end, he'd have what he'd always wanted. Power.

Perhaps he'd share it with the beautiful Miss Baker.

He looked down at the heavy lump of gold on the little finger of his right hand. Three full-ounce Krugerrands had been melted down into a ring that was so big it swallowed his knuckle. He smiled, admiring the shine and the sheer size of it.

"We set up a photo op with the governor," Greer said, flipping through a notebook. He was a young man, eager to please, with dark hair slicked close to his head and the blue suit and striped tie that comprised the perfectly correct uniform. He was the kind of man Miki knew how to break in fifteen minutes. The kind with too much at stake, career, reputation, who had never suffered, never been tempered in the heat of adversity. These things made him weak and malleable. And useful.

Miki watched in silent amusement as Greer adjusted his black-rimmed glasses, a frequent gesture. "And the mayor, that Bonner guy, has been a pain in the ass about pictures. So you'll probably have to do a meet and greet with him, too."

Miki shrugged, not caring. He liked having his picture taken. He was an important man, after all. "Fine. Whatever is necessary."

"Good. I've worked out the schedule with A. J., and you should still have time to enjoy yourself."

He intended to, and Miss Baker was high on his list of pleasures. She appealed to him, as did the promise in her eyes. Something he could guess but couldn't quite name, like fire blazing beneath frost.

She was young enough to be his daughter if he'd had one, but she had a maturity, a hardness he found intriguing. No doubt she felt the same. He'd never had trouble with women. Almost sixty, he prided himself on looking fifteen years younger. Trim and fit, he had style. *People* Magazine had named him one of their top fifty bachelors two years in a row.

He twisted the Krugerrand ring, enjoying the weight of it on his hand. Tonight he would press Alex. He would see if that cool, knowing look in her eyes was just an empty promise. She would be ready, excited from the success of her event, flush with vodka, exhausted after the strain of playing hostess.

And he would see that she relaxed.

He smiled, completely satisfied. Oh, yes, he'd see to it.

3

When Hank arrived, Sokanan's WBRN studio was in a lull between the six and ten o'clock news broadcasts. He introduced himself to the guard at the reception desk, was escorted into the work area by a producer, and eventually handed off to an intern, who made him a copy of the Baker house tour, including all the B roll—the pickup shots of backgrounds and extras that might or might not have ended up in the final piece aired that night.

In a small viewing room Hank went through the tapes, starting with the edited broadcast. He quickly found the section that had caught his eye: A. J. Baker in front of a floor-to-ceiling bookcase crammed with books, curios, and pictures. Behind her sat a framed photo of a man and a girl. Something about the man had seemed familiar, but even when Hank slowed the tape to stop-frame speed, he couldn't be sure if it was Luka Kole. He ran through the rest of the footage but found nothing else of this particular scene. Imagining things? Probably.

Only one way to find out.

Half an hour later, he swung into the drive leading to the Baker home. Peter Newcomb was at the entrance, stopping vehicles and checking them in. He signaled for Hank to roll down his window.

"Didn't know you were working this gig, Bonner. You're not on the list." Newcomb held up his clipboard. A thirty-year veteran, he was nearing retirement, a balding, big-bellied stereotype. All he needed was a donut.

Hank shrugged. "I'm working a case."

"Here? Tonight? Are you crazy?"

Hank didn't feel like explaining. "Thanks for the vote of confidence, Pete." He headed toward the house, Pete's shout of protest lost in the sound of the car engine.

He had a brief argument with the parking valet, who insisted Hank hand over his keys, but his badge quickly put an end to that. Hank parked his car where he could get to it easily and strolled into the house.

Joe Klimet met him inside the door. "What are you doing here, Bonner?" He eyed Hank suspiciously, and Hank thought briefly about lying. But he'd have to fill out a report, and Klimet would find out anyway.

"Chasing down a lead."

Klimet's eyes narrowed. "What lead?"

Hank bit down on a rush of annoyance. "Tell you if it pans out."

Hank tried to pass, but Klimet blocked his way. "You make trouble here tonight, you'll have the whole town on your ass."

"That a threat, Joe?"

"It's a goddamn promise"—Klimet flashed his adolescent grin—"Hank." He pivoted to let Hank pass. "Don't go screwing this up for everyone," he called to Hank's back. "This town needs a boost."

Christ, if he had a nickel for every time he'd heard that in the last month, he, too, could afford the flower-covered oil rig dominating Alexandra Jane's entrance. Renaissance Oil was a gilt-wrapped gift waiting to be opened by everyone in Sokanan. He just hoped that when they did, the package didn't explode in their faces.

He navigated around the sculpture and plunged into the crowd. Waiters in hard hats and yellow jumpsuits embroidered with the blue Renaissance Oil *R* passed trays of food and drink. Hank snagged a couple of stuffed mushrooms and chomped them down while he oriented himself.

The garden she'd shown him earlier was to the right. Maybe the den was on the left. He strolled in that direction. The house was crowded; he heard snatches of what sounded like French and Russian in addition to plain old-fashioned English. He found a large living room with a photographer set up in the corner. The governor was there, shaking hands, surrounded by several aides in conservative suits. And in the midst of it all stood the mysterious A. J. Baker.

Hank paused to watch her, compelled by something he couldn't name—a shimmer of hair, the curve of a shoulder. He'd always had a soft spot for self-assured women, from his mother on down. Even his wife, who'd been so self-assured she'd ultimately discovered no need for him, was someone he remembered with fondness, if not regret. Alexandra Jane seemed stamped from a similar mold, but right now more sensual, her head bent to hear something the governor said, then thrown back in a laugh, the light gleaming off her silvery dress.

A tall, thin man stood on the other side of her. He wore a smooth black jacket and a black turtleneck that draped his slender torso like silk. The effect was high fashion, not informal, the trendy look completed by a thick head of long, silver-gray hair dramatically swept back from his forehead, the light hair a contrast to heavy black brows. In another situation, Hank might have pegged him as an artist—or a thug trying to look like one—but Hank knew who he was from the long media coverage of Renaissance Oil. Miki Petrov. One arm wrapped around Miss Baker's shoulders.

She looked up at Petrov, the angle calculated to set off her face to its best advantage. Hank saw Petrov fall for it.

Interesting. Something going on there, below the surface. Were they lovers?

They made a dramatic picture, Petrov's darkness against her frosty glimmer. Dramatic but unsettling since Petrov was old enough to be her father.

Not that Miss Baker's sex life was any of his business.

Without warning, she glanced toward him, and he ducked behind a wall. He wasn't eager to reveal his presence, especially after telling her he wouldn't be there tonight. Besides, he hadn't come to see her, not really. He'd come to check out that photo.

He scanned the layout, picked a direction, and saw the mayor of Sokanan approaching. Damn.

"Hank!"

Too late to run, too late to hide.

Benton Bonner dashed up, his crisp navy suit, ocean blue shirt, and red tie the perfect political costume. And from the look on his face, he was as surprised to see Hank as everyone else.

"Hey, Ben."

Ben frowned. "What are you up to? Mom said you weren't working the party. What's going on?"

Hank repressed the flash of irritation his older brother always seemed to arouse. "Nothing."

"Then why aren't you home with Mom and the kids?"

The irritation deepened. "Last time I looked, I didn't have to answer to you, mayor or no."

Ben's face reddened, and a tiny bolt of guilt jabbed Hank. No matter how annoying Ben got, he'd never pulled rank.

"I just meant—"

"I know what you meant."

Ben drew in a sharp breath. "Look, can't we even say hello anymore?"

Hank shrugged. "Doesn't look like it."

"You know, if Mom sold the farm, she and the kids could move into a normal house, a place she could take care of. Then you wouldn't have to—"

"She's not selling, and you damn well know it." Hank gritted his teeth, knowing the argument chapter and verse. "That place has been in Dad's family for two hundred years."

"Well, Dad is gone, and two centuries is long enough. Look, she can't make it anymore. You know it, I know it. There's cutthroat competition on the wholesale level and cheap imports flooding the market. What our workers earn in an hour is a week's salary to the Chinese. No one can match their price. And you can't make a living selling apples to tourists."

"Ben—" He clamped down on angry words and, shaking his head, tried to walk away. But Ben grabbed his arm, swinging him into a corner.

"If you'd just let me show you the figures. Land around here is going to boom in light of this oil deal. I've already talked to several developers. She'll never get a better price. Hank, it will be a small fortune. More than enough to set her up carefree for the rest of her life."

"I don't have time for this, Ben."

As usual, Ben was oblivious to anything but his own agenda. "Make time. Talk to her. She listens to you."

"Only because she knows I'm a disinterested party."

"What is that supposed to mean? Are you implying I have some sort of backdoor deal in the works?" Fury flashed in Ben's eyes. "This has nothing to do with me. It's for her, for the kids, even for you, dammit."

"Right. And as mayor, development has always been your top priority, not widows and orphans."

Ben's voice tightened with anger. "You think I'm going to get some kind of political windfall from selling Apple House?"

"You always said you wanted to go to Washington."

Ben looked as if he'd been slugged, and Hank started to retract what he'd said—Christ he had a big, stupid mouth, and Ben brought out the worst in him—but his brother leaned in, his voice low and full of venom. "And you always said you weren't a quitter."

Hank felt the blood drain from his face. "We're not talking about me."

"Oh, yes we are. Quitting your job, your life. Taking the safe road and crawling back to Momma."

Shame grabbed Hank's gut and twisted into rage. "You don't know what the hell you're talking about."

"I'm talking about you, little brother. And the way Tom Stiller left you one of the walking dead. Christ, he might as well have killed you, too."

The words struck deeper than Hank cared to admit, and to deflect their truth he balled his hands into fists. But before he could use them, a commotion went off over his shoulder. Raised voices. Shouts.

Drunken shouts.

In an instant Hank was back outside his brother-in-law's toolshed, the afternoon sun beating down on him like a search light. His sister and her husband were barricaded inside, and he could hear Tom's out-of-control drunken raving as he smashed anything he could lay his hands on.

In the next instant Hank was back at the party. It was evening. Smoke and talk swirled around him and he found himself moving toward the sound of the argument.

Alex turned in horror as the angry sounds of dispute reached her.

"Russia is the greatest country on the earth!" a male voice insisted loudly in Russian, the words an angry slur. "Always we will be the greatest country. We don' need America's help." She turned to see one of Miki's entourage red-faced with fury and leaning drunkenly into the governor's aide. "Fucking asshole," he said clearly in English.

Alex scanned the crowd. Heads were turning, reporters and photographers swiveling to see who was making a scene. The drunk raised his fists and a flush of horror raced through her as headlines appeared in her imagination.

"Mikail," she said sharply to her companion. "Who is that?"

"Yuri," Miki growled, then muttered a curse in Russian.

"Get rid of him."

He looked around, as though searching for someone else to handle the situation. "I can't get involved. Not in front of the media."

His gaze caught Jeff Greer's, the State Department's liaison, who scuttled over to Yuri and put a calming hand on his shoulder. The drunk jerked the arm away, then bent over Greer in such a threatening way that the smaller man almost tipped backward.

Damn him. She dropped Miki's arm and hurried toward the commotion, hoping to pacify the man herself, but she'd gone only a few steps when someone else appeared next to the drunk.

The cop from earlier in the day, the one who'd told her about Luka. He'd said he wasn't on the security detail; what was he doing back here?

As if watching a scene play out on a movie screen, she saw the policeman—what was his name?—lean over and say something to Yuri. Yuri turned his attention to the cop, staggering as he shifted position. With a snarl, he said something she couldn't hear, and the cop—Bonner, that was it, Detective Bonner—put a hand on Yuri's neck.

And like that, Yuri was cowed. Cooperative. His hand still in place, Detective Bonner led Yuri through the crowd and out the door. The whole thing was over in seconds. Reporters returned to interviewing the governor, waiters resumed serving guests. The party was back on track, disaster averted.

She swallowed and glanced back at Petrov. He was already occupied by someone else—a fawning reporter from *Business World* magazine. He wouldn't miss her. And she needed a break from his obsessive clutching. She felt sticky from his touch; he'd barely let her out of his sight all evening.

This morning, she would have been delighted by his persistence, but now, after she'd heard about Luka, her plans had changed. She had hoped to go back to Manhattan with Petrov. Her invasion of his business was going well, but the assault on his home, his life, and especially his computers still needed to be done. But now she would have to put him off. *Luka, Luka. What happened?*

She wove her way to the front door and met Detective Bonner as he was coming back in. Her instincts on high alert, she fought to keep the anxiety off her face. Why was he here? "What did you do to Yuri?"

"Pressure points." He pointed them out on his neck. "Works every time. I left him sleeping it off in one of the limos." He seemed calm enough, though a faint sheen of sweat filmed his forehead.

"That was very discreet. Thank you." He nodded and gave her a measuring look that sent a flush of heat through her.

A wash of resentment quickly followed. She had no time for distractions, especially when they came packaged in good-looking cops with ridiculously wide shoulders, compelling faces, and sharp green eyes. "You said you weren't going to be here tonight. You had plans."

"Yeah, well I changed them."

"Why?" A beat of fear. Was it something to do with Luka?

But the detective didn't say a word about Luka. Instead, a lazy grin crossed his face. "You're not going to make me say it, are you?"

"Say what?"

"Why I changed my plans."

She studied him. She didn't like playing games, not unless she could control them. "I'm afraid I am."

He gave her a sheepish look, which she would rather not admit was charming on his big craggy face. "Isn't it obvious?" He leaned in. "I wanted to see you again."

A teasing light shone in his eyes. Careful. She had to keep her distance. But she also had to find out if he was telling the truth.

"Are you flirting with me, Detective?"

"Hank. And I'm just being honest."

"Honest."

"You know. Like in truth and justice. What I'm sworn to uphold." He propped himself against a wall, watching her. "Occupational hazard."

She nodded sagely. "I see." Maybe he was telling the truth. Maybe the calculation she saw in his eyes was just masculine conceit. Maybe he was no threat, and she could dismiss him and get back to her real quarry.

And maybe not.

She shivered and touched the locket at her throat.

Give me strength, little sister.

"Cold?" He started to remove his jacket, but she forestalled him.

"I'm fine. Too much vodka, probably."

"Maybe you should eat something. I haven't had dinner. Bet you haven't either."

He took her arm, and she let him lead her into the library, where a large table was laden with food. His touch was warm, his hand large and sure. A responsive zip raced through her. She ignored it. She couldn't afford to do anything else.

She wasn't particularly hungry, but she filled a plate and followed him to an empty corner. He ate, and she pushed the food around her plate.

What are you after, Detective Bonner?

He looked around. "Your home is striking. How long have you lived here?"

Interrogation or something innocent? "Thank you. I bought the place several years ago."

"Must have cost a small fortune."

"Snooping into my finances?"

He laughed. "Why not? Just as easy to marry a rich girl as a poor one." He winked, and she was sure it was another attempt to disarm her. "How did you get involved with all this anyway?" He gestured with his fork, indicating the clamorous party.

"By way of Harvard Business School and some lucky guesses in the emerging Russian market."

His brows rose in an I'm impressed look, then he scanned the room, his gaze lingering on the floor-to-ceiling bookcase across the way. Her collection of Russian folk art—matryoshka dolls and bottle-cases, boxes decorated with lacquered miniatures—were scattered over the shelves. From where they stood, details were obscure, but the hand painting was bright and colorful.

"Must have been some pretty lucrative guesses."

How much to tell, how much to hide? The story of her life.

She nibbled on a mushroom while she made her decision. "Are you a gambler, Detective?"

"I've done my share."

"Well, the new Russia is like one giant game of high-stakes poker. I arrived there six years ago, as a representative of Lyon, Peterson Financial."

"And they are . . ."

"Investment bankers. Old Wall Street firm. My first job out of Harvard. I speak a little Russian, so I asked them to send me to Moscow."

"I didn't know Russia was any great place for business."

"Once the Soviet Union fell, it was—is—probably one of the fastest moneymakers in the world."

He raised his brows in surprise. "Hard to imagine Boris and Natasha doing much but stepping on their own feet."

"Boris and Natasha?"

"Sure. You know—the bumbling spies on *Rocky and Bullwinkle.*"

"Rocky and . . . who?"

He gaped at her. "You've never heard of *Rocky and Bullwinkle?*"

A flutter of nerves went through her. He was looking at her so strangely. Had she just made some horrible mistake? Rapidly, she reviewed the possibilities, landing on what seemed the most obvious.

"What are they—characters in a book?"

"Cartoon."

How could she tell him that her childhood hadn't included American cartoons? She laughed it off. "Oh, well, I never did like cartoons."

"Also a movie with Robert DeNiro."

She shrugged. "Perhaps I was out of the country when it came out."

"Perhaps." The word seemed overly enunciated. Was he making fun of her? No, he was nodding thoughtfully, trying to figure things out.

Moving the conversation to safer ground, she said, "You should update your perceptions of Russians, Detective. The Soviet Union is dead, and as you can see"—she gestured out toward the party—"the new Russia is doing quite well."

"And taking you with it."

She shrugged. "I have a strong tolerance for risk."

A shadow crossed his face, but was gone so quickly she thought she imagined it.

"Ah, that gambling instinct you mentioned."

"Precisely." How much longer would this continue? Surreptitiously, she looked around, searching for a way to excuse herself. Before she could do so, he shifted positions, effectively blocking escape.

"So, Moscow was the place to be?"

"Moscow was a free-for-all. A Wild West town."

"And you came riding in with your deck of cards?"

"I came riding in with a nose for bond trading."

"Government bonds? No one gets rich on bonds."

"I did. GKO's. Russian Treasury bills. Short-term yields were astounding at the time, as much as 22 percent. You could earn more in three months than in ten years investing in US T-bills. I made Lyon, Peterson millions, and they gave me a bonus with lots of nice zeros."

He whistled, and she smiled, enjoying his sticker shock. "People expect women to marry or inherit their money. Not earn it."

He held up his hands in surrender. "More power to you. Any way that works is fine by me. Though you do seem kind of young to have accomplished so much."

"Do I?" She couldn't help another smirk. "At the time, Moscow was ripe for young people. The World Bank's International Finance Corporation sent hundreds of twenty-somethings to Russia to help with economic reform and privatization. I just happened to be in the right place at the right time."

"So is that how you moved on to oil?"

"I had the connections and the credentials to broker a deal, yes. A deal that should be profitable for everyone, including Sokanan."

"But expensive. What was the initial investment?"

She didn't hesitate. Why should she? She'd been giving press conferences on this stuff for months. And far better to talk about business than herself. "Three and a quarter billion split between Petroneft—Miki Petrov's oil company—and North American Petroleum, a joint venture between three US companies." She turned to point out a few relevant players, powerful men in their own right.

He didn't seem intimidated. "Lot of egos there. And you right in the middle. A den mother."

She looked at him blankly. "Excuse me?"

"A den mother. Cub Scouts."

Another cultural phenomenon that seemed to have passed her by. "Sorry," she said stiffly, tired of fencing with him. "I never was a Scout. Or a boy."

"No, ma'am." He grinned, but the innuendo was quickly undercut when he laid down his plate and wandered over to the bookcase. "So you have another bonus in the making. Going to spend it on special collections?"

She followed—what was he looking for?—and picked up one of the figurines. "I have a weakness for Russian folk art. Like Clever Vania here. See the detail? A perfectly rendered peasant carved out of lime-tree wood and hand-painted. And inside . . ." She opened the case and smiled. "Just enough room for your secret stash of vodka."

"I know a couple of guys down at the station who could use one of those. Handier than the old bottom drawer trick."

"And much prettier."

"I don't think the guys worry about pretty, if you know what I mean. Me, on the other hand . . ." He crossed his arms and studied her, and she forced herself not to squirm under his intense scrutiny.

"So you speak Russian."

With slow, precise movements, she closed the case and replaced it, all in an effort to buy time. He'd changed the subject. Why? "I have an ear for languages."

"How do you say"—he gazed at her mouth, then slowly, back up to her eyes—"you are beautiful?"

Heat spiked in her cheeks, but she met his gaze head-on. "It depends on whether the 'you' is a man or a woman."

"Definitely a woman."

Coolly, she said, "You're flirting again."

He shrugged as though helpless in the face of her charms. "It's that bonus. It's gone to my head."

She surprised herself and laughed. Outright. She hadn't done that in a long time.

"Laughter looks good on you," he said. "You should do it more often."

"The world is a serious place, Detective."

The smile faded from his eyes. "Yes, it is." And suddenly she knew he was thinking about Luka.

"The man who was murdered today," he said. "Luka Kole. He spoke Russian, too, didn't he?"

"I . . . I wouldn't know. Did he?"

"He was an immigrant from Russia."

"Was he? Well, I'm sorry for him then. To come all this way and to . . . to die like that. What happened exactly?"

He shrugged, but observed her closely. "Looks like a robbery. We've had a number of them over the past month."

"Any suspects?"

"One or two."

Just then, a jumpsuit-clad waiter came up and murmured that the governor was leaving.

She turned to Hank, grateful for the interruption. "Will you excuse me?"

"Of course."

Hank watched her go, unsure what to think. He'd flirted with her because he couldn't divulge the real reason he'd come back. And hell—he might as well admit it—because he'd enjoyed it. Especially watching the heat flood her normally cool, controlled face. She'd handled him well, maintained her composure despite the telltale blush, but then, maybe she was just a good liar.

He turned toward the bookcase. The framed photographs he'd seen earlier were all gone.

He frowned, studying the case. The doors on the bottom might prove interesting. He looked around. For the moment, he was alone. Opening the cabinets, he discovered more wooden carvings lined up inside, but no photographs. Disappointed, he scanned the room for another likely hiding place. There were probably a million of them, but none he could search just then, with the crowd looking on.

But later, after the party, someone would do a perimeter check outside and a final walk-through inside. Hank would just have to make sure that someone was him.

He strolled through the public areas, examining walls, shelves, and tables for the missing photograph, or for something that would confirm Alex was either lying or telling the truth about Luka Kole. His head told him he was wasting his time, but his gut told him to hang in there.

He did, watching the party flow, then ebb hours later. Finally, well after midnight, only A. J. and Petrov were left.

Hank spied them in a corner in the next room, heads bent together. They hadn't seen him, and he edged closer until he could hear their conversation, but the murmurings were all in Russian. Petrov stroked her arm, then her face, cajoling her into something, but she shook her head, regretfully, it seemed to Hank.

"Not tonight," she said in English. "I'm too tired, and I have too much to do tomorrow."

"You disappoint me," Petrov said.

"I'm sorry, Miki. I'll call you. We'll have dinner."

She tucked her arm through Petrov's and escorted him to the door, caressing his face and kissing him good-bye. A kiss meant for his cheek, but Petrov turned his head at the last minute, catching her mouth with his. Alex stiffened, then leaned into the kiss, her body pressed against the older man's. Again, distaste flickered through Hank. There'd been something slick and scheming in the way Petrov had taken advantage of a simple good-bye.

Not that Alex seemed to mind.

Hank shook his head. Who she kissed and who she didn't was not why he was there.

Petrov walked out the door and as soon as it was closed, Alex wiped her mouth with the back of her hand.

Hank raised his brows. Now, that was interesting.

Then she picked up the skirt of her dress and ran toward the back of the house.

Quickly, Hank stepped outside and told a surprised Joe Klimet that he would do the interior walk-through. It was late, and everyone was eager to get home. Hank's offer meant one less man had to stay behind. For once, Joe didn't argue.

Hank had just finished his inspection, as well as a fruitless search for the missing photo, when he saw Alex, now in a pair of dark slacks, dash past the library door. Racing out of the room, he was in time to see her bolt outside.

Where the hell was she going?

Hunches on alert, he ducked outside and two minutes later, a car came roaring down the drive. He could just make out Alex behind the wheel. Hank checked his watch—1:27 A.M. Pretty late in the day for a spin.

Hank sprinted down the steps to his car. In seconds, he'd turned it around and followed Alex.

He tailed her to the Taconic Parkway and drove north for two hours. The parkway was unlit, a two-lane winding nightmare swathed in nothing but moonlight. Hank could do little more than concentrate on the road.

When she pulled off at last, it was onto an exit marked Lakeview. Hank doused his headlights, using the moon to light his way. Even darker than the parkway, the crow black murkiness made his skin crawl. It was six-months-old superstitious crap, a remnant from his deadly bout in the toolshed. The shrinks had told him the fear would fade, but anxiety still clutched at him, drying his mouth and sending his pulse into overdrive.

Five minutes later, Alex drove into a gas station, a small setup with two old-fashioned pumps and a tiny run-down store that advertised fishing bait. Dim light illuminated the parking area.

With relief, Hank eased into a cluster of trees at the side of the road. He got out of the car and crept closer, keeping to the shadows.

Flattened against the side of the rickety store, he sneaked around back until he could see her. She was standing in the shadows, talking to a man. Sixty maybe. Or older. Wearing a pair of rumpled khakis and an equally rumpled shirt. A scruffy pickup faced Alex's car, fishing rods mounted on a rack at the back of the cab. Hank squinted but couldn't make out the plate number.

He focused on Alex. Her hands waved in the air, her body shook. Was she crying? The man handed her a handkerchief. He seemed to be trying to calm her down. Fatherly arm around her shoulder, he led her to the pickup, put her inside, and leaned in as if talking to her. His back was toward Hank, blocking Alex's body.

Explanations flitted through Hank's mind. Uncle? Father? Older brother? Much, much older. But why drive all the way out here? Why not pick up a phone and call? And what had upset her so? She'd seemed perfectly composed during the party.

Whatever Uncle Fisherman was saying, it didn't last long. A few minutes, and Alex was back on the road, heading the way she'd come, while the older man drove off in the opposite direction.

The glow of the pickup's taillights disappeared into the curtain of blackness, and Hank stared after it, trying once more to catch the plate number. But the truck was too far away. He thought about following, but the road was unfamiliar, narrow, and deserted, and the risk of being seen too great.

He trudged back to his car, wishing he had a bead on the guy in the pickup. Not to mention his relationship to Alexandra Jane Baker.

4

Apple House was dead quiet when Hank finally made it back. He let himself in, sneaked down the hall to his room, and was so tired he collapsed on the bed before he got his clothes off. Images of flower-covered oil rigs and dusty pickups swirled in his head, but at last he dropped off to sleep.

What seemed like seconds later, a wail jerked him awake. Disoriented, he took a second to fix the sound. Then he hurried across the hall and pushed open the door to Mandy's room.

She twisted in her bed, another nightmare making her quake and scream. Guilt snaked through Hank, and he gathered the small body into his arms.

"Hush, baby," he whispered. "Everything is all right. Shh." He gave her the lie, crooning so she would believe. She whimpered and sank into his chest, still sleeping, and he held her against him until she quieted.

Tucking her in, he pushed her stuffed dinosaur close under the covers so she could feel it. Above the pink-and-purple comforter her face looked small and defenseless. What happened when she found out he couldn't keep her safe? That no one could? That safety was an illusion as flimsy as smoke.

He rubbed a hand down his face, the fear of letting her down palpable as his own skin.

Returning to his room, he tumbled into bed and didn't sleep much. When the sun rose, he got up bleary-eyed, helped his mother get the fruit stand opened, then drove the kids to school. Mandy had her headphones draped around her neck. Tapes, television, books—they were all part of her arsenal of escape, a way to keep the dangerous world at bay. Trey sat beside her, scowling out the window.

Hank glanced at his nephew in the rearview, hesitated, then plunged in, a smile on his face, a friendly tone in his voice. Nothing ventured, nothing gained.

"Nana said you have a social studies test today, Trey. I thought we could go over the material on the way." Truth was, his mother had also mentioned her doubts that Trey had done much studying for it. She was worried he wouldn't pass sixth grade at the rate he was going.

But Hank didn't care about the test for its own sake. He just wanted an opening. Something to talk about, to let Trey know he was interested. "So, what do you say?"

Trey said nothing. Head turned away, he continued to frown, enclosed in silence. Hope sank, and Hank debated whether to try again, but Mandy whispered loudly instead.

"Trey, don't." Her small voice held a pleading note. She hadn't mentioned the nightmare; he didn't know if she even remembered it. Or wanted to.

Through the rearview, Hank saw the boy stir as though Mandy's plea hadn't fallen on completely deaf ears. That was good. But then he resettled himself in the corner and didn't answer.

"We're starting a play in school today," Mandy said into

the void. Her voice was a little too eager, her smile in the rearview mirror a little too strained. She was trying to make up for her brother's intransigence, trying to make everything calm and smooth and all right. As if it ever could be all right.

"That's great, Mandy. Maybe you'll get a part."

"Everyone gets a part," Trey said sullenly.

Hank bit down on a sharp retort. Trey seemed to be itching for a fight, and a fight first thing in the morning was not what Hank had in mind. "That's good. No one feels left out."

"Yeah," Mandy said softly, "no one feels left out." Which in Mandy's world meant everyone would be happy. Satisfied with that, she sat back, placed the earphones on her head, and plugged into her tape.

He dropped them off at the front of the school and watched them go, Mandy to fourth grade and Trey to sixth. They were slipping away, Hank felt it as keenly as if the kids were dangling over a precipice with only his two hands to keep them from falling. Which one would he drop? Trey, who fought him with every breath, or Mandy, who pretended nothing had happened? Christ, he wasn't up to this.

But of course he had to be. He had no other option. But as he made his way to the station downtown, the doubts continued to swirl.

His route took him past Grove Street Plaza, the ghost mall littered with vacancy signs. He remembered how excited everyone had been when it opened ten years earlier. Newspaper articles had touted Sokanan as a model of development. A grand opening ceremony with bunting and speeches had drawn a crowd. It had been his last year on patrol before his promotion to detective, and he'd been assigned to the event. He'd stood at the edge of the makeshift podium, listening to the Sokanan High School band play

"Stars and Stripes Forever," and felt proud and hopeful as anyone.

The optimism had gone with the GE plant closing, and Grove Street had gradually suffocated to death. Last year, a fire in one of the abandoned stores had left half the mall a burned-out hulk, an eyesore that had the city council in an uproar and the responsible parties vying over who would pay the cleanup.

When he got to the station, the squad was gearing up for the daily meeting. The Sokanan Police Department had ten men in the detective division; they handled all major crimes from homicide to robbery to sexual assault. It was a lot for a small city, but no one sat around. Times were bad, and crime was up. And since Sokanan was at the end of the Metro North train line from Manhattan, they got a lot of spillover.

Hank poured himself a cup of coffee and wandered into the small squad room. Three men and one woman milled around drinking coffee, chatting, and waiting for Parnell to begin.

They greeted Hank with a nod and pity in their eyes. Most had been supportive after his family had been blown apart. No one had accused him of screwing up, but their silence seemed loud as an accusation.

Joe Klimet called to Hank from across the room. "Hey, Bonner—you get that lead chased down last night?" His eyes glinted with malicious pleasure as several heads turned Hank's way. "Our boy here showed up at the Renaissance Oil thing. But the only lead I saw him chasing was—" Joe mimed a woman's curvy body in the air.

A few wolf whistles and catcalls greeted this.

"Couple of weeks and you'll have plenty of time for

chasing those kinds of leads," a voice said over the din, and everyone laughed.

"And do it better than you, Fenelli." A pang washed through Hank. The closer he got to leaving, the more that seemed to happen. He felt like he was deserting everyone.

A quitter. Like Ben had said.

He clenched his jaw. Not quitting. Just doing what had to be done.

For Trey and Mandy.

For everyone.

Lieutenant Parnell burst out of his office. He was a spare man; Hank always thought he looked as though he'd been honed by the wind. Not sixty yet, he'd gone gray early, and now a layer of white hair covered his head. But that didn't make him any less sharp. He looked down at a yellow pad. "How'd the Renaissance Oil thing go?"

"No problems," Joe Klimet said.

"Good." He crossed something off on the pad, then looked at Hank and asked about the Luka Kole murder. Before Hank could respond, Mike Fenelli spoke.

"A uniform picked up Big Mac McTeer twenty minutes ago."

McTeer, who had argued with Luka Kole the day before, was at the top of their lead sheets. "What's he got to say for himself?" Hank asked.

Fenelli shrugged. "You and Klimet caught the case. We left that for you."

"What about ballistics on the round from the vic?"

"Haven't come back yet. Neither have the phone records."

"Canvass on the neighborhood around the store?"

"Deaf and dumb all around," Klimet said.

"How about a lead on the home address?"

"Clerk had no idea," said Fenelli. "This Luka Kole kept a profile lower than the ground. No one knows anything about him."

"We're working through his credit card statements," Klimet said. "Bills we found in the office, stuff like that. So far it's all tagged to the store."

"Keep digging," Parnell said.

The meeting moved on to other things, and when it was over, Fenelli turned to Hank.

"Uniforms said McTeer's a real tough guy. Not too cooperative."

Klimet wandered over, balled one hand into a fist. "I like tough guys."

Hank exchanged a look with Fenelli, suppressing his irritation at the younger man's bravado. He picked up the phone, punched in the number for the jail upstairs. "You got a McTeer up there. Bring him down to Interview Two."

He let Joe go in alone, watching from the observation room behind the two-way glass. A few minutes later, McTeer was escorted in, a wiry white guy with a black do-rag pulled low on his forehead.

From his record, he was nineteen, an unemployed high school dropout with an address in the projects on the north side of town. He wore baggy jeans that sagged over a pair of expensive Nikes and an old Knicks game shirt with Sprewell printed on the back.

He sauntered toward the table in the center of the room, hip-hop to the max. "Yo, when you gonna cut me loose?" He danced right up to the two-way mirror, as though Joe were insignificant and the real players behind it. "I ain't done jack shit." The accent and body language were perfect homeboy black.

Not one to be easily dismissed, Joe grabbed the kid by

the back of the shirt and shoved him toward the table. "I'm over here, big shot." He forced him into a chair. "Sit."

McTeer exploded, jumping up the minute Joe let go. "You ain't got no right to be all over me with that shit."

So the kid had a short fuse. Had it exploded over Luka Kole yesterday?

Joe shoved him back down again; this time a heavy hand forced McTeer's head to the table. "I said, sit."

McTeer stopped struggling.

"Ready now?" Beneath Joe's hand, McTeer nodded. Joe let him go.

The boy raised his head slowly, resentment written all over his face. He glared at Joe, and Hank saw generations of abuse staring out of those stark, dangerous eyes.

"Where were you yesterday about five P.M.?"

McTeer continued to stare.

"You want to get out of here, you'll cooperate."

McTeer crossed his arms, leaned back in the chair so the front legs lifted off the floor. His face was hard and expressionless. He'd been here before.

Hank sighed, poured two cups of coffee, and let himself into the interrogation room. He set one cup in front of McTeer. "Coffee?"

McTeer eyed him suspiciously.

"Black or—" From his pocket he took out a couple of packets of sugar and a small tub of nondairy creamer, threw them down in front of McTeer and waited for him to coffee up.

"You like the Knicks?" He grabbed a chair and, turning it around, straddled the seat. "That Sprewell, he was something wasn't he?"

McTeer picked up the cup, sniffed it as though it might be poisoned. "I ain't done nothing," he said sullenly.

Hank shrugged. "No one said you did."

McTeer shot a hostile glance over at Joe, then back at Hank.

"But see, we got ourselves a problem. A man was killed yesterday at the convenience store on Rossvelt. We heard you had words with him earlier in the day, and we have to check it out. So helping us is really helping you. We just want to clear all this up so you can go home."

Distrust still rife in his eyes, McTeer said, "What man you talking about?"

"Luka Kole. The man behind the counter."

"That dumb-ass old man, don't speak English?"

"That's the one."

McTeer looked up at the two-way. He opened a pack of sugar and emptied it into his cup. He mixed it with the red plastic stirrer Hank had brought. Added cream. Sipped.

Klimet tensed, hands fisting, but Hank threw him a warning look and for once he backed down. Repressing the same inclination to throttle McTeer, Hank waited through the dumb show while the kid figured it out.

"The sucker shortchanged me, you know?" McTeer said at last. "I give him a twenty, he give me change for a ten. Fucking foreigner. So, yeah, we ex-change some words." He overemphasized exchange, moving his head from side to side as he did so, as though it were two separate words, ex and change. "He was throwing all kinds of foul shit at me. I ain't taking that shit. But I ain't killed no one."

"So where were you around five last night?"

His jaw set. "Nowhere. Hanging."

"With who?"

He shrugged. "I got peeps to hang with."

"Which people?" Hank studied the boy. He had no idea if

the guy was lying; chances were he was. But Joe took down names and addresses, and they let McTeer go.

Hank sighed. Scouring the projects for deadbeats was not his idea of fun.

Alex dressed quickly, pulling on a pair of dark slacks and a black silk sweater, then grabbed a wide tote bag. She hadn't slept much and felt sluggish; if she could, she would have stayed in bed all day. But she had much to do, though she was dreading it.

A small army was cleaning up under Sonya's watchful eyes. Alex picked her way through an obstacle course of mops, dust cloths, and huge plastic trash bags, already half-full.

"You go to city?" Sonya asked, following her to the door. Her wrinkled face was calm. No sign of last night's concern lay in the soft lines.

"No, dear. I have some errands to run." She made her tone placid, but had a hard time pretending everything was all right.

"The party, it was good?"

"Very good." She kissed the old woman on the cheek to forestall more questions. "Don't wait lunch."

"Lunch?" Sonya scowled. "You don't eat breakfast?"

"I'll stop for a cup of coffee."

Sonya shook her head. "And dinner?"

"I don't know. Don't worry about me. I'll grab something if I'm hungry."

Sonya tsked tsked her, shaking a finger in a fond scold. "You are too skinny."

Alex smiled. Sonya was always trying to feed her, but food was the last thing on her mind at that moment. She rummaged in a drawer for a set of keys, swung a light jacket over her shoulders, and waved good-bye.

Once inside her car, she tried to breathe normally. For a moment, she laid her head on the steering wheel and took a deep breath. She didn't know if what she was doing was a good idea or not, but it had to be done, and soon. In fact, it might already be too late.

Last night Mason had told her not to assume that Luka's death had anything to do with her. He promised to look into what had happened and told her not to panic. But panic was unavoidable.

Hands trembling, she turned the ignition and headed for the highway into town. Fifteen minutes later, she parked at the Wal-Mart and set off.

It was a two-mile walk to Luka's apartment. Plenty of time for regrets and recriminations. Plenty of time to wonder if the price of justice was too high. It had claimed her youth, kept her apart from other people. Besides Sonya, she had no family, no roots, no relationships of any weight. When other girls had giggled over boys, gone on dates and to dances, Alex had stayed behind. Getting close to people meant sharing secrets, and hers could never be revealed.

She bit back the sob that threatened to choke her. A week ago, Luka had called and said he'd found something. Something that would lead them to the proof they'd been seeking for thirteen years. Proof of her father's innocence. But what it was, he'd refused to say, and now he would never tell her.

She didn't believe for a minute that he'd been killed in a robbery. He died because he'd uncovered something. And if it had killed him, it must be important. But what?

Head down, she wound around as many back streets as possible. Every few minutes, she glanced over her shoulder. No one followed.

It was a cool spring day, but she was sweating by the time she reached Luka's run-down apartment complex. The units, painted dull turquoise and dirty yellow, crawled around a crescent road. Luka's was in the back, hidden from the street.

He could have lived better. He could have afforded it on his own, never mind that she'd offered to help a thousand times. But lying low had been a way of life with him. Harvard, the house she'd bought, the public splash she'd made—he hadn't been happy with any of it.

She teared up remembering the arguments. The way he'd sigh in the end, call her Sashka in his own gruff way and pat her head. *Kazhdomu rostku svoyo vremya,* he'd say. Every seed knows its time.

She went through the parking area with its series of covered slots and crossed the grass until she was out of sight of the road. Carefully, she jogged to the end, where she climbed a staircase, fished in her tote for the keys, and inserted them in the door.

She needn't have bothered; it wasn't locked. With the first touch of her fingers, the door creaked open. She paused. Luka would never have left the door unlocked.

Cautiously, she pushed the door open the rest of the way.

A cry of dismay escaped her. Every inch of the apartment's front area was covered with overturned furniture, upside-down drawers, papers, clothing, and the remains of a smashed television set.

Slowly Alex picked her way through the debris. Whoever had done this had been thorough; nothing had been left intact. Every closet, cabinet, and drawer had been emptied. Every cranny pried open. A blast of fury ripped through her. The damage made her angry in a way she hadn't been over the news about Luka. As though the death itself were something she couldn't face yet, but this, this . . .

She wanted to howl, to screech. Her chest rose and fell as she took in huge gulps of air.

With ironclad control she forced herself to calm down. No use getting upset; she'd only lose her ability to think.

Her foot hit something that rolled across the floor and butted up against the edge of a slashed sofa cushion. She stooped to picked it up. A can of vegetable soup. Vegetarian vegetable. She couldn't picture Luka eating anything as bland and ordinary. A hearty meat-and-potatoes dish yes, but vegetarian? The image made her giggle. The giggle turned into a laugh, then she couldn't stop laughing. She laughed so hard, tears pricked her eyes, and suddenly she was sobbing, clutching the can of soup to her chest.

She was sixteen again, staring down from the sixth floor at the small body below. Her father's body. Someone was screaming, screaming like an unnatural thing, and Luka hit her and the screaming stopped. And then he was wrenching her away from the window, her father's driver and bodyguard pushing her out the office door, down the back stairs.

They had to escape.

No one could ever know she'd been there. Heard the argument. Her father's accusations. Thief. Betrayer.

Luka, Luka. What would she have done without him?

Now she would find out, she thought as she sank onto the cushionless couch. Just as she'd found out all those years ago what it was like to face a harsh world without the warm security of her father. Then she had Luka, now she had only herself.

Except this time she wasn't a child.

She was an adult, with power and resources of her own.

Alone, but she'd been alone for a long time. Why cry about it? Emotional scenes were a waste of time.

Breath unsteady, she sniffed back a sob and ruthlessly searched for the ice deep inside, forcing it to the surface. Feel nothing. Do something.

When she was in control again, she rose and began to search through the wreckage.

Miki Petrov put down the phone at his desk and frowned at the glass case across the way. Inside was a collection of antique swords. An English navy officer's saber, a Russian light cavalry saber, a French dragoon's weapon. All nineteenth-century. Not his best, of course, but good enough to display. If it wasn't good enough to show off, it wasn't good enough to own, a philosophy he freely applied to people as well.

To Alex Baker in particular.

After last night he wanted to show her off, but she was not in her office or at home. He'd been annoyed enough that she'd refused to come home with him last night. Now he couldn't even reach her.

He rose from the desk and glided to the huge window overlooking midtown Manhattan. He liked the view from the ninety-eighth floor. Cars and buses, people—everything in miniature, toys in his own private playing field.

Except Alex, who wasn't available for play. Was she avoiding him?

Impossible.

Women didn't avoid him, they sought him out. Why should Alex Baker be any different?

A knock sounded on his office door.

"Enter," he barked in Russian. He wasn't in the mood to be interrupted.

Behind him the door opened, but he stared out the window, a rush of petty anger surging through him and keeping whoever it was waiting. And waiting.

At last, the person spoke.

"You . . . uh . . . wanted to see me?"

Slowly, Petrov turned. A pasty-faced Yuri stooped in the doorway. As always, he wore a black leather coat over black shirt and slacks. The inky color made his face appear even more sickly. He had a half-smoked cigarette in the corner of his mouth, which he sucked in and removed with a shaky hand.

"You made a fool of me last night," Petrov snapped, sticking to their native tongue and making the man stand when he clearly longed to collapse in one of the upholstered chairs in front of the desk. "Repeat that performance, and I'll send you back to Russia."

"*Da, tovarish'nachalnik*," Yuri muttered.

Petrov returned to the desk, sat down, and steepled his fingers together. Over his clasped hands, he scowled at Yuri, stabbing him with a look Petrov had used on countless victims. A look that said you were standing there by his leave, and if he wanted to, he could make sure you never stood again. "What did you find?"

Yuri squirmed. "I tore Kholodov's place apart. Emptied drawers, cabinets. I searched everywhere, even pried up floorboards. There was nothing about you."

Petrov growled. That could mean Yuri was an incompetent fool.

Or Kholodov had been bluffing, and there was nothing.

Or they just hadn't found it yet.

None of which were options Petrov liked.

"I did find this." Yuri trudged over, took something from inside his coat, and with two fingers slid it carefully across the desk as though afraid Petrov might cut the digits off.

A photograph of Alex.

Petrov glanced sharply at Yuri. "Where was this?"

"In a nice silver frame on top of the TV."

What did this mean? How would a runt like Kholodov come in contact with one of the most talented business-women in the country?

Petrov studied the photograph. In black and white, it looked like a blowup from a newspaper article. Well, Alex was a beautiful woman. Maybe Kholodov just wanted a picture of her.

Maybe.

He felt Yuri's gaze on him. "Stop hovering."

The man tensed. "What do you . . ." Yuri licked his lips. "What do you want me to do?"

"When I decide I'll let you know. Get out." Yuri started to obey. "Wait. Go over to Miss Baker's building and tell me when she arrives. And don't let her see you."

Yuri bowed slightly, a relieved expression on his face. He backed out, and Petrov had forgotten him before he disappeared through the door.

He picked up the phone. "Get me Jeffrey Greer."

While he waited, he stared at the picture. Alex stared back at him, her smile cold and meaningless, for the camera only.

He would like to warm that smile. Melt it. Heat it.

Discover the mystery behind it.

"Greer." The State Department aide's voice broke into Petrov's thoughts.

He didn't say hello, didn't identify himself. "What do you know about Alex Baker?"

"She's a brilliant mind who made a name for herself in the newly formed Russian market?" He turned the statement into a question, as though this were a game.

Petrov growled. The only games he played were of his own making, and this wasn't one of them. "What do you know about her that I don't know?"

"I—I'm not sure I understand." Greer hesitated, and Petrov pictured the man shoving back the black frames of his glasses. "What is this about, Mr. Petrov?"

"I want you to find out everything you can about Alex Baker."

"Why? Is there a problem?" Worry edged Greer's voice. Renaissance Oil was his project, the first he'd been given to handle from start to finish, and he had a personal stake in seeing it through to a positive outcome. "She's perfectly respectable, has all the right contacts, speaks—"

"Just do it. And Greer?"

"Yes, Mr. Petrov?"

"If you want to ensure the future of Renaissance Oil, don't tell anyone what you are doing."

"But—"

"Am I clear?"

"Yes, Mr. Petrov."

"I'd hate to tell your superiors you haven't been cooperative."

"No, Mr. Petrov."

Miki grunted in approval. "Good." He appreciated a man who was easy to manipulate.

Hank's morning hadn't gone well. Neither he nor Klimet had found any of the mopes McTeer had alibied up with. At ten, he got a call from Ricky Garza at Juvie. Trey had got into another fight at school and, while supposedly cooling his heels in the principal's office, had managed to cut out altogether. A patrol unit had caught him downtown, breaking windows and spray-painting the back of the municipal building. They'd brought him in, and Hank spent the rest of the morning dealing with the damage.

A good portion of that time was used up in a fruitless attempt to talk to Trey about what had happened, but the kid clammed up like McTeer in the interview room with Klimet, and no appeal to the Knicks or any other topic broke the kid's silence.

Hank didn't want Trey to end up a tough guy like McTeer. And he didn't want himself to turn into a bully like Klimet. But if things didn't improve, he was afraid they were both headed down that road.

After dropping Trey off at Apple House, where he was put to work under Rose's watchful eye, Hank drove back downtown to pick up the keys they'd found in Luka Kole's pocket. Through a cable TV bill, Fenelli had tracked down Kole's home to a west side apartment complex in a scruffy part of town, once solidly blue-collar, now edging lower. A lot of GE plant workers had lived there, and when the plant closed the neighborhood had slowly deteriorated. Riverside Towers was no exception.

He stopped by the manager's office for directions, got back in his car, and cruised slowly down the road toward the back end of the development. He found the apartment easily enough, on the top floor of a two-story structure in need of a new coat of paint.

He inserted one of the keys from Kole's key ring in the lock, but the door swung open. A human sound, like a gasp, hit him and without thinking, he pulled back against the outer wall and drew his weapon.

He faced the sun, which simmered and pulsed, a bright ball of Mojave heat. Sweat beaded up. The last time he'd burst into an enclosed space where he knew someone was waiting for him, people had died. Deep inside his head he heard his brother-in-law's taunts, the tinny sound of a heavy weight hitting metal. He hadn't known it then, but that had been Maureen going down, her body bouncing off the side of the toolshed.

The scar on Hank's chest seemed to throb beneath his shirt, and he rubbed the place where Tom Stiller had plunged the screwdriver in. Christ, his hand was shaking.

Unless whoever was in Kole's apartment wanted to risk breaking a leg or worse by jumping out a window, there was no way out except the stairs, an exit he now controlled.

"This is the police," he called. "Come out, hands on your head." Silence.

Who was inside? Rapidly he ran through the options. The killer coming for more. A burglar. A relative. Harmless, not harmless. Armed, not armed. He'd been lucky once, would his streak hold? He thought about the randomness of the universe, the sad, sick fact that no matter what he did, survival boiled down to chance and fate.

He had to move. Had to stop debating, second-guessing and just plain move. A year ago he wouldn't have been having this little heart-to-heart with himself. He'd already know what to do and done it.

He made himself breathe. Steady. Too much adrenaline, and he'd be no good to anyone.

He inhaled. It was like taking in his own life force—shivery, icy hot. Pushing through the terror, he forced himself around the corner and back outside. What had he seen?

A woman frozen in place holding an empty picture frame.

A familiar woman.

Relief flooded him. He grabbed a moment to compose himself, then, mouth dry, he stepped into the apartment, gun still drawn.

Alex Baker stared at him, face flushed, gray eyes wide with shock.

Well, at least he'd gotten his answer—she'd lied. As the totality of her deceit washed over him, he saw her stiffen. The disbelief in her face mutated into haughtiness. He had to hand it to her—the look she gave him made him seem the trespasser.

But they both knew who didn't belong. And all her Russian millions couldn't change it.

5

"What are you doing here?" Hank holstered his weapon but gave Alex a look that was equally intimidating.

She opened her mouth, but nothing came out.

He fisted his hands, opened them. "You know, I'd like to wring your neck, but I'll take this slow and easy. One, you obviously knew Luka Kole, or you wouldn't be here. So you lied to me." A beat of silence. "Don't say anything," he said dryly. "Just nod when I get it right." She didn't move. "Fine. I'll take that as a yes. Who is he? What is he to you?"

"I . . . I don't know what you're talking about."

A lousy bluff if he ever heard one. "You just happen to be here ravaging a dead man's apartment? A dead man you claim not to know?"

Her skin, already pale, was nearly dead white. She dropped the picture frame she'd been clutching and began gathering things—a tote bag, a purse. "I don't have to answer to you. I haven't done anything wrong." Her voice was cold; that lady-of-the-manor thing again.

"Except lying to the police, breaking and entering. Oh, and destroying private property."

"I didn't do this." She made a move toward the door. He blocked her way.

"Yeah? Who did?"

She didn't reply.

"Who is Luka Kole? What do you know about him? What's your relationship to him?"

"Let me pass."

"Dream on, Countess."

"You can't keep me here." She was quivering, the fine tremors rippling through her. She struggled with them, raising her head and squaring her shoulders, working to conquer the fear. He admired that, but admiration wouldn't get him where he wanted to go.

He stepped forward. She backed away. "Who is Luka Kole, Alex?" Her jaw tightened, but she didn't answer. He took another step, she stepped back. "Did you have anything to do with his murder?"

"Don't be ridiculous."

"Then what are you doing here?"

"I . . . I—"

He raised his voice. "Dammit, who is Luka Kole?" She bumped up against the remains of the couch. A small push, and she landed on it. Braced on the sofa's arm and spine, he loomed over her. "Talk to me, Alex, or I'll cuff you and take you to the station and put you in a holding cell."

She gazed up at him, cool and resentful. But below the surface he saw something else, despair or hopelessness. An opening, one he took.

"Who is Luka Kole?" He bore down on her, voice hard and unforgiving. "Why did you lie to me? What do you know about his murder?"

"Nothing."

"Stop lying."

"I'm not lying."

"Yes, you are. Who is Luka Kole?" He shook the couch,

and her body jerked forward and back. He shouted at her. "Who is Luka Kole? What do you know about him? Who is he?"

"My father," she shouted back. "All right? He was my father." Her voice cracked. "He was my . . . my father." She looked away, out toward the chaos of the room, as though she didn't want him to see the tears.

Slowly, Hank released her. Jesus Christ . . . "Your father? Luka Kole was your—"

"Yes. How many times do I have to say it?"

"His name is Kole. Yours is Baker."

"My stepfather's name. Luka and I . . . we are—were—estranged. I haven't seen him in years."

He sank on the couch beside her. "Why didn't you tell me? Why did you lie?" Her hands were clasped tight as though holding her together, and he fought against a surge of pity.

"You come to me on one of the most important evenings of my life with a scandal that could have led to bad publicity or worse. What did you expect me to do? My father was not a nice man. I don't care who murdered him. He probably deserved it. I don't want to have anything to do with him."

"Why are you here, then?"

She was silent for a moment. Figuring out her story or steeling herself to tell the truth?

"He had something that belonged to me. I wanted it back."

"What?"

She held up the empty picture frame. The silver sides caught the light. "A picture of my mother."

Hank studied her. Was she lying again?

"She died when I was six. I have no photographs of her. Luka refused to give me one."

"So you ripped the place apart looking for one?"

"I told you, I didn't do this. The door was open. This was how I found it."

"If that's true—"

"It is."

"Then who did do this? What were they looking for?"

"How am I supposed to know? I told you, I haven't seen Luka Kole in years."

He appraised her. Even in distress she dazzled. The color had returned to her face, and the exotically slanted eyes, now gray, now blue, had a bruised look. He had a swift urge to pull her against him, tell her it was okay, he believed her.

But he didn't.

"Where were you yesterday around five o'clock?"

"You can't seriously think I had anything to do with—"

"Where were you?"

She gazed down at her clenched hands, and as though realizing they were a sign of weakness, she pried them apart. When she looked back up, whatever softness or vulnerability he'd seen in her face had vanished. The ice princess was back.

"I was at home getting ready for the party. At least twenty people can attest to that." She looked at him as though he were some lower order of insect.

He didn't let it bother him. Instead, he pulled out a pocket notebook and a pen. Tossed them in her lap.

"Good. Write them down."

Alex picked up the pen and prayed he couldn't see her hand shaking. Her brain was thick with confusion; desperately she tried to keep all the lies she'd told straight in her head. And she fought to remember even one name—the florist, the caterer, bartender, waitstaff. Plenty of people had seen her. They filed by inside her head in a blur. Sonya. There was always Sonya.

She started to write Sonya's name at the top of the list, then crossed it off. She couldn't let the police question the elderly housekeeper; it would frighten her to death. After her experience with the Moscow authorities, Sonya had a natural dread of officials.

God, what if he asked for proof that Luka was her father? What would she do then?

But that at least was closer to the truth than the rest. Luka had been like a father to her. He'd gotten her out of Russia, seen that she attended the best boarding schools, that she was safely hidden away from all her father's enemies. And if he didn't bring her home for Christmas or the summer holidays, if he never wrote or sent cookies, at least he'd kept her alive. What more could she have asked of him?

Emotion clogged her throat again, and she fought to clear it. She would not break down in front of Hank Bonner.

As if he knew she was thinking about him, he said, "What's taking so long?" He knelt down in front of her and glanced at the almost blank page. "Look—write down Edie's Flowers. I saw their truck outside your house yesterday."

He was watching her closely, but something had softened in his face. For a moment it almost seemed as if he felt sorry for her.

"Edie's Flowers," he said gruffly. "Write it down."

Slowly, her fingers formed the letters. Her brain cleared, and she remembered the caterer's name. The rest soon followed.

Hank said nothing more while she wrote, but she felt him there. A small inner voice urged her to tell the truth and ask for his help. The longing to lean on someone was suddenly overwhelming.

She gripped the pen tighter; trust no one had been her motto for thirteen years. She couldn't abandon it now just because a pair of green eyes had looked kindly at her for a moment.

Finished, she handed the list to Hank. He skimmed it, nodded. "Okay, I'll check this out."

She rose, collected her things, and with as much dignity as possible, walked to the door.

"I'll have the coroner call you about the body."

She stilled, something freezing inside her. "What do you mean?"

"Someone has to bury him. You're next of kin."

An overwhelming sadness gripped her. Burying Luka would be the last kind thing she could do for him. But it was also the one favor she couldn't grant. Not if she wanted to keep her distance. "I refuse the honor." She laced the last word with a touch of acid.

Contempt flew across Hank's face and shamed her. She raised her chin. Who was he to judge her?

"You're not going to lay this on the city. Not with all your millions."

She stiffened at the rebuke in his voice, and used whatever frost she could muster to reply. "If it's merely a question of money, I'll pay for whatever is necessary. But make the arrangements with my lawyer. I'll have him call you."

"Fine."

She reached for the knob, desperate to get away.

"Don't go anywhere I can't find you," he said.

She ignored that, sailing out into the day. Down the stairs, over the scrap of grass, through the parking areas.

Running, she was running, gasping, until the apartment was out of sight.

At the main road she stopped, a hand to her pounding chest, and gulped in huge mouthfuls of air.

Hank stood in the doorway and watched Alex sprint across the parking area and disappear around a corner. Something nagged at him, but he couldn't figure out what. A buzz of anger vibrated inside his chest, but below it he felt something else. Something unexpected and not entirely welcome. She'd frozen like a cornered rabbit in there—small, white, and trembling. And for a moment some damn soft spot inside him had wanted to hold her the way he held Mandy after one of her nightmares.

That would have been a stupid move. All he needed was to fall for her. Falling for *anyone* was a risk he wouldn't take, let alone a suspect in his murder case.

A damn cold-blooded suspect. Kole must have been a pretty bad guy to turn her off like that.

Bad enough to want him dead? Want him dead enough to kill him?

He closed the door and faced the mess inside the apartment. He had to admit he couldn't see Alexandra Jane creating this vast swath of destruction. He examined the tear in a cushion. A deep gash, as if it had been slashed with a knife. But not a precise cut. If she had wielded a knife, the cut would no doubt have been careful and meticulous. As careful and meticulous as every move she made.

But if she hadn't trashed the place, who had? Someone who had been desperate to find something. What?

And what did her mysterious roadside chat in the middle of the night have to do with any of it?

He picked up the silver picture frame she'd dropped

when he entered. The photo had been ripped out; paper edges stuck to the sides.

And then he realized what had been nagging at him: She said she'd come for pictures of her mother. Had she taken any with her?

Still shaky, Alex reached her car and let herself in. What had just happened? How had she let herself be caught like that? Stupid, stupid, stupid.

She desperately wanted to get away as fast and as far as possible. Putting the car in gear, she drove off, no clue where she was going. The hunger to run—to escape—overwhelmed her.

Her relationship with Luka had been exposed. How soon before it became public knowledge? How soon before it got back to the wrong people?

She found herself southbound on the Taconic. The winding parkway with its tree-lined landscape soon gave way to the exhaust-filled rumble of the interstate, and to the toll booths and bridges that led to the complex world of Manhattan.

She ditched the car in the garage a block from her office on Madison and Sixty-first Street. Trying to shake her feeling of foreboding, she walked to the sleek glass tower, anonymous among so many other lofty structures. The security officer recognized her and waved her in. She took the elevator to the ninth floor and let herself into the office of Baker Financial.

Letty Birnbaum looked up in surprise from her post outside Alex's office. "Thought you weren't coming in today." Letty's acid red hair was teased into new heights, her dress tight and cut low enough to glimpse a bit of cleavage. Not exactly the pin-striped conservative who should be representing Alex's business to the world, but something about Letty had struck Alex from the first. An openness, a free-spiritedness Alex longed to possess.

"Changed my mind," she said.

Letty snorted in disbelief. "You just can't bear to take a day off." She smiled and leaned forward conspiratorially. The glimpse of cleavage increased to an eyeful. "So, how'd it go last night?"

If she only knew. "Great. No problems." Alex riffled through the pink message slips Letty handed her. Smolov, her contact in the Russian Duma, had called twice. Was there a problem? He'd assured her there was enough support in the Parliament for the tax legislation they needed. Was opposition gathering again?

"Well, you were a hit in one quarter." Letty nodded over to the office. Through the open door, Alex saw a huge bouquet of flowers covering the center of her desk.

"Who are they from?"

Letty pulled back in shock. "You think I looked?"

Despite her distress, Alex smiled. "Absolutely."

Letty sighed. "You know, you should trust people more." The mournful look she threw Alex turned into a wide smile. "Okay, so I'm busted. They're from Petrov." She waggled her brows suggestively, which Alex ignored.

"Okay. Thanks." She started toward her office.

"Okay, thanks? You get flowers from one of the hottest guys on the planet—even if he is old enough to be your father—and that's all you can say?" Her voice took on a note of concern. "Are you all right? You look, well . . . tired."

Alex forced herself to smile. She didn't like that her distress was so clear on her face. "I'm fine. Late night. Lots of excitement."

"Want me to hold your calls?"

"Thanks."

Finally, Alex escaped into her office, closed the door, and sank onto the pale green leather couch. She was thinking more clearly now, the fear of discovery settling in as undeniable fact. Fact she had to face and deal with. Hank Bonner knew about her relationship to Luka, so where did that leave her?

Absently, she stared at the flowers. A thick bunch of gaudy hothouse blooms, they were showy in an overblown way, like an overdressed woman with too much makeup. Miki had probably spent a fortune on them. Then again, he wouldn't think them worth much if he didn't pay through the nose. Money was the only arbiter that mattered in the new Russia. She thought of the old joke she'd heard time and again in Moscow. One new Russian tells another about a pair of shoes he bought for five hundred dollars in Paris, and the second businessman calls him a fool; he could have bought the exact same pair for a thousand dollars up the street.

She closed her eyes. Her mind refused to stay on the problem of Luka. Hank knew about Luka or thought he did. She'd lied to him. Again. And someone had searched Luka's apartment down to the floorboards. Had they found what they were looking for? What had it been? What had Luka discovered? Whom had he told?

The questions wound through her like an endless maze, up one blind alley and down another.

She sighed, picked up the phone and called Moscow. It was after ten P.M. there, so she rang Smolov at home. He answered the phone himself.

"Sasha!" His big bear voice boomed Russian in her ear. "I thought you would never come to work. I hear you had quite a night. Petrov is pleased."

She glanced at the flowers. "So I understand. Is that why you called? For congratulations?"

He cleared his throat. "Not exactly. I wanted to let you know that Dashevsky is making noises again." Dashevsky was the Russian prime minister and a lukewarm supporter of favorable tax legislation for foreign investment in Russian oil. The vote would take place in a few months, and it was vital that the bill pass. "I don't think he was pleased with the splash your little party made. Pictures of the Russian consul shaking hands with your governor were in the morning papers."

She massaged her neck. One more problem was all she needed. "He's blown hot and cold before. Is this a real threat?"

"With Dashevsky, who knows?"

"Find out. And if it is serious, find a way to shut him down. We need that vote."

She disconnected and began to punch in another number when a knock sounded.

Letty poked her head in. "You have a visitor." Her brown eyes sparkled mischief, and Alex groaned silently. She needed time alone to think and plan. She opened her mouth with a polite excuse, but another voice spoke first from behind her secretary.

"Hello, darling." Miki Petrov pushed the door open wider and stepped into the office, his smile clearly indicating that she should be delighted to see him.

Letty's brows rose at the word *darling*. She winked at Alex and backed out, tactfully closing the door behind her.

Alex's heart sank. She didn't have the energy to fend off Miki today. But she didn't have a choice either. She stood and extended her arms, pasting on a smile. "Miki! What a nice surprise."

He strode across the room, thick silver hair contrasting with his pitch black brows. He kissed the tops of her hands, then her cheeks. "I couldn't wait to see you again."

"The flowers are lovely. And so unnecessary."

"It is always necessary to say how much one appreciates excellence." Still holding on to her hands, he pulled away to admire her. "You were marvelous last night. The papers are full of it. Fantastic job. Let me take you to lunch to celebrate."

Alex's stomach turned. "I'd love to, but I'm swamped with catching up. Can we do it another day?"

Petrov shook a finger at her. "I won't hear of it. You work too hard. A relaxing meal with a glass of wine will do wonders. Come. I will not let you refuse." He tucked her arm in his and walked her to the door.

Alex couldn't think of a way to separate herself without making him suspicious. "All right. Where shall we go?"

Petrov tapped a finger against the side of his nose. "Let's make it a surprise."

She stopped at Letty's desk on the way out. "Looks like I'm being kidnapped."

Letty looked at Miki with approval. "Well, don't expect me to ransom you."

Outside the building Miki's limousine was waiting at the curb. A giant of a man in a long black leather coat stolidly guarded it.

Yuri the henchman.

His eyes were bloodshot, and she hoped he was feeling as lousy as he looked.

Wordlessly, he opened the car door and as he reached for the handle she noticed a series of crude tattoos on his massive knuckles. Jailhouse souvenirs. One, a dollar sign tattooed in the web between thumb and forefinger, meant he'd served time under the Soviets for hard currency speculation.

Everyone was in the money game.

Apprehension brushed her, but Yuri was docile as a lion on a leash and stood at attention while she and Miki got in. Then he closed the door behind them and slid into the driver's seat.

6

The limousine headed uptown. There were any number of restaurants on the Upper West Side that Miki favored, all trendy and overpriced. But the car stayed on the East Side, finally stopping at a sedate building two blocks from the Guggenheim.

Miki's apartment.

She would have liked to protest, but couldn't. Getting into his home had been one of her key objectives from the beginning. But to have the goal slide into her lap so easily, and on today of all days, was a bit daunting. Her stomach did a nervous flip as he helped her out of the car. "Come, my dear. I have the most marvelous meal planned."

He spoke in Russian, and she answered in kind. "You've been plotting this, haven't you?"

He held a hand to his heart in mock repentance. "You have found me out."

Oh, if only that were true. "You've gone to such trouble, Miki. The flowers, now this. I don't know what to say."

"Say whatever you like, *dorogaya*." The Russian word for *darling* rolled off his tongue, deep and smooth. "You have the most marvelous way of speaking. Like a schoolgirl and also like a native. Where did you learn your Russian?"

A buzz of warning vibrated inside her as the uniformed doorman opened the door for them. She was on Miki's ground now, his territory, and she had to walk carefully. "I have an ear for languages. I studied in school, of course, and college. And spent several years in Moscow. You know that."

"Of course. But someone once told me you have family there."

"In Russia?" The alarm started to clang. "No. My family was from Boston. My parents died in a car accident when I was sixteen."

He leaned toward her, close and intimate. "Then it must be true what I hear about you."

She met his eyes, fear thumping behind her ribs. "And what dreadful rumors have people been spreading about me?"

"That you are as brilliant as you are beautiful." He smiled, a wicked gleam in his coal-dark eyes. Tucking her arm into his, he escorted her into the elevator.

Relief was quickly swallowed by the door closing. Escape blocked, she shivered.

As though he knew and understood why, Miki rubbed her hands. "You are so cold, *dorogaya*."

"Ah, but that is my charm."

He blinked, and she felt a second of satisfaction for surprising him, but it was quickly overwhelmed by Miki, who threw his head back and roared with laughter.

He was still smiling when the elevator opened, and she stepped onto a lush carpet in shades of charcoal and pale gray.

A harsh tang greeted her immediately. Leather and steel. The furniture was night black, and, even without touching she could tell, butter-soft. A globe of twisted metal stood on a sculpture stand at the entryway. Across the room, a collection of swords stared back at her from the wall, hilts of ivory, silver, and brass intricately carved.

Miki followed her gaze. "Interested?"

Again, surprise laced his voice. The race of blood she felt looking at the collection surprised her. But the sight of so many lethal objects in proximity to Miki Petrov held definite appeal. "Of course."

He led her across the room and took one down, a long, curved sword with a carved hilt. Stepping back, he slashed the blade through the air, his lithe body as gracefully lethal as the weapon he held. The blade whistled as it cut through space, a haunting, mournful death song, and the sound seemed to please Miki. He smiled with approval and presented the weapon with two hands and a short bow, laying the blade flat on her outstretched palms. "Careful, now. It's sharply honed."

"What is it?"

"A Cossack *shashka*. A curved saber." He traced the arc of the blade in the air. "This one dates to the sixteenth century. The hilt is bone. Legend has it, human." He watched for her reaction, and she was careful not to pull away.

"Fascinating."

"Note the engraving on the blade."

She ran a finger over the Cyrillic letters incised into the polished metal and spoke the words aloud. "Die enemy from my hand."

For a second she was tempted to put the weapon to good use and split Miki Petrov in two. *Die enemy from my hand.*

She hefted the sword—it was lighter than she'd imagined—and sliced through the air, as he had done earlier. The blade keened its sharp song, and Miki eyed her.

Did he feel her hatred? She turned the blade on him, laying the tip against his chest. Their gazes locked.

"Should I run you through?" A goblin voice inside her head hissed, *yess, yess*.

"If you'd like us to kill each other, *dorogaya*, I can think of far more pleasurable ways," he said softly.

Carefully he took the weapon from her, replacing it on the wall, and as if the last moment hadn't happened, coolly pointed out a Russian hunting dagger, an eighteenth-century sword that had once belonged to one of Catherine the Great's guardsmen, and a wickedly curved Persian saber with a blade of Damascus steel called a *shamshir*.

With shaking hands, she gripped her purse, hoping he wouldn't notice. She could have killed him. She could have plunged the blade into his heart and everything would have been over.

Except her father's name would still be sullied.

She swallowed hard and tried not to think about what Petrov could do with those swords if he found out about her link to Luka. Instead, she calmed herself and studied the layout of the apartment, a huge, spacious home that took up the entire eighth floor. But though she expressed interest in seeing all of it, Miki demurred.

"Lunch first, then we'll tour."

Lunch turned into an all-afternoon affair, with a meal that dragged on for hours, every tidbit accompanied by Miki's subtle probing. Where did she grow up again? What did her parents do? What happened to her after they died?

She sidestepped what she could and when she couldn't, she repeated the stories she'd told for years.

"My family was from Boston, where my father was a doctor, my mother a housewife. They were simple, ordinary people. After they died an aunt took care of me. She also passed away."

He peered at her closely. "You have had many losses."

"Yes." She returned his gaze easily. It was the truth after all, though the losses she'd sustained were not what he imagined.

"And so you grew up in Boston? I have been there. Very historic city."

She smiled, recognizing the probe for what it was. "I went to boarding schools mostly." She leaned toward him, hoping to deflect the rest of the interrogation. "You can't possibly want to hear all this. It's quite boring."

An animal watchfulness slithered across his face and into his dark eyes. "You could never bore me, *dorogaya*."

She forced herself not to turn away, and thankfully, he did, returning to the Chilean sea bass on his plate. "So they packed you off to boarding school. In Europe?" He spoke casually between mouthfuls, but she knew there was nothing casual about the continued questions. And nothing casual about her stream of practiced answers.

"Oh, no. Right here in this country. Briarcliffe in New Hampshire."

He gave her a long, measuring look. "Yes. I can see you there. All bundled up in a hat and wool mittens. Me, I went to the school of hard knocks, as they say here."

"We each have our own path," she murmured, suppressing the anger that rose at his bid for sympathy.

"I suppose we do. And yours. After, what was it—New Hampshire—tell me, my dear, where you learned such brilliance."

"Princeton and, as you well know, Harvard." The truth came as easily as the lies.

"And were you top of the class?"

"Of course." She repressed a jolt of fear. What more was he after?

He smiled and took another bite. "The fish is marvelous. Really, you must eat some."

Dutifully, she nibbled, his sharp gaze searing her from beneath those formidable black brows as though she were the object of all his desires.

"So, Boston. Tell me what that was like." And the interrogation began all over again.

By the time she extricated herself, she was exhausted, palms damp, blood like frost. Worse, she'd seen enough of the apartment to know he kept nothing of interest there. No files, no computer.

"This was wonderful," she told him at last, gathering her purse. "But it's late, and I still have to drive home."

"Oh, no. Please. You must let me take you home." Miki's long, thin fingers wrapped around her upper arm like a manacle, the lump of gold on his little finger digging into her flesh.

"Please, darling, don't fuss." She gave him a diminutive pout and twisted in his hold, pecking him on the cheek and forcing him to drop his hand. "This has been marvelous, truly glorious. Thank you. But my car is here, and I'll need it tomorrow."

His black eyes gleamed with barely concealed displeasure that stopped her breath. Would he really let her go?

"You drive a hard bargain, *dorogaya*."

"That is why I'm so useful." Folding her arm through his, she led him to the door. "Come now, don't sulk. If you insist on being helpful, Yuri can drive me to the garage."

In the end, Miki settled for that, escorting her into the elevator and out to the curb where the limousine waited. He performed the attendant duties himself, opening the door for her with a flourish. "We will see each other again," he promised.

"I look forward to it." She gave him a last cool smile and slid into the car. He closed the door and stood at the curb to watch them leave, dangerous as one of his sword blades.

Finally free, she sat back against the seat, weak with relief. She forced herself to breathe slowly, in and out. She thought about home, eager to get to her refuge.

But the trip to the garage was a hellhole of taxicabs, buses, and cars that clogged every avenue. After she'd transferred to her own car at last and left the city behind, traffic continued thick, expanding the usual drive home to over two hours. All the way up the interstate the back of her neck prickled as though someone were following her. But when she stared into the rearview mirror all she saw was an endless stream of anonymous cars packed on the roadway like ants.

Daylight was dwindling into evening by the time she turned into her gravel drive. Steering up the familiar tree-lined path, she anticipated closing herself up behind her own walls where welcome silence waited.

But what she found when she turned the last curve and the house came into view set her pulse hammering. A police car, blue light flashing, stood in front of the bay window.

Her first thought was for Sonya. Something had happened to Sonya.

Alex bolted out of the car, up the steps and through the door. "What happened? What's going on?"

The florist must have come because the oil rig from the party no longer stood there, giving her a clear view of the room. A heavyset policeman stood in the entry trying to talk to Sonya. A huge boulder lifted from Alex's shoulders. The housekeeper was safe.

But near hysteria.

Wringing her hands, the elderly woman broke into a cloudburst of Russian the minute she saw Alex. Something about a dead rat and the florist?

"Hush, darling," Alex said, putting an arm around her. She looked up at the officer. "What happened? Why are you here?"

"Someone called in a complaint," a new voice said from behind her. Alex whirled to find Hank Bonner at the door. Just what she needed to top off the day from hell.

The detective strolled in, nodding at the uniformed officer by way of greeting. "Officer Newcomb."

"Well, if it isn't Detective Bonner. Didn't think the detective division was necessary. It was a raticide, not a homicide."

Hank gave the officer a deadpan look, as though he were used to this kind of ribbing. "What's going on, Pete?"

The officer produced a plastic bag, holding it up by its contents. A tail. A tail attached to a dead rat. "Someone pinned it to the front door."

A spasm of revulsion gripped Alex, and Sonya went into another paroxysm of Russian. "I told them not to call the police. I told them we didn't want—"

Of course Sonya wouldn't have called the police. "Who? Who did you tell?"

"The people with the flowers. The florist. They came to take the decorations down and they found the . . . the . . ."—she nodded in the direction of the plastic bag—"on the door and I told them not to but they insisted . . ." She shot a fearful look at the uniformed officer.

"Calm down. No one's going to hurt you."

She twisted her hands together. "But who would do such a thing? Don't tell me, I know. They are here, they are back.

They won't stop until they kill us all. We must leave this place. We must . . ."

"It's all right, *nyanya*," Alex murmured. "Look at me. Look at me." She forced the older woman to face her. "You are safe. We are all safe. Hush now." She stroked the woman's head. "Hush."

Hank Bonner was watching her. Even while she concentrated on calming down Sonya his gaze bored into her back. The gaze that meant questions. Always questions.

Bonner asked his first. "Who do you think did this?"

She held Sonya's hand, stroked it. "I have no idea."

"Maybe someone doesn't want your oil deal to happen."

"That's nuts," the uniform said. "Everyone in town wants it to happen."

"Maybe it has something to do with Luka Kole," Hank said, dropping the name into their midst like a grenade.

"Who's Luka Kole?" Newcomb asked, but the question was nearly drowned by Sonya's half scream.

"What do they know about Luka?" She clutched Alex's hand, her Russian fast and desperate. "My God, my God. How do they know about him?"

"Sonya, please—"

"Something has happened. Something has happened to Luka."

Alex looked up at the two policemen. "Please, can I take her to her room?"

The uniformed officer shrugged. "I got everything I need."

"Go ahead," Hank said quietly.

"Come, dear." Gently, Alex led Sonya toward her room. "I'll give you something to calm you down. You can rest. We'll talk later. Hush now. Everything is all right. Hush."

Hank watched Alex—cool, calm, unfeeling Alex—wrap

a comforting arm around the shriveled old woman and escort her away. So she did care about something, even if it wasn't her own father.

The two women had spoken Russian, so he didn't have a clue what they said, but he didn't need a translator to understand fear and distress. And whoever the older woman was—grandmother, aunt—she'd been terrified of something. Or someone.

And the name Luka Kole had been key.

"So, Detective, what do you want me to do about our friend here?" Newcomb wiggled the bag with the rat, eyeing Hank with amusement.

"What have you done so far?"

"Not much. Turns out the florist's people made the call. The old woman wasn't much help. But I questioned the guys who called. No one saw or heard anything until they were leaving. They opened the door and whammo—welcome home, Ricky the Rat."

"Did you get their names?"

"Yeah, sure. But they had another job to get to, so I let them go."

"All right. Turn in the, uh—"

"The body."

"Yeah, turn it in. I'll take it from here."

"Anything you say, Detective." Newcomb turned to go, and Hank walked him out, stopping on the other side of the door.

"Show me where you found it," Hank said.

"Well, they'd already taken it down when I got here, but there's a nail hole in the door. Kind of small, like a finishing nail or maybe a strong thumbtack. Anyway, figured that's where they strung him up." He showed Hank the hole. "This kind of thing—gotta be kids."

"Probably." Hank thought of Trey. Was this the kind of stunt he'd be pulling in a few years if Hank didn't get through to him?

Newcomb left, and just for grins, Hank went to his car, opened his trunk, and took out the crime scene field kit all detectives carried. If it had been more serious, he would have called for a uniformed techie, but he thought he could handle this one on his own.

He dusted the door for prints and found hundreds of partials. Multiply the number of people who had gone in and out of the party the night before times fingers on two hands and he'd get months of latent analysis that would probably add up to nothing.

Same for footprints. He searched the grounds for tracks and other trace evidence, but found nothing useful.

After replacing the field kit, he returned to the house. Alex was coming back from wherever she'd stashed the old lady.

"She all right?" Hank asked.

"I gave her a sleeping pill."

"Your grandmother scares easy."

Resentment flared in Alex's eyes. "She's old and set in her ways. She's spent a lifetime caring for other people and deserves her peace and quiet."

Well, well, well. Quick to the defense.

"And she's not my grandmother. She's my housekeeper."

Not even a relative. And here he thought Alexandra Jane was such a cold fish.

As if trying to prove him right, she turned that haughty tone on him. "Is there anything else I can do for you, Detective? If not, I'd appreciate your leaving."

But Hank had no intention of leaving. Yet. "You're not interested in who might have harassed you?"

"I'm sure it was a prank, nothing more."

Hank agreed with her but didn't say so. Instead, he studied her, and she returned his gaze, unflinching. There were tiny lines around her eyes, lines of weariness. Must have been a tough day for his ice princess.

"Thought you'd like to know," he said. "I checked out the names you gave me. You're clear."

"Well, I'm infinitely relieved." A little sarcasm there? "Now if you'd please—" She gestured to the door, but Hank didn't budge.

"I tried calling you earlier to let you know. You weren't home."

"I went in to the office."

"You weren't there either. I tried."

"I'm a busy woman, Detective."

"I told you not to go anywhere I couldn't reach you."

"I don't have to check in with you every minute of every day."

"Where were you?"

Briefly, her mouth compressed into a thin line. She didn't like being interrogated, and who could blame her?

"If you must know, I was with Miki Petrov."

Doing what? A flash of ridiculous jealousy ran through him like fire. "He's the Russian end of your oil deal." As if he didn't know.

"That's right."

"How did that happen?"

"How did what happen?"

"How did you hook up with Miki Petrov?"

She got all stiff and proper. "I don't see how that's any of your business."

"Everything's my business until I figure out who killed your father."

A blink of surprise, then recovery—so quick he wasn't sure she'd reacted at all. "You mean Luka."

Man, she couldn't even refer to him by their rightful relationship. "Yeah. Who else?"

"Look, you've verified my movements at the time of the murder. I already told you Luka and I were estranged. I don't see what my relationship with Miki Petrov has to do with any of this."

"Maybe nothing. Maybe something. You lied once, you could lie again. So humor me."

She looked away, toward the living room, where the furniture was back in place, everything neat and calm as if the party the night before had never happened.

"Can we sit down? I've had a long day."

She did look tired. "How about some dinner?" The words were out of his mouth before he knew he was going to say them. That damned soft spot working overtime.

He thought of everything he should be doing—going home to Apple House, helping Mandy with her homework, talking to Trey about what happened in school, helping his mother put the kids to bed—and he knew he was going to let them down. But he was a cop for one more week and he had a lead to explore.

"I'm not hungry."

"Come on." He flashed her his trademark grin. "You gotta eat."

She was stiff as a tree limb, neck rigid on bunched shoulders. Suddenly his hands itched to massage those tight muscles, to feel her soft, pale flesh beneath his fingers. Lead hell. If he was AWOL from Apple House, it would be for more than professional reasons.

7

Alex repressed an urge to scream. She'd already endured a meal with one man she detested, now here was another badgering her with food.

Oh, but not quite. She glanced at those teasing green eyes and an unwelcome pulse started thrumming.

"I'll take you someplace you've never been before."

Damn her, she should loathe him. Why didn't she? "Are you making a pass at me, Detective?"

He gave her an innocent look. Too innocent. "I'm following up on a lead. Think of it as your civic duty."

"But I'm a liar."

He shrugged but didn't deny it. "A challenge."

"And you like a challenge?"

"I don't like mysteries."

That stopped her. Green eyes aside, which would be safer? To stay away and hope he never solved this one, or to bring him closer and control what he knew?

Years of keeping her distance had honed her instinct for detachment. But before she could refuse again, he spoke.

"Look, I don't think you killed anyone. But you could help me find out who did." For once he was neither bullying nor flirting. His voice was quietly sincere, his face sober. Earnest.

She should be taken out and shot for falling for it. "One drink."

He shrugged. "Fine."

"And I want to change."

His gaze flicked over her, a quick assessment that made her heart race a little too fast. "You look great, but have at it."

She rolled her eyes and pivoted, heading off to her room.

She showered quickly, scrubbing off the smell and feel of Miki Petrov. A quick stint with the blow-dryer took the worst of the wetness out of her hair, leaving the rest to air-dry. She redid her makeup, then reached into her closet for a pair of slacks. But her hand landed on something else instead. Slowly, she held it up.

She'd bought the skirt ages ago but had never worn it. Light and airy, it was pale blue with tiny green buds and pink roses splashed across it. The skirt looked fresh and feminine and suddenly she was eager to have it swirling around her legs. She didn't stop to ask why, and if a picture of Detective Hank Bonner rose in her mind, she quickly repressed it.

To distract herself she slipped it on, enjoying the glide as the material sashayed over her thighs. Rummaging in her dresser, she found the matching sweater, a soft, silky green the exact color of the buds. It slid over her shoulders and hips like a cloud, cool and smooth against her skin. For the final touch, she draped the three sisters necklace around her neck, the jeweled ornament settling nicely into the sweater's deep V.

Watch over me, little sisters.

A final peek in the mirror to smooth down her still-damp

hair. She appeared soft and vulnerable, and she hoped Hank Bonner wouldn't think it anything more than a costume.

On her way out, she stopped in Sonya's room, saw that the housekeeper was asleep, and left her a note just in case she woke before Alex returned.

Then she walked toward the entry and the man waiting there.

Hank Bonner's brows rose in surprised admiration when she stepped into the room, and her face heated. Denying his reaction as well as her own, she spoke coolly.

"I don't want to be away long. If Sonya wakes up, she'll worry."

The edges of Hank's mouth tilted up ever so slightly. "You went to a lot of trouble for one drink."

She frowned; she didn't like being found out. "I put on a skirt and sweater. I assume you've seen them before."

He cocked his head, that small knowing smile still in place at the corners of his mouth. "Well, I thought I had. Now I'm not so sure."

She definitely didn't want to respond to that. "Can we go?"

He opened the door and gestured her out.

He wasn't kidding when he said he'd take her somewhere she'd never been. Buddy's was a burger-and-beer joint in Redpoint, twenty miles or so west of Sokanan. A wailing blues song was pounding out a beat as they came through the door. Guitars and harmonicas decorated the walls, tins of peanuts adorned the tables, shells crunched under their feet as they walked to a table.

He grinned as she surveyed the place. "Not exactly champagne and caviar."

"I do know how to drink beer, Detective."

He raised a brow and despite her protest that she wasn't

hungry, ordered two burgers to go along with the beer. "Guess you'll have to prove that."

They'd barely sat down when a phone rang. Hank retrieved a cell phone from his pocket and spoke into it. The music had just ended, so she could hear him, brusque and in command. "Bonner." A beat, then, "I'll be home soon, Mandy." The crispness in his voice had softened to marshmallow. "No, you won't. Not tonight. Pickles is there to watch out for you. And Nana. And when I come home, I'll make sure the nightmares have gone." Another pause. "Promise. I'll be there when you wake up. Put Nana on the phone, and go to sleep. You'll be fine." Despite the softness in his voice, his jaw was tense, a muscle working. "Don't worry about it," he said in a new, more adult voice. "Ma, it's okay. I don't mind." He sighed. "All right. I'll be there soon as I can."

He ended the call, put the phone back in his pocket, and took a long swig of the bottle the waitress had just brought.

"Who is Pickles?"

His gaze slid over to her, the green eyes shuttered. "Bodyguard. Guardian of Sweet Dreams. In the shape of a huge purple dinosaur. Stuffed."

"Your daughter?" She tried to imagine him married with children. A flash of something like anger lit her up. What was he doing here with her if he had a wife and child home waiting?

"Niece."

Oh. "Where's her own daddy?"

"Dead." The word was curt, the tone a roadblock.

But the glimpse she'd had of another side of Detective Bonner had been revealing. The gruff kindness that had slipped out at Luka's apartment wasn't an act he put on for her. It was genuine. She pictured the little girl and her purple dinosaur, remembering a time when she, too, had nightmares. Something fluttered inside her chest, sadness and sympathy. And an urge to return the kindness.

"It appears you have a previous engagement, Detective. Maybe we should get down to business. How can I help you?"

"What do you know about Miki Petrov?"

A pulse jumped inside her. Why did he harp on Miki? Had he made a connection between him and Luka and wanted to trick her into confirming it? "Why? Do you think he had something to do with Luka's death?" A film of dread settled on the back of her neck, cold and unpleasant.

"I don't know. I'm going on gut here. I don't have anything that ties them together except a newspaper article we found in Kole's wallet about Renaissance Oil."

"So you're fishing."

He shrugged. "I'm exploring possibilities. It's a long shot, but then, so were you, and look who you turned out to be."

She peered down at the table to hide a flush of embarrassment. So much to hide. So much she couldn't say.

"So tell me about Petrov. Who is he?"

She tried evasion by telling him what he already knew. "A *Novy Russky*, a new Russian. One of the new breed of Russian capitalists."

"And how does a capitalist get started in Russia? It takes money to start a business. Where did initial investment capital come from?"

"Back in the late eighties, early nineties, through tiny companies sponsored by the State that were allowed to operate as privately owned businesses. Anything from bakeries to construction companies to small lending operations. And there was always a huge underground economy."

"The black market."

She could see the wheels turning in Hank's head as he made connections. Too bad they were the wrong ones.

"So Petrov was a black marketeer?"

She ran a finger down her beer bottle, tracing a line in the dew on the glass. "Not exactly."

"You're not going to tell me he got his start baking cookies?"

She smiled wryly. "Oh, no. Miki Petrov never wanted to work that hard. Not when he could punch his way in."

He paused, working the clue. "Punch? Like in smack, hit, beat up?"

She sighed. No way to avoid it now. "Like in threat, interrogation, torture, and exile." She braced herself for his reaction. "He's ex-KGB."

She wasn't disappointed. His eyes widened in surprise, and he leaned back in his chair and whistled. But before he could react further, their food came.

The burgers were thick and juicy, grilled on chunks of French bread, slathered with mayonnaise and ketchup. Succulent slices of ripe tomato and leaves of crisp green romaine peeked out from beneath the bread. The smell was outrageous—meat, charcoal, and spice—and surprisingly, her mouth watered. All of a sudden she was starved. She bit in, finding it as delicious as it looked.

Hank grinned, wiping sauce and juice from the corner of his mouth. "Worth the drive and the company?"

"I hate to admit it, but yes."

They chewed for a while in silence, then Hank put down his sandwich. "So how does a thug for the Russian secret police become the money behind Renaissance Oil?"

She'd hoped he would have forgotten, but not Hank Bonner. "Come on, Detective, figure it out. This is right up your alley. How do most thugs get ahead?"

"By stealing their way up the ladder."

She shrugged: Give that man a cigar.

"You're saying he stole his millions?"

"Who else but the KGB would be in a position to grab what it could when the Soviet Union fell?"

He tilted his bottle back and swallowed a mouthful of beer. "Yeah, but we're talking millions here."

She shook her head. "You're thinking small, Detective. Believe me, there was much more for the taking."

"How much more?"

Careful. Tread softly. "The entire treasury of the Soviet Communist Party for one. Billions of dollars in gold and cash, all of which disappeared in 1991 and has never been found."

He stared at her, his expression stunned. "You mean it just . . . vanished?"

"Into thin air. Or into someone's pocket." In the far distance her father's voice echoed over the years. *Thief. Betrayer.*

"And you think Petrov—"

"No one knows for sure, but only the KGB had the power and influence to get that money out of Russia and into foreign banks. And Miki Petrov was the KGB's golden boy in Moscow. Rumor has it he did anything he was asked. Anything. No qualms, no questions. Service like that gets rewarded. And no one knows where Miki got his initial stake."

"You're serious."

"It's as good a theory as any." And true, though she couldn't prove it. Yet. A pang went through her. She was so tired of tilting at windmills.

"Then why are you working with him?"

She pushed the plate away, her appetite gone. "Because, as Willy Sutton said about why he robbed banks, that's where the money is."

He looked disappointed and shame pricked her. She didn't like being judged, especially when he didn't know the whole story.

Then again, whose fault was that?

She picked at a french fry, moving it around on her plate. "Look, the US wants to wean itself of its dependency on Middle Eastern oil. Russia has huge arctic tracts of multibillion-barrel oil and gas fields, all undeveloped because Russians lack the money and experience to tap them. Without Western resources and expertise, those fields will remain undeveloped. But despite that there's been huge resistance to foreign investment in Russian oil."

"Why? If what you say is true, they need us as much as we need them."

"It's a question of control. There's a faction that's afraid of giving foreigners control of a vital resource. Think about it. How would you feel if Russians owned a controlling stake in Ford or GM? Or in the Alaska pipeline?"

"But Petrov doesn't care?"

"No. All he cares about is the money he can make." She tried keeping the contempt out of her voice and wasn't sure she succeeded.

"So Petrov's a traitor as well as a thief."

"Not if you look at it from a global capital perspective. From that point of view, he's a hero. He's bringing investment and development to an industry and country that needs them."

"With money he stole from the country itself."

She gazed at the thick wooden table, at the dozens of

names and dates carved into the surface, and it struck her how eager some people were to proclaim their identities.

But she didn't have that luxury. It was time to pull back, muddy the waters, inject some doubt.

"Who knows? It could all be Miki's myth-making machine working overtime. Moscow in the nineties was like Tombstone in the 1880s. Maybe Miki is a Russian Wyatt Earp—a legend built from a speck of truth surrounded by a fistful of fairy tale."

"Except Wyatt was on one side of the angels, and Petrov is on the other."

"Don't think black and white, Detective. Think gray. Always shades of gray."

He polished off his sandwich and sat back. "So what does your father have to do with any of this?"

Panic surged into her throat. "My fa—" Then she remembered. "Nothing. Luka has nothing to do with it."

Hank's eyes narrowed. "I thought you said you hadn't seen him in years. How would you know?"

Damn. She had to be so careful with him. "I don't. I just meant that Luka didn't move in those circles."

"He owned the Gas-Up."

"An immigrant ambition. Hardly the stuff that puts a man on the same rung as Miki Petrov."

"Then why did he have the article in his wallet?"

"How should I know? Maybe he thought Renaissance Oil would be good for business, bring lots of people to his Gas-Up. Or maybe he was hoping to turn the Gas-Up into an RO franchise. Maybe he thought his connection with me would get him a better deal."

Hank was studying her. "Would it?"

She sighed. "Maybe. If only to get him out of my life as quickly as possible."

"I guess you don't have to worry about that now."

A chill settled inside her. "No."

"By the way, your lawyer called. He wants the body released for burial on Monday. I passed his name on to the coroner's office."

She nodded. She didn't want to think about burying Luka. "Have you made any progress on the case?"

He shook his head. "Nothing I can talk about."

Oh, he was good, this Detective Bonner. He extracted an encyclopedia of information from her while divulging nothing of his own. Well, she was through with his history lesson. "On that note, maybe it's time to go. You have someone waiting at home."

At the reminder of his niece, he signaled for the check.

"Thanks for dinner," she said quietly.

"Thanks for the information."

Once again she fought an absurd compulsion to tell him everything. But that would have been foolish beyond belief. She might have been many things—a liar, a manipulator, an avenging demon.

But she was no fool.

Hank noted Alex's pensive mood on the way home but didn't press her about it. Instead, he sifted through the information she'd provided. The more he thought about it, the more it seemed he was chasing air. He'd seen Luka Kole's apartment. Wrecked though it had been, it was no penthouse suite. If he'd had access to the kind of money Petrov blew in a week, he wouldn't have been living in a working-class hovel.

No, something else was behind Kole's murder. Something as simple as an out-of-work troublemaker with a beef. He thought of McTeer. Klimet had rounded up one of Big

Mac's alibis, but he'd been stoned to the eyeballs. Klimet wasn't sure if the guy knew what day it was, let alone remembered the day before.

Hank dropped Alex off at her front door. "Hope your housekeeper is all right. What's her name again?"

Alex hadn't said her name before, but it would be there on Pete's report. "Sonya."

Hank nodded. "Hope she's feeling better in the morning."

"Thank you."

She glided up the few steps, tall and royal. What was it about the way she carried herself? As if her skin were the only thing between the tough world outside and the tender secrets within. And why did he find that so compelling?

His hands tightened on the steering wheel. If he let go, she might pull him in after her, a great feminine tide that made him want to edge closer, drink deeper, despite the danger and bad luck he could bring her. As though she had some indefinable something, some hidden music only he could hear.

She used a key to open the door, turned briefly on the landing for a small wave, then disappeared inside.

Or maybe she was just one cold, distant bitch, and the music was just her ice cubes jangling. Better the latter. That way, he didn't have to feel so sorry for her.

A car was parked out back of Apple House when Hank pulled in. He groaned silently. The last thing he needed was an evening with Ben.

He pushed open the back door into the mudroom. The place was redolent of cinnamon and sugar, which meant his mother had spent much of the afternoon and evening baking apple pies for the weekend rush at the fruit stand. And just in case his nose didn't tell him what she'd been doing, a pie stood on the kitchen counter, one thick wedge missing.

The slice sat on a plate on the table next to his brother's hand. He leaned over their mother, pastry ignored, maps and brochures spread out in front of them.

"This is the best time to sell, Ma." Ben's voice was smooth and persuasive. "And I can arrange the sale so you can choose who gets to develop the farm."

Hank entered and Rose looked up, face tight, mouth pinched. Her hair sagged in its banded ponytail, the end drooping over one shoulder.

"Ben, it's late." Hank poured a cup of coffee from the never-empty pot on the counter and set it down in front of his mother. "Mom's had a long day. Why don't you table this for now?"

Ben glared at Hank. "I don't want her to be left behind."

Rose laid a hand on Ben's. "I don't want to sell Apple House, Ben. I promised your father. Please try to understand."

"I know how you feel, Ma. This place has been in the family for generations. But times change, and if we don't change with them, they roll right over us."

"I don't want to sell."

"But if you'd just look at these—"

"Ben," Hank interrupted. "Sit down, eat your pie, drink your coffee. Pretend you're a son and not a salesman."

He'd said it with a teasing tone, a lightness meant to take the sting out of his words, but Ben didn't hear it.

"That's a shitty thing to say."

Hank sighed. He didn't want to fight tonight. "You're right. I'm sorry."

Ben gave his mother a last close look, then folded up the maps and stacked the brochures in a tidy pile.

"How are Lori and the kids?" Hank asked by way of a further apology.

"Fine." Ben's voice was curt, his body stiff. "Josh told me Trey got into another fight at school."

Hank sat down, rubbed the back of his neck. He was suddenly bone tired.

"You know, this isn't working out," Ben said.

"It's what we decided," Rose said. "Let's not rehash it tonight." Using the table for support, she launched herself up with a sigh of effort, then shuffled to the counter, where she began covering the rest of the pie with plastic wrap.

"I'll be here full-time in another week or so," Hank said. "We'll make it work." How, he didn't know. He only knew they had to.

Ben gathered up his coat and briefcase. "There is another option. This place puts a lot of pressure on everyone. It doesn't have to be this way. I wish you'd think about it."

He kissed Rose on the cheek, and she patted his face, giving him a wan smile. "Love to Lori and the boys." She handed Ben the pie, and he left.

Silence settled over the kitchen. Rose swiped at the counter with a sponge, and Hank ate a forkful of his brother's pie. It was rich and sweet, and tasted like all the days of his safe, innocent childhood. With a pang he remembered the kids whose childhoods would be forever altered.

"Mandy get to sleep all right?"

"Uncle Hank's voice does wonders," she said with a smile.

Hank didn't know about that, but he didn't want to argue either.

"You're good with her, Henry. She'll be all right. You'll see."

Hank shrugged, doubtful. His mother had always been his biggest cheerleader.

She disappeared into the back, where a cold-storage room held apples and a refrigerator held all the confections for the weekend rush. Most of them she baked herself; Rose Bonner's pies were famous. But she also had an army of women who baked for her, from apple tarts to apple breads to apple butters. Even in spring, when apple season was long gone, the cooking continued.

Hank followed, leaning against the doorjamb and watching her go through her Friday night ritual. Counting pies.

"She had another one last night."

Rose paused in her tally. "Did she?" His mother's gaze caught his, concern warring with understanding. "The doctor said to expect nightmares. You know that. None of us get over that kind of loss without a few side effects." For a moment her mouth trembled, and he was acutely aware of her own loss. Her own child gone. Then she composed herself, gave him a brave smile. "Now go on. Eat a piece of pie. You'll feel better."

Hank wandered back to the kitchen, saw the pile of brochures Ben had left behind. Slick and glossy, they portrayed homey collections of houses, each one glowing with family warmth. He felt the irony clear down to his toes.

"Trey awake?" he asked, when his mother returned to the kitchen.

"Probably." She gathered up the coffee cups and placed them in the dishwasher. Picking up the half-eaten piece of pie, he started toward the hall. His mother's voice called over his shoulder.

"Don't let that boy eat you alive, Henry."

"No, Ma." But they both knew it was easier said than done.

Hank sauntered upstairs to Ben's old room. It was Trey's now, and he'd turned it into a shrine to basketball and hip-hop ghetto music. A picture of Eminem emblazoned the door. The rapper stared from the poster, ski cap pulled low over his forehead, eyes dark and dangerously intense. Was that how Trey felt—furious at the world? Hank could hardly blame him.

He knocked on the rapper's nose and waited.

"Yeah?"

He braced himself, hoping for the best, expecting the worst, and let himself in.

Trey cut a glance toward the door, saw who it was, and went back to whatever he'd been doing. Drawing, it looked like. On a notebook he probably should have been doing homework in.

"Nana made apple pie. Want a piece?" He held out the plate.

"Already had some." Trey's hard tone said he knew the food for the bribe it was.

Hank bit back a sharp response and set the plate down. "You get the assignments from the classes you missed today?"

Trey shrugged but didn't look at him.

Hank sat on the edge of the bed. "Trey," he said softly, "this has got to stop. Fighting at school and breaking windows, vandalism . . . it's just going to get you more trouble. Trouble you won't like, believe me. You'll get kicked out of school for one thing. And if that's what you're hoping, trust me, you won't like the alternative. McPherson is a day in the park compared to Alterman."

He couldn't bear the thought of his skinny nephew thrown into the alternative school, moving among the druggies and the tough guys, all the kids whose lives had fallen apart.

Trey's chin sank to his chest. Over and over again, he rubbed the same sharp lines of the basketball player he'd drawn on his notebook.

"Trey, your mom would be heartbroken if she were here. You know that."

His head snapped up, Maureen's blue eyes on fire. "She's not here. And don't give me that bullshit about how she's looking down from heaven."

"Trey—"

"I'm sick of that stupid school. Sick of the stupid kids. I hate it."

"You didn't hate it six months ago."

Trey didn't respond.

"Everything's different now, isn't it?"

Silence.

"Life sucks, Trey. I'm not going tell you different. You caught the baddest break there is. But you can't keep taking it out on other people."

"Why not? What are you going to do about it? Lock me up?"

Hank studied the anger in his nephew's face, remembering another angry face he'd seen that morning. In the interview room at the station. "I might, Trey. If you don't cut out the crap, I might end up having to. Is that what you want?"

Trey didn't answer.

"You know, that's pretty much the question here. What do you want?"

The obvious answer hung between them, pulsing and loud though it was unspoken. He wanted his mother back. He wanted his life to be the same as it had been and everything that happened to be one hell of a bad dream.

"I can't give you back what you lost," Hank said. "But if you figure out what you want now, from this point, playing the cards you were dealt, I'll break my back to see you get it."

Trey plopped down on the bed, turning away from Hank. "No thanks. I saw the kind of help you give. And so did my mother and father."

The words came out sharp as a knife blade. Hank felt them going in, the cut bone deep.

8

Morning broke cool and clear, a hard, crystal nugget of a day. Though it was Saturday and Hank didn't have to go in to the station, he was on call, so he hooked his phone to his jeans, turned it on, and hoped it would remain dormant. He had plenty of other work to do; Saturday was the busiest day of the week at Apple House, and everyone worked.

He roused the kids, and they ate a quick breakfast. By eight they were out at the farm stand, setting out cakes and pies, rolling heavy barrels of cold-storage apples to the front, heaping spring lettuce and peas from local farmers into attractive piles.

He was glad of the work. Anything to take his mind off the muck bubbling below the surface. The information Alex had provided was fascinating, but what was the connection between her international business deal and his small-town murder? Between Miki Petrov and Luka Kole? None as far as he could tell.

And yet the two things sat inside him, begging to be linked.

And then there was Trey. The morning warmed as they worked, but Hank couldn't say the same about his nephew.

He'd always liked the orchard and the fruit stand—that, thank God, hadn't changed. He'd been coming there since Maureen strapped him to her chest in an infant carryall, and he still jumped in with enthusiasm, hauling apples and flats of spring flowers without a word of complaint. But aside from the necessary grunts, he spared no words for Hank.

Hank shrugged it off. He wasn't giving up, Christ, he couldn't give up. Not on his own flesh and blood. But he didn't have the energy for another confrontation, not after last night.

For a moment he gazed out at the orchard. The fruit stand was set in a cleared patch of ground surrounded by trees on either side. Blooming thick and fragrant, the branches wore their delicate flowers like young girls in new clothes. In the distance he could hear the faint buzz of the bees brought in to pollinate the blossoms. Another week and the flowers would drop and they'd pick up the bees and return them to their keepers.

The task was a routine part of apple growing, and it happened despite human catastrophe. Trees bloomed, bees propagated, apples grew. Regular and predictable, through death and loss and their aftermath.

There was comfort in that.

Maybe that was why Trey liked the stand and the orchard so much. He could depend on it.

If the weather held and the insects stayed away.

A gamble of a different kind, Hank realized. Still ruled by chance and luck, even here.

He gazed at the crates of apples to organize by color and type and the bales of hay to strew over the ground. The sun was up, the day brightening, and if he had to, he could pretend with the best of them that everything was fine. He got to work.

It was almost noon when he saw Alex. He was driving the tractor, pulling the hay wagon from the orchard to the stand. Every spring they gave Apple Blossom tours to people who came up from the city and the surrounding suburbs, families mostly with schoolkids. It was a way to draw business to the stand in the off-season, when the previous fall's apple crop was nearly gone and the coming harvest was still months away.

He was returning from a ride with a load of visitors in the hay wagon when he caught a familiar head bent over a display of pansies. He braked, swung down from the seat, and paused to observe, slipping off his heavy canvas gloves and readjusting his ball cap.

The sight of her in tailored slacks and a pink glimmer of a blouse set off a trip wire inside him. What was she doing here? She looked as though she should be on a city street or in a fancy art museum, not a mud-strewn farm. Oblivious of his scrutiny, her face relaxed, the haughtiness gone, though the reserve remained. Did she ever truly unwind?

As he watched, Mandy appeared at Alex's elbow. Mandy was their flower expert, and she happily pointed to several pots. If Alex wasn't careful, Mandy would sell her the whole lot.

He helped his riders dismount, then strolled over just as his niece was claiming that the yellow pansies with the purple centers were her favorite.

"Purple's my favorite color," she said.

"I like purple, too." Alex's face had softened even further, sending an odd twinge through Hank's chest.

"I'm a red man myself." Alex turned, and he enjoyed the surprised look on her face when she saw him.

"Uncle Hank!" Mandy gave him a gap-toothed smile.

"This is my uncle Hank. Don't you think pansies are the cutest flowers?"

"Yes, I do, Mandy. How about you, Miss Baker?" He couldn't decide if he liked seeing her there, among the mire and the peasants, or if he preferred her pristine and remote in her stone-and-wood castle.

"They're very sweet," she said, recovering her composure more quickly than she had a right to.

"And yet, you don't seem like the sweet type." What was it about her that brought out the tease in him?

Her eyes cooled, and at the same time her face flushed, a combination that was unique in its ability to get to him.

Luckily, Mandy let her off the hook. "Everybody likes sweets," she piped in. "My nana makes the best apple pie. Have you ever tried it?"

Hank decided to let Alex off, too. "Why don't you get her one, Mandy. Pick out the best. On us."

Mandy gave a whoop and ran off, leaving the two of them alone.

"What are you doing here, Alex?"

The question came out a little more belligerent than he'd intended, and she blinked at the tone, then slanted him an amused, catlike glance.

"Buying apples, Detective. What did you think—that I was stalking you? That last night wasn't enough, so I've hunted you down for more?"

He smiled. "A guy can dream, can't he?"

"Not about me."

Shot down, right through the heart.

He looked away from her, squinting over at the new group of folks waiting for the next ride. Just as well. He needed a reminder that flirting with her was risky—to her and his case—since he seemed unable to stop. "Yeah, well, I guess I was surprised to see you here."

"I'm as surprised as you," she said briskly. "It's not every day you discover Sokanan's finest has a secret life."

"Not so secret. Just family."

"I come here often. I had no idea this belonged to you."

Her gaze scanned the area, and he followed it, seeing the colors pop out—the apple reds, from cherry to crimson, the vegetables, pale green to forest, flowers, pert yellow and white and that deep velvet pansy purple. The spectacle sent a warmth through him, the kind of feeling that came with familiarity and belonging.

"Not to me, not per se. It belongs to all the Bonners. But mostly to my mother." He nodded over to the stand, where Rose was juggling fruit and customers, her stolid form in its red-and-white Apple House apron like the roots of a tree dug deep.

On the far side, Mandy was studying a display of cakes and pastries, as if picking one was the most important decision in the world.

"Is that your niece? The one with the dinosaur for a body-guard?"

He nodded. "Amanda. Mandy."

"She's adorable." Just then, Mandy looked up and grinned, and Hank's breath hitched. Some days it seemed as if everything was going to be all right.

"Henry! You got people waiting!" Rose's voice boomed across the yard, and Alex's blue-gray eyes crinkled with laughter.

"Henry?"

It was good to see her laugh about something, even if it was him. He returned her mirth with a long, dignified look. "We all have our burdens to bear."

Rose strode up to them, the sharp-eyed look she threw Hank vying with the hint of a smile at the corners of her mouth. "Quit flirting with the customers and get back to work."

"Yes, ma'am." He tugged the brim of his ball cap, half-relieved and half-disappointed to be leaving. Putting his gloves back on, he went to load the hay wagon with kids and their parents.

Alex turned to the older woman, who stuck out a solid, no-nonsense hand. "I'm Rose Bonner, Henry's mother."

"Alexandra Baker, Henry's . . ." What? Suspect? Informant? Mystery? "Friend," she finished lamely.

A thick-set woman in jeans and a yellow sweatshirt, Rose was discreet enough not to ask the questions so obviously there between them. *Who is this woman? How does she know my son?* Instead, she watched Hank help a toddler into the arms of her father, who was already in the hay wagon. Alex followed her gaze.

A pair of faded jeans were slung low on Hank's hips, a washed-out red T-shirt tucked into them. Muscles bunched as he lifted the child, and Alex found herself looking away so she wouldn't be tempted by the sight.

She gazed around the fruit stand, trying to place Hank there. To imagine him growing up among the acres of trees that stretched outward from the stand in two directions, their blossoms deliciously scented and fluffy as clouds. Did he bring friends to the white farmhouse in the distance? Bring a girl to kiss under the apple trees? A keen nip of envy bit into her. What would it have been like to grow up surrounded by people who loved you? Who celebrated your greatest triumphs and saw you through your utter failures? To know you weren't alone and never would be?

For an instant she imagined what it would be like to live

like that. To let go of hatred and revenge and live free of the past. But she'd spent so long pursuing justice, she wasn't sure she'd know how.

"Trey!" Rose called to a gangly teen who was crossing the field in front of them. "Go help your uncle Henry with the hay wagon."

The boy trudged over, and between the two of them, they got the tickets collected and the wagon loaded. The boy jumped to the ground, and Hank set off.

"That's my brother," a voice at her waist said. She looked down to find Mandy at her side, a brown paper bag at her feet.

"Is it?" She studied the boy. He appeared to be three or four years older and completely the opposite in coloring— light while Mandy was dark. "You're lucky. I always wanted an older brother."

"I always wanted a younger one," Mandy said.

"Oh, you just want someone to boss around." Rose's stern look was soft at the center.

"Well, sure," said Mandy. "Isn't that the whole point?"

Alex laughed. "I always thought a sister would have been nice, too."

"You don't have a sister either?"

She shook her head, trying not to feel bereft. "Just me."

"And your mom and dad." She said it with a touch of wistfulness, and Alex recalled that Hank had said her father was dead. She wondered how fresh that wound was.

"No, just me. My mom died when I was a little girl. And my dad . . ." She paused, remembering the net of lies she'd woven around herself, and opted for the most basic truth. "My dad is also gone."

Mandy stilled. "Really?"

Alex nodded, and she saw Mandy's face change, her gaze turn hot and intense.

"What is it?"

"My parents . . . my parents died, too." The admission came out in a hoarse whisper, as though wrenched out of her.

Alex's stomach turned over. Parents. Then both were . . . She exchanged a glance with Rose, and immediately Mandy sensed the tension.

"But it's all right," she said quickly. "It's fine." She smiled, and the pretense of it, wide and false, nearly broke Alex's heart. "We live here, now. With Nana. And Uncle Hank. And everything is wonderful."

Oh, no, malishka, *no it's not.* Alex stooped so she was on a level with the girl. "Then you really are lucky. I was sad for a long time."

"You were?"

Alex nodded.

Mandy looked at her feet. "Did you cry?"

"Buckets."

"I have bad dreams." Her voice was small, as though she were afraid to say it out loud.

Something tightened in Alex's chest. "I had nightmares, too."

"You did?" She searched Alex's face for the truth, and Alex gave it to her.

"For a long time."

They stared at each other, understanding instant between them. Suddenly, Mandy threw her arms around Alex. "I like you," she whispered.

"That's enough, you," Rose said, and Alex heard a tremor in the older woman's voice.

"It's all right," Alex said. And then she whispered to Mandy, "I like you, too."

"Go on now, see who needs help with the flowers."

Mandy started to run off, then turned, walking backward. "I brought her a pie, Nana." She pointed to the bag on the ground. "It's a present from us. Uncle Hank said so."

"Well, if Uncle Hank said it, it must be so. Scoot."

Rose turned to Alex, a troubled look on her face. "I'm sorry. We've had a lot of losses in the last year. She didn't mean to burden you with them."

"She didn't. Please don't apologize."

"Well, you were kind to her. And that means a lot to us." She noticed a line forming at the register, and shook her head. "Sorry I can't talk."

"Go ahead. You have customers."

"Why don't you stay for lunch? Nothing fancy, we just set up in the orchard and take turns eating, but we'd love to have you join us."

Alex shrank back. She was already too close, too involved. And involvement meant questions, lies, secrets. She had to cut this off now, before she wasn't able to. "Oh, I couldn't possibly."

"Couldn't possibly what?"

She turned to find that Hank had returned from his tour and parked the tractor. He came up behind her, slapping his gloves against his thigh and clearing them of dirt and hay from the wagon.

"Henry, I have to go ring up those folks. See if you can talk her into staying for lunch."

Rose hurried away, and Hank's brows rose. "You work fast. I was barely gone and already you got yourself invited to a meal."

She looked away from the grin on his face. She couldn't

get sucked in. Not by him or his family. "It's not necessary. I just stopped by for some apples. Sonya is making an apple *kissel*—a kind of fruit drink—and she thinks Bonner apples make the best."

"Sonya does?"

She felt her face heat. "Well, I do, too, of course, but . . ." She backed away before she made a complete fool of herself. "I should be going."

Mandy ran up, breathless. "Nana says you're invited to lunch. Is she going to stay, Uncle Hank?" Mandy turned to Alex, slipping a hand into hers. "You are, aren't you?"

She opened her mouth to refuse, then saw the hopeful look in the little girl's eyes. How could she disappoint her?

Hank saw the split-second change come over Alex. More than that he saw a bond where once there had been none. A tie that had somehow developed between remote A. J. Baker and his own Mandy girl. Wonder of wonders.

Something went off inside him, an odd little burst of pleasure. That compulsion rose up again, the unwanted desire to draw Alex in. He was playing with fire, tempting the universe, daring it to bring her close without immolating her.

He should know better.

But the day was so fine and Mandy looked so happy.

And there was something in Alex's face, a kind of yearning as though all she needed was a little push to stay.

So before he changed his mind, he gave it to her. "Oh, she'll stay." He grinned down at his niece, then at Alexandra Jane. "Not for me, Mandy girl. But for you, yeah, I think Miss Baker would do just about anything."

Sonya grunted as she mixed the ground beef. She did it with her hands, her fingers digging into the raw meat, blending in the cooked onions and rice. The effort cost her, and she breathed heavily. Aleksandra would have given her a long-handled wooden spoon, but what did that child know about food? You had to get in with the bare hands and feel the ingredients.

Sonya couldn't say why she wanted to make *golubtsy* that day. Her head was fogged from the sleeping pill Sashenka had given her, and she had a pain in the center of her chest as though her heart were afraid to beat.

Preparing the stuffed cabbage rolls comforted her. Later, after her Sashenka returned, she would make a rich *kissel* with the apples she brought. Both were mementos of the old days, and Sonya so yearned for them. For the time when everyone had been safe.

But *nyanya*, Sashenka always said with a frown, those days were not the best; many people suffered. In her mind, Sonya could hear the irritation in Aleksandra's voice.

It was a truth she preferred not to know. To her, the past was haloed. Back then, before the world changed, her hands never trembled. She always had meat on the table and every year Comrade Baklanov gave her a new coat for the winter.

Nyet, nyet. She paused, hands mired in the meat mixture. There were no more comrades. Why could she not remember? Sashenka would be very angry with her.

She sighed, added salt and pepper and a bit of dill. Everything was different now. The whole world was different. Sometimes she got confused, as mixed up as *golubtsy* stuffing. More and more it was easier to remember the past, the good time, the safe time.

She mixed in a bit more salt, then clumped a ball of meat and set it in the center of one of the cabbage leaves she'd already boiled. Hands clumsy, she tucked in the ends and rolled it up.

This was the safe time. She was far away from Russia, she had nothing to fear.

Then why did her heart bang against her ribs? Why did they send a dead rat to her door?

She'd told them what they wanted to know. Years ago. She was an old woman, she deserved her rest. Why could they not leave her alone?

She rolled another leaf around a ball of meat. Were those unsteady fingers hers? She wiped her face with the back of one wrist. She was sweating. It was so hot in the kitchen.

She tried not to think about the rat nailed to the door. Sashenka said it was a trick done by children, but Sonya knew better. If only she could wish it away like a magic baba-yaga in the old stories her mother had told her long ago.

Her heart thumped with a wild pain, and she paused, her fingers formed around a bit of meat. Flashes of memory went through her, memories she thought she had buried deep. The cold, sterile room, the long metal table, the uncomfortable chairs.

The light had hurt her eyes and the questions had seared into her brain. Who had Comrade Baklanov spoken to? Where had he gone? Who had called? Come to visit?

They had put things on her. Small pieces of metal attached to wires. And when she couldn't answer, or when the answers didn't please them, they jolted her with them. Burned her so she jumped and jerked uncontrollably. Until she sobbed and names came out of her. Names she didn't even know, names she had heard in passing. Names that made the pain stop, that got her sent back to the dank, dim room with the lock on the door.

A rush of shame went through her, even after all this

time. What had she done? What had happened to the people whose names she'd cried out?

No one ever told her, and she hadn't had the nerve to ask. She didn't want to know. She begged forgiveness from the great unknown, hoping no one had been punished because of her.

Eventually, they'd let her go. Her hair had gone snowy though she didn't know it until she'd seen herself in a dirty mirror in the train station on her way back to Moscow. She'd looked old. An old, ragged peasant woman whose hands shook.

She'd made her way to Baklanov's apartment, but of course, Baklanov was no longer there. The apartment manager, a fat, pinched-faced pig of a woman, pretended not to know her.

With nowhere to go, Sonya had been forced to throw herself on the mercy of her sister, who was already squeezed into a tiny apartment with her daughter and her daughter's husband and new baby. They had welcomed her, but not without a tinge of resentment, and Sonya could hardly blame them for that.

No one had ever questioned her again, though for years afterward she felt people watching her. Men in black leather jackets, with hard faces and nasty hands, would stop by her street stall for her *golubtsy* or *pelmeni*, the hearty little meat pies she was allowed to sell. They asked for the spiced honey cake called *medovnik* or the *romovaya baba*, the rum cake with nuts, which she made only when the ingredients were available. And she'd wrap the food, give it to them, and decline the fistful of rubles they offered.

But then her Sashenka had come. All grown-up like a warrior queen, sweeping down with her American clothes and her American dollars.

"I have been looking so long for you, *nyanya*," she had said, her voice catching on a whisper.

And then the nightmare was over. They left Russia and came here, to this beautiful house. It was all done in great secrecy. Her Sashenka had many friends, many contacts. No one would know who Sonya was or who she'd been. She would be safe here.

But those burned by milk blow on cold water. Sonya knew they were still out there.

Wasn't the dead rat proof? They had found her, they would take her once more, question her. She rolled up another cabbage leaf, her heart going crazy again.

And then she heard it. Footsteps outside the kitchen. She stilled, the blood beating into her chest like thunder.

"Sashenka?"

No answer.

"Who is there?" Her voice came out on a quiver, no bigger than a mouse's. "Who . . . who is there?" she whispered.

But she knew. She'd always known. Evil never went away.

Hands shaking, she grabbed the knife she'd used to cut up the onions. She felt light-headed, dizzy, the thump in her chest violent and erratic.

Footsteps outside the kitchen drew closer.

The door opened.

The monster stared at her, clad in black leather, huge as she remembered, the face cruel and vicious as all the others. A different monster, but the same. Always, always they were the same.

He looked at the knife she clutched, her grip so tight her fingers hurt. A smile worked the lips on the monster's face. A smile she remembered well. Amusement at her pain, laughter that she could ever be a threat, ever be anything more than a beetle to squash.

And then it spoke, the words tumbling out like a breath of poison. Russian words, as though she needed proof.

"Are you going to kill me, old woman?"

She lunged, and her breath hitched. A pain snaked up her arm and burst inside her chest.

She was falling, falling.

Alex disconnected the call on her cell phone and stared at the rickety picnic table. It was set amidst a clutch of ancient apple trees whose sweet-smelling blossoms permeated the air with a luscious bouquet.

"Problem?" Hank spread a white cloth over the table and lifted a cooler.

"Sonya didn't answer." She frowned. Had Sonya stepped out for a few minutes? Sometimes she enjoyed sitting on the patio in the sunshine. But when Alex left, the elderly woman had been boiling cabbage for *golubtsy*. Had she finished cooking already?

"She's probably in the bathroom. Give it a few minutes and call back."

Alex nodded, an uneasy feeling sifting inside her. But she pushed it aside when Mandy grinned at her from above a huge chocolate cake with caramel frosting.

"No apple pie?" Alex asked.

"Uncle Ben and Trey like chocolate," Mandy said.

"Uncle Ben?"

"My brother," Hank said, handing her a pile of paper plates. She put them on one end next to a pile of napkins anchored by a stone. "He'll be here for lunch, too."

More Bonners. A wave of strangeness shot through her at the thought of so much family, so many connections and support. She felt dizzy with the closeness and, to cover it, focused on the one Bonner she understood. "What about you, Mandy? Apple or chocolate?"

Mandy giggled. "I like chocolate, too."

Alex felt a goofy smile etch itself across her face, and noted with alarm that Hank had lifted an amused brow. What was happening to her?

She ducked her head so he could no longer see her expression, and set out hunks of cucumbers and tomatoes, cheese and bread with homemade apple butter and preserves, sliced meats and a bowl of red Bonner apples. To drink, there was cider. Several gallons of it, in old-fashioned glass bottles.

"Hand-pressed," Hank said, with an edge of family pride.

When they were done, the table looked like a true peasant's feast. Nestled among flowering apple trees that looked like they had stood for centuries, the scene held a magic glow, one of her Russian miniatures come to life. All it needed was a cluster of women with embroidered skirts and beribboned tambourines to dance around a troika.

But instead of a troika, an SUV drove up the lane and parked off to the side a few yards from the impromptu dining room. Hank nodded over in its direction.

"There's Ben now."

She watched with interest as a man and woman with two boys got out, bringing a load of lawn chairs with them. Trey wandered over, grabbed a couple and set them up.

"We share the work as best we can," Hank added. "I do the mornings, Ben's wife Lori helps in the afternoon. Weekends are the busiest."

The newcomers got closer and Alex recognized them with a start of surprise. "The mayor is your brother?"

"Like I said," Hank muttered, "we all have our burdens."

Of course. Why she hadn't put two and two together? Everyone knew Ben Bonner's connection to Apple House. And then the new family was there, milling and greeting each other, and introductions had to be made.

"Of course I know the mayor." Alex smiled and shook the hand Ben Bonner offered.

"I didn't know you knew Hank socially." He eyed Hank suspiciously. "You haven't dragged her here to harass her about some case, have you?"

"Ben," Lori scolded gently. A pert blond in navy slacks and a white tennis shirt, she looked like a youthful coed.

Ben ignored his wife. "Has he been hassling you, A. J.?"

She looked to Hank, saw tension there, and wondered about it. "Of course not. I stopped by the stand to buy apples—you do know that Bonner apples are the best—and your mother invited me to stay."

That didn't explain much, but before Ben could interrogate further, Mandy spoke. "She doesn't have any parents either."

A leaden hush greeted this.

"Shut up, Mandy." Trey gave his sister's shoulder a little push.

"Well, she doesn't."

"So what?"

"Trey—" Hank's voice held a warning note.

Trey flicked his uncle a look that surprised Alex with its contempt. Then the boy plucked an apple from the bowl, bit into it, and sauntered away.

Ben and Hank exchanged glances, and all at once Alex realized that the family she had been idealizing was as real as her own. Complete with cracks and holes. And trouble.

"I'm going to help Trey at the stand." Ben's oldest, Josh, started after his cousin. His mother stopped him.

"Have some lunch first." Something about the way she said it made Alex think Lori didn't want her son anywhere near Trey.

"But Mom—"

"I don't want you and Trey getting into trouble."

"We won't—"

"Lunch first. Then you can come with me while I do my shift." And where I can keep an eye on you, was the unsaid rest of the thought.

Josh plopped down on a lawn chair, face marred by a resigned frown.

An embarrassed hush ensued. To cover it, Alex asked, "Have you always taken turns like this?" She was surprised by the way the Bonners worked. Sokanan was no Manhattan, but this kind of small-town support seemed unusual.

Lori paused, then spoke in a low voice. "Well, when Maureen and Tom were alive, we didn't need to help out as much."

Another pall. Maureen and Tom. Mandy's parents?

"Which is why," Ben said with exasperation, "we should sell the place and have done with it."

Sell Apple House? How could they sell the Bonner family legacy?

"Do we have to go over this every time?" Frustration pierced through Hank's low voice.

Apparently, Lori agreed. "Josh, Randy, come and eat lunch," she called, interrupting whatever Ben was going to say next.

But not for long. He turned to Alex. "With Renaissance Oil coming soon, this whole area will be booming. It's the perfect time to sell, don't you agree?"

She hesitated, not wanting to be dragged into a family row. "I—"

"Ben, not now," Lori said.

"But I'd really like to know your opinion, A. J. You've done a lot for this community, and—"

"Cut it out, Ben," Hank said, his voice rising.

Ben not only matched Hank's tone, he took it a notch louder. "You just don't want to hear the truth, do you, little brother?"

The tension was palpable, and it sent an ache of loss through Alex. She wanted her fantasy, wanted to know a warm, kind, and loving family existed even if it wasn't her own.

Lori thrust a plate in her husband's hand. "Not now." She gave a meaningful look in Mandy's direction.

The little girl was hunched on the picnic bench, face bent low over the table. Alex thought she would burn a hole in the spot she traced over and over in the cloth. The sight sent a rush of sympathy through her, and a helpless look across Hank's face. Everyone else glanced away.

Hank slid onto the bench next to his niece. "Why don't you see if Nana wants to take a break?"

Stubbornly, she shook her head.

"I'll come with you," Alex said softly.

That seemed to cheer Mandy up. She sighed, slunk off the bench, and slipped a hand into Alex's.

They walked slowly, Mandy plodding along. "Why does everyone always have to shout?"

"I don't know, *malishka*." And she didn't. She had no idea why there was such sorrow and grief in the world.

"What does that mean? Malish—what you said."

"*Malishka*. It means 'little one' in Russian."

"Are you Russian?"

A pang stabbed her. "No, but I speak it."

"Really?" Her face brightened with interest. "What's my name in Russian?"

Alex thought a moment. "Well, there isn't a good translation of Amanda. But I could call you Masha. Or Manya."

She spied her grandmother and dashed up to her. "Guess what? My name is Manya."

"Manya?" Rose was packing jars of apple butter into a paper bag for a customer. "What happened to my Mandy?"

"Mandy is ordinary. Manya is Russian." Mandy gave the last word theatrical importance.

"Oh, I see," Rose said, with a wink that made Alex smile.

She would have thought Mandy had forgotten the unhappiness of a moment ago; but when she peeked over her shoulder at the picnic table, the same haunted expression crossed her small face.

"Uncle Hank says you're to take a break now."

"Does he?" Rose gazed over at the group milling around the distant table under the trees. From the heated gestures it looked as though Hank and Ben were still arguing. Mandy looked away, and a small frown pierced the good humor on Rose's face. But only for a moment. She handed the bag of jam to the customer waiting for it, then ruffled her niece's hair. "And who's going to help the shoppers while I'm sitting down?"

"I will." She lowered her voice. "But only if you call me Manya." She uttered the name in an exaggerated, throaty voice accompanied by a dramatic, sweeping curtsy.

Rose sniffed. "Well, I think I'd better send someone to assist you, Your Highness." She took off her apron and somehow, Alex ended up with it. Rose shuffled off, and a few minutes later, Hank joined them.

He eyed the apron still clutched in her hand. "I see my mother has already put you to work."

Flustered, she looked around for a place to set it down.
"Oh, I didn't mean to—"

"Let's see how it looks."

"But—"

He slipped the apron around her neck, turned her, and
tied the strings behind her back. "What do you think?" he
asked Mandy.

She eyed Alex critically, then, with a grin that reminded
Alex of her uncle, said, "Perfect."

And so for a little while, Alex found herself completely
absorbed by the tasks at the fruit stand. She had no time to
think about Petrov or Luka. No time to worry about who
knew what, or what she should do about it. Loss and death
seemed to belong to another world. Another time. Another
life. All she thought about were apples and pies, change and
paper bags. It was the most mundane job in the world, and
she enjoyed every minute of it.

Eventually, Lori and Ben came across the field with the
two boys in tow. Alex turned over her apron, Mandy disappeared with her cousins, and as she and Hank made their
way to the picnic table, she saw Ben greeting customers,
chatting and shaking hands, while Lori worked the register.

"Just one more stop on the campaign trail," Hank said,
following her gaze.

"He certainly is good at it. I can see why he won so hand-
ily. But I'm surprised he wants to sell. This must be a great
political base for him."

"The orchard isn't doing as well as it used to. Imported
apples have taken over the market. We just can't compete."

"And you're shorthanded."

He shrugged. She could tell he didn't want to get into
that.

"Tom and Maureen were Mandy's parents?"

He nodded.

She slanted a look at him, debating whether to push. His face had closed up, and she decided not to pry. She knew about keeping secrets. Some were better left unsaid.

They'd reached the table. Rose was clearing the remains of the previous diners, tossing paper cups and plates into a garbage bag. He filled a plate with food and handed it to her.

She held up her hands. "No. Really. I should get home. Sonya will be worried."

"Try her again. I'm sure she'll understand."

She dug her phone out of her purse, punched in the number, and frowned when no one answered, her earlier uneasiness returning. She put the call through again. No answer. She looked around, suddenly confused, light-headed. Where was her car? "I . . . I think I'd better go."

"Is everything all right?" Rose asked.

"I don't know. It's not like her not to answer the phone."

"Maybe she took a walk," Hank suggested.

"She never takes walks. She never leaves the house." Uneasiness was building to dread.

"Want me to come back with you?" He had that earnest look about him, the one that said he not only took these things seriously but could handle them. Could be counted on. Leaned on.

But instinct kept her at arm's length. He was still a cop. He could still ask questions she didn't want answered. "No, that's . . . that's not necessary. It's probably nothing."

"Are you sure?" Rose's face was concerned. "Henry can take a few minutes. It's no trouble."

"No, it's fine. I'll be fine."

"But—"

"Ma, she said no."

Rose scowled at him. "I heard. I may be old, but I'm not

deaf." She scraped leftovers into the trash. "At least take some apples back with you."

"I got it covered," Hank said, rolling his eyes with more affection than irritation.

He walked her back to her car, stopping to retrieve the apple pie Mandy had chosen and to fill a bag with apples.

She slipped in behind the steering wheel while he put the bags in the back. He closed the car door, then leaned in, strong arms braced against the car roof. "Next time, bring Sonya with you. I have a feeling my mother would like to hear about that apple drink she makes."

She smiled, trying not to let fear take over. "I'm sure Sonya would love telling her about it."

He backed away, and she turned on the engine and drove off, leaving him in the yard among the apple blossoms, the bustle and the tumult of his family.

Her heart beat in time to the rhythm of the tires. *Please let everything be all right. Please let everything be all right.*

9

Thirty minutes after Alex left, Hank's phone vibrated against his hip. He'd been finishing lunch, trying not to dwell on the image of her under the fruit trees, the strangeness of it. And the unexpected rightness, too. He had the queasy feeling that the universe was getting ready to play another trick on him.

He pushed his plate away and unhooked the phone. "Bonner."

Lieutenant Parnell was on the other end. "Hank, we got a DB on Highbridge. Where the Renaissance thing took place the other night."

A dead body. At Alex's. Cold washed through him, quickly followed by heat. He bit down on the rush of panic. "Who is it?"

"Housekeeper. Death was unattended, so we're doing a rough crime scene. The homeowner, this Miss Baker, she's pretty upset. Said she'd been with you this morning. Is that true?"

Hank avoided the question. "Hold on. I'll be right there."

He domed up, slapping the light on the car roof, and, with the siren blasting, what should have taken twenty minutes took ten. He tore down her drive, brakes squealing to a stop.

An ambulance stood at the front door along with a patrol car and Parnell's department issue.

Hank darted out of his car, up the steps. More commotion inside. A couple of uniforms, hefty and young, looking uncomfortably like they weren't sure what they were doing there. Two EMTs, waiting for word they could take the body.

"Where?" he said to one of them.

He nodded with his chin. "Kitchen."

"And Miss Baker?"

"In the living room with the lieutenant."

Hank headed for the kitchen, opting to find out what had happened before he confronted Alex. He traced his steps with deliberate care, but nothing appeared changed from the last time he'd been there.

Except for the apple in the hallway.

Carefully, he stepped around it, and it led to another and another. And then he came to the bag with the rest of the fruit he'd handpicked, lying open at the kitchen doorway where it must have fallen from Alex's hands along with the apple pie. The bag had split open and apples pooled around it, bright and red as fresh blood. He stared at them, imagining the shock and pain Alex must have suffered coming home.

Inside the kitchen, Greenlaw was already suited up in his white clean-room garb, booties and all, field kit open.

Hank stood in the doorway and called to him as he was carefully pulling off a pair of latex gloves, rolling the tops down over the fingers so as not to contaminate the scene with trace evidence of his own. "What do you have so far?"

The highly trained patrol officer tiptoed over. "Got a knife from the floor near her hand. But she was cooking, so that's not out of line. No sign of a struggle, no visible wounds. I don't know. Probably a natural. Looks like we'll have to wait for the autopsy."

"I'm coming in."

"Okay, but put on some booties."

The officer handed him a pair from the field kit, and Hank complied before moving into the kitchen.

The white-haired woman was on the floor where she'd fallen. He scanned the scene, took in the position of the body, the counter with bowls of meat and rice, onions glistening in a pan on the stove. The smell lingered, boiling cabbage, onions, some kind of herb, dill maybe. But no blood. Unless you counted the raw meat she'd been mixing.

He asked to see the knife, gloved up, and removed an ordinary kitchen knife from the evidence bag, maybe four inches long. The kind you might use to chop vegetables. He sniffed along the blade, thought he caught a faint oniony whiff. He rebagged the knife and stared down at Sonya.

What happened to you?

She gazed back at him, face frozen in a grimace that could have been terror. Or just death playing tricks. Secrets. The dead always kept secrets.

He recalled Sonya's fear yesterday and how Alex had put her arm around her, gentled her, comforted her. He swallowed hard.

"Whatever develops, I want to see it before you do."

"You got it, Detective."

Hank stepped out, removed the shoe coverings, placed them in a crime scene trash bag and went to look for Alex.

She was in the living room. He remembered it as it had been the night of the party, with the governor shaking hands, photographers flashing pictures, and Alex cozying up to Miki Petrov.

Now she sat on a couch, still and white-faced, misery etched in every line of her body.

Parnell stood when Hank entered and met him before he reached the couch. The lieutenant's body was an effective blockade, and Hank squelched a flash of impatience.

"How is she?"

"Pretty torn up."

"You baby-sitting?"

"Until I figure out what's going on. What was she doing with you?"

"She came to the fruit stand. I was there. I showed her around. End of story."

"Why the special treatment?"

Rapidly, Hank tallied his options—zip it or spill it. He didn't like keeping things from Parnell. First off he usually smelled a con. Second, he was good at what he did, and Hank respected that. But he opted for the former anyway, though he couldn't say why. Didn't want to know why. "I questioned her about the Luka Kole case. We found an article about the Russian oil deal in his wallet. It mentioned her. I followed up."

"Is that the lead you were chasing the night of the party?"

"More or less."

Parnell frowned. "Why the hell didn't you say something about this?"

"It didn't pan out. I was going to write it up." Eventually.

Parnell nodded but was clearly unhappy. "I don't like being kept out of the loop, Hank."

Yeah, wait until he found out the rest. The way he'd caught Alex at Kole's apartment, her relationship to Kole. Protecting Alex or his case? Either. Both. Besides, it wasn't as if he was going to ruin his career.

"Yes, sir." He tried not to gaze over Parnell's shoulder at

Alex. He couldn't exactly plow down his commanding officer, but he was itching to get to her. "You want me to handle this?"

"You're on call, it's yours. Looks like natural causes. The autopsy will tell for sure, but shouldn't be too much of a problem."

Hank cleared his throat. "Can I . . . uh . . . see her?"

Parnell looked back at Alex, who still sat stiff and quiet. "She doesn't have much to say, but yeah, sure. I have a baseball game to go to anyway. My youngest is playing." He started to step aside, then stopped. "I don't want you harassing her. You got a buzz up your ass about the Kole murder, keep it to yourself. One thing has nothing to do with the other."

"No problem, boss."

"And keep me informed. Of everything. Even the stuff that doesn't 'pan out.'"

Hank recognized the dig for what it was and nodded.

"She's important to this city," Parnell said, "so keep the kid gloves on and the VIP treatment up."

Hank nodded. "Yes, sir. Absolutely."

And then Parnell was gone, and only Alex was left in the room.

He walked up to her slowly, letting her get used to the sight of him. People in shock were sometimes startled by the slightest things. But Alex didn't say or do anything as Hank eased himself on to the couch next to her. Her eyes were dull, and she stared out toward something across the room, though he doubted she was seeing much of anything.

"Alex, can I call someone?"

Alex heard his voice, but wasn't quite sure what he had said.

"I'd like to call someone to stay with you."

The sounds penetrated, but not the meaning.

"So you're not alone. Can I call someone?"

Finally, the words took shape, made some kind of ironic sense. He wanted to find someone to comfort her, to stand vigil with her. She almost smiled. Poor Detective Bonner with his endless stream of relatives. He had no idea, did he? "No. There's no one to call."

"Are you sure? How about . . . " He hesitated, then, "How about Petrov? You seemed . . . close to him."

A joke. He was making a joke. Petrov to comfort her? He'd killed Sonya. Just like he'd killed everyone else.

A wail went off in her head. Why had she pushed so hard? The past was over, done. She couldn't change it, what did it matter? But she had insisted. She had pressed and shoved and finally brought Petrov down on all of them.

"Please, no." She had done this. Her. All her fault. She thought of the body lying on the kitchen floor, and almost shattered with remorse. "Just go. Let me be."

So cold. She shivered with it.

He disappeared, but like a bad dream he came back, bringing a sweater with him. It was Sonya's, from the closet by the front door. He wrapped it around her shoulders, and she inhaled the fragrance of the past. Of the last living link to it.

Who would call her Sashenka now? She would be Alex, forever cold, cold Alex.

She felt a tear slide down her cheek, heard a muttered curse.

"Who is your doctor, Alex? Let me call him and get something for you. To help you sleep."

Sleep? She couldn't sleep.

In a corner of her mind she knew the police were there,

doing whatever it is they did to old dead women. To her *nyanya*. Her nanny, her friend.

If she sat still long enough, eventually they would go. They would take Sonya with them, and there would be no one. Nothing.

Just silence and revenge. And maybe only silence.

Someone was tugging her up. Oh, yes. Hank. Detective Bonner was here.

Dangerous. She mustn't talk to him.

But he didn't ask any questions. Gently, he pulled her up, led her through the hallways. He had his arm around her. That was strange.

Uniforms passed by in a blur, dark blue and white, and then she was in a different room. He sat her on the edge of a bed.

"Stay here. I'll be right back."

It took a minute to realize she was in one of the guest rooms. She rose but couldn't remember why. Then he returned, and she found herself sitting again.

"Here. I found these in one of the medicine cabinets. Take one. It will help you sleep."

She stared at the pill in his hand. At the glass of water.

"Take it, Alex. Lie down for a bit. Let the shock wear off."

The thought of sleeping made her stomach turn. How could she sleep when Sonya would never wake? "I can't."

He set the pills and the water on the bedside table. "Alex, I'm sorry for your loss. So sorry."

"Go. Please. Just go." She couldn't bear to look at him, at the concern stamped on his face.

"I won't let you stay here alone. If you won't let me call someone, come to the farm with me."

The farm? If she hadn't been distracted by him, if she

hadn't allowed herself to be enticed by apple blossoms and little girls, she would have been here with Sonya. She could have protected her, prevented whatever had happened. She wouldn't go back to the farm. She would never go there again.

"I'm going to check on what's happening," he said, when she didn't answer. "Stay here. Lie down."

She nodded, glad to see him go.

Obediently, she lay down on the bed. Tears leaked across her face and rolled down her neck. She despised them. What was the use of crying?

She closed her eyes against the wetness, but the tears kept coming. With a keening moan she rolled over and let them come.

Hank watched the medics push the gurney with the black body bag toward the waiting ambulance. He dismissed the two uniforms, then checked on Alex.

Wrenching sobs came through the closed door, and he backed away, moved by her grief. She'd always seemed so self-contained, it was hard to hear her break apart like that. People always said it was good to get it out, but he knew that getting it out was sometimes more painful than holding it in.

He left her alone and went back to the kitchen, where the apples still sat on the floor.

One by one, he picked them up and put them in the refrigerator. Then he scraped the pie off the floor and threw it away.

The mess on the counter would have to be dealt with. He debated whether to wait for Alex; it would give her something to do. But in the end, he did it himself, dumping the meat and cabbage and taking the garbage out of the house.

By the time he was through he hoped Alex might have

calmed down. When he checked on her, the sobs had stopped, but she didn't answer his knock. He cracked open the door and peeked in. She was asleep. The heavy drugging kind of sleep, he hoped, which would give her some relief for hours.

He called Apple House, told Rose what had happened. She clucked in sympathy. "Of course you should stay," she told him.

"Ma, don't be crazy. I can't do that."

"She shouldn't be alone."

"She's asleep. She won't even know I'm here."

"I'll know. Do it for me, Henry, if not because it's the right thing to do."

Christ.

He hung up the phone, trapped by his damn sense of decency and his mother. A grown man no less.

Grumbling, he checked on Alex again. She was still out. He left her that way, and returned to the kitchen. Quiet had descended like snow, muffling and oppressive, and he wondered why Alex had buried herself away like this.

The answer was there, somewhere in the house, and he found himself searching for it. With bands of glass that opened on to dense forest, her home was rambling and big-roomed. Too big for two people, let alone one. How did she deal with the isolation?

Pushing farther into the house, he found what was probably her bedroom. Spacious enough to set up house in, it had a separate sitting room, both wallpapered in huge overblown roses on a black background. Fascinated, he stood in the doorway. What did the décor say about her?

He would have predicted something cool and white, something unemotional. But the roses were passionate and the dark background sensual. Another side to his ice princess? A side she kept hidden like so much else?

And then he was overtaken by an underground impulse. A cop's impulse. He hadn't forgotten that picture he'd spotted on the news. Could it be here, somewhere in her room?

A rhythm quickened in his head. Any search he conducted would be entirely illegal.

Then again, he already knew Kole was her father, so turning up the photograph wouldn't be evidence he'd need.

So why do it?

He scanned the room, chary of entering, and tried to answer the question. Curiosity. A need to know more about her. A need he didn't understand, but was compelled to honor.

For some reason. Some unknown, hidden reason.

Secrets. Always secrets.

Was there was a link between Kole and Petrov? If so, what did Alex know about it?

But there was no link. Hadn't he already come to that conclusion? Hadn't Parnell told him to back off?

But his feet were already taking him inside her room, his hands already opening drawers and closets.

She wouldn't like him for this.

Yeah, well, she didn't like him for a whole lot of other things anyway.

He found the box high up on a closet shelf, back behind a slew of shoe boxes. Gingerly, he took it down, then opened it.

The photograph he'd seen during the WBRN broadcast was right on top. A much younger Alex outside what looked like a school or university, and Luka Kole, all dolled up in an ill-fitting suit and tie.

Hank smiled. He liked being right.

Lifting out the framed picture, he saw piles of other snapshots below it. Several more of Kole, and then many of Alex as a child with another man. And then several of the three of them. Kole, a teenage Alex and the second, unidentified man. Her stepfather? No, not in a picture with Kole. The three of them stood outside an official-looking building, the men in clumsy suits with lapels the size of bus fenders. Another showed them on a porch with a lake in the background, the unidentified man dressed in dark slacks and a droopy sweater that looked like a remnant from World War II. And there they were again, in front of a huge, black car with little diplomat flags on the front end, the men wearing those same square-cut suits.

He checked the backs. Some were dated, some weren't. A couple had handwritten labels, but they were in Russian, which he couldn't read.

He found a picture of Sonya, too. Much younger, with brown hair and smiling blue eyes. Alex was in her lap, grinning at the camera. Her front tooth was missing.

The picture sent a spasm of grief through him. For Alex and all she had lost.

He dumped the photos on the bed, remembering those clawing, tortured sobs. Who were all these people? Alex always seemed as though she'd sprung whole from the mind of Zeus, a perfectly formed adult. But she hadn't. She'd had friends, family. A childhood.

And if pictures didn't lie, her estrangement from Luka must have been fairly recent, though she said she hadn't seen him in years.

Toward the bottom of the box he found a wedding picture. The unidentified man in the picture with Kole and Alex, and a woman. Beneath it were more pictures of the other woman. She had the look of Alex about her. Her mother?

Why wasn't the groom Kole? And why had Alex said she had no pictures of her mother?

He sifted through the snapshots again, spreading them out on the bed. The frame she'd been holding in Luka Kole's apartment, the frame with the picture ripped out of it, had easily been eight-by-ten. But there was no picture that looked like it had been torn out of its moorings, sides shredded. No eight-by-ten photograph of a woman here at all.

Would she have put it somewhere else? Maybe she was getting it reframed. Why would she have torn the photo out of the frame anyway? Why not just take the whole thing?

Instinct, that ingrained cop sense, told him something wasn't right. Too many unanswered questions were piling up.

He replaced the pictures and the box and went to check on Alex. Since she was still sleeping, there was nothing he could do about his uneasiness, so he hunted in the kitchen for coffee, made a pot, then slapped together a sandwich from some cheese and bread he found. He discovered a TV in a room off the kitchen and turned it on. The Mets were playing the Phillies, and he watched with half an eye and the sound off so he could hear if Alex stirred.

He didn't remember falling asleep, but he woke with a start at three A.M. His empty coffee cup lay on the floor, the plate with his half-eaten sandwich sat on his chest, and the light from the TV screen flickered in the darkness.

Stretching, he retrieved the dirty dishes, turned off the TV, and shuffled into the kitchen. Alex was there, standing over a half-full bottle of Stolichnaya and a shot glass.

She startled as he came into the room, and he stopped dead still. She'd changed out of her clothes and wore a silk robe in ashen blue, the whole thing belted carelessly so he could see a wide sweep of pale skin leading from her throat to her breasts.

He looked away. "Sorry. Didn't mean to scare you."

"I thought you'd left." Calmly, she poured a shot of vodka, as usual recovering her poise as quickly as she'd lost it. She had that cold, no-trespassers look about her again. And yet her hair, like frosted gold in the dim kitchen light, was wild and loose, and so at odds with the carefully controlled persona she normally projected.

He tried a smile on her. "My mother told me to stay."

"Your mother?" Her brows rose in sardonic disbelief.

"Yeah, can you believe it? Over twenty-one and still listening to my mother."

Unimpressed by his attempt at lightness, she responded by downing the shot.

He changed tactics, dropping the grin. "Look, I didn't want you to be alone."

Her mouth twisted into a bitter parody of a smile. "Oh, but I am alone."

He caught her eye, spoke softly. "Not tonight, Alex."

She held his gaze for a moment, and in that half a second he saw the fragility those sobs had hinted at.

Then she brought another glass down from a cabinet, poured the vodka, and pushed the shot toward him. "Good. Drinking alone is so déclassé."

He stared at the cool, clear liquid, then at her shadowed gaze. "You feeling better?"

"That's what the vodka is for." She pronounced it strangely, with a slight accent. She did that now and again, said words in a funny way. Almost like a foreigner. And then, like that, whatever he'd heard would disappear and she sounded like any other red-blooded American.

"Say that again."

"What?"

"Vodka."

She repeated it, the foreign inflection gone.

"No, say it the other way. The way you said it before."

"I don't know what you're talking about."

Didn't she? Where were those pictures taken? The photos of her as a child?

"How long did you live in Russia?"

She stiffened, drank down another shot and slapped the glass on the counter. "Three years."

"That's all?"

"That was enough. Why?"

"What about before? When you were a kid. Ever live there then?"

She gave him the snooty look. "What are you talking about?"

"I don't know. Just wondered."

"I grew up in Boston." More frigid condescension.

"Boston? Luka Kole took you to Boston?"

"My parents were divorced. I told you that. My mother remarried. Until they died, I grew up with my mother and stepfather in Boston."

Well, that explained the occasional British-sounding thing.

"How did you and Sonya meet?"

She eyed him frostily. "I'm not in the mood for an interrogation, Detective. Drink up or go." She nodded at the booze, and, deciding to humor her, he picked up the shot she'd poured him and kicked it back. The stuff burned going down, but left a nice glow in its wake.

She poured them both another glassful. And as if the drink was the key that unlocked the treasure chest of all her secrets, she shared one with him. "Sonya was my mother's nanny. She took care of me after my mother died."

"You knew her a long time then?"

She wavered, eyes watering. "All my life."

He looked away. Christ, he felt pulled down by her grief. It flowed into and melded with his own, so heavy he could have drowned in it. He drank the second shot of vodka, struggled for balance and air.

"Your mother brought her here from Russia?"

Instead of answering, she swallowed her own liquor down. Before it cleared her throat, she reached for the bottle again. Wobbly, she knocked it over.

"Careful." He caught it, set it aside.

Reaching for dignity, she righted herself and almost succeeded. Almost.

His brain stuttered to a stop. What the hell was he doing? The booze was only going to make him more morose, and it sure wasn't doing her much good. "How about we call it a night?"

Those blue-gray eyes bored into his. "I don't need a baby-sitter, Detective." Her words slurred, the foreignness back in her voice.

"Yeah? Doesn't look that way to me." He capped the bottle and, when she lunged for it, swept it out of reach. "How about some coffee?"

"How about you go fuck yourself? *Proklyatiy sukin sin.*" The Russian came out naturally, the anger and contempt obvious in the curse.

"Whoa there, Natasha. I think you've definitely had enough."

Her eyes flashed. "I say when I've had enough. A long, long time, I've been taking care of myself. I don't need help."

She lunged for the bottle again, and, again, he swept it out of reach. "Everyone needs help, Countess."

Her head snapped up. "My name is Sashenka."

"Sure it is."

"Sashenka. Say it!" A tear slipped down her cheek.

"Alex, don't do this to yourself." He spoke quietly, wanting desperately to pull her back from the rim she was edging up to.

"Sashenka. Say my name. Say it!"

"Alex, I'm not going to—"

"Say it, you goddamn son of a bitch. Say it. Say it!"

All at once, she was crying again, those jarring, bone-chilling sobs wracking her body.

He stared at her helplessly, knowing what he was going to do, moving forward even as he knew he shouldn't.

And then she was there in his arms.

"Say it," she sobbed, fists pounding against his back. "Sashenka. My name. Say it, say it."

"All right, Countess, all right. Sashenka. Okay?" It didn't sound nearly as nice rolling off his tongue.

She moaned, a hard wailing sound, and sank into him, her legs gone. He supported her, then in one swift motion, bent and lifted her into his arms.

He couldn't explain the sudden thrill of having his hands beneath her body. It mixed with the weight of grief, an odd little jarring bump of his heart that he acknowledged and ignored.

As if she understood, she curled into him, wrapping her arms tight around his neck like a heartbroken child. Needing him the way Mandy needed him. Cloying, clinging, pulling him under.

Something caught in his throat, that awful fear of not getting there in time, of letting her down, of not doing the right thing; and he fought to hold it back, all the while carrying her to her bedroom.

The roses bloomed on the walls and on the bedspread, huge puffs of blush pink and crimson. Fecund, primal. Speaking to the core of him, so that while his heart broke for her, his body was aware of her shape beneath the thin silk covering. Of the white valley of skin between the edges of the pale blue robe.

He laid her on the bed and backed away—Christ, could he get far enough?—but she grasped his wrist. "Don't leave me," she whispered.

How could he?

He dropped to the bed and she came to him, pressing herself against him in desperate need to be held. And he held her, tight, so tight. A bulwark against the pain. As if he'd never let her go.

His fingers traced the plane of her back beneath the cool silk, the wash of hair against her neck, and he battled desire.

Crooning softly, he rocked her, knowing bone deep that nothing he did would matter. He couldn't stop her from breaking apart. He couldn't save her; couldn't save anyone. And the thought, and the sounds of her sorrow were like a knife in his ribs.

"Shh, hush now. Hush. I'm here, it's going to be all right. Shh." The words were a lie, but what else could he say? That she would hurt forever? That you never recovered from some losses?

And slowly, so slowly, the sobs eased. She relaxed against him, a lifetime of waiting, until only the raw ache of breathing was left.

She slid away, collapsing on the bed, her face to the wall. "I'm sorry," she whispered.

"God, Alex, don't apologize." He stroked her hair, sweat damp at her forehead. So sweet, so sad.

And him so helpless to fix anything.

He eased away, thinking to leave her alone, but her hand groped for his. "Stay," she whispered.

He couldn't. Not and keep some part of himself safe from guilt and failure.

But even as he knew it, he slid down, wrapped his arms around her, and pulled her against him. She sighed, a hitched, breathy sound, laid her head on his shoulder, and slept.

10

Morning found Alex tangled in the sheets, arms and legs entwined with someone else's. Her mind blanked, a low headache looming at the back of her head. Then she eased herself up, saw Hank, and remembered the vodka and the tears. And him.

For a moment the weight of grief pressed her down. She lay back, hearing him breathe, wishing it were real and he was her lover. That outside the room, children waited, Sonya, an aunt or uncle. A web of people to love and care for. Who would love and care for her.

A bleak shadow stole through her. Wishing was a waste of time. Things were what they were. She untangled herself, slipped out of bed quietly so she wouldn't wake him. He had shown her such kindness last night; the least she could do was let him sleep.

Silently, she gathered clothes. Linen slacks, pressed sharply. A charmeuse blouse, which would drape but still look tailored. Protective covering in hand, she turned toward the bathroom to shower, but her gaze stuck on him sprawled on her bed.

He slept on his back, the arm that had held her all night now thrown out, hand strong, finished in blunt ends. It was the kind of hand that could shift a heavy bushel of apples or comfort sorrow away. Strong. Dependable. A hand she was tempted to grasp.

His sandy hair was mussed in a charming way that brought a tiny smile to her lips. For half a second she yearned to brush the fallen locks back from his forehead as if she had the right.

A big man, he filled the bed. Would she let him fill her? Desire buzzed her. At least she thought it was desire. She'd had little experience with sexual passion so she wasn't sure. Her passion had been for other things. Achievement, so she could be in the right position at the right time; wealth, so she could have money to grease the wheels of power. Above all and leading from all, her passion had been for revenge.

And now that was all she had left.

For a flicker of a moment the thought of letting go drifted over her. Forget revenge and live life. Be a woman. Chase a man. Uncharted options down an uncharted road.

But that was a dream for children, and she was no child. She hadn't been a child for thirteen years.

Turning away from the bed and the fantasy it held, she went into the bathroom and switched on the shower. The warm needles of water pounded her back, a reminder to bury grief and hold on to resolve.

Petrov would pay. Somehow, someday, if she died doing it, he would pay for what he'd done to everyone she'd ever cared about.

The vow strengthened her, gave her purpose. By the time she was dressed she was Alex again. Cold, determined Alex.

She was making coffee when Hank sauntered in, sleepy-eyed, rumpled, and infinitely good to look at. Which was why she glanced away, busying herself with the cof-feemaker. Normally, Sonya would have done all this, and for a second Alex's breath snagged as she remembered. But then she concentrated on the filter, the coffee measure, the water. This was a kitchen, not a death zone. If Sonya had died there, she had also lived there, and if she had to, Alex would remember only that.

"Morning." Hank threw her a lazy smile, and she wondered what it would be like to see that smile every morning.

"Coffee will be ready in a minute."

He helped himself to a cup and leaned against the counter, waiting for the drink to brew.

She peeked at him, then away. "I . . . I want to thank you for last night."

He nodded, studying her, and she felt the force of his gaze clear down to her toes.

"Back on track now?" He looked . . . almost disappointed. Well, what did he expect? For her to fall apart and stay that way?

"It was very generous of you to stay, especially since I . . . since I behaved so badly."

"Not so bad." His eyes were soft. "Considering."

She didn't want to consider; she wanted to move on. Without softness, without him. She couldn't afford anything else. "Well, I appreciate it. But I'm fine now. I'm sure you have plenty to do. You don't have to stay."

His brows rose and that teasing glow lit up his green eyes. "You're throwing me out without breakfast?"

She struggled with politeness. "Of course not. I'm . . . I didn't mean . . . I'm sure we have some eggs." She opened the refrigerator and the contents blurred in front of her. "Sonya usually . . . " She caught herself, and suddenly she was trembling again.

And like that, he was there, as though he knew, as though

he understood. He shoved her gently aside, peered into the box, and took out a dozen eggs.

"I know there's cheese because I made a sandwich last night. How about an omelet?"

She shook her head. The headache had eased, but her stomach rebelled at the thought of food. "No really, I'm not hungry. But please, you go ahead."

She retreated as he took out three eggs and a slab of herbed cream cheese. She found him a mixing bowl and with those deft, capable fingers, he broke the eggs into it and whipped them with a wire whisk he discovered in a drawer. Pans hung from a rack over a central workstation, and he chose one, set it on the stove, turned up the heat, and dropped in a lump of butter to melt.

She was amazed at how quickly he worked. Before she knew it the eggs were cooking. "You like to cook." It was more observation than question, a little discovery. He didn't seem the domestic type, and yet there he was, missing only the apron. It spoke to that other side of him, the one that included Mandy and Rose and Apple House.

He didn't seem to think it so special. He shrugged. "I like to eat. Unless you're going to depend on other people, one goes with the other."

By that time the coffee had finished brewing. She poured herself a cup and eyed him over the rim. His big body filled her kitchen the way it had filled her bed. Rolled-up shirt-sleeves exposed muscles in forearm and wrist that bunched and rippled as he worked. Again something stirred inside her. A longing for the touch of his hand, the warmth of his body.

It would be so easy to tell him everything. He would understand, he would help her. She felt the words on the edge of her mouth, the urge to share the burden so powerful.

And then he spoke. "Alex, if you can, tell me what happened when you came home yesterday."

This was her chance. If she could only open her mouth, get the words out. Tell all. But she wavered, not wanting to relive those awful moments.

"I know you don't want to think about it, but we don't know what happened yet. It looks like Sonya might have died from natural causes—a heart attack or a stroke. Did she have a weak heart? Complain of dizziness?"

It wasn't her heart, Detective. "She didn't complain about anything, but she did get confused a lot. I always attributed it to the culture difference."

"She'd been here a long time, though, hadn't she? If your mother had brought her over."

Damn, why couldn't she keep the lies straight?

If she just told him the truth, she wouldn't have to.

"I guess some people never fully adjust."

He was looking at her closely, and she turned to the coffeepot, refreshing her cup to get out of his view.

"So, as far as you know, she had no medical history that might explain a collapse?"

Would a bout of torture and interrogation at the hands of the KGB count? She was sure it would; why couldn't she tell him so? Instead, she shook her head.

He jiggled the pan, redistributing the eggs, and turned to her, relaxing against the nearby counter as though he belonged there. Did he?

"It's probably nothing," he said, "but I want to make sure. Just in case something else went wrong, I'd like to know how you found her."

She loved him like this. The way his face turned sober, intent but humane.

"Did you touch her, pick her up?"

She thought back, trying not to let sorrow rip her apart. "I . . . I pulled her into my lap, tried to wake her . . ." Her voice caught.

"It's all right. Take your time. I know how hard this is."

She saw compassion in his face, imagined how he'd look when she'd told him everything. As if he could spin back time and make it all go away.

She took a ragged breath. Composed herself. "I tried to revive her. Unsuccessfully. I called an ambulance. The patrol car arrived. Then Lieutenant Parnell, then you."

"And when you first came in, when you first walked up to the kitchen door, did you notice anything unusual or out of place? Besides the obvious, that is. Anything at all?"

"Nothing. And even if there were, I was too distracted to notice."

He nodded thoughtfully. "Okay. Then we'll just have to wait and see what the coroner turns up."

He checked the pan again, then spread a generous spoonful of cheese in the center of the eggs, rolled one side over the other, and slid the omelet onto a plate.

"Sure you won't have some?"

She nodded, not even sure she could speak. Something huge quaked inside her. Aside from the people who'd been there all those years ago, she'd trusted no one with the whole truth. Now she was on the verge of altering the habits of half a lifetime, and it terrified her.

Don't do it.

Tell him.

Don't.

He poured himself a cup of coffee and pulled up a stool at the counter. Without thinking, she gave him a fork and a cloth napkin, and suddenly he was eating breakfast in her kitchen as if he did it every day. And despite herself, she liked it.

"So, what are your plans?" He chomped down a forkful of eggs.

"Plans?"

"For the day. What are you going to do? I'm not going to let you rattle around this house alone."

She blinked. Was she going to confess today? "I . . . I don't know. I haven't thought about it yet."

"Why not come back to the farm with me?"

The farm? That dream-filled place of apple blossoms? "I . . . no, I couldn't."

"If you won't come with me, let me take you to Lakeview. Whoever that guy is out there, you seemed pretty close to him. Let me take you to him. Or call him to come here."

Her heart nearly leaped out her throat. "What guy?"

He threw her a look: Don't con a conner. "The man you met the night of your party."

Before she could think, she blurted, "How did you—" Dawning horror rose in her voice. "You followed me." Her stomach cramped. He knew. He'd known all along. "You followed me."

"Who is he, Alex?" It was spoken quietly, but she heard the demand underneath. A cop's demand.

All the weakness of a moment ago, the compulsion to confess, the certainty that he would understand—God in heaven, how close she'd come. The man was a cop after all; how could she ever forget that?

Her armor clanked into place. "I thought you were my friend."

"I am. That's why—"

"Friends don't spy on friends."

His eyes hardened. "Friends don't lie to friends either."

He tossed a photograph on the counter. "You said you had no pictures of your mother."

Ice froze her veins. Sirens screamed in her head. "Where did you get that?"

He remained mute, the answer obvious.

"You came here pretending to comfort me, and all the while you used what happened to search my house? That's not only illegal, it's despicable."

He had the grace to look ashamed, but not enough to deny it. "I don't want to hurt you, Alex. God, you must know that. If you're in some kind of trouble, I can help."

"Help? Is this the kind of help you give? Betrayal, lies? I don't need that kind of help."

His face turned white. "Maybe you don't." He pushed his plate away. "And maybe you do."

"No maybes about it." She tried to brush past him, but he grabbed her wrist and pulled her back.

"Who's the man out by the lake, Alex? What were you doing in Luka Kole's apartment? Not looking for pictures of your mother, that's obvious."

She wrenched her arm away. "Get out of my house." She swiped the plate and his cup off the counter and dumped them in the sink. They rattled like gunshots.

"If you're hiding something, it's only going to make things worse."

"Is that a threat? Are you threatening me?"

"I'm trying to help you!"

"I curse your help, Detective. I curse you. Get out. Get out of my house. Get out!"

He stared at her, mouth pinched white around the edges. Then he threw down his napkin and stalked out of the kitchen. A second later, the front door slammed.

Trembling, she collapsed onto a stool. When the shaking

had subsided, she reached for the phone, punched in a four and two ones. When the operator came on, she was quick and blunt.

"Sokanan. The number for Ben Bonner."

Outside the front door, Hank ran a weary hand through his hair. That went well.

He trudged to his car, removed the dome light, and got in. Christ, he shouldn't have sprung all that on her. Not this morning.

Okay, so the timing might not have been ideal, but what was the ideal time to confront her lies?

Maybe not the day after she lost someone close to her.

He punched the steering wheel, furious at himself. Fuck it. Fuck him. Fuck the whole damn thing.

How did things go, Henry? his mother asked in his head.

Swell, Ma. Just swell.

He should go back to the farm, but he couldn't face Rose yet.

Coward.

You got that right.

Instead, he drove into the heart of Sokanan, to the home he hadn't seen in a few days. It sat atop the hill on Webb Street, an aging beauty of a bungalow with enough exterior molding to ice a cake and a sweet little porch that sagged only a bit in the center.

He eyed it from the curb, seeing the details through the dreariness of the exterior. The paint was peeling, the porch steps broken. Poor thing, it fit right into the rest of the rundown neighborhood. There were blocks and blocks of houses like his, all with great lines and bad posture, ancient beauty queens on the edge of gentrification. He'd bought his for a song, did a hell of a job on the inside, but the outside needed more TLC than he had time for now.

I should have been better to you, sweetheart.

He sighed, strolled up the cracked concrete walk toward the steps. Someone had knocked down the FOR SALE sign in the yard, and he set it upright again.

Mail had piled up on the floor beneath the mail slot. He pushed the envelopes and papers aside with the door, then swooped to pick them all up. Leafing through, he saw most of them were advertising circulars dated a week ago. The important things, bills and a couple of magazines, he kept. The rest he dumped in the trash.

He went into the living room, a snug area at the front of the house that he'd spent much time and money on. He'd refinished the hardwood floor himself, cleaned up the chair rail and the molding on the windows, pulled out the drywall that a previous owner had used to cover over a built-in bookcase, and repainted. It was cozy now, filled with comfortable chairs and a small, overstuffed sofa. Leaving it was going to be harder than he thought, which was why he didn't think about it. He shoved that pending loss into the same dark corner he shoved the fiasco of the morning, dropped onto the sofa, and checked the messages on his cell phone. Greenlaw, the uniform who'd done the crime scene at Alex's, had called. And there was one message from Ben.

Thinking it might be about the farm, and feeling guilty he wasn't there, he called Ben back first.

His brother lit into him. "I just heard from A. J. Baker. What the hell do you think you're doing?"

Hank paused, taken aback by the vehemence in Ben's voice. "What are you talking about?"

"The future of this entire city depends on her goodwill. If she wanted to, she could have taken this Renaissance deal anywhere. She brought it here, to us, because she's community-minded. But that won't go far if the community—and that means you, little brother—alienates her."

Anger pumped through him. That cold bitch. Siccing the mayor on him. "What the hell did she tell you I did?"

"Questioned her. Tried to implicate her in this convenience store murder. She just lost her housekeeper, for Crissake. What's wrong with you? Miss Baker has nothing to do with your case. You have a suspect, don't you?"

"We have suspicions. I wouldn't say he's a suspect."

"Well, make him one. Do your job, Hank, and leave Miss Baker alone."

Ben disconnected, and Hank put down his phone, fury subsiding into something else. He knew desperation when he heard it, and Alexandra Jane must have been beyond desperate to call in the troops. He stared out the window, the stained glass he'd restored there bending the light into prisms of pale yellow and lavender. He was getting close. But to what?

Within the last four days, two Russians had turned up dead. Two Russians with a clear link to Alex. A fluke? Possibly. Especially if Sonya had died of natural causes.

But in his line of work, coincidence often panned out to be something else entirely.

But what? And what did Alex have to do with it?

Hank sighed and picked up the phone again. Greenlaw answered on the second ring.

"I got a list of the items we placed in evidence," the patrol officer said. "Thought you'd like to see it."

Between Saturday night and Sunday morning? Crime scene investigation was one way out of patrol, and if Greenlaw was bucking for detective division, Hank would give him two thumbs up. "Anything stand out?"

"Maybe. Any smokers in the house?"

"Not that I know of. Why?"

"Found a butt on the ground off the front steps. Marlboro. Like whoever smoked it stood on the porch, took a last drag, and threw it away, either before entering or just after leaving."

Hank remembered doing a perimeter search for trace evidence right after the incident with the rat. He hadn't seen a cigarette butt.

"Think it means anything?" Greenlaw said.

"I don't know. What kind of profile can you get from it?"

"DNA for sure. Don't know how much that will help without someone to match it to on the other end."

Hank thought back. He could have easily missed the butt. Any one of the guests at the Renaissance Oil party could have dropped it. From what he'd seen, lung cancer didn't translate into Russian.

Then again, someone could have dropped it between Friday evening, when he did his search, and Saturday afternoon when Greenlaw found it. Someone who'd come to the house. A repairman? Neighbor? Or someone with more sinister intent.

Intent to do what? Scare an old woman to death? If Sonya'd had a heart attack, there was no crime to investigate. And tests were expensive.

"Hold off on the lab work until we hear cause of death."

"You got it."

"And fax me the list."

"Sure thing."

Hank gave him the number and went in to turn on the machine. A few minutes later, the pages came through.

Greenlaw had done a thorough job, listing the evidence by type and location found. Hank scanned the sheets; nothing popped out except that cigarette butt, and he wasn't sure that meant anything either.

Just as he was finishing up, the phone rang.

"Bonner."

"This is dispatch, Detective. Got a woman with information about someone called McTeer. Ring any bells?"

Attention caught, he said, "Yeah. What's she want?"

"I've been telling her to call back tomorrow when the division is staffed, but she just isn't listening. Called back six, seven times. Making a real pain out of herself. I threatened to send a patrol over there, arrest her for harassment or something, but thought I'd better check with the on-call first."

He frowned. If someone came forward on McTeer, this whole thing with Alex would go away. And right now, he was highly in favor of that.

"All right. What's her name and address?" He scribbled the information into the small notebook he always carried. "If she calls back, tell her you're sending someone over."

He showered, found a clean pair of jeans still in his closet and a much-washed, soft blue oxford whose sleeves he rolled up and whose tails he left hanging. People in McTeer's neighborhood weren't exactly the Brooks Brothers type, and besides, he'd have to head out to Apple House after and he might as well be dressed for farm work. There was still a section of winter pruning that needed disposal, and Rose had been after him to start the mowing.

The address was on the north side of town. He couldn't remember if the number was the same as McTeer's, but it was in the same complex. Called St. Martin's Square, it was a low-rise collection of fake wood apartments surrounding a mostly dirt courtyard. At one time there'd been swings at the east end. Now the swings stood bereft of seats, chains hanging like arms without hands.

He parked the car and trudged up to the door. A chocolate-skinned woman answered, still young enough to be in high school, pretty despite the suspicious stare she was giving him. In her arms, she held a swaddled infant.

Hank glanced at the paper he'd scrawled the information on. "Shatiqua Williams?"

Velvet brown eyes narrowed. "Who wants to know?"

He reined in his temper. "Sokanan PD. Look, Miss Williams, you asked to see a police officer."

"You don't look like the police."

He lifted his shirttail, showed her the shield on his belt. "Detective Bonner."

Distrustful, she eyed him a minute, then made her decision, stepped back, and let him in.

The apartment was tiny and halfway to falling apart. Plaster peeled off the walls, and water stains marked the ceiling. But it was neat and clean, free of clutter. A beat-up brown couch stood behind a scratched coffee table with a GED workbook in one corner. Across from the couch sat a crib with a blanket spread out at its feet like a picnic, a couple of baby toys scattered on top. The place smelled like babies and Sunday dinner, chicken and dumplings and gravy.

"Smells good," Hank said, and watched Shatiqua preen.

"I'm roasting a chicken. Mac, he like my roast chicken."

"Mac. That's Big Mac McTeer?"

She nodded. "My baby's daddy."

From the way she said McTeer's name and the way she smiled down at the infant, Hank was rapidly recalculating the type of information she had.

"Ain't he pretty?" She pulled the blanket away from the

infant's face, showing him off. Hank peeked; the baby was sleeping. Didn't all babies look pretty when they slept?

"He's fine-looking."

"We call him little Mac. Mac, that's big Mac, he don't like me calling him Adulous. Says that's too big a mouthful for such a little bean."

Hank nodded. He was having trouble imagining McTeer calling anything a little bean. "Miss Williams, you said you had some information about McTeer."

She looked up from the baby, caution in her face again. "He's a good man, Mac is. A good daddy."

Hank shrugged, trying to remain impassive. But any hope this woman was going to pin Luka Kole's murder on McTeer was rapidly fading. "If he's such a good guy, where is he?"

"Working."

Hank's brows rose in surprise. "On Sunday?" Hell, he didn't expect McTeer to be working any day.

"He's painting for Mr. Mundy. Gets overtime for weekends. I asked him not to work on the weekends, but little Mac, he needs stuff." She put the baby in the crib, and he gave a tiny squall of protest, then was silent.

Shatiqua turned from the baby to Hank. "He didn't do nothing to that old man. He's got a temper, I tell you what, but that don't mean shit. We need every cent. So when Mr. Kole over to the Gas-Up shortchanged him, Mac, he got mad. But he didn't hurt no one."

Hank sighed. "Look, I appreciate the character reference, but—"

"He was working. Like today, for Mr. Mundy." She disappeared into the kitchen and came back with a crumpled-up receipt. "He waits at the parking lot at the CVS on Main, and Mr. Mundy, he picks him up. Mac, he has to be there real early. Like maybe six. Gets up at five, walks to Main. There's a shitload of men waiting for jobs, but Mr. Mundy, he picks Mac most every time."

Hank stared at the receipt. It was a crude pay stub written on brown paper like someone had torn it from a lunch bag. Date, amount. Hank knew about the black market day labor workforce. Knew about the various pickup points throughout the city. Everyone did. Employers had a steady supply of the unemployed, and they didn't have to pay social security, payroll taxes, or health care. Workers got paid in cash, so there was no official trail for city, state, or federal income tax. They all turned a blind eye. Times like these, with so many out of work, the police department didn't make it a priority.

He looked up from the makeshift pay stub to the young woman in front of him. She was watching him, hope and distrust warring in her face.

"Why didn't Mac tell me this himself?"

"Says he'd get Mr. Mundy in trouble and lose his job. He be real mad at me for telling, too, I tell you what, but he ain't done nothing. We got cops asking questions and bringing him in and shit so he can't work, and it ain't fair. Mac, he's doing everything he can for me and little Mac, and he still has to put up with this shit. He needs a break. I can't do much, but I can do this."

Hank nodded, touched.

"He don't do drugs. He don't drink much. He coulda asked me to get rid of little Mac, but he didn't." Her mouth trembled, but she controlled herself. "He didn't do nothing. Leave him alone."

Hank pursed his lips, trying not to think too hard about what this meant for the rest of his case. "I'll have to take this with me." He held up the receipt between two fingers.

She shrugged. "I made me a copy over to the library yesterday."

"Okay." He took a last look around the apartment, at the crib with the sleeping baby and the young woman struggling hard to hold on to this fragile sliver of life she had with McTeer. "Enjoy your dinner," he said, and left.

Outside, the air felt sharper, as though the encounter inside had honed his instincts. Made him more aware of . . . what?

Loyalty and trust.

A far cry from what had happened at Alex's that morning. He recalled her words, her rejection of his help, her accusation of deceit and betrayal.

Looked like he could learn a thing or two from Big Mac McTeer and Shatiqua Williams.

11

Morning came early. On the last Monday of his last week as a cop, Hank rolled out of his childhood bed at four-thirty, tugged on a pair of jeans and work boots, and finished chopping the debris he'd pruned the month before. Yesterday he'd gotten a head start on the mowing, but it would take another four or five days working full-time, maybe a week, to finish it all. Last night, he and Ben had talked Rose into hiring someone to do it.

The kids were getting up as he trudged inside. He heard the rush of water through pipes and the sound of pounding footsteps over his head as they washed and dressed. His mother, bless her heart, was already up and working on breakfast. He smelled coffee and bacon as he came in through the back door.

She eyed him as he entered the kitchen. "You're up early."

"Finished chopping." He poured himself a cup of coffee and let the hot liquid go down smooth.

His mother tsked and turned to him, but he forestalled her arguments.

"It had to be done. I did it. Let's not argue about it."

But Rose never did take a hint well. "I appreciate it, Henry, you know I do. But not if it's going to kill you."

"You looking at a ghost?"

"You know what I mean. You've been a police officer for a long time. You worked hard, moved up. You've done a lot of good, protected a lot of people."

He stiffened. "Not my own."

"You did the best you could," she said quietly. "You always have."

"I don't want to talk about it."

"Maybe you need to."

He stonewalled. "I did my share with the department shrink."

"Henry—"

"Gotta go. I'm late." He poured himself another cup of coffee and escaped with it into the bathroom, drinking while he shaved. One more week of this madness and he'd be free. One job, one life. No recriminations.

He ran the water, waiting for it to heat up, and looked at himself in the mirror. Boy, his dad must be loving this. He was probably hooting and hollering in heaven knowing Hank would finally be what he'd wanted him to be all along. Joe Bonner never did like to lose an argument.

Hank lathered up, wincing at the picture of himself on a tractor day in and day out. Oh, he loved the place, no doubt about it, it was home. But would he ever get used to the routine of it?

He fended off the answer and hit the shower, the hot water obliterating all thought. Half an hour later he was ready to drive Trey and Mandy to school.

The kids slung their backpacks into the trunk, then traipsed in, Trey closed-mouthed as usual, Mandy with a book to bury herself in. But she didn't open it. Instead, she sat in the back, unnaturally quiet. They hadn't gone far when she piped up.

"Did you see Alex yesterday?"

He flicked a glance in the rearview mirror. Her forehead was furrowed with worry. "Yesterday morning."

"Is she sad?"

He remembered the weight of tears, the way Alex had broken apart. Then he remembered the way they'd parted, and a flicker of shame ran through him. "Yeah, Mandy girl, she's sad."

Mandy thought about it a while, then leaned forward. "Maybe we could visit her this afternoon."

"Geez, Mandy, you're such a dork." Trey didn't even look at her, but stared out the side window.

"I am not. Sometimes visits can cheer people up."

"Yeah? Did a visit ever cheer you up?"

Mandy was silent, and Hank's chest constricted at the truth in Trey's words. Grief didn't disappear, and nothing helped but getting through it. He just wished he knew there would be an end. Someday. "I don't think she's ready for company yet, Mandy. But it was a good idea. And very thoughtful."

He dropped the kids off and headed on to the station. The minute he walked into the detectives' area everyone turned and looked at him. Klimet smirked.

"Loo wants to see you."

Loo meant Lieutenant Parnell. Klimet always talked liked he was on *NYPD Blue*. "What about?"

Klimet shrugged, but Hank could tell he was enjoying this. "I don't know, but I don't think it's going to be fun."

Great. If Parnell wanted to see him first thing Monday morning, something was definitely up. Three guesses what it was.

He stepped into Parnell's office.

"You wanted to see me?"

"Close the door, Hank." The command jacked up Hank's dread quotient. Closed-door meetings were usually personal.

Hank shut the door and turned to face Parnell. He was a fair man, solid and thorough, with almost thirty years' experience behind him. He'd been the hands-down favorite to lead the department, and Hank didn't like letting him down. But that didn't mean he liked taking lumps from him any better.

"You remember what I told you about VIP treatment?"

Hank nodded, suspicions confirmed. "Yes, sir."

"You do?" Parnell shook his head. "Well, I would've sworn you didn't because I got a phone call from the mayor *and* the chief of police telling me you're being an asshole about Miss Baker." He leaned forward, pinned Hank with a look, every one of those thirty years staring out from his eyes. "Are you?"

"No, sir."

"You got something solid to connect her to the Kole murder?"

"Not solid like concrete. But something."

Parnell waited. Hank debated.

Shit.

"She's Kole's daughter. Estranged daughter."

Parnell's brows rose, and he sat back with a thump.

"You're telling me A. J. Baker is related to the victim?"

"I found her in his apartment the day after the murder. The place had been ransacked. Not by her, I don't think, but by someone."

"And when were you going to tell me this?"

"When I had it figured out."

Parnell took it in. He knew what it was like to run a case, to hold his cards tight. But he also believed in teamwork. And he hated not knowing what was going on in his own department.

"What was she doing there?"

"I don't know. Not for sure. She gave me some story about looking for a photograph of her mother, but that was mainly bullshit. The real reason?" He shrugged, shook his head. "I don't know yet."

"Jesus H. Christ." Parnell rubbed his forehead. "I knew something bad was going to happen today."

Hank threw him a bone. "She's clear of the murder as far as I can tell. But she knows something. I can't prove it. I don't even know what it is I'm trying to prove. But she's connected. Somehow."

"But she's clear of the murder? You're sure?"

"As sure as I can be. Must be fifty people saw her that evening."

Parnell's face brightened. "Then lay off. She's got her panties in a wad, and I've got your brother and the chief on me. I don't like it. Stay away from her."

Hank looked down, not gathering his courage exactly, but bracing for Parnell's reaction. Then he gazed back at his boss's face, telling it straight. "Can't do that, sir."

Parnell returned the look. "Why the hell not?"

"She's tied in somehow." He scrubbed a hand down his face, wishing he could scrub all this away. "I think she knows the killer."

Parnell sighed. He clearly didn't like hearing this. "And you think this . . . why?"

"She's running scared."

Parnell scrutinized him, gaze boring in. Then he spoke, voice soft, careful. "What's this really about, Hank?"

The tone of voice, the piercing look. Hank spotted the psych-out, Big Daddy routine a mile away. He appreciated the intent, but he'd endured more of it than he could stand after he'd screwed up with Tom and Maureen.

"It's about solving the case."

"Is it?" Parnell rose, came around the desk, and perched on the end. He was a smaller man than Hank, lean where Hank was broad, but he had the air of command about him, and Hank respected that.

"Look, you know how I feel about your decision to leave. Frankly, I think it's a bad one. I gave you this case hoping it might help you see that. Has it?"

Hank stiffened, not wanting to talk about it now any more than he had at breakfast with his mother. He'd made up his mind, why was everyone always trying to change it? "One thing has nothing to do with the other."

"Then you're still determined to go?"

"Yes, sir."

Parnell nodded slowly, the disappointment in his face merging into thoughtfulness. "You know, most people slack off right before they leave a job. But you—" He shook his head. "Are you sure this grandstanding isn't some last-minute effort to leave under a winner's halo? Solve the murder and be the hero one last time?"

The hero? Not him. Not likely. "Look, I didn't ask for this case. I didn't want it. But now I've got it, and I just want to do my job."

Parnell sighed. "Then do it. Without pissing people off. I don't have to tell you how important the Renaissance Oil thing is to this town."

"No, sir."

Parnell gave him a last searing look. "Okay." He nodded toward the door. "Get the squad together."

Hank pivoted, then turned back. "One more thing."

Parnell's brows rose in question.

"McTeer's out."

Parnell muttered a curse under his breath. "How'd that happen?"

Briefly, Hank reviewed his interview with Shatiqua Williams. "I spoke to Mundy last night. He confirmed."

"That means we're back to square one."

It also meant Alex was now hanging from that limb alone. But Hank didn't say so.

The coroner's report on Sonya Ranevskaya came in later that morning. Heart attack. Hank read the medicalese, half of him glad and half of him disappointed. The postmortem results strengthened the coincidence theory and loosened any tie he was trying to uncover between Alex and whatever bad guys were out there. But it didn't take away his misgivings. And it didn't explain what Alex was really looking for in Luka Kole's apartment or why she lied about it.

At noon, Klimet came in, an excited look in his eyes. "We got latents." He threw down a report on Hank's desk. "A partial print at the Gas-Up matches one at the apartment after the ransacking."

Hank scanned the report. "No ID?"

"It's not Kole's, and it's not Baker's." Because of her securities work, Alex had been bonded, which meant her prints were on file.

"But we don't know whose they are?"

"Not yet. But at least we know the same guy was in both places."

A conclusion that would have been easy to draw, prints or no, though he didn't bother pointing it out.

"We also have the ballistics and the phone analysis."

Klimet handed Hank the two reports. The list of phone numbers contained both incoming and outgoing calls from Kole's apartment and his office. Hank scanned the list. Most were local, though a few were regional. Upstate. Manhattan.

Klimet said, "I'm going up to Karlsbeck. They started a joint task force with the rest of the Hudson Valley to find this convenience store killer. Parnell wants me on it." His voice had an edge to it, a note that said he'd be going, not Hank.

Hank shrugged. "Have at it."

After McTeer had been eliminated as a suspect, and Parnell and the rest of the planet had warned him off Alex, the department's theory had rotated back to the original—that Kole's murder was one in a string that had hit the Hudson Valley over the last few months.

Hank didn't dispute the validity of the theory, but he didn't put any weight in it either. And since he wouldn't be around to help with a task force, he wasn't surprised Parnell had sent Klimet.

And it got the man out of his way, which suited Hank fine.

Klimet sauntered out, and Hank returned to the two reports. Ballistics listed the ammo as .38 caliber. But the bullet had been so damaged, they couldn't pin down weapon make or model. Which meant Hank didn't know whether the shooter had used an automatic or a wheel gun. A revolver would explain the absence of shell casings. Anyone could be the shooter. But if it was an automatic, the shooter might have been smarter than average. He would have had to pick up his shell casings, and how many convenience store killers stopped to do that?

The issue unresolved, he turned to the phone list. He'd asked for coverage of the last month, so there were pages of listings starting with most recent. He took a breath and committed himself to the drudgery of calling and identifying each one.

Halfway down the middle of the third page was a number answered by a female voice first in Russian, then English. "Petroneft USA."

Pay dirt. So Luka Kole *had* had some business with Miki Petrov's company.

"Hello? May I help you?"

Hank only knew one person at Petroneft. "Miki Petrov."

"Who may I ask is calling?"

"Detective Bonner, Sokanan Police Department."

"One moment, please."

A new voice came on the line. Male, this time, heavily accented. "Mr. Petrov is in a meeting. You want to leave message?"

He'd leave a message all right. "No, that's okay. I'd rather deliver it myself."

He debated whether to drive into Manhattan or take the train. Driving in the city was a pain, but if he drove, he could make a stop along the way.

He got in the car and, knowing he shouldn't, headed out toward Highbridge anyway. He took the turn into her drive with a sinking feeling. Alex wasn't going to like seeing him, but he owed her this.

It took her a few minutes to come to the door. When she did, she tried to slam it shut again, but he wedged himself inside the jamb.

"I just want to talk to you."

She released the door and scurried away. "I have nothing to say." She pulled a handbag from a nearby closet and fished out a cell phone. She was already punching in a number—his brother's, the police chief's, maybe she had a direct line to God himself.

"It's about Sonya."

Her head snapped up, and her eyes went dead with grief, then alive with caution. "What about her?"

"I got the coroner's report. She wasn't murdered, Alex. She died of a heart attack."

She looked at him hard. What were those eyes telling him? That she didn't believe him?

"Christ, Alex, you think I'd lie about that? It's true."

"Yes, I'm sure the coroner was very thorough. Now get out."

"Look, can't we just—"

"Get out, Detective. I have nothing to say to you, and you no longer have any business with me."

He shrugged, raised his hands in surrender, and backed out.

Alex closed the door behind him and sank against the wall, trembling again.

Damn him. And damn her for being such a fool about him.

She gazed at the cell phone in her hand. Tightening her hold, she resurrected her determination and punched in a number.

"He was here again. I thought you said you would do something about it. All right. Yes." She disconnected, then sank to the floor. Leaning her head back, she closed her eyes, wishing it were tomorrow and this awful day was over.

Hank drove into Manhattan, trying not to think about the anger in Alex's face as she kicked him out. How many phone calls was she making this time?

Well, the more she fought, the more certain he was that

she knew something. Something important. Did it have anything to do with Miki Petrov?

With Kole's phone records, he could now establish a link between Luka Kole and Petroneft. Didn't mean Kole had spoken to Petrov. But it didn't mean he hadn't either.

Petrov owned a swank midtown high-rise graced by a huge blue brushed steel *R* for Renaissance Oil. His company, Petroneft USA, occupied the top two floors. Security was tighter than ever since 9/11, but Hank's badge got him inside the building and into the elevators. At the large, curved Petroneft reception desk, he had to browbeat the receptionist a bit, but eventually a bulky man he recognized from the party came to the reception area.

"Hey, pal," Hank said. "How's the head?" The hangover must have been a doozy.

The man—Yuri, that's what Alex had called him—didn't respond, and Hank figured he didn't recognize him.

Too far gone to remember much of anything, eh, pal?

With slow, ponderous steps Yuri walked him to a private elevator and used a key to access it. The ride up was heavy with silence and the smell of cigarette smoke. Was that Yuri's cigarette Greenlaw had found? And if so, when had he left it?

Hank spotted a telltale bulge under the black leather jacket. An automatic or a revolver? Impossible to tell. So Yuri was what—a bodyguard? A thug? The symbols etched into his knuckles indicated an ex-con if nothing else. Hank didn't know what the Cyrillic letters meant, but he knew prison tats when he saw them. What kind of businessman needed an ex-con armed guard?

The kind with enemies.

Had Luka Kole been Petrov's enemy? Was Alex?

Hard to believe after the way she'd thrown herself at the

oil tycoon at the party. Then again, she had wiped her mouth off.

Secrets within secrets.

Petrov's suite consisted of an outer office with several desks and a beautiful woman occupying each. Heavily made-up, they were dressed in clothes that stretched tightly across breasts and revealed an airstrip of leg. Both were tapping halfheartedly on computer keyboards with fingers tipped in highly polished nails that were so long they curved.

Yuri stopped to talk to one in Russian. Sloe-eyed and sulky, she glanced over at Hank, lifted a phone, and spoke into it, also in Russian. Jesus, why didn't these people speak good old-fashioned English once in a while?

Two other men lounged around the room. Both immense white guys, they wore black track suits and black leather jackets. Heavy gold chains glittered around their thick necks, and bulges similar to Yuri's enlarged their waists. Buzz cuts leveled white-blond hair to near-scalp level. Aryan homeboys, they watched Hank through impassive blue eyes.

Cindy Crawford over there put down her phone and exchanged a few more words with Yuri, who nodded in Hank's direction.

"Mr. Petrov will see you."

"Nice talking to you again." He grinned, friendly, eager, the perfect small-town sucker. Yuri took it at face value, said something to his two compatriots, and everyone laughed.

Fucking asshole.

But Hank went in humbly, playing his part.

"Mr. Petrov." He extended a hand. "Nice of you to see me." His gaze swept the office, took in the wall of window with its bird's-eye view of Manhattan, the gold-framed artwork on the walls, the museum case that held—what? Old swords, he thought. So Petrov was a collector. What else did he collect? Debts? Dead bodies?

The air was rich with quiet, sound absorbed by the velvet plush of the gold-and-red carpet thick under Hank's feet. Petrov rose slightly, extended a hand, and gestured for Hank to take a seat across from his desk. He sank into the upholstered crimson chair and wondered who had paid the price for Petrov's luxury.

All of Mother Russia, if Alex's rumors proved true.

"It is always my pleasure to help the local police," Petrov said.

Yeah, he'd just bet. He hadn't forgotten the rest of what Alex had told him. Ex-KGB and probably cagey as shit.

"So, Detective . . ."

"Bonner."

"Ah, yes, Detective Bonner. What can I do to help you?" Hank had heard him speak before—on TV and at the party—and though the accent was strong, the English was fluid.

"You are from Sokanan, as I understand. Perhaps you are looking for a donation to the department?"

Hank laughed and waved the offer—the bribe?—away. "No, no, nothing like that."

"Then what can I do for you? You are a distance from home." Translation: you're out of your jurisdiction. True, but Hank pretended otherwise.

"It's about this phone call." Hank began on a hesitant note, as if he wasn't sure how to begin.

"A phone call?"

"This man back home, Luka Kole, he made a phone call to you, and—"

"To me?" He looked taken aback, but mildly so. "I do not know a—what was the name?"

"Luka Kole."

"Ah yes. Kole. No, the name is not familiar."

"Well, he called Petroneft about two weeks ago. I have this list from the phone company here." Hank fumbled with the papers, slid them under Petrov's nose, then slid them away again before he could get a good look. "And it says right there that he made a phone call to you."

Petrov spread his hands in a gesture of helplessness. "We get a lot of phone calls here, Detective. Petroneft is a very large company."

Hank chuckled again as though Petrov had made a joke. "Well, I know that, Mr. Petrov, but the thing is, this man, this Luka Kole, well, he got himself shot a couple of days ago, and we were wondering, since he did call you, well, you know, what it was about."

"I have no idea. If he called the company, he could have spoken to anyone."

"So you never heard of this Luka Kole?"

Petrov smiled indulgently, a city cat staring down a country mouse. "I am afraid . . . no."

Hank frowned. "Well, I'm sorry to hear that. Miss Baker, she'll be sorry to hear it, too."

His eyes sharpened. "Miss Baker?" That ruffled his fur.

"Yes, I believe you know her. A. J. Baker? Don't you and she have some kind of business thing together?"

"Yes. Renaissance Oil." His eyes had narrowed, his attention focused.

"That's right. Been reading a lot about that in the paper."

"And what does Miss Baker have to do with this man, Kole?"

"Well, seems she was Mr. Kole's daughter."

That got a reaction. Petrov took in a sharp breath, quickly controlled himself, and smiled. "I did not know Miss Baker had relatives in Sokanan. I understood she was from New England."

Hank shrugged. "I don't know about that, but she says she's his daughter. She's burying him today."

"Is she?"

"Well, not by herself, of course. We've got a cemetery, and they do all the heavy lifting, but she's paying for it. At least, the city's charging her for it."

Petrov looked at him, a sympathetic smile on his face, a smile that meant nothing. "I will have to send her flowers. I had no idea. She must be terribly upset."

Upset was an understatement, but not about Luka Kole.

"So, you're sure you never heard of the man?"

"Luka Kole? No, I am sorry. But I can have my secretary do some little research for you and see who he might have spoken with."

"Would you? That would be a big help." Hank handed him his card. "You can contact me anytime. Thanks."

"My pleasure."

He rose, walked Hank to the door. "Give your police chief my regards. We are playing golf next Sunday."

As if he might actually move in those circles. "Oh, sure. Will do." They shook hands, and Petrov released him into Yuri's custody. The bodyguard escorted him to the elevator and back down to the lobby.

At the door, Hank stopped, patted his pockets, and looked sheepishly at Yuri. "Spare a smoke?"

The other man looked as though he'd rather spare a left hook, but with a grunt he reached into his inner jacket pocket and pulled out a pack of Marlboros.

Bull's-eye.

"American." Hank winked. "They're the best."

Yuri shrugged and shook the pack to free up a cigarette. "Thanks, pal."

Hank stuck the cigarette behind his ear, walked through the revolving door and out into the street.

So Yuri smoked the same brand as the butt Greenlaw had found. So what? A million other nicotine addicts smoked Marlboros. And even if a DNA profile came back on Yuri, that butt could have been dropped anytime. Hank had a feeling it hadn't been, but he couldn't take a hunch to court.

He stopped outside the building and gawked up at the heights of glass like a rube from the sticks. Out of the corner of his eye, he saw Yuri leave to return to his master.

Okay, Miki. Let's see what you do next.

Ensconced in his office, Petrov stared at the case holding his swords. The dragoon officer's saber grabbed his particular attention. It dated to 1841, and unlike the hilt of the regular soldier's weapon, the officer's sword glittered with gilt. Petrov kept the gold highly polished, though it was mere decoration. A gloss hiding the base metal underneath.

Was it the same with Alex?

The information Detective Bonner had so casually dropped zipped through Petrov like a lit fuse.

Alex, Luka's daughter?

Impossible.

Kholodov had no children.

Even if he had married while in hiding, any child born could have reached a maximum of only thirteen years.

He opened the case, took out the dragoon's saber and frowned at it.

A relative perhaps?

A niece maybe. That idiot detective had gotten mixed up.

But what if he hadn't?

Petrov took a fighting stance and whipped the sword through the air. The blade sang with sharpness. A deadly sound. A comforting one.

Why would Alex claim to be Kholodov's daughter? And if she was his daughter, why tell him she was raised in Boston by a physician?

He slashed the sword through space again, cutting it three times.

The last time he'd seen Kholodov had been thirteen years ago. The day Comrade Baklanov . . .

He stopped, midswing. A picture formed in his memory, fuzzy at first, but sharper as he brought it into focus.

Kholodov pulling someone away from the body. A screaming child. No, not a child. A girl. A young woman.

Petrov didn't quake often, but he was nearly quaking now. Not with fear, Miki Petrov was afraid of nothing. But something . . .

He stared at the sword, at its honed edge and gleaming hilt.

Gilt over metal.

There was meaning in that. But what?

He leaned over his desk, punched a button on his phone, and ordered Svetlana to find Jeffrey Greer.

In minutes, Greer's voice echoed into the office from the speakerphone. "Mr. Petrov. How nice—"

"What have you found about our Miss Baker?"

He'd wasted no time on preliminaries, and Greer was slow to respond. "Uh . . . just a minute, let me get the file." The sounds of shuffling paper came through the receiver, driving a sliver of impatience through Petrov.

Miki rotated his wrist, watching the blade twirl. Would Jeffrey Greer enjoy seeing what could be done with a blade?

"Here it is," Greer said. "Okay, let's see. Graduated summa cum laude from Harvard Business School. Prior to that, she was at Princeton, where she also graduated at the top of her class. After Harvard she—"

"I know all this. Where was she thirteen years ago?"

"Thirteen? I don't understand."

He gazed along the blade edge, contemplating the drag as it slid across Greer's throat. "You don't need to understand. The question is a simple one. Where was she thirteen years ago?"

"Well . . ." More paper shuffling. "Oh, here we are. She was in Boston."

"She went to school there?"

"Well, no. Briarcliffe in New Hampshire. I have her senior transcript. Graduated with a 3.87 G—"

"And before that?"

"Before that?"

"Yes, *before* that." He heard his voice. The tone was silky, calm. Deadly. "Where did she go to school *before* that?"

"You mean when she was what—six, ten? You want to know where she went to school as a child? How can that possibly have any relevance to—"

"Find out."

"But, Mr. Petrov—"

"Find out, Greer. I don't have to tell you the consequences of disappointing me." Idly, he drew the blade across a pad of paper on his desk, carving it in two.

"No, sir."

No, sir. Jeffrey Greer was becoming more and more to his taste.

Petrov disconnected the call and paged Svetlana again. "Send Yuri in."

Yuri poked his head in, looked from Petrov to the sword and back again. Fear sliced across the big man's face, and Petrov smiled.

"Come in. It won't bite. It's not hungry. At least . . . not yet." He replaced the sword in the case, closed the glass door, and locked it. Then he turned to Yuri, who stood like a lump of clay waiting to be shaped.

Petrov signaled for him to sit. "Comrade Baklanov—what do you know of him?"

A flash of surprise in Yuri's eyes. Surprise he was wise enough to cover. "He was a thief and a traitor."

Petrov waved this away as irrelevant.

"He killed himself."

"Yes, yes, but what do you remember about him before he killed himself?"

Yuri's face brightened. "He was a big man. A fat man. I remember that. Probably splattered when he fell."

Petrov frowned. Subtlety never worked well with Yuri. He got directly to the point. "Did he have a daughter?"

Yuri thought about it. "I remember something about a child. Could have been a girl."

Could have.

"What happened to her?"

"I don't know."

"Find out. Call Moscow. Use the back door to Dashevsky if you have to."

Yuri's brows rose, but he was smart enough not to comment.

Petrov swiveled his chair around to face the windows. From this vantage point all he could see were clouds and sky. He liked being up high. Liked the danger of it. And being above everyone. He'd worked hard to arrive at this place where he and the sky were one. He was not about to risk his position.

"Kholodov is being buried today in Sokanan." He spoke slowly, softly, thinking it through. "Send Vassily to the cemetery. I want to know who goes to the funeral. Use the camera."

Behind him, Yuri said, "*Da, tovarish'nachalnik.*"

"And tell him not to let anyone know he's there."

12

The Sokanan cemetery was twenty miles or so from Apple House. Hank wanted to see who turned up at Luka Kole's funeral, but first he thought he'd stop by the farm and check on his mother.

He was five minutes away from the turnoff to the orchard when a black Ford slithered out of the roadside trees and caught up, butting against his tail.

A warning ticked inside Hank's head. He glanced in the rearview mirror, saw two men inside the other car. What the hell were they doing? It wasn't as if the road was heavily traveled. In fact, there was no one on the road but Hank and the Ford, which was sticking like glue to his rear.

He slowed down, waved the car to pass, but instead, the Ford sped up and bumped Hank's.

What the—?

He struggled to maintain control of the car, but a second hit sent him careening off into the side road.

Trees came at him in a blur. He gripped the wheel. Braked the shit out of the pedal.

And came screeching to a halt half an inch short of a thick maple tree.

Jesus H. Christ.

He caught his breath, lucky to be alive playing its old song in his head.

Weapon drawn, he bolted out of the car, the hot sting of adrenaline pumping madly. Using the vehicle as a shield, he called to them. "What the hell do you think you're doing?"

The two men were already approaching. They were big, bigger than Hank and he was a big guy. Both were dressed carefully in conservative suits. Dark blue, gray.

"That's far enough." Hank tightened his hold on the weapon, stopping the two before they barreled down on him.

The driver held up a hand.

"Calm down."

"Calm down? Fucking asshole, you almost killed me."

"But we didn't," the passenger said. "So put the gun away, Detective Bonner."

Like hell he would. "Who are you? How the hell do you know my name?"

As if he hadn't heard and didn't care that he was facing an angry cop with a gun, Driver peered at him, face expressionless. "We're here to deliver a little message."

"From who?"

"Stay away from A. J. Baker."

"You're kidding." He looked between the two impassive faces. "What are you—more of Petrov's goons?"

"You have your suspect," said Passenger. "Follow up. Leave Miss Baker alone."

"Or what?"

"Or you're not going to like what happens," Driver said.

"Your family has a farm around here," Passenger said.

Hank's gut tightened. "You're threatening my family?"

Driver shook his head. "You're doing that by poking your nose where it doesn't belong."

The two men stared at him, faces cold and impassive.

Driver said, "¿*Comprende?*"

"Yeah, sure. I understand."

"Good." They turned and walked back to the car.

Hank watched them go, neat, pulled together, confident of getting their way, and very, very American.

Not Petrov's goons.

They had the walk, the talk, the smell of Feds.

Passenger saluted as the car whizzed past Hank. He ground his teeth. Looked like Alexandra Jane had more pull than he thought.

And was much, much more afraid.

With shaky fingers, Alex pulled on the long navy skirt and equally dark blouse. The clothes clung, the skirt straight and slim, the blouse high-necked and long-sleeved. They surrounded and trapped her, and she wished she were wearing the floaty skirt she'd put on for Hank.

Hank. How did that name sneak into her head?

Ruthlessly, she squashed it. She wasn't going to a blues bar, and she had to dress accordingly. She buttoned the blouse, fingers still trembling, and hid the matryoshka necklace as though it would give her away. She squeezed her hands shut, then straightened them, but her fingers remained wobbly.

She had to get hold of herself.

Not likely. Not today.

She stared in the mirror over her dresser. She'd bundled her hair up and out of the way, and against the midnight blue of the blouse, her face appeared washed-out. But that was fine; no one would see her face.

Setting a wide hat on her head, she adjusted the angle and pulled down the veil so her face was obscured.

Mason's words throbbed in her head, a drumbeat of warning.

Stay away. Stay away.

But how could she?

She picked up a pair of black gloves from the dresser. Between the veil and the gloves, the long sleeves, and the narrow, ankle-length skirt, she would be covered from top to bottom. A mystery. One nobody would solve.

At least that's what she told herself.

And what would she tell Mason when she showed up?

She had depended on him a lot these past few days, but in this, she would go her own way. She would take a cab, not risk even having her car seen, but she would be there.

He had suspected as much, hence his warnings in their last phone call. Remembering that he'd promised to take care of Hank, a flush of shame ran through her.

She slipped on the gloves, pushing the tight silk over her unsteady fingers. She wouldn't think about Hank Bonner. About the compassion on his face when he told her about Sonya. His strong hands and good intentions.

Dangerous. So very, very dangerous.

She hoped Mason had done what he promised.

She hoped he hadn't.

She turned away from the mirror, half-muddled and confused.

For the first time in her life, she didn't know what she wanted.

Sokanan's Gates of Hope cemetery sat on the south end of town, on the edge of the Van Dekker Country Club's golf course. An odd place for a cemetery, but the graves had been there long before the country club bought the land and carved it into hillocks and sand traps for GE executives. The executives were long gone, but the country club hung on, and the graves remained forever.

Hank had spent more time at the cemetery than he would have liked and so was painfully familiar with it. He knew you could see the golf course from the gravesites; rather than sing hymns and listen to some minister's well-meant words, he'd spent whole moments watching golfers swing.

That was why he headed to the country club first, flashing his badge as his entry fee and making straight for the small rise on the golf course's sixteenth hole.

The only golfers that time of the afternoon were down around the ninth hole, so Hank had the sixteenth to himself. He sank to the ground, flattened against the manicured grass, and gazed out at the graveyard. He'd brought a pair of binoculars with him, and from that vantage point, saw the upturned earth of Luka Kole's grave and his coffin above it. Only one mourner was there. Hank started as he recognized him. The man Alex had met in the middle of the night after the Renaissance Oil party.

Uncle Fisherman.

That stirred his curiosity, but he held back, scanning the area around the gravesite to make sure no one else was there.

Would Alex show up?

He had his doubts; she was adamant about having nothing to do with the funeral. But still, he wanted to make sure. If she did turn up, he might have to revise a few more things about her and her so-called estranged father.

When no one else appeared, Hank scrambled down the rise. A flash of color caught his eye.

A man. Skulking toward the freshly dug grave. A man in black. A leather jacket perhaps?

Hank held up the glasses again, brought the figure into focus.

One of the homeboys who'd been in Petrov's office with Yuri.

So there *was* a connection between Petrov and Kole. Why else would Miki P. send one of his thugs to scout out the funeral? The guy wasn't paying his respects either; he kept well away, hidden behind a large headstone.

But he had a camera. And he was taking pictures.

Well, well, well.

Hank grinned as he made his way back to his car. He drove from the country club to the cemetery and got to the grave just as the coffin was being lowered.

Uncle Fisherman was still there. And though he couldn't spot him, Hank felt Homeboy's presence, too.

As he and Uncle Fisherman were the only two at the grave, and it would seem odd not to, Hank stuck out his hand and introduced himself.

Uncle Fisherman looked mildly amused, but he shook Hank's hand. "Oh, yes, the persistent Detective Bonner. I should have expected you." His graveled voice promised roughness, yet the phrasing was polished and articulate. He'd exchanged his scruffy khakis for a neatly pressed suit, and his silver hair, which had looked half-combed in the early-morning darkness, was now tidy and in place. Up close, he was taller than Hank had thought, ranging as high as Hank's own six-two, and the hand that gripped his was strong and robust. Altogether, Hank had the impression of competence and utter reliability.

"Yeah? How come?"

"I'm afraid Miss Baker has told me quite a lot about you."

Miss Baker. Of course.

His gaze locked on to the other man's. It was returned, as measuring as his own. "And how did I come across?"

"You know how it is." He chuckled, a sound that was both friendly and not. "Always better in person."

He'd just bet. "And you are . . . ?"

"Edward Mason, Miss Baker's lawyer."

Her lawyer? At two in the morning he must keep very odd office hours. Not to mention the office itself—a deserted gas station way the hell out and beyond. "Of course. I passed your name on to the coroner."

"And I appreciated it."

The coffin sank into the ground, suspended on some kind of pneumatic device. He'd seen plenty of that in the last year, and he still couldn't get used to it. But Mason was watching him, so he pulled himself away from the coffin's unhurried, final journey and turned to the other man.

"Practice around here?"

Mason smiled as though he knew a fishing expedition when he heard one. "I'm retired. An old family friend."

"From Boston?"

"Well, I live here now. I have a fishing cabin up by Lakeview. As I think you already know."

Hank didn't admit that, though if Alex had run to Mason after breakfast yesterday, they both knew he did.

"You've known Alex a long time, then?"

"I knew her family, yes."

"She said she was estranged from her father."

Mason acknowledged this with a small shrug. "It's such a shame when families can't get along. The modern tragedy and all too familiar, I'm afraid."

"What happened between them?"

"Oh, you know how it is." Mason spread his hands in a gesture of helplessness. "Divorce breeds bitterness. Misunderstanding. Estrangement." The coffin was in place. Mason turned to stare at the gaping hole. "Would you excuse me?"

Hank stepped back. "Of course."

Mason walked toward the grave, lifted a fistful of dirt from the pile surrounding the hole, and threw it in. The earth clattered on top of the coffin and sent a wintry ripple down Hank's spine.

Mason repeated the gesture twice more. As the last handful fell, he murmured something, but Hank couldn't catch what he said.

Was it because he was too far away, or because he was speaking something other than English?

Finished, Mason rubbed his hands together to cleanse them and turned to Hank.

"Thank you for coming." He walked away without a backward glance.

His pickup sat on a nearby path not too far from Hank's car. The dust and mud he'd seen the other night were gone. Looked like Mason had cleaned up his truck along with himself.

Bitterness ripped through Hank. Why did everyone always dress for death? As if it were a prize and not the lump of coal at the end of the rainbow everyone knew it was.

Alone now, Hank drifted to a more familiar landscape. He hadn't intended to visit Maureen, but he wasn't surprised to find himself at her grave.

The afternoon was waning, and old headstones cast long shadows over the grass around them. He bent down, cleared a bouquet Rose had probably left. Apple blossoms. Maureen had loved the fragrance.

"How you doing, sis?"

He listened to the silence.

They'd buried her next to their father, but Tom was on the

other side of the graveyard, over by the Stillers. Separated in death as they should have been in life.

He stared at her headstone, remembering how hard they'd all tried to get him help, and when help didn't work, didn't ease the temper or the drinking, tried to get him out.

But he was a nasty SOB. Always had been. Even when he was throwing touchdown passes to Hank back in high school, even then he was quick on the trigger. The slightest thing would set him off.

Christ.

He'd brought Tom home. Introduced him to Maureen.

The nausea he hadn't experienced in months came lurching back, and for a moment he felt as though he were going to be sick. Sweating, he leaned into the top of his father's stone so the cool granite bit hard into his hands. After a minute, the queasiness passed.

Sorry, Maureen. So damn sorry.

He stumbled away, wondering for the ten thousandth time why he was alive and Maureen wasn't.

The unknowable, unanswerable question. A rusty knife in his soul that could lift the scab off the wound and draw fresh blood at a moment's notice.

He swallowed it down, tramping on. Afternoon sun glinted off grave markers, but the chill of the place cut through the warmth. He shivered, still yards from his car, and saw her. Dripping in dark widow's weeds that covered her from head to toe.

He didn't need to see her face to know who it was; he'd held her body in his arms, watched over her through much of a long, nearly sleepless night.

She stood straight and stiff. Beside her, the business of filling the grave had begun, a small front end loader doing the work by rote—mechanical, impersonal. Normally, they waited for the family to leave before completing that task, and he could only assume they'd begun before she arrived and that she allowed them to continue while she stood there.

He had the odd thought that the machine's presence was wrong, the engine hum and metal clank out of place. Devoted hands should cover the grave, the last human act we could do for those we loved.

But there were no people to do the hard work of filling Luka Kole's grave. Only one raucous contraption.

And her.

He paused, wanting desperately to turn around and leave. Forget she was there and what it meant about her relationship to Kole. Forget her lies and everything she'd ever told him.

Forget he was a cop for four more days.

But a flicker of movement caught his eye.

The cameraman.

At that moment, Alex tilted her head. Hank couldn't see her face but he knew by the way she recoiled that she'd seen him. Fear seemed to lash through her body; she picked up her skirt and ran.

Right toward Petrov's homeboy.

Hank covered the ground between them in three fast strides. Grabbing hold, he spun her around. She raged at him, struggling to break free.

"Let me go." She muttered something in Russian. More curses, he guessed.

"Stop it. Don't." He wrapped his arms around her so she couldn't flail at him, and spoke low. "There's a man with a camera."

Immediately, she ceased thrashing.

"Wh—what?"

"One of Petrov's thugs. He's behind a headstone with a

camera. No, don't look!" He dragged her in the opposite direction, led her to his car, and pushed her in.

She started to lift the netting over her face. He stopped her hand.

"Leave the veil on."

In ten seconds he'd zoomed away, Bonner to the rescue as if he'd never learn.

Stunned, Alex's grief-stricken brain moved like mud. Hank there. Someone with a camera. And below it all, the awful clank of the machine filling in the hole over Luka.

She closed her eyes, every inch of her bowed down by weariness. Her face felt stretched, dried tears making the skin taut. Luka gone, Sonya gone.

And now this.

The car slowed, turned. Stopped.

A voice penetrated the fog. "Okay, you can come out now."

Fingers lifted the dark veil and she opened her eyes to find Hank as close as a breath.

"Tell me what's going on, Alex." His voice was low, his face full of concern and that intense earnestness she admired.

"I don't know what you're talking about," she managed to get out.

He looked away from her, out the window as though searching for another way into her head, her soul.

He sighed. "Well, maybe you're right. Maybe holding on is smart. God knows I'd love to wash my hands of you." His wistful tone took the sting out of the words. "But for some reason"—he laughed, curt and sharp, almost astringent—"for some reason, I can't." He turned, looked at her with those serious green eyes. "You're in trouble. Let me help you."

"You can't. No one can."

"Try me."

She gazed down at her hands, which were clasped tightly in her lap, any place to avoid that penetrating look he was giving her.

"Try me, Sashenka."

The way he said her name, so foreign-sounding on his tongue, yet so sweet. Tears welled, and she tensed, willing them away.

"Trust me. Let me help."

She was so tired of the tears. And the lies. So very tired.

"How does Petrov know Luka?"

"Petrov . . ." She swallowed, the words drying in her mouth. "Petrov killed him." Her stomach twisted, she felt sick with exposure. "He killed Sonya, too."

"No, Alex, she had a heart attack."

"He killed her! I can't prove it, but I know, here"—she thumped her chest where her heart was thudding dully—"that he's responsible. He killed my father, he killed everyone I've ever cared about."

Hank was silent.

She'd spewed out the bald truth, and he sat staring out the window. For the first time she realized they were parked in the middle of the orchard. In all directions, pinkish white puffs of blossoms floated on trees.

She had a strange impulse to run and hide in their thick branches, cover herself with blossoms and disappear.

She opened the door and got out of the car. The air was warm and tinged with a heady fragrance. The earth smelled alive with promise, new life beginning even as old life waned.

Walking blindly, she ended up beneath a tree, her back against the hard trunk. She removed her hat, dropped it to the ground, and unpinned her hair, letting the spring blow through it, fresh and unsullied.

Hank came after her, his step slow and deliberate, as though working it all out, trying to make sense of what she'd just told him.

But it didn't make sense, and she didn't want to wring meaning out of it either. So much better to forget, to drift away on spring and apple blossoms.

"What kind of apples are these?"

He glanced up at the branches. "Jersey Macs. They're early fruit. Summer harvest. Very soft and hard to keep. We don't grow many."

"Why grow any if they're such a bother?"

He smiled, a little knowing curve of his mouth. "Once you've tasted Jersey Mac pink applesauce, you won't ask that question."

"And over there?"

He turned to look where she pointed. Dozens of trees faced them, their pink-tinged white fur swaying in the breeze. Blossoms danced on branches or floated leisurely to the ground. A pale carpet was beginning to form.

"Macintosh. And those are Spartans, Honey Crisp, Cortlands." He pointed in several other directions. "We have Red and Golden Delicious on the other side, Northern Spy, Ida Reds. And over here"—he turned in the opposite direction—"there's Winesaps, Romes, and Fujis."

"It's so beautiful."

"Yes, it is."

"How could anyone give it up?"

That mouth of his went to work again, this time the smile wry. "Once you get beyond the pretty façade, it's just hard work. And it doesn't always pay off. Do you remember the freak hailstorm we had two years ago in June?"

She shook her head.

"No, why should you? A summer hailstorm to most folks is just a weather oddity. But it was devastating to us. It took three-quarters of the apple crop. Almost put us out of business."

"But you hung on."

"Yeah, we hung on." He shifted impatiently. "Alex, what does this have to do with—"

"And now things are . . . different."

He shrugged. "Look, can we get back to Petrov?"

She peered down at her hands. Miraculously, they'd stopped shaking. "I've told you everything I can."

"You've told me that Petrov killed Luka Kole, but you didn't tell me why or how you know."

She looked away, out toward the magic of earth and tree and blossom. "I can't talk about that."

"Why not?"

"Why can't you talk about what happened here, with your family?" She turned back to confront him, and his eyes grew cold. "See? We all have secrets we'd like to keep."

He gave her another terse, sardonic laugh. "It's no secret. It was in the paper, on TV, radio. I'm surprised you don't know about it."

"I was in and out of Moscow most of last year. What did I miss?"

Hank opened his mouth, but the words caught in his throat. "My sister was . . ." He took a breath, willing his voice to stay calm and even. "My sister was married to a guy with a lot of trouble in him."

"Maureen was your sister?"

He nodded.

"And Tom, that was her husband?"

Tom. The name still conjured up that nightmare face

coming at him, lips contorted in a crazed grimace, arms rigid, hands fixed on the screwdriver with a cast-iron grip.

"Tom Stiller. We were high school buddies. On the football team. He was the big shot quarterback. Never did get over that taste of celebrity. He was always looking for a shortcut to fame and fortune."

"And did he find it?"

He shook his head, bitterness bubbling up. "No, he got Maureen pregnant and that was that. They got married and ran Apple House. He started drinking, and the drinking got worse, and then he started shoving Maureen around, and"— he shrugged, cutting the litany short because who'd want to hear all that pain and who'd want to tell it—"it was a mess."

"Why didn't she leave him?"

Oh, the dozens of times she'd tried. "It never stuck. He always crawled back. I think she'd become his excuse for failure, and he needed an excuse. We tried counseling, rehab, anger management, you name it. Finally, Maureen had had enough. She filed for divorce. The day the papers showed up, so did Tom. Drunk. Wild. Raging. They must have been going at it for hours before Trey called me."

He remembered the panic in the boy's voice. He couldn't get the words out fast enough.

"Slow down," Hank had told him.

"You have to help her," the boy screamed into the phone. "Who? Help who?"

"Mom. He's got her. My dad. Please. Please, help her."

Help her. Christ. He'd been a big help.

"By the time I got there, Tom had dragged her into the toolshed behind the house."

"What happened?"

He felt the sun on him again, hot as a spotlight as it bounced off the white metal shingles of the shed. He remembered the sweat, the nail-tearing fear. The sound of his heart like a cannon in his ears. Could he talk Tom out or would he have to break in? If he broke in, could he get to Maureen before Tom did?

He should have gone in sooner. The familiar rebuke burned through him. He should have gone in sooner.

"I broke into the shed. He came at me with a screwdriver. Nearly killed me. I . . ." Another pause, another breath. Another wave of regret. "I shot him."

A shock wave ripped through Alex. He'd killed Mandy's father. His own brother-in-law. "And Maureen?"

"She was already dead, though I didn't know it. He'd thrown her across the shed. She fell on a scythe, and the tip tore through her brain."

"My God." Images swirled, making her stomach flop.

"Yup. Pretty much of a screwup all around."

"I'm sorry." She knew how inadequate those words were. People had said them to her often enough.

He blew out a breath, as though exhaling the deep emotions, and swooped down to pick up a fallen branch. He cracked the branch in two, then in two again, and, with a brutal toss, flung the pieces into the field as though throwing away the ache.

He turned to her. "So"—his mouth twisted into a wry semblance of a smile—"now that I've shown you mine, how about you showing me yours? Why do you think Petrov killed Luka?"

The moment had come. She had to make a choice. Other pictures crowded her head. The cold, black hole she'd just left Luka in; the similar place she would soon leave Sonya. They had paid for her revenge. Would he?

She searched his face; he looked so strong. Invincible.

But no one was immune. Death stalked all.

Would he be safer knowing what he was up against? Or was it better to leave him in the dark?

People stumbled in the dark. Fell.

She didn't want him to fall, didn't want another grave on her conscience.

"Luka knew . . ." She licked her lips. "He knew something Petrov didn't want him to know." Her voice came out hoarse and forced.

"What? Some kind of proof against him?"

She shook her head. "I don't know exactly. That's why I was in the apartment. I thought . . . maybe I could find whatever it was."

"But what could Luka know that would hurt Miki Petrov? How are they connected? And what does it have to do with you?"

The last barrier. Was she ready to breach it? Blood pounded in her ears. She was drawing him into her perilous life. Pushing him closer and closer toward a sharp-edged precipice. She saw him tumble over, an endless, hopeless fall. She heard the scream that she never wanted to hear again.

She froze, lungs clogged. She couldn't speak, couldn't make the words come. All she could do was shake her head.

He muttered a curse under his breath. "If you're right, whatever Luka knew killed him. If you're tied into it, you could be in danger, too."

Another cold wind rippled through her. The man with the camera. Did he take pictures of her? Would Miki recognize her? Would he make the connection? And if he did, what could Hank do about it but get caught in the cross fire?

"I can't. Please. Don't push."

"Push? There was a man with a damn camera back there.

I'm not the one doing the pushing." His jaw tightened. "I could subpoena you, bring you in as a material witness."

"Handcuff me and throw me in jail? Somehow I don't think you'll do that."

"Why not?"

"Just a hunch."

He ran a hand through his hair, and she wished she could recapture her fury of the previous morning. Anger was as good a defense as any against him. But when she reached for it, she discovered it gone. As though it had been buried along with Luka.

"They threatened my family."

"What?" She looked at him sharply. "Who?"

"Those federal boys you launched at me. They made a veiled threat against my family if I don't butt out."

She felt the blood drain from her face, then flood right back. Mason. "I . . . I didn't mean . . . I didn't know . . . I would never—"

"So they did come from you."

She opened her mouth, saw the gleam of satisfaction in his face. Dammit, she'd fallen right into his trap.

"Don't you want to see the bad guys punished?"

She swooped down and picked up her hat. Breathing time was over. "More than you'll ever know, Detective. But you're not the one who can do it." She marched back to the car.

He followed, keeping pace easily. "I think you just insulted me. What's the matter—don't think I'm man enough?"

"Oh, you're plenty man enough." Her face heated, and something exploded between them. Quickly she doused it. "But you're a small-town cop, and this is way over your head." She reached the car, opened the door. He closed it.

"I'll say it again, Alex. Try me."

"No." She crossed her arms, as if that could protect her from his tenacity. "I've said enough. Take me home."

"And then what?"

Then what? What did he think? "Then I carry on as before."

"Carry on? Clanking around in that huge castle in the forest? I don't think so." He opened the car door and nudged her in. "I'm taking you back to the farm. My mother would love to lavish sympathy and attention on you anyway. And Mandy has already made up a visitation schedule."

She didn't argue; truth was, she didn't really want to go home to an empty house. Too many memories. Too much sadness.

He slid behind the wheel and sat for a moment. "Look, I think I should tell you. I saw Petrov today. It's my fault he sent a goon with a camera. I told him you were Luka Kole's daughter and that you were burying him today."

"What?" Her whole body stilled.

"What's the harm, Alex? Why shouldn't I tell him? Oh, because you think he's responsible? Because you don't want him to know of your relationship with Kole? Which one is it, column A or column B? And how am I supposed to know if you don't goddamn tell me?"

She was silent. Would Miki believe him? What would he do?

"I want the truth, Alex. All of it."

But she couldn't tell him and keep them both safe. Not yet. Not ever.

13

Alex stared out the window as Hank drove through the orchard, the car bumping over what at times was only a narrow dirt path. The trees seemed to go on forever, petals in every direction. She let her gaze drift over them. She didn't want to think about Miki. About death and revenge. Or what he would do with the information Hank had given him, or what her next move would be.

She wanted to pretend she didn't have to move. She wanted to think about apples, about roots and family tradition.

"Will you sell?"

He cut a glance her way, but went along with the change of subject. "I don't know. My mother doesn't want to, but as the summer progresses, I'm not sure we're going to have much choice."

Who did? "Why don't you hire someone?"

"These days who wants to come out and run an operation for someone? Everyone wants their own piece of it, and who can blame them?"

"There must be someone out in the great wide world who needs a steady job, a home, roots, and who might trade labor for training." She heard the longing in her voice, knew it for the fantasy it was. Her own, ready-made to block out whatever was coming next.

He cut a glance her way. "Bonner's job corps?"

"Why not?"

He shrugged, his expression thoughtful.

By that time they were at the farmhouse. Trey was playing basketball at a hoop in the back. He stopped to watch them drive up and park.

"Hey, Trey." Hank called his nephew over. "You remember Miss Baker."

"Hello, Trey." She tried a smile on him, but he only gave her a sullen nod and went back to playing.

Hank frowned and opened his mouth to reprove him, but she stopped him. "It's all right. I don't mind. He's just being a boy."

"He's just being a brat." But there was an edge to the pronouncement. Worry, frustration. Even affection. Lucky boy to have someone care that much about him. Even if he didn't seem to know it.

Hank escorted her into the house. They came through a mudroom with a concrete floor and a series of hooks crowded with coats, hats, and scarves. Boots were scattered against one wall, and opposite sat a long wooden bench for putting them on and taking them off. A shovel, a pile of newspapers, and a rusted pail lay about. It was a mess, but a mess made by many people living and working together, and it welcomed her.

Since it was spring and mild, neither she nor Hank were wearing boots or coat so they passed through and into the kitchen. Warm and lived-in, the room was festooned with leftovers from decades past. A countertop lined in well-worn black-and-white octagonal tiles. Long, deeply hung cabinets with plain fronts painted yellow. In one corner a round table sat snugly. Edged in chrome, it had a flecked gray surface and red leatherette chairs with matching chrome trim. In another corner, Rose's stolid form hovered over a pan on the stove.

"Look what I brought home," Hank announced, and Rose turned. Her face broke into a smile when she saw Alex.

"I'm so glad." She opened her arms and embraced Alex. "We were sorry to hear about your housekeeper. And worried about you." After a brief hug, she broke off and stepped back, examining Alex. "How are you? Really."

Alex opened her mouth to assure the woman with some meaningless phrase like "fine," but Rose gazed at her with genuine concern.

"Tired," Alex said at last. "Worn down."

Rose squeezed her hand. "That's what happens. Grief is exhausting. Let yourself get plenty of rest." She ushered Alex to the table. "Come sit down. Get her something to drink, Henry." She turned to Alex. "Coffee? Henry's got some beer in the fridge, I think. And there's always apple cider."

"Cider would be nice."

Rose found glass and bottle, which she set in front of Alex. The juice was cold and sweet and tasted like summer.

"Excuse me a minute," Hank said. "I'll go find Mandy."

When he'd gone, Alex turned to Rose. "Are you making dinner? What can I do to help?"

Rose frowned. "Not a thing. What did I say about rest?"

"I'm not an invalid. Besides, I'd rather not sit here feeling sorry for myself. I can cut and chop. And I'm good at fetching things."

"Well, I do need a couple of jars of green beans. They're in the pantry. Through the mudroom and turn right."

She followed the directions and ran into Trey, who was

just coming into the house. He looked startled to see her; his face colored, and she wanted to put him at ease.

She smiled. "Your grandmother sent me for a couple of jars of beans. I think I'm lost. Can you help me out?"

He stiffened, then, "They're in the pantry. Here." He showed her the door, opened it, and stepped through. "The beans are up there." He pointed to a top shelf filled with a bounty of home-canned fruits and vegetables in mason jars.

"How does your grandmother do all this and run the orchard, too?"

"She doesn't. Those are last year's."

Something about the way he said it caught her attention, a tensing of his shoulders, a hitch in his voice. Last year. When his mother had been alive.

"Special then," she said softly.

He shuffled his feet and looked down. "My mother did those. She grew them in the garden and canned them herself."

There was a small silence. A rush of pity went through Alex.

"You must miss her very much."

Trey shrugged.

"I hardly knew my mother. She died when I was six. Sometimes I wish I could have known her. Wish I could have had her through all the rough times."

"Doesn't do much good to wish, does it?" His voice was biting, and as though he heard the tone and didn't want to say more, pointed to the jars above him. "Want me to get those down for you?"

"All right."

He clambered up a step stool and brought down two jars of beans, handing them to her one at a time.

"I appreciate you letting me share your family for a little

while. I hope you don't mind. Your uncle is trying to help me."

He snorted. "Better watch out, then."

This wasn't the first time she'd seen him express contempt when it came to Hank. "What do you mean?"

He gave her that sullen shrug again, his gaze roaming the room, anywhere but on hers. "I don't know."

"I think you do."

He looked at her defiantly, eyes hot. "I thought he'd help, too, but it didn't exactly work out that way."

She thought back over what Hank had told her about his sister's death. "You called him that night, didn't you?"

He peeked at her truculently. "So?"

"So I was wondering. Who are you really mad at? Him? Or yourself, for making the call?"

His face went white. Without another word, he dashed out of the room, barreling into Hank, who was coming in.

"Hey, what's the matter?"

"Nothing. Let me go!"

He wrenched himself away and ran past.

Hank swung around from the empty doorway to her, his eyes wide and astonished. "What happened? Was he rude? He can get pretty mouthy."

"No, no. He was fine." She glanced down at the mason jars she was carrying. For Trey—for all the Bonners—they contained memories as much as anything else. She wished she hadn't spoken. "It was my fault. I shouldn't have said anything. I hit a nerve."

"He's all nerves these days, so hitting one isn't too hard." He sighed. "We used to be good friends, Trey and I." He stared out the doorway, regret all over his face.

"Why don't you go talk to him?"

"That never seems to work too well."

She hesitated. Who was she to get mixed up in this? She'd already said too much, gotten too close. Look at the mess she'd made.

But she plunged in anyway. "This time you might try telling him it wasn't his fault."

"What wasn't?" Hank unloaded the jars from her arms and led her out of the pantry.

"What happened to his parents."

They were crossing the mudroom toward the kitchen when they heard a door slam. Hank winced.

"He doesn't blame himself. He blames me."

"He made the phone call, Hank. You only answered it."

Hank slowed to a stop. "What do you mean?"

"You're the detective. Think about it."

Slowly he turned toward her as though still absorbing what she'd said.

"Stupid kid," he muttered. He piled the jars back in her arms and left her standing in the mudroom.

The door to Trey's room was shut tight when Hank got there, but he could hear the music pounding through. He knocked, and when Trey didn't answer, knocked again, louder. When there was still no answer, he opened the door.

The sound hit him like a tidal wave, raw, rhythmic, and deafening. Trey lay on his bed, staring at the ceiling. He took one look at Hank, and said, "Go away."

Hank raised his voice. "Turn off the music, I want to talk to you."

The CD player sat on a shelf above the bed. Trey reached up and turned the volume higher.

"Trey—" Hank practically had to shout. With a snap of his wrist, he switched off the machine. The music cut out in midnote.

Trey jumped up. "You can't do that. This is my room."

He reached for the CD player, but Hank grabbed his arm before he got there.

In every interrogation there were times to be soft and times to be hard. Looked like this was one of the latter.

"I said, I want to talk to you." He shoved the boy back on the bed. Trey bounced a little on the mattress, and Hank saw tear tracks on his face.

And just like that, Hank's plan to use strong-arm tactics vanished. He sat on the edge of the bed. How was he ever going to make this right?

"Look, Trey—"

"I don't want to talk to you."

"I get that. So don't talk. Listen." He paused. How the hell to find the words? "None of this is your fault, Trey. None of it."

His nephew stared ahead, stone-faced.

"Whatever you think you did or didn't do, or should or shouldn't have done, what happened to your parents was not your fault. Blame me if you have to blame someone. Just don't blame yourself."

The stone face began to crumble into tears.

"Ah Trey . . ." Hank did what he would have done with anyone, what he'd done a million times for Mandy: he took the boy in his arms.

"It's not your fault, Trey."

"I'm like him." Trey's voice broke on a sob. "I'm just like him."

"God no, Trey. You're you."

"I get so mad all the time. And I hit people. Just like he did."

Oh, God. Is that what was really bothering him? Hank pulled away so he could see his nephew. "Trey, look at me. Look at me." His heart broke at the sight of Trey's thin, narrow face, so like Tom's and now flushed with tears and confusion. "Your dad made a lot of bad choices. He hurt a lot of people, including you. But that doesn't mean you'll make the same choices. You can be like him or not, Trey. It's up to you. Nothing is written in stone. You can choose."

Trey peered down, his voice snagged. "What if . . . what if I make the wrong choices?"

"Do you think you will? Really?" Hank hooked a finger under the boy's chin and raised his tear-stained face. "Look inside yourself, Trey. Your mom lives there, too. Do you think she'd let you do that? When you get mad, listen to her voice. When you want to hit something, remember her. She never hurt a thing in her life."

Trey sat, breath hiccuping, and Hank hoped to God he'd heard him.

"I love you, Trey," he said softly. "I know it's not the same as having your mom here. And I can never be your dad."

"Who'd want to be?" Trey looked at him glumly.

"I would. My own version, not his." He hesitated. "I . . . I'm sorry I took him away from you. Whatever he did, he was still your dad."

Trey picked at a piece of skin on his thumb, focusing on his hand as if it were vitally important. "Grandma said you had no choice."

The memory flashed, quick and bright as summer lightning. The crazed look on Tom's face, the strength in his arm as the screwdriver plunged into Hank's chest.

"I didn't think so. Sometimes that's how it works out."

He nodded. "Life sucks."

"Sometimes. But sometimes it can be pretty damn good. If you let it."

Trey threw him a look Hank could only describe as adult. "You mean like Miss Baker?"

Hank blinked. Then he laughed. "Yeah, Miss Baker is definitely one of life's pluses. Not to mention that she's also a royal pain in the ass."

"Most women are," Trey said with grown-up forbearance, and Hank repressed another smile.

In the distance, Rose called them to dinner, and Trey scrubbed at his face with the bottom of his T-shirt.

"Don't tell Mandy, okay?"

"Don't tell her what—that you think she's a pain? She already knows that."

"That I was such a crybaby."

Hank's heart hitched. In spite of everything, Trey was still a boy after all. "Not a chance, pal. Not a chance."

Whatever had happened between Hank and Trey, dinner was a pleasure for Alex. The food was plain but honest—pot roast and mashed potatoes, a simple salad made from pale green spring lettuce.

She found herself smiling more than she'd done in a month. Mandy pestered her about Russian, and before the meal was over they were all counting to ten—even Trey, who'd been reluctant at first, and Rose, who couldn't always get her mouth around the exotic sounds. A whole roomful of Bonners booming, *"Odin, dva, tri, chetyre, pyat, shest, sem, vosem, devyat, desyat!"*

"Eleven," Mandy yelled. "What's eleven?"

"Too much to remember," Rose said, her face stern, her eyes twinkling.

"If we learn everything tonight, she won't have a reason to come back," said Hank, winking and making Alex blush.

Everyone rose at once to take plates to the sink. The clatter and scrape of chairs and dishes, the clink of silverware and glasses all mingled with babble and laughter, sounding strange and familiar at the same time. For far too long she'd been a hungry little girl, nose pressed to the window of other people's lives, and now there she was, right in the middle of that bright, warm fantasy. It was overwhelming, overpowering, and very, very nice.

But after leftover chocolate cake and, of course, apple pie, it was time for the fairy tale to end. Alex asked to be taken home.

"I've imposed on you too much already," she said with an apologetic tone to Rose.

"No, you haven't," Mandy said. "We like you."

Trey rolled his eyes. "Uncle Hank likes her."

"Well, I do, too." Mandy's stubborn assertion made them all laugh again.

"I'm glad," Alex said, and meant it. "I like you, too, Manya."

Mandy giggled.

"And she's not going home," Hank announced.

Alex turned from the little girl to her uncle. "Oh, but I must."

"Not tonight. You're staying here. We have plenty of room."

Mandy jumped up and down, clapping her hands. "Yes, oh yes, please stay."

Trey shook his head but didn't offer an opinion, which Alex took as a good sign, and Rose only nodded.

Alex sighed. How could she let herself be persuaded so easily? How could she not?

"It's very kind of you, but—"

"There's nothing at home for you, Alex." Hank's voice

was low, the look he gave her deep and understanding. "There's no reason for you to be alone."

Alone. The word rattled inside her like wind in a cold, empty room. She looked around at the warm circle of faces gazing back at her.

"You might as well do what he wants," Trey said dryly. "He won't stop yakking at you 'til you do."

Hank raised his brows as if to say, See? Might as well give in.

Resistance crumbled. For once she would do what she wanted and not what she should. "At least let me go home and get some clothes. If I have to wear these things another minute, I'll scream."

"You got it." Hank grabbed his keys and gestured for her to precede him.

"Trey, you and Mandy help Nana with the dishes. Then homework. I'll be back to help with that if either of you need it."

A scowl crossed Trey's face, and he opened his mouth in what was sure to be a loud protest. But something passed between him and Hank, some kind of newfound understanding. He closed his mouth and nodded slowly. "Okay."

"I appreciate it," Hank said quietly. Then he grabbed her hand, his own large, hard, and warm. "Come on. Everything looks good here."

Outside, the night was just crowding into the day, twilight deepening into blackness.

"Thanks for the tip on Trey. I owe you one."

"Does that mean you worked it out?"

"Let's just say we made some real progress."

She got in the car, and he switched on the engine, turned around and headed down the drive toward the road in the distance. Behind her, the lights of the house grew smaller and smaller until they were tiny pinpricks of brightness in the dark.

"You're very lucky," she said.

"Lucky?" She heard irony in his voice and knew he was thinking about his sister. But no matter how much he'd lost, he still had so much left.

He cut a glance her way, "How about you? Didn't you have a fabulous Boston childhood?"

She didn't want to lie, and she couldn't tell the truth. So for now, simple answers were best. "No."

"You didn't spend much time in Boston, did you?" His tone was quiet, the answer already there in his voice. "I saw the pictures, Alex. You, Luka Kole. Some other man. And they definitely weren't taken in Boston."

She licked her lips. "No."

"Russia?"

"Some of them."

"And the others?"

She was silent. Her hands were suddenly clammy. "Different places."

"You're going to tell me, aren't you? I mean, sometime before the close of the century."

God, he was persistent. "I don't know. Maybe." She sighed. "Probably." When it was safe. An eon from then, when it was safe.

"Maybe you need a little of that Dutch courage back in your kitchen."

"Dutch courage?"

"Russian courage would be more accurate in your case. That bottle of Stoli you tried to drown yourself in the other night. We could open it up and finish the job. And you could tell me your life story."

Or maybe this time, he'd take her to bed and do more than hold her while she cried.

A flush of heat rippled through her, and she closed her eyes against the warmth. She was moving through mud, getting in deeper and deeper, and all she could see was the way down.

"I think we should probably leave the vodka alone."

He didn't respond, but the small smile at the corners of his mouth promised otherwise. Deep inside her, a pulse beat a rapid dance. Was he remembering her thin robe and the feel of his hands on her? If he touched her again, what would she do?

Fifteen minutes later, they approached the turnoff to her home, and all thought of touching seemed to disappear. He slowed to make the right, fingers gripping the wheel in a taut, white-knuckled grasp. His face tensed as they pulled into the drive.

"What's the matter?"

"Nothing."

"Nothing? You look like you're expecting an army of goblins to jump out."

"I said it's nothing," he snarled.

She stilled, taken aback by his hostility. "All right. I didn't mean to pry." Which was a whole lot more than she could say for him.

He pulled up to the front, braked, and turned off the engine, then sat there a second staring out at the night, arms draped over the wheel. "I have this thing about places I can't see into. Leftovers from . . . from the toolshed."

"I see." And she did. He'd trusted her with something private, something deeply personal. If only she could do the same. But his secrets couldn't change the past, while hers could alter the future. And the transformation could be deadly, getting him hurt or worse.

If he saw the difference or the danger, he didn't say. "So now that I'm an open book, how about you? What nasty little secrets are you hiding?"

She opened the door and got out. "Too many to tell."

She crossed the drive to the front door. The night had deepened into black and the thick forest surrounding the house only made it more so. If it spooked him, he did a good job of covering it up, though his gaze was watchful, his body alert.

She let him into the house, and he headed for the kitchen. As she crossed to the windowed hallway that led to the low steps at the back of the house and her bedroom, she heard him mutter, "Where's that Stoli when I need it?"

She smiled. If they were going to move beyond silence and secrets they'd need help. Would vodka be their matchmaker?

A wave of giddiness hit her, making her feel girlish and foolish at the same time. Maybe she'd change out of her clothes and into the blue robe. Maybe she'd lead him into her bedroom. Maybe she'd—

A loud gasp stopped Hank at the kitchen doorway. Instinct had him pivoting, weapon drawn. "What is it?"

Alex stood frozen at the foot of a long, glass-lined hallway. He trotted over, gaze working the area, but didn't notice anything unusual until he was beside her.

Great masses of broken glass lay in heaps at her feet. What once had been a wall of window was now shattered. Jagged holes let in the night and the floor glistened with splinters and ice floes.

A sudden awareness tightened his stomach. "Stay here." He edged closer, trying not to crunch on the glass, and examined the destruction. Someone had deliberately smashed the window; he could see the pattern of hits.

Had the creep struck and fled? Heartbeat revving upward, Hank peered into the opaque darkness down the hall. It was like peering into his past.

Mouth like cotton, he started down the corridor.

Alex grabbed his arm. "Don't."

He shrugged her off. "Quiet." His voice was barely a whisper. "I'm going to see if—"

A shot blasted.

14

Hank froze. Wall plaster pinged and chipped beside him in exquisite slow motion. From far away, Alex cried out.

Somehow, instinct took over, and his arm moved, his body followed, and without conscious thought he shoved her against the wall, blocking the shooter's line of sight.

And then, as though he'd been sucked through a vortex and spit out the other side, the world spun back to real time. To the sour stench of sweat beneath his shirt and the solid weight of steel in his hand. To Alex's body quivering at his back and the sick realization of what her cry might have meant.

Swallowing dryness, he shot a fast glance behind him. Her face was tight with fear. "Are you hurt?"

"I . . ."

"Are you hurt, dammit!" To his ears the hoarse whisper rang out like a shout.

"No." But she sounded dazed. Christ, had she been hit? Had his sluggishness gotten her hurt? He hadn't seen any blood, but with the dim light and her dark clothes, he could have missed something. He buzzed with terror, with the lightning-quick vision of another woman dead in his arms.

"Are you sure?" He turned back to her, fighting the need to run hands over her.

She nodded, face pale but calm. Thank God for her fabled composure.

Another round spit into the wall by his ear. Whatever relief he might have felt was quickly obliterated. They were sitting ducks.

"We have to move. Go—" He nodded toward the front door. "Now!" He shoved her backward, forcing her to scuttle against the wall.

Another shot zinged near his head.

Jesus Christ.

Behind him, she gasped, part scream, part intake of breath. One hand squeezed hers, pushing her forward, the other returned fire.

"Police officer! Drop your weapon!"

A fourth blast answered, close enough to feel its heat.

They were almost at the foyer. Sweat slicked his back. He didn't want to think about the open space between the hallway and the door. About the randomness of chance and fate, the time bomb ticking the minutes of her life away.

"Don't stop," he told her. "Get out the door and into the backseat of the car. I'm right behind you."

"All right." He heard the tremor in her voice and the effort to control it, and he couldn't help a flash of admiration.

At the corner, he held her back one split second. Then he aimed into the darkness behind them and let go of her hand, her fingers slipping away like a last chance. *Count yourself lucky.* The doctor's words echoed inside his head.

He started firing. "Go! Move!"

She raced across the open space of the foyer and he followed, easing backward and providing cover. The continuous roar and blast in the enclosed space was deafening. He lost count of the rounds left in his clip, prayed he'd have enough to get Alex out.

The front door slammed against the wall: Alex flinging it open. He focused on the invisible shooter, hoped to God she'd made it through.

Backing up, he shouldered through the entrance, pulling the door closed behind him so the shooter wouldn't have a clean window.

No bodies, no blood; she must be in the car.

He backpedaled, gaze riveted on the house. Was that movement behind a window? The car was only a few feet away, but felt like a mile. The scar underneath his shirt seemed to glow like a lit target.

Then his hand was on the car door, key in the ignition, engine turned.

In seconds, they were careening down the drive.

Black silence between them. The roar of the engine filled it. The bounce of tires on roadway, the whoosh of trees speeding past. Blood pumping, heart pounding. Hands glued to the wheel.

He grabbed the radio, spit out his location and the situation. "I took rounds. Shooter still inside the house. Got a civilian with me. I'm getting her out."

Gaze everywhere. The thick ebony of forest; the pitchy blind ahead lit by headlights; the coal black hollow behind lit by nothing. Murky. Dense. Who did it hide?

Then the highway. Tires slipping easy on smooth blacktop. Heartbeat ratcheting down from frenzied to frantic, fear like an aftertaste in his mouth.

How had they escaped?

His soul was on fire, needing frantically to know.

Bad aim or near misses? Accident or intentional?

Count yourself lucky.

Lucky. When would his luck run out?

Then Alex's voice was in his ear. "Is anyone following?"

"Get down!"

"Where are we going?"

"Get the hell down and stay down!"

"We can't go back to Apple House." Alex's voice was urgent. "I can't bring this to your family."

She was right. "We're not going to Apple House. I have a place downtown where you'll be safe."

"No."

"No? Fine, I'll take you to the station. Protective custody. Think a jail cell will be safe enough?"

She climbed over the back, wriggling into the front seat.

"What the hell do you think you're—"

"I know a better place. Pull over."

"What?"

"Pull over. I'll drive."

"I'm not pulling over, and I'm not letting you drive."

She was silent, which was good. He needed every ounce of concentration to push away the shakiness.

But the silence didn't last. "No one followed us, did they?"

"No. They seemed more interested in getting rid of us than finding out where we were going once they did."

"Then turn left up ahead."

He spared her a glance. When was she going to stop giving orders? "What for?"

"The entry to the Taconic is a quarter mile away."

"The Taconic?"

"North."

She didn't have to say it; instantly he knew where she wanted to go. Lakeview.

The name spun in his head, scrutinized from all angles.

The place was farther away than his house or the station, an isolated dot on the map. All around, it seemed as good an idea as any. Maybe better.

But dammit, it pissed him off. Royally. He felt like a blind man heading down an unfamiliar street, no dog, no cane, nothing to get him through but chance and instinct.

And those were odds he didn't like.

"You want to go north? You tell me what the hell is going on."

She stiffened. "When we get there."

Rage filled his veins, hot and furious. He braked and the car squealed to a stop. "No." He rounded on her, grabbed her by the chin, and swung her face toward him. "Now."

Her eyes challenged him, cool to his heat despite the grip he had on her. "When. We. Get. There." Voice quiet and reaching for firm but not making it. Oh, she was determined, that was clear, but she was also trembling. Quaking right beside him. Scared to death, and he knew how that felt. Knew, too, he was making it worse. Shame pricked him, and he released her.

"You know you're goddamn fucking lucky you're not dead."

Alex watched out the window as he started the car, then slowed to make the turn onto the parkway. Oh, she knew how lucky she was. Knew, too, that if Petrov had wanted her dead, she'd be dead.

She huddled into herself, wishing she could blend with the night, turn herself into inky air and disappear.

Then she wouldn't have to reveal anything. Wouldn't have to expose herself.

But she was already exposed. Luka gone, Sonya gone.

Alone, she hung by a thread, with nothing left to hold on to but the truth.

The truth Hank deserved. The truth that could cost him his life.

But it was too late for secrets. Those bullets could have hit him as well as her. Lies couldn't protect him. Not anymore.

But the long drive to Lakeview and the anticipation of what lay at the end of it coated her skin with icy dread.

Beside her, Hank was working on calm, but it took a good fifteen minutes for the sweat to cool. Hands fixed to the wheel, he sped into the night, thankful Alex was still and silent.

He hoped she stayed that way. Even fell asleep. He could use a shot of oblivion himself. Darkness was a good time for ghosts, and his were rising out of the grave.

He stared at the twisted black highway, powerless to stop them.

Because the truth was he couldn't save anyone anymore. Couldn't protect anyone. Not with love or good intentions. Not even with guns and bullets.

By every law of God and man he should be dead and Maureen alive. She was the one with a place in this world and children who needed her.

But she'd ended up under the ground, and he'd walked away.

Emotion tightened the back of his throat and he gripped the steering wheel, white-knuckled and desperate.

If she'd fallen an inch east or south she might have walked away with nothing more than a bump on the head. An inch, the difference between life and death. That same little bit, applied to the arm of a madman with a screwdriver, had saved his life.

Why had that fluke killed her but kept him alive?

Why?

The question seared through his brain, burning a well-worn channel, the same unsatisfying answers in its wake.

Random chance.

God's will.

Luck.

Fate.

Take your pick. None of it made sense. Life was one big crapshoot, and everyone played. Everyone gambled. And someday when he needed it most, his lucky streak would end.

Because the universe was going to redress the imbalance that had left him whole. Reset the scales, right the wrong. The final outcome decided not by what he did or didn't do, but by whatever joke the cosmos played on him.

He only hoped to God no one else got killed along the way.

He hit the gas, speeding into the night as though the whoosh of hot air outside the car could burn away the thoughts inside his head.

The car raced ahead, and he made the exit in record time. Past the one-pump gas station, down a two-lane winding country road that upped and downed like a carny ride. To hell and beyond was no exaggeration.

"Up ahead, make a right."

He followed her instructions and in a few minutes, water appeared to his left, glistening in the moonlight. He hugged the shore's arc, easing around the north side where dark shapes morphed into cabins that hung over the lake. An hour earlier, she'd made a phone call, and as they drove up the dirt road in front of one, Mason came out to meet them.

"Pull around back," he called, waving his arms to point the way.

Hank drove into what passed for a driveway—a track channeled into the dirt by truck tires. He braked, and Alex was out of the car in a heartbeat.

Mason shook his head. "This is not a good idea, Sasha."

Alex responded in Russian and Mason switched over. Hank couldn't say he was exactly surprised to hear the Slavic sounds coming out of the other man's mouth, but he hadn't been expecting it either.

For a few minutes, Hank listened to the two of them argue close and low. Then fury rising, he clapped his hands to get their attention.

"Enough. Enough!"

They broke off to look at him as though he were an appendage they'd forgotten.

"English." He drilled them both with a look he'd honed in years of uniform patrol. It was a look that said he was about to get nasty if whoever he was addressing didn't calm down and cooperate. It hadn't failed him yet. It didn't fail him this time.

Mason jerked his head in the direction of the cabin. "Inside."

"Wait," Alex said. She turned to Hank. "I . . . I appreciate everything you've done. But Edward can handle things from here." She gave him that regal smile. Polite, cold. Go away, it said.

A low rhythm beat in his head. A voice urging him to get in the car and drive away. Let someone else take care of her. Someone who wouldn't get her shot, wouldn't get her killed.

But then there was that other voice. The one that reminded him he was still a cop with a case to solve.

"I don't think so." He returned Alex's smile grimly.

"Go home. Your family needs you."

"Nice try, Countess, but we have a deal. A couple of hours ago someone tried to kill us, and I'm not leaving until I find out why."

15

We can argue about it inside," Mason said.

Wordlessly, Hank tramped into the cabin. A single room functioned as both living room and kitchen, both bare-boned and unfinished. One side held an old leather recliner, several coolers, including one that doubled as a coffee table and held a pile of fishing magazines. Scattered over the area were reels, rods, fishing line, and a tackle box with several wicked-looking knives sitting on top. The kitchen side had the necessary appliances plus a wooden table and a couple of chairs.

Hank leaned against the table and while he waited for the other two to troop in, he called home.

Trey answered. Ordinarily, Hank would have asked to speak to Rose, but in a split-second decision, he plunged on with his nephew, giving him the consideration he hoped he deserved.

"Trey, I need a big favor." The kid was silent. Hank didn't know how far their new truce would hold, but he'd already bet on it so he continued. "Look, something's come up, and I may not make it back tonight."

"Where are you?" Suspicion rimmed Trey's question, but Hank ignored it.

"I don't have a lot of time for explanations, but I'm trusting you now, man to man. I need you to tuck in Mandy and if she wakes up in the night, to settle her back down."

"Why? What happened? Are you all right?" Fear replaced caution in the boy's voice.

"I'm fine." He put all the reassurance he could into his words; the last thing Trey needed was someone else dying on him. "But Miss Baker is in a lot more danger than I thought. I have to get her somewhere safe. Do you understand?"

"Sort of."

"I'm counting on you, Trey. Are you up to it?"

"What do you think?" Vestiges of the old bravado came through the phone, and Hank was glad to see his nephew hadn't done a complete one-eighty.

"I think you are or I wouldn't have asked."

"I can take care of stuff tonight, but what about tomorrow? How will we get to school?"

"Call your aunt Lori. Tell her I'm working on a case and see if she can take you. And don't mention Miss Baker, okay?" All he needed was Ben breathing down his neck. "Just say what I told you—that I'm working on a case."

In the background, Rose's voice drifted through as though she'd just entered the room. She wanted to know who Trey was talking to. In front of him Alex and Mason were settling in, waiting.

"Look, I gotta go. Tell your grandmother I'll touch base tomorrow." He was about to disconnect, when Trey spoke.

"Uncle Hank!"

"I'm here."

A pause. "Be careful."

A burst of warmth flew through Hank. "Back at you, kid."

He ended the call and returned the phone to his pocket. In other circumstances he might have dwelled on Trey's last piece of advice and what it meant for the two of them. But right now, he couldn't afford the distraction. So he tucked it away where he could examine it later and addressed Mason.

"I want to know what's going on. Who are you? And don't give me that lawyer crap."

Mason opened a cabinet and took down a mug. "Coffee?"

"Explanations."

Mason poured a cup from a carafe on the counter and handed it to Hank anyway. He poured another cup for Alex and one for himself. Hank knew what he was doing—inserting a little civility into what could be a rude confrontation. Hank ignored the cup, and Mason set it down.

"As it turns out, I am a lawyer." Mason replaced the carafe and removed a container of cream from the fridge, poured a dollop into his cup, and set it on the table where Hank and Alex could reach it. Neither of them moved. "At least, I graduated with a degree in international law. But I didn't spend much of my career in a courtroom."

"Where did you spend it?" Hank eyed him. Mason was calm, in control. When he answered, it was matter-of-fact.

"The Soviet Union mostly."

Surprise, surprise. "Doing what?"

Mason shrugged. "That's classified information, son."

Hank paused, Mason's words conjuring up the host of images he'd intended, all of which Hank didn't like. "State Department?"

"No."

Hank's eyes locked with the other man's. There weren't many other alternatives with "classified" in their description. "CIA."

"Forty years. Now retired." He sipped his coffee, watching Hank over the brim of his cup.

"And that's where you met Alex."

At the sound of her name, Alex looked down at her hands. From the minute she'd entered the cabin, her body had frozen into a block of ice. The time had come. It was here. She would have to tell him everything.

"I . . . I met Mr. Mason when I was sixteen." Her mouth wasn't working, her lips tight, her tongue thick. "Luka took me to him."

She was throwing Hank off that cliff, letting him free-fall into the danger that was her life and hoping neither of them paid the price.

"Luka Kole," Hank said.

"Kholodov," Mason corrected. "Luka Kholodov." He smiled. "We thought it best to Americanize the names."

Hank looked from her to Mason and back again, brooding assessment in his eyes.

"So you're not Baker."

"No."

"And you're not Kholodov. Will the real Alexandra Jane please stand up?"

She flushed, ashamed that she'd lied to him though it couldn't have been helped.

Mason said, "Meet Aleksandra Ivanovna Baklanova."

The name sounded distant, foreign. A memento of another person. Another life.

"Ivan is, of course, Russian for John," Mason said. "John became Jane. A nice, unobtrusive American name that works well with Baker."

Hank didn't respond. His gaze remained on her, the look penetrating. *Who are you?* it said. *I'm waiting, tell me*.

She crossed into the living area, needing distance. Somehow she thought it would be easier if he couldn't stare at her that way. "My father was Ivan Baklanov. He was treasurer of the Communist Party."

She risked a direct look at Hank. His eyes remained keen and measuring. She sat on the arm of the recliner and focused on Edward's tackle box. On the knives lying on top. A sudden image of the sword in Petrov's apartment rose in her head. *Die enemy from my hand.* "You remember I told you that all the party assets disappeared?"

"I remember."

"The money didn't just vanish. Someone was held responsible. Someone was accused of stealing them."

"Your father." It wasn't a question, but a confirmation of the conclusion he'd already drawn.

She nodded. "He . . ." She closed her eyes, squeezing out the memory. "He fell from his office window soon after the scandal broke."

"Fell?"

Her face heated. "Threw himself, or at least that's what everyone said."

"Unless he had a little help on the trip down," Mason said.

Hank's jaw tightened. "Petrov."

Mason acknowledged the name with a nod.

"I was there that evening," Alex said. "In a small room off the main office." Despite her efforts, the pictures came anyway. The little anteroom with its tiny desk, the stand with the ancient mimeograph machine. The smell of the ink and waxy blue paper.

"Because of my father's position, I went away to school and didn't see him very often. But that week, I was home. It was my sixteenth birthday, and my father had thrown me a huge party."

She smiled, remembering the fancy dress he'd gotten her in Paris. Absently, she touched her throat, where the little sisters necklace lay beneath her blouse. Her father had given her the necklace at the party. "We spent the next day together."

She remembered waking up early, their special breakfast with *klubnichnoye varenye*, homemade strawberry preserves on wafer-thin slices of bread, the surprise when her father handed her the envelope with the tickets.

"That evening, we were going to the ballet, but first he had a brief meeting in his office. I came with him and sat in the little room reading a fashion magazine he'd given to me." Another rare, wonderful gift. She could still remember the cover: Nadya Novikova wrapped in white fur, shoulders bare.

"After a while, I heard the door open and thought my father's appointment had arrived. I heard nothing at first. Then they began to argue. Their voices grew angrier, they were shouting at each other. I heard a crash, like they were fighting, then a . . ."

She swallowed, clutching her hands together in hopes that would keep her voice steady. "I heard a long, terrifying scream." The sound echoed in her head, an endless, world-shattering siren. "I couldn't move. I couldn't breathe." She felt that way now, frozen in time, eyes fixed on Nadya Novikova's shiny pink lips. "I let Petrov get away."

"And probably saved your life, Sasha," Mason said softly.

But she didn't want to admit that. She only wanted to remember that if she had moved faster, she might have prevented Miki Petrov from escaping.

"When I finally crept out, the window was open, and my father . . . my father was six stories below, on the ground."

The horror rose up from the place she'd hidden it, her father's broken body, bloody and mangled.

Papa. Papa.

She heard the moan. Who was moaning? Were those her teeth chattering? She was so cold. Papa, so cold.

And then he was beside her, holding her, saying her name.

"Alex. Alex, you're all right."

Not her papa.

"Look at me. Shh. Look at me."

With gentle pressure he forced her head to turn. To face him. Lean against him.

Hank.

She sank into his arms.

"I've got you," he whispered, and pressed her tight against his chest. "It's all right."

He felt so good, so strong. Slowly she stopped shaking, and Hank stepped back, tilted her chin. "All right?"

She missed his warmth but nodded. Edward handed her a cup of coffee. She wrapped her hands around the cup, letting the heat seep into her ice-cold fingers.

"Kholodov got her out of there," Mason said, giving her more time to recover. "He was Baklanov's bodyguard. They came to me."

"You? Why you?"

"Kholodov was afraid Petrov would find out she'd been there. He wanted to get her out of the country. He needed help. We were comrades in arms, so to speak, though on opposite sides."

"You and Kholodov?"

"He was KGB until the Soviet Union fell. Then like many in his position, he hired out as freelance protection. Russia was a dangerous place. Assassinations and mob hits were endemic. Here and there Kholodov had been useful to us, so I did what I could. I got them out of Russia, got them new identities, new lives." He turned to Alex, his face suddenly hard. "I gave you a second chance, Sasha. Don't screw that up."

"I won't let him get away with stealing my country's assets and murdering my father."

"He already has. Short of revealing yourself to him, which is suicide, there's nothing you can do."

"There's a lot I can do," she snapped. "Luka called me two weeks ago and told me he had something we could use on Petrov. He refused to say what it was, just that all of this would be over soon."

"It is over." Mason was blunt. "For Luka."

She felt her face drain of blood. Bad enough to accuse herself, but to hear it said out loud was like being pierced by an arrow.

"That's enough, Mason," Hank said.

"It's the truth, and she'd better face it." Mason's rough voice softened. He put a fatherly arm around her shoulders. "Leave it alone, Sasha. Move on, enjoy yourself. You're a beautiful woman, you have your whole life ahead of you. Don't throw it away on a pipe dream."

Pipe dream? Outrage boiled up. Getting Petrov was no fantasy. It was her life's work. "Fine." She disentangled herself. She'd made a mistake coming here. She could see that now. She'd relied too much on Edward, expected too much. There'd be no help here.

She stalked toward the door. Outside, the car waited. She was alone again, but there was nothing new about that.

"Whoa!" A hand pulled her back. Hank spun her around. "Hold on. Where are you going?"

"Out of here."

"Really? How are you getting there?" He held up a hand. Car keys dangled from one finger.

She swiped at them, but he jerked them out of her grasp.

"You can't keep me here." She glared at him. "I'm not a prisoner. I'll call a cab." She started toward the kitchen; Hank blocked her way.

"Look, you told me that Miki Petrov was responsible for Kholodov's death. You also told me why. He has the means and the motive. Let me prove he had the opportunity."

The words were out of Hank's mouth before he knew they were coming. Christ. When would he learn? If she wanted to jump off a rooftop, who was he to stop her?

He was a cop. With a job to do.

A job that hinged on a string of dead ends and only four days left to make them pay off.

A lot could happen in four days.

Yeah. All of it trouble.

As if she'd come to the same conclusion, Alex's eyes narrowed, and indecision warred in her face. She didn't trust him, and who could blame her?

"Prove it how?"

He shook his head. Bad idea on top of bad idea. He felt the universe stir, that old, cold gust of fate blowing through him. Reluctantly, he reviewed what he had. The cigarette that could have been dropped anytime, the damaged bullet that didn't lead to a weapon, a set of partials that were dubious at best. A house of cards on top of a moving train. But the flimsy nature of the evidence didn't matter as long as he could use it to stall her. Keep her there where she'd be safe and out of the way until he came up with a better plan.

"I've got a chain of evidence that could link back to Yuri."

"What evidence?" Mason asked.

In for a penny, in for a pound. "A cigarette butt at Alex's house. Ballistics I can try to tie to Yuri's gun. A partial set of latents found at the store and Kole's house. If I can bring Yuri in, maybe I can flip him."

He heard himself. I, I, I. As if he'd be there to do it. The hero, the protector, the saver of worlds.

Alex snorted with derision, a perfect response. "You think Yuri will turn on his boss? That will never happen. He knows what Petrov would do to him. Besides, what does any of that prove?"

Carefully, he built the case, going with the theory even if he couldn't prove it. "That Yuri was there. At the store, in the house. That he had something to do with Luka's death, with Sonya's."

"Sonya died of a heart attack," Alex said. "Even if Yuri was there, and believe me, I'd bet he was, you can't hold that over him."

"Yes, I can." He cocked his head, leaned against the kitchen table. Hoped she'd go for it. "It's called felony murder. If someone dies, even unintentionally, during the course of a crime—let's say a burglary—the burglar can be charged with murder. If Yuri was there, he entered your home illegally. That's a crime."

Alex turned to Mason, who nodded in confirmation.

"But he was at the party," Alex said. "Smoking. A hundred people saw him, including you. Yuri could have left the cigarette then, and any defense attorney would say so."

A pang of frustration and admiration hit him. God, she was smart. Wasn't going to be easy putting anything past her.

She shook her head. "You're grabbing at straws."

"Better than throwing yourself into the lion's den," Mason said, then turned to Hank. "What else have you got?"

Not much, but he didn't say so. "Ballistics. Luka was shot with a .38." He didn't bother with the fact that he didn't have a lead on the weapon. "If I can tie the gun to Petrov—"

"Petrov wouldn't do the job himself." Alex waved the idea away with an impatient flick of her wrist. "He doesn't work that way. Second, whoever did do it—let's say Yuri or Vassily, or one of his other thugs—wouldn't have kept the weapon. And even if you found it, the gun would be untraceable. Have you found it?"

"No, but—"

"It's a start," Mason said. "At least let him—"

"I've got prints," Hank said, a desperate, last-ditch effort. "Give me some time to check them out."

"Partials, you said. Nothing solid."

"You never know. All I need is a few days."

Alex shook her head. She was tired of talking about it. "No. None of that's going to work. Even if it did, you'd only have Yuri, and we're back to him betraying Miki, which will never happen."

"Look, Mason and I agree." Hank signaled to the older man. The two of them were nodding at each other, a brotherhood of testosterone lined up against her. "We follow the evidence, put the pressure on—"

"He'll make a mistake, Sasha, you'll see, and—"

"You're right." She looked between the two men, her goal suddenly clear. She saw Miki's face at the party, the invitation in his eyes. Sexual. Lethal. That part of her scheme had always gone as planned. And if he hadn't killed Luka, she would have followed through. Gone home with him. Slept with him. Twined her way into his confidence. Bled him dry. "Leaving would be foolish."

Hank exhaled a breath of relief. "Good. That's good. You'll be safe here, and I can—"

"We'll bring Petrov to the cabin."

Her statement stopped the discussion like a shot.

Hank's eyes narrowed to a slit of green. "What for?"

"If I bring him here, I can get him to confess."

Mason threw up his hands. "That's crazy, Sasha. No."

"Confess? How? Hypnosis? I don't think so."

She raised her chin, determined. "He wants me. He's always wanted me. It's time I give him what he wants."

Hank glowered at her through disbelieving eyes. "What—you're going to do a little cha-cha with him? You think he'll give himself up over some pillow talk?"

"He's not stupid, Sasha."

"Stupid? No. But he's blinded by arrogance, and that's a kind of stupidity." She stared out the porch window into the night. Could she do it? Could she make herself do it?

Why not? It's what she'd intended all along. She reached for the ice she'd nurtured over the years, the frozen shell that kept her true feelings carefully shielded, but found a tremor of horror threatening to overtake her. She struggled to suppress it, and Hank grabbed her arm.

"Forget it." He dragged her from the door into the living room. "You're not going near Miki Petrov." He bulldozed her into the recliner, where she gazed up at him.

"I'll do what I have to," she said, perfectly calm, perfectly composed. Now that she'd made her decision, fear oozed to the edge, replaced by a numb certainty. This had always been the way. Always the plan. In the chaos that had surrounded her lately she had almost forgotten. Petrov had tried to rattle her. He had almost succeeded.

"What if he already knows who you are?" Hank said. "What do you think those shots were about?"

She didn't flinch. "If he knew who I was, I'd be dead. Those shots were about something else."

"Lousy shooter," Mason said.

"No. He's stirring the pot. Miki likes to get people off-balance. See if they'll trip themselves up. Reveal something useful."

Hank said, "You don't know that."

She rose, feeling sure and in control for the first time in days. "Ah, but I do. I've done business with him. I know how he thinks. I know what he wants. He'll take the bait." She circled the room, a predator plotting the kill.

"He'll take it and gobble you up," Mason warned.

"Tell me this." Hank stepped in front of her. "How the hell will you stop him from shooting you point-blank?"

"I won't." She watched him, sadness breaking through her iron will. She could no longer protect him; he was part of this now. "You will."

16

Hank's blood chilled. Images flitted through his brain. The screwdriver plunging toward him. Maureen dead on the toolshed floor. "No. It's too risky."

Alex smiled, cool and confident. "I have a high tolerance for risk, remember?"

Damn, it was like talking to a brick wall. Or a steel one.

"It's a bad idea, Sasha."

She rounded on Mason, smoky eyes hot. "It's the only idea we've got. Whatever proof Luka had is gone. Hank's evidence is flimsy at best. We have nothing. Only me." Her voice deepened, passionate and unwavering. "Miki Petrov killed my father. He killed Luka. He probably hurried Sonya's death. I'm not letting him off the hook this time."

"He'll kill you." Mason didn't mince words.

She shook her head. "That's why you're both here. You'll stop him."

Another earthquake rocked through Hank. "No. We won't. I won't. I don't want your life in my hands."

"They're strong hands, Hank. I trust them." She gazed into his eyes, the look softly determined.

"Then you're a fool." He looked from her to Mason, who gazed back with sympathy. "Excuse me."

He walked out into the night. The fresh air cooled the sweat he hadn't even known was filming the back of his neck.

Christ Almighty. His hands were shaking.

Mind whirling, he stumbled the ten yards down to the lake. Moonlight silvered the surface, glazing the water with a hard sheen.

How did he get caught up in this mess? It had nothing to do with him. Luka Kole—Kholodov—was killed because of something that happened years ago in another country. It had nothing to do with the Hudson Valley, Van Dekker County, or the Sokanan PD. A few more days and he wouldn't even be a cop. He should walk away. Now, while he still had the chance.

Chance. The word reverberated inside him. Take your chance. Chance of a lifetime. Game of chance. He closed his eyes, acid coating his mouth.

Footsteps sounded behind him.

"Better lock up your keys." Mason positioned himself beside Hank and stared out at the lake. Behind him, Hank felt Alex's spirit lurking like a heavy weight.

"Has she always been suicidal?"

Mason smiled tightly. "Pretty much. Determined to clear her father's name at least."

"And get her revenge."

"That, too."

They stood in silence, the breeze making the water gurgle against the bank.

Hank's gut churned. "She's going to do this, isn't she? With or without us."

"Probably."

Damn. He was afraid of that.

"I've seen her with Petrov. She's right—he's . . . smitten."

"Unlike you?"

Hank turned his head. Mason was scrutinizing him with a dispassionate gaze that stripped Hank of pretense and exposed everything he wanted to hide. Even from himself.

He looked away. "She'll need help."

"She'll need someone who isn't emotionally involved."

Hank squinted out over the gleaming water in front of him. How well he knew the dangers of getting too close. Of not thinking clearly, of response time slowed to a crawl, of doubt and indecision, and the gamble of luck. Not that he had much choice. She'd rolled the dice and it had come up him. She could die with his help, but she could also die without it. Besides, he still had a case to solve. One last bad guy to catch. Much as he wanted to, he couldn't make himself walk away.

"That's tough. She'll have to settle for you. And me."

A slow smile crept across Mason's face. "I've still got contacts. I'll arrange to get some men out here."

"We'll need audio surveillance."

"I can handle the wires, too."

"Good. It's too dicey to involve the department. As it is, I'm going so far out on a limb I'm sitting on air." Glumly, Hank turned to gaze back at the cabin, where Alex's shadow was outlined in the front window. "This is a bad idea, Mason."

"I know."

"Then why are we doing it?"

"Because we're all she's got."

Mason clapped him on the back and trudged to the cabin. Hank took out his cell phone and called Parnell.

It was just past midnight and the lieutenant answered in a sluggish voice.

"It's Bonner."

Parnell asked him to hold while he took the call in another room. A minute later, he was back. "Okay, Hank." His voice had shaken off the sleep and sounded keen and alert. "Where are you?"

Instead of answering, he asked Parnell about the shooting at Alex's house.

"We sent over a team. They didn't find much. Shooter was gone but trashed a couple of bedrooms. The place was a mess. Any idea what they might have been looking for?"

Oh yeah, he had a good idea. But he didn't say so. "I'm working on it. How about our guys? Did they find anything useful? Brass? Prints?"

"No prints and no shell casings. This guy is slick."

Damn. When were they going to catch a break?

"Where are you now?" Parnell asked again.

"I've got Alex stashed. She's safe."

"Bring her in. We can use a rotation of uniforms if you think she needs round-the-clock protection."

"She'll never agree. Too many people who could talk. To say she's skittish is an understatement. She's good here. I've got some help."

"What kind of help?"

Hank hesitated.

"What kind of help, Hank? Where are you? At what point are you going to tell me what this is all about?"

Hank pictured his boss's face, with its whip-smart eyes. He didn't imagine Parnell was happy about any of this. "When it's over."

"I don't like the sound of that."

"You wouldn't believe it if I did tell you."

"Did your hunch about her connection to the Kole murder pan out?"

"In more ways than one. Let's just say you can take

Klimet off the Hudson Valley task force on the convenience store robberies."

Parnell was silent. Hank was positive his boss wasn't happy about what he was hearing.

"You're way out of procedure here, Hank."

"I know." He gazed at the lake, at the dark shadows of boats rocking against their docks. He knew what he had to do, but the words stuck in his throat. "Cut me loose if you have to. It's only four days short."

"Dammit, Hank."

"Hey, what's one less dick in the grand scheme of things?" He spoke lightly, but the words wrenched like a chain pulling out his heart. Funny. He couldn't wait to be free, and now that the time had come it actually hurt. Christ, he was a fucked-up mess.

"Look, Hank, this is bullshit and you know it. You're a good cop. I don't want to lose you. But right now I've had it up to here with you. I'm running blind. I don't know what the hell you're up to, except it involves a key player in this town's recovery. It's not just your job on the line here. It's mine, too. Not to mention the whole damn town. Now haul your ass down here and fill me in."

"Sorry, sir. Can't do that."

"Why the hell not?"

He picked his words carefully. "I don't know what's going to happen. Could be okay. Could be a bad pile of shit. You don't want to get your feet dirty. Cut me loose. If things go wrong, the heat's on me and the department's in the clear."

"You got it all figured out, don't you? I'd like to say I'll have your badge for this, but you've already thrown it in my face."

There was a beat of silence. He liked Parnell. It was hard disappointing him.

"What are you trying to prove, Hank?"

"Just trying to keep all those balls in the air."

"I think it's something else. What, I don't know, except that you don't have anything to prove. Not to me or anyone. And especially not to yourself. You got that?"

"Yes, sir."

"You coming in?"

"No, sir."

Parnell swore softly, but all he said before disconnecting was, "Watch your back."

Hank flipped the cell phone shut. For a smart guy Parnell was dead wrong. Hank had everything to prove. And he was scared to death to do it.

Yuri knocked on the penthouse door, flushed with excitement.

Petrov answered it, his silk robe flashing black and silver as he moved. "What happened?"

"What you wanted. A few broken windows, and a little something extra. A small shoot-out with the locals."

"Who?"

"The detective. Bonner. She was also there."

"Casualties?"

"Nyet."

"Good. A little fear stimulates the system, but we don't want our dear Miss Baker out of the picture. Yet. Soon she will show us whether or not she can be trusted."

"She won't have to." Yuri threw down a set of photographs, proud at his accomplishment. "You can call off Dashevsky. I took the liberty of conducting a search. She's Baklanov's daughter all right."

*   *   *

Hank and Mason split the night watch, Hank taking first shift and Mason snoozing in his beat-up leather chair. Riven with the sharp suspicion that he couldn't keep Alex safe and the unbearable weight of trying, Hank couldn't have slept anyway.

Sometime between two and three, headlights cut across the cabin window, and Mason was instantly awake. He took one careful look out the window and signaled Hank to open the door.

The newcomer had a long, rat-shaped face and appeared to be older than Mason, who towered above him. "Kiley!" Mason greeted him with a smile and an outstretched hand. "Thanks for coming." He turned to Hank. "Our soundman. Local law," he said to Kiley, indicating Hank.

Kiley grunted a dismissive greeting, gaze already working the room. A wizened, scrawny scrap of a man, he didn't look like he could find his way through a phone book, let alone a complicated audio surveillance schematic. A pair of huge black-rimmed glasses sat on his pointy nose and a large metal suitcase swung from his hand.

He dropped the suitcase with a thud. "What do you got?"

"Two rooms," Mason said. "Here and there." He nodded toward the bedroom, where Alex slept.

Kiley stepped farther into the cabin and turned a measured circle to see it from all angles. A man of no words, he returned to his case, knelt beside it with the energy of a far younger man, and popped it opened. Pulling out switches and fuses, cable, wire, and tools, he placed everything in precise piles on the floor. It was like watching a circus clown car empty. More stuff came out than the case seemed able to hold.

Starting in the kitchen, he moved to the living area, then

to the bedroom, where he worked without waking Alex.
Hank and Mason vacated each room to accommodate him,
but though they watched constantly, he said nothing to
them.

Instead, he muttered to himself, grumping about outdated
circuits and used equipment, about retirement and being
kept out of the loop. He worked steadily, fueled by the endless cups of coffee Mason shoved into his hand.

"Where'd you dig him up?" Hank whispered at one point
to Mason.

"Best sound man I ever worked with. Forced into retirement ten years ago."

By six he was finished, by six-fifteen he'd pointed out
the five hidden microphones—one in the kitchen, two in the
living area, one in the bedroom, and one in the bathroom,
just in case someone needed privacy for a phone call. By
six-forty-five he'd taught them how to turn on the recorder,
which he'd hidden inside one of Mason's coolers, using the
switch he'd disguised as a fishing reel and attached to one of
the rods against the wall. He was gone by seven, a phantom
chugging away in a 1972 Chevy Nova.

Hank stared after him, then turned slowly to examine the
walls and floorboards for signs Kiley had been there, but the
man had made the wiring disappear in plain sight.

Mason looked on, amused. "Told you he was good."

Sleep seemed an impossibility, but it was Mason's turn to
stand watch. Hank sank into the recliner, closed his eyes,
and must have drifted off because when he opened them
again the sun was blazing through the front windows and the
smoky tang of bacon lingered in the air.

"Morning." Mason handed Hank his service weapon,
which they'd each carried in turn.

"No trouble?"

Mason shook his head. "Peaceful as a snowfall."

"Where's the countess?"

Mason nodded toward the closed bedroom door. "Changing. I gave her an old pair of pants and a shirt. She's going to need some clothes."

Hank stood and groaned as muscle and bone realigned themselves. His head felt thick, so he slogged to the kitchen and poured a cup of coffee. The caffeine went down hard and fast, a jolt that helped wake him. "You tell her about the surveillance?"

Mason nodded. "Taken care of. She knows where the switch is and how to turn it on. I'm heading out. Just waited for you to finish getting your beauty sleep. Can you handle things here for a day or two?"

An evil wind clawed up Hank's back. He didn't want Mason leaving him alone with her. Too much responsibility. Too much could go wrong. "I don't think that's a good idea."

"We don't have a choice. I need to round up a few people, and I don't want to do it over the phone."

"How many people?" Alex stood in the doorway, a pair of prehistoric khakis sagging over her hips and rolled up at the ankles. A faded flannel shirt, knotted loosely at her waist, swam on her.

"Two. With me and Hank that gives us four. The cabin is small. One man per wall should cover it."

She nodded calmly. He would have thought she planned for war every day. "I'll need supplies. Champagne, fruit, caviar. And some decent clothes." She rolled up her shirtsleeves. "I can't seduce Miki Petrov in this."

Coffee roiled in Hank's stomach. She looked sleep-tousled and appealing, and the thought of her and Petrov made him nauseous. "You're not going to seduce him at all. He won't give you time."

She straightened her shoulders, an imperial gesture that came through, despite the clown-sized clothes. "I'm not going to argue about this all day."

"Of course not, Your Highness."

She smiled. "I'm too happy."

The smile transformed her face into something radiant and luminous. Stunned, Hank stared at her. "Happy? What the hell are you happy about?"

Before she could answer, Mason spoke. "You two kids work this out when I'm gone." He poured coffee into a thermos and started for the door.

"Wait. Let me give you a list of things I need." Alex grabbed a paper towel and used a pencil hanging from a string near the phone to compose a list. "Make sure the champagne is French and the caviar Russian. Miki is very particular."

"Just write it all down."

The effort took longer than it should, and Mason growled at the delay.

"You can't possibly need all that."

"Trust me, I'm only skimming the surface." She handed him the paper. "If I think of anything else, I'll call."

"Anything else?" He skimmed down the list. "I don't think there's anything else in the Western Hemisphere." He pointed to an item. "What are . . . tap pants?"

Alex crossed her arms and pursed her lips, her expression thoughtful. "You know what?" She slid the list out of Mason's fingers, tore it in two, and handed Mason the smaller half. "Why don't I let my secretary buy the clothes? I'll arrange for her to overnight them. Would that work better?"

Mason winked at her. "You always were smart."

Not smart enough. "Petrov might be watching her," said Hank.

"That's all right," Mason said. And then to Alex, "Tell her to expect a call from a friend. I'll take care of the rest." He opened the door, then turned back to Alex, his face serious. "Don't give Hank a tough time, now. Listen to him. Do what he says." And to Hank, "Don't let her stray." Then he was gone.

Alone, Hank gave Alex plenty of room. He had a ridiculous but overwhelming compulsion to run his hands over her and make sure she was all right, which was why he stayed away.

She hummed as she poured herself coffee, and Hank watched, irritated. "For someone about to walk in front of a firing squad, you're in a damn good mood."

"You wouldn't understand."

"Try me."

She sipped at the coffee, scrutinizing him. The silence between them was familiar; her secrets had always outweighed her frankness.

But something happened this time. She hitched her shoulders in a small shrug as though giving in. "You're the first person I've told the truth to in thirteen years." She sounded anything but defeated. In fact, she sounded almost buoyant. "I feel . . . free." Face pink with embarrassment, she crossed to the door and opened it, gazing out at the lake. "I like the feeling. No more secrets. No more lies."

Despite the anger and the fear that simmered beneath it, Hank's annoyance began to crumble. What would it be like to blurt out his own truth, to tell her he was terrified of failing her? Relief, indeed. A liberation.

He joined her at the doorway, and she tossed him a mischievous grin. "Dare I risk a walk? The lake is so beautiful."

She looked eager, but he shook his head. "It's not a good idea to be seen. By anyone. You never know who's hanging around asking questions."

"You're right. Of course." But she looked so disappointed he felt like a son of a bitch.

She sighed, backed away from the door, paced the kitchen.

With every move her scent wafted toward him, spicy and sharp. He didn't imagine she'd brought perfume along. How did she make soap and shampoo smell so tantalizing?

He tore his gaze away from her. Poured himself another cup of coffee. Stared out the window.

But he felt her there. A heat source and him the missile that wanted to seek it out.

He escaped onto the porch. How was he going to get through the day?

Alex gazed wistfully out the door. The sun was bright. Such a welcome counter to the darkness lying in wait beyond it.

She had so much left to do. Figure out how to turn this mess of a fishing cabin into something inviting and seductive. Prepare herself to contact Miki. Convince him to come up here.

Embrace him, kiss him, let him touch her.

She swallowed her aversion.

All that was ahead of her.

Right now the sun shone on the lake, turning it silver. She was free, nearly all her secrets told. And she wanted one hour to enjoy it. One hour to throw her arms in the air and explore every crevice of this new world.

She grabbed a hat and an old jacket from a hook near the door and slipped out.

Hank frowned. "Where do you think you're going?"

Striding off, she thrust her arms into the jacket and jammed the hat on her head, quickly shoving her hair inside. "For a walk."

"Dammit, hold on!"

She made it to the end of the dock that linked the cabin to the water before he caught up with her. A thick ring of lily pads encircled the lake. The wide band of broad green leaves gave the lake an exotic feel, like something out of a storybook. Far in the distance, an island floated in the center, partially blocking the view. Two boats sat in deep water, men with rods silhouetted against the morning light. What would it be like to forget revenge, shrug off the burden of the past, and sail away?

Hank shattered that thought. He grabbed her arm. "Get back in the cabin."

"I just need some air."

"Get back—"

"Hank. Please." She said it quietly, looking at him from under the brim of Edward's silly hat. "I know how dangerous Miki Petrov is. But this is important to me." She pulled the hat lower on her forehead and yanked the oversized jacket away from her body. "Besides, no one's going to know who's under all this."

Hank looked from her to the lake and back again. She was probably right, but she appeared so outlandish everyone was bound to notice her. On the other hand, he was more comfortable out here than stuffed in the cramped cabin with her. At least here there were other things to watch. But he kept his hand on the butt of the gun shoved in his waistband underneath his shirt.

"All right. But stay close."

They sauntered in silence for a few minutes. Alex gazed out at the lake, as though she'd never seen the sun rising over water or men in fishing boats. As though the girl she'd lost so many years ago had been reborn overnight.

Swooping down, he picked up a pebble and threw it into the water. It landed beyond the lilies, sinking without a splash.

"Why does Mason call you Sasha?"

She turned from the water, her face dreamy as her eyes met his. "It's a diminutive for Aleksandra. Like Billy for William. My father sometimes called me Sashka. Sonya used Sashenka." She colored, and he knew she was remembering the night Sonya died.

In an instant he remembered it, too. Carrying Alex in his arms, the dip of her robe, which revealed a wide ribbon of satin skin. The same skin now revealed in the smooth curve of her neck beneath Mason's hat.

"I'm afraid I made a bit of a fool of myself over that," she said. "Sashenka was a childhood nickname, and she knew me as a child."

"In Russia?" He concentrated on the lake, seizing on something else to think about besides that patch of skin.

"Yes. She was our housekeeper. After my mother died, she practically raised me. We took her everywhere until my father's death."

"Everywhere?"

"My father was in the diplomatic corps before working for the CPSU."

"CPSU?"

"Communist Party of the Soviet Union."

"Ah."

The names and the world they conjured were so alien, her experience so foreign from his. Yet he could easily imagine her as the privileged child of a privileged class. What had it been like to lose that? She'd run to another country, merged into another culture, a new language, new customs. A child with no family and few friends. No wonder she seemed so isolated. As alone as the island in the middle of the lake.

"We lived in England and America. I went to elite schools. Diplomats and party bosses always had special perks. I learned English very early, which was why Luka took me to an English-speaking country."

"That explains the accent."

"What accent?"

"Exactly. Your accent is almost nonexistent. Here and there, a slight something, but otherwise . . ."

"Yes. I worked very hard at that."

Once again, she stopped to admire the view of water glistening under the rising sun. To their right a grassy area held a copse of trees. Tulip and locust from the looks of them. It was a pretty setting, perfect for a lakeside picnic. He had a flash of himself and Alex lying on a blanket beneath the boughs. She was smiling that open smile he'd seen on her face that morning, and he was holding her, kissing her, touching . . . His body tightened, blood pulsing wildly, and he coughed, cursing silently. To distract himself, he asked another question.

"What happened to Sonya after your father died?"

"Petrov and his KGB thugs arrested and interrogated her." Her voice caught. "They were very cruel."

He wanted to put an arm around her shoulder and squeeze her close, but didn't dare. The image of the two of them on that blanket was still too fresh.

"I'm sorry."

Tears welled in her eyes, but she smiled through them. "She was very dear to me."

And then he couldn't help himself. His arm went around

her, and he pulled her into a tight, brief hug. He would have left it at that, but she slid her fingers into the hand he'd draped over her shoulder, and he was stuck. Right where he wanted to be.

"Thank you," she said quietly.

"For what?"

"For being here."

Alex turned in his embrace and gazed up at him. She didn't know why she'd done that. Why she'd put her hand in his. She should be thinking about Miki, plotting her next move.

But Miki was far away, and Hank so very close. All of a sudden, a giddy, foolish feeling struck her. The same feeling she'd had right before she discovered the broken glass in her house. Hopeful, excited. Not knowing what was coming next but eager for it to happen.

What had happened next was gunshots. Reality strafed her, a reminder as quick and brutal as the bullets had been.

And then the sun glided through a cloud and glinted off the lake. Edward was gone; Miki in Manhattan. She had time. A little while before she had to act. She gazed up at Hank, breathless.

He stared down at her, mesmerized. "Alex," he murmured. "Sasha."

The name came out unexpectedly, but it felt right. Close and intimate. Something to call the woman he kissed. The secret, hidden woman he wanted to take into the trees, whose remaining core of ice he wanted to melt.

He caressed her face, her forehead under Mason's hat, her strong jaw. She trembled beneath his fingers, and that quiver sent a sudden wave of hot fear through him.

What was he doing?

He was a decoy, a death trap. A prank the universe

played on the people he cared about. He couldn't let her fall for it. He had to maintain distance. A cool, detached perimeter.

He cleared his throat, but as if she'd read his mind, she led him to the copse of trees.

She scanned the area, gauging its potential. "This would be a good spot."

Hank's pulse quickened. "Good spot for what?"

"For my date with Miki Petrov."

His stomach dropped to his knees, his detachment shattered. He shot her a hard look. "I wouldn't call it a date. More like a disaster."

"You say tomato, I say tomahto."

The joke went flat. His whole mood had gone flat. "The trees aren't wired for sound, Countess." He grabbed her hand, tugged her out of the grove, and started the march back to the cabin. "Just for grins, let's say your whole crazy scheme works. You do . . . whatever the hell you do"— his mind shied away from picturing it—"Petrov is arrested, discredited, your father's reputation restored and you're still alive."

"It could happen." She said it calmly, too calmly for his taste.

"In your dreams. But let's say by some small miracle, it does. What happens with Renaissance Oil? Sokanan is counting on that deal going through. Everyone in the whole damn county is counting on it."

She had the grace to flush. "I can't promise anyone will have the wherewithal or the will to replace Miki. But if there's a chance to save it, I will."

"Well, that's encouraging."

"It's the best I can do right now."

"Terrific. I'm not only helping you commit suicide, I'm doing the same for my hometown."

She touched his arm. "I'm sorry."

"Yeah, me too."

He pulled her into the cabin and dropped her hand, leaving her in the doorway. He would have liked a nice shot of whiskey or some of that Stoli she was so fond of, but he poured himself a cup of coffee instead. The liquid hit his stomach like battery acid.

The hell of it was, he couldn't stop thinking about those trees. And her beneath them.

With him.

With Miki.

With him.

Shit.

A hand on his back. He flinched and turned to find her behind him, close enough to take in his arms, to kiss. He stepped away, and a pleading expression crossed her face.

"I've spent my whole adult life working to bring Miki Petrov down. Please try to understand."

He sighed. "I understand fine. I just don't like it."

He left her in the kitchen. Keeping his distance. Keeping his head clear, or trying to. It wasn't easy, filled as it was with things he rarely thought about: Russians, communists, KGB. All swirled with thoughts that often occupied him: opportunity, means, and motive. If he could just put all the pieces together in one clear picture that didn't include her and Miki Petrov in that grove of trees.

He eased into the recliner, using the chair as another barrier. He had to keep away from her. Had to find neutral ground, something dry and unemotional to talk about.

"What do you think happened to the missing party money? Have you tried tracing it?"

Alex sat on a cooler, desperate to forget their argument. She couldn't stand fighting with him. Not now. Not when she felt so . . . so weird and wonderful. Not when they had so little time. Miki was out there. She only had to call him, and the end would begin. But not yet. Not yet.

"The missing money, Alex. Have you tried tracing it?"

She forced herself back to the cabin. Away from the future and back to the past she'd been living with all these years. "Better heads than mine tried and failed. Yeltsin hired an international private investigation firm to find it. They ran up a huge bill and came up empty. They needed the cooperation of the KGB and their underground sources, and couldn't get it."

"Why not?"

She drifted away again, remembering the look in his eyes, the buzz in her body. His hand on her face.

"Alex, Sasha." The sharpness in his voice snapped her back. "Why not?"

"If Petrov and his KGB buddies were behind the theft, it wouldn't be in their interest to help, would it?"

"So you think there were others who benefited—not just Petrov?"

"Probably."

"Any idea who?"

Oh, she didn't want to talk about this. She wanted to talk about that moment outside. When he touched her face and the world stood still.

"Who, Alex?"

She sighed. He was right, of course. She needed to concentrate. Focus. "Antonin Dashevsky for one."

"Who's that?"

"The prime minister."

He stared at her, and his shocked expression almost made her laugh. "You've got to be kidding."

"Why not? He wasn't always prime minister." She left the cooler and perched on the arm of the chair, feeling the heat he generated.

But he tensed, rose, and walked away. "Christ, this gets worse and worse."

"Look, Dashevsky is a banking genius who began to gather wealth at the very onset of perestroika, when he was still in university. He was probably the only one who not only knew enough about moving large sums of money, but had the contacts to do it."

"You're butting heads with the likes of the KGB and the prime minister of Russia?"

"I'm butting heads with murderers and thieves. Their pedigree is irrelevant."

"You're crazy, you know that? Stark raving insane."

Forget Miki Petrov, Hank would kill her himself. But before he could, the phone rang. Alex crossed to pick it up. She listened briefly, ran down the half of the list she had retained, listened, murmured something approvingly, then hung up.

"That was Letty. My secretary. She said the clothes should be here in the morning."

The morning. Who knew what else the morning would bring? "What a shame." His voice dripped sarcasm. "I'm going to miss the bag lady look."

"Miki Petrov won't." Alex was sorry the minute she said it. She wanted to forget Miki. Not forever, but for a moment. For now. While Hank was here, and they were alone.

"I don't give a damn about Miki Petrov." He knelt in

front of the chair, shaking it. "What you're doing is crazy. It's dangerous and reckless and—"

She leaned forward and took his face in her hands. "And the only idea we've got," she said softly.

Her touch startled him, and his heart took off like a shot. He was caught, trapped, and part of him couldn't care less.

Hands cool against his skin, she peered into his eyes so he couldn't look away. "I know you're worried. I understand. I'll make you a promise, all right? I won't call Miki or arrange anything until Edward gets back and our plans are set. If it looks like we can't get our end together, I won't contact him."

Relief burst inside him. Mason wasn't due back for another day, maybe two. If she held off contacting Miki, that meant he'd have time to talk her out of this madness.

"Okay," he said.

"So can we stop arguing about it?" Her fingers were moving now, in his hair, around his neck and back on his face. Everything was rushing inside him, blood, breath, thought. "There's so much else we could be doing."

Their eyes met. Hers were soft, hungry, blurred with desire. His mouth dried up.

"Not a good idea, Countess."

She traced his lips. He tried not to vibrate with her touch. "Why not?"

A thousand reasons, all ending in tragedy. "Too distracting. We need to keep our heads clear."

"My head is clear, Detective." She leaned closer. "Clearer than it's been for a long, long time."

Her mouth was close, almost on his. *Christ.* His heart was thudding like a jackhammer.

Don't do it.

The warning was loud as a bullhorn, and he heeded it. He would not touch her, hold her, then watch her die.

No, sir. Not again.

He wrenched himself away. "I need a shower."

17

Letty Birnbaum frowned as she ran her fingers over the silk-and-lace tap pants at Belle Monde. They were delicately beautiful, skimpy enough to be sexy, but so very, very white. She tsked at the virginal color. And the price! Wickedly expensive. For her money, she'd rather buy something on sale at Macy's, something red or hot pink. Leopard skin was nice.

She sighed. But that's not what A. J. had asked for. In fact the whole morning's shopping had been an exercise in boring taste. She glanced down at the mess of bags at her feet.

Someday, she was going to give her boss a complete makeover. Get her out of those old lady suits and into something that showed a little cleavage and lot of leg.

But right now . . . Grumbling, she found the right size, gathered up the panties, a couple of fragile bras that looked as if they'd fall apart if you breathed on them, let alone wore them during hot wild sex and, ignoring the snooty look of the salesgirl, paid for everything with the company credit card.

She added this package to all the others, then hailed a cab to the Marriott Marquis Hotel. The place was a tourist mecca, and the lobby was crowded. She looked around for a bellman, saw one to her left, dashed off to catch his attention, and ran head-on into a large, sexy, and very well muscled man wearing a long, black leather coat. Packages flew out of her hand, but she was too distracted to notice. She loved a man in leather.

He smiled at her, and she smiled back. Visions of new plans for the evening flitted through her brain.

"Sorry," the man said. He had a charming accent. She loved foreign men.

"That's okay."

He gathered up her bags and handed them to her.

"Thanks."

He nodded and disappeared into the crowd. She gaped after him, an arrow of disappointment shooting through her.

Oh well.

As instructed, she snagged a passing bellman and told him that the packages were for an E. Mason, a guest who was checking in later that day. She exchanged the purchases for a baggage claim ticket, which she left in an envelope at the front desk.

Job done, she practically raced through the lobby, hoping to run into the leather-clad foreigner. But he had vanished.

Petrov stared at the pictures Vassily had taken at Kholodov's funeral. One showed a woman draped in dark clothing whose face was obscured by a veil, but who Petrov suspected was Aleksandra Baklanova. The Sokanan detective who'd paid him an unexpected visit occupied the second photo.

He gazed at a third picture, the one Yuri had liberated from Alex's house. Ivan Baklanov and his daughter. Shortly after her father's death, the daughter disappeared. Years later, she surfaced in the United States. How had that happened?

Petrov picked up a fourth picture, also taken by Vassily at the funeral. Was this man the link between those two events? Only a man like this would have had the contacts and skills to move Baklanov's daughter and bury her deep.

Petrov drummed the table in his office, then punched in the number for the State Department.

"I've just heard an old friend may be close by," he told Jeffrey Greer.

"Oh?"

"He's a colleague. We used to be, shall we say . . . business competitors. I want to renew our friendship, and I need you to discover where he is, how to contact him."

"Uh, Mr. Petrov, I . . . I wouldn't know where to start."

Petrov did. "Try Langley. Discreetly, of course. The name is Edward Mason."

Yuri watched the redhead from a safe distance, seeing without being seen. He'd been with her all morning, and the only thing she'd done was shop. He'd suspected she was using the stores as a rendezvous, but she'd met no one. She never even disappeared into a dressing room. And with each store, the packages had added up.

He'd seen what she bought. Underwear mostly. Nothing significant. In his belly he'd felt tailing her was a waste of time.

Until she left the packages at the hotel.

Now he had to choose. Clothes or redhead? No time to linger over a decision. She was leaving, and if he let her go, she'd disappear. For the moment he knew where the packages were. He headed for the exit.

But he didn't want to face the consequences of making

the wrong choice. Petrov didn't like independence. Yuri followed the woman out of the hotel, but punched a number on his cell phone's speed dial.

Petrov picked up on the first ring, and Yuri explained what had happened.

"You are sure all she did was shop?"

"Da."

"Why would she shop all morning, then drop the packages at a hotel?"

Yuri told him the only conclusion he could draw. "Maybe she was shopping for someone else."

A long thoughtful silence. "Stay with her. I'll send Vassily to the hotel."

Fifteen minutes later, a foreigner in a black track suit and gold chains appeared in the lobby. He scoured the crowd, trying to match faces to the pictures he'd brought. But none of them showed up. Not in an hour, not all day.

Alex heard the water in the shower, the sound crisp and clear even through the closed bathroom door. But everything was clear now. Clear and bright, with knife-sharp edges.

She knelt on Edward's bed and gazed out the window at the deepening twilight. She knew Hank thought her crazy. But that was only his concern speaking. It was natural for him to worry, for worry to make him pull away from her. But he didn't understand how everything had changed. What it meant to be released after long imprisonment, what it meant to be herself. The self she was born to be: Aleksandra Ivanonva Baklanova. Sasha. Sashka. Sashenka.

She had nothing left to hide. Or almost nothing. Instinctively, she reached for the matryoshka necklace, her hand clasping the pendant.

Are you happy for me, little sisters?

She looked toward the closed door, fixing on the sound of water streaming in the shower. She imagined the drops glistening on Hank's body, each one a diamond, precious, beautiful.

Hurry. Please, hurry.

She didn't want to spend the day waiting for him. She felt as though she'd been waiting for him all her life.

But the water streamed on as though he were drowning himself in it.

To keep busy, she bounded off the bed and attacked the living room, stacking magazines, clearing the clutter, making it into something halfway decent for when she brought Miki inside. Her hand brushed against the fishing rod with its secret switch, and all the while, her ears were tuned to the whoosh of water.

When the shower finally stopped, she stopped, too. Slowly she straightened, arms around one of the coolers to move it.

He was finished. Any moment, he would come out.

Hank jerked on a pair of Mason's old khakis. The man didn't seem to own much else. He ran a towel over his wet head. The shower had felt good, but had done little to lighten his spirits. Alex was determined to throw herself in front of a speeding train, and he was helping her do it.

A sliver of fear split him down the middle. What if his luck held and hers didn't?

All the more reason to forget that look on her face and the touch of her hands. Mason was right, he was already too involved; any more, and he'd be paralyzed with it.

He scraped the towel over himself, letting the harshness burn away whatever soft feelings he might be harboring. Yet when he was finished and dressed, with his gun at his back, he stepped into the living area and found that the sight of her undermined all his good intentions.

She'd straightened the cabin, gathered the fishing magazines and stacked them neatly in a corner. The rod Kiley had rigged now stood a little apart from the others and within easy reach of the recliner. When he came in she was struggling with a cooler, trying to move it against the wall.

He ran to help, grateful for something to do beside stare at her. "Here, let me get that."

Their hands touched as she transferred the bulky object to his arms. An electric jolt leaped from his fingers into his chest. At this rate, he would never make it through the next two hours, let alone the next two days.

Talk. Keep talking. He lowered the cooler to the floor, ransacking his brain for something to say. Rising, he looked around the room.

"This place will never look Martha Stewart good."

She followed his glance. "It has to look better than this. If I bring Miki in here, he has to believe it could belong to me."

Miki. Christ, he was sick of that man's name.

"If you have any chance of making this work, at least map out a plan."

She shook her head and moved closer. She was taut with emotion, a filly at the starting gate straining at the bit. "I don't want to plan."

Whatever state she was in, it wasn't calm, cool, or collected. And he needed her thinking, needed the old, cold Alex back. He stopped her with outstretched arms when she was a foot away. "Too bad. You're going to." He turned her around and pushed her into the chair. "So, I'm Petrov, and you're—"

She looked at him through lowered lids. "If you're going to be Miki, at least say his name correctly."

"What—Petrov, how hard is that?"

"It's Pe*trov*." She put the emphasis on the last syllable, rolling the "r".

He frowned. "Petrov, Pe*trov*, either way he's still the snake that's going to bite you."

"Not unless I bite first."

"And how do you plan on doing that, Countess?"

She gazed at him, eyes narrowed in a feline pout. "First, maybe I'll do this." She rose from the chair and slunk toward him. Even in the baggy clothes he saw the hips sway, the legs glide, imagined the curves melding. He suppressed a groan and backed away, but she kept coming.

"Then maybe I'll do this." She slung an arm over his shoulder and pulled herself right up against him. Her breast brushed his chest, her face tilted toward his, her mouth pink and moist. He started to sweat.

"Do you think that will get his attention?"

Reaching behind, he locked his fingers on the weapon stowed at his back. "Maybe. But this should definitely get yours."

She froze when the muzzle touched her rib.

"Bang, you're dead."

Her mouth tilted in the barest hint of a smile. Ignoring the gun, she pressed closer, crushing her breasts against him. "Do you really think he'll waste the moment on violence?" She gazed right into his eyes, deep and penetrating. "Would you?"

Then her mouth was on his, and he was lost.

He tumbled so fast it was laughable, if he could have laughed. If he could have thought at all, he would have. But all he could do was feel her. She melted against him, no iceberg now, but pure heat and fire. She was everywhere, his mouth, his arms, his chest, his heart. She was his. Every piece of her. Alex Sasha Jane Ivanovna Baker Baklanova. They were all his, each a flame in a bonfire of secrets. He plunged into the heat and was consumed.

First taste, first touch. Alex trembled with it, her whole being awash in sensation. He kissed her lips, her cheeks, her jaw. He whispered her name, a spell, an incantation.

Sashaaa.

Every sliver of ice inside her melted. She was liquid, a creature without form or shape.

And yet he held her. His arms came around her, embracing what was left of her. His hands traced her shoulder, caressed her breast. She shuddered with his touch, with the slick wetness of his mouth and tongue.

"God, Sasha." He breathed, chest heaving, and pulled away. "I can't. We c—"

"*Da, miliy.* We can." She stroked his face, the word she'd used—dear one—sinking in as she kissed him. He was dear. Basic as air. Vital as water. All she had and all she needed.

His mouth was warm, his groan welcome. She ran her hands under his shirt, and in one fluid motion, he pulled it over his head. She gasped at the beauty of him. The wide shoulders, muscled and hard, his taut back. So big.

She tasted his skin, her tongue flicking over his neck and chest. She wanted to inhale him, become him, wanted him against her, skin against skin.

And he did, too, because her shirt was gone in an instant. His hand flicked open the clasp of her bra and she sighed as those large, hard hands cupped her, his mouth heating her, turning her inside out, flesh over flesh, no bones, nothing to keep her standing.

And when she would have collapsed with the rush of

feeling, he bent and swooped her up, taking her into the bedroom.

"Sasha," he whispered, as he laid her on the bed, his hands slipping easily into her too-big, borrowed pants. His fingers found her, found the heart of her and lit her up in a blaze of sensation.

She arched into his touch, breathing hard, wanting more—to be bound, to merge, to be one creature newly formed. With no past and no future. Only now, this moment.

"Come with me, *liubimi*," she whispered, calling him sweetheart. "Be me. Let me be you."

She tugged at his pants as he pulled away hers. She kissed the hands that held her, covering her face with their strength as he entered her.

And then they were one. She gasped with the feel of him, opening her, becoming her. His strength was hers now, the weight of him, broad-shouldered, muscled. Her warrior, her lover.

Tears hovered behind her eyes. She was no longer alone. No longer cold. Cut off. Every nerve ending pulsed, every place they touched radiated. He whispered her name, his mouth breathing the sound into hers.

And all the while he moved inside her, around her, stroking, caressing, making her body sing with pleasure until thought dissolved into ecstasy. Into heat and desire and him. Only him.

She'd been darkness, the night, the hidden one, but far in the distance, the sun beckoned.

His body was bringing it to her, stoking her, heating her. His lips tasted of it, hot and warm with belonging. Together they would find the light.

She wrapped her legs around him, bringing him closer,

fusing skin and bone, blood and heart. There, almost there. Almost—

She exploded with light, splintered with heat. All her secrets shattered.

All her secrets gone.

All her—

She breathed. Lungs back in her chest. Fingers attached to hands, ribs in place, skin, hair. It was all there. She was all there, but new, different, reborn.

And Hank was gazing down at her, a stricken look on his face.

"Oh, *dusha moya.*" My heart, my soul, she'd called him, her voice low and soft. She heard the emotion in it and couldn't mask it. Didn't want to. She rubbed her mouth with his. "It's all right. Don't worry so. It's fine. Everything is fine."

He smiled, but it was tinged with sadness. "Yeah? Says who?"

Those green eyes were troubled now, and she wanted desperately to make him forget the danger.

"Kiss me, and I will make you believe."

He did, and it was like spring, new and filled with promise. She flung her arms around him, drawing him close. Tears welled.

Oh my God.

She loved him. Loved him.

And that was far more precious than revenge.

18

"Tell me about this." Hank's finger traced a line from her naked shoulder to her throat, the tip skating below the jeweled pendant hanging from the gold chain around her neck.

"It's a matryoshka—a replica of the nesting dolls in Russian folk art. This one is the three smiling sisters."

"Matri—"

"—Oshka."

He repeated it, his tongue making hash of the word. But she smiled at the effort; it was endearing.

They were in Edward's bed, scrambled in his sheets. They'd been there for hours. Now twilight beckoned from the window. Hank was propped on one hand, his bare shoulder and chest solid and hard, the scar in the center large and still vivid. It scared her, that scar. His body was so big and strong and had been pierced so easily.

"You've worn it before."

"It was a gift from my father."

"From Baklanov?"

"Yes."

His hand moved lazily, over her breasts, down her belly, and back again, leaving shivers in its wake. "Be precise. I don't want to get confused again."

"You are rather easy to confuse."

He nipped at her lip. "You're just a very good liar."

She smiled. "Practice makes perfect."

He ran his fingers around the necklace, circling the little sister and giving Alex more shivers. "A Christmas present? Do Russians have Christmas?"

"A birthday gift. My sixteenth." She sobered remembering. "My father was killed a few days later."

He pushed the hair back from her forehead, a world of comfort in his touch. "Ah, it's precious, then."

"Very."

She wrapped her fingers around the pendant, felt it warm with the contact, her one final secret safe. He watched, eyes sharp with perception. She loved that look, loved knowing that he saw past her secrets with understanding and compassion.

All except this one.

Should she keep it or let it go?

Her gaze drifted past his face to his chest. She caressed the jagged line where the skin had been broken and was suddenly lashed by a whip of fear. What if something happened to him?

She'd lost everyone else, would she lose Hank, too?

If she gave up her revenge she could keep him out of danger. But could she give up what she'd spent so many years pursuing?

He leaned over, his lips rubbing her cheek. "What's going on in there, Sasha? That calculating look is back."

"Is it?" She'd spent years perfecting the art of deception. How was it he saw through her so effortlessly?

"Uh-huh."

"Well . . . I was just wondering." She wrenched her gaze away from the scar. "Do you still think this was a bad idea?"

Another troubled expression crossed his face. "Yeah. I do." But he kissed her anyway, and she thawed against him, the ice inside her gone the way her secrets had.

The phone rang, and he tensed.

"Let it go," she whispered.

"Wish I could." He untangled himself from her arms. "But it might be important."

Hank stumbled off the bed and out of the room; their clothes, his cell phone, weapon, everything lay on the floor by the recliner.

Guilt staggered him. Guilt and the knowledge that he'd made a mistake, a terrible lapse of judgment. The knowledge sank inside him, a hundred-pound weight assaulting his conscience the way the insistent ringing of the phone battered the silence.

He rummaged in the pile, found his phone and punched it on. It was Mason.

"Everything all right?"

Not really. Hank wasn't sure anything would be all right again. "Yeah, everything's fine."

"Sasha giving you problems?"

He thought about that, about the problems she'd given him all afternoon. Heat and pleasure and trust.

"No, she's . . . she's okay." He closed his eyes, sweating as he remembered her touch, her softness, the smooth arch of hip and leg. She was fire and light, a cushion against the darkness inside him, and he was so far gone he couldn't find his way back with a map. But he couldn't tell Mason that.

"She agreed not to make a move toward Petrov until we've lined everything up."

"Been trying to talk her out of it?"

"Yeah."

"She listening?"

"Nope."

A beat of silence, as though they both recognized the problem and the power of the woman.

"Okay, then," Mason said. "I got two guys lined up. Matt Pruitt and Danny DiMarco. They should be there tomorrow."

Tomorrow. Reality crashed into him. "So I don't shoot them first, what do they look like?"

"Familiar. You had a little roadside chat with them. I'm sure you'll remember."

He remembered all right. His jaw tightened. "Just make sure they don't come in like a couple of James Bonds. This isn't a CIA action, and keeping Alex safe is all that matters."

"Cool your jets, son. They're okay. They were with me when I brought Alex over—young guys just starting out. They like her. They're not going to do anything that puts her at risk."

That soothed him. A hair. "I need ammo."

"I'm on my way. I'll bring some with me. What do you need?"

Hank told him, and they disconnected.

He stood still a moment, staring at the phone in his hand. Hours had passed, and he hadn't checked his messages, hadn't called home or Parnell. Hadn't done anything but make love to Alex.

He ran a hand through his hair, his heart pumping out a thick, dull drum line. He was going to get her killed.

This was what came of falling in love.

The realization ruptured inside him, not a surprise, more an acknowledgment of what he'd known all along.

Fool.

Lucky man.

A bolt of dread stabbed him.

"Hank?" Her voice from the bedroom. "Who was that?"

He found his pants in the pile on the floor, slid them on, and retrieved his weapon. The phone call had been a warning. A reminder that his luck could be someone else's curse.

"Who was it?"

Her voice was nearer and he turned to find her in the doorway, smooth and pale, naked from head to toe, every curve a temptation.

"Mason." He threw her the pants and shirt she'd been wearing. "Here, get dressed."

She caught the clothes and dropped them. "Why?"

He eased into the armchair. It was positioned away from the bedroom, so he couldn't see her. "Just get dressed."

"Is everything all right?"

"Everything is fine. Mason's sending two guys up tomorrow. Says you know them. Pruitt and DiMarco."

"Matt and Danny? Yes, I know them. I haven't seen them in years, but—"

"Great. It'll be a hometown reunion. But first you have to get dressed."

Her hand reached over the back of the chair and stroked his head. A quiver of awareness ricocheted through him.

"No, I don't." She sidled around, wormed her way onto his lap, and nestled against him. "Come back to bed."

"I have to check my messages. Call the department. Let Rose know what I'm doing."

She nuzzled his neck, and he breathed in sharply, her touch igniting a conflagration under his skin.

"Do it later."

Christ, he was hard again, wanting her again. "Look, I don't think we should—"

"Don't think." She kissed him.

"Petrov—"

"Doesn't know where I am. We're in control. Until I contact him, we're in control."

She kissed him again, her mouth liquid and soft. Resistance crumbled. Thought crumbled. Wrapping his arms around her, he lifted her up and carried her back to bed.

The gravelly sound of male voices penetrated Alex's brain. She opened her eyes in darkness, felt the empty bed beside her and made the connection between sound and source. The bedside clock read two-twelve. Hurriedly, she slipped on Mason's shirt and khakis, pushing the sleeves up over her wrists, and peeked out.

Hank and Edward were hunched over the kitchen table. A rush of heat went through her at the sight of Hank's broad back, his muscled shoulders flexed, his strong arms braced on the tabletop. She remembered the feel of him beneath her hands and for a long moment wished Edward had stayed away for another hour, another day, another lifetime.

"When did you get back?" She leaned against the doorframe. How much did Edward know? Had he caught Hank in bed with her? Would he care? Did she? She ran the idea around her mind. Not only didn't she care, she hoped he did know. She wanted everyone to know.

"Five minutes ago." Mason stepped back and nodded in the table's direction. "Had a few things to drop off."

She saw what lay on the table and froze. Black and gray steel with muzzles and triggers. Wicked-looking bullets.

The weapons and ammunition made the looming confrontation with Petrov all too real.

She met Hank's gaze, remembered the scar he bore, and once again, her need for revenge shifted inside her, no longer clear or certain.

"Your friends should be here in a few hours." Hank's gaze drilled into her. "That gives us our four men. The surveillance is in place. The weapons are here. Mason brought the wine, and the clothes you wanted will be delivered. We're all set." Face grim, he crossed his arms. "Are you?"

Now that the moment had come she only wanted to put it off. "I . . . I'll need more than that. Rugs. Something to cover the walls."

Mason fished a cell phone from his pocket. "I'll call Danny. See what he can find." He punched in the number and walked out onto the porch to make the call.

Hank's gaze never left her face. She flushed and turned away, but his unspoken words whispered in her head. *Don't do this.*

Could she listen? The urge to let go had sneaked up on her, but now it was there every time she looked at Hank. The man who had broken through all her barriers. Who had freed her from the secrets of the past.

Could she have her revenge and Hank, too?

Or would one cost her the other?

The bleating of a cell phone scattered her thoughts.

"Bonner." His tone was flat, unemotional, a cop's voice. *"What?"* Shock erased the impassivity.

She swiveled around to face him. He'd gone white. Slowly, he sank into one of the kitchen chairs. She crept closer, a lump of fear forming inside her.

"Are you sure it's him? I just can't believe . . . there's got to be a mistake. A mix-up . . . Okay, all right. No, I'll notify her. Yes, I'll take care of it. And I appreciate the heads up. Thanks." He disconnected.

"Who was it?"

He sat staring at the phone.

"Hank! What's the matter? You're scaring me."

He looked up at her, his face a portrait of confusion. "Lydia from dispatch."

"Why? What's wrong?"

"It's . . . it's Trey. He's in trouble."

The lump grew, a cancer of terror spreading inexorably. "What kind of trouble?"

He rubbed a hand down his face. "He and a couple of cronies, they . . . they broke into a bike shop. Shattered the storefront, took three bikes, damaged four more. The others got away, but the owner caught Trey red-handed. The story's still a bit garbled, but evidently Trey . . ." He shook his head as though trying to shake the words loose. "He assaulted the owner with a brick."

My God. She gripped the back of his chair. "I'm . . . I'm sorry."

"They're bringing him in." He said the words as if he didn't believe them. Couldn't believe them. It broke her heart.

"You'd better go."

"I thought . . . I thought we'd finished with that. He was coming around."

"I know." She knew what he was thinking. That he should have been there. He should have been with his family instead of baby-sitting her.

A chasm of guilt opened up. "You should go."

He turned his head to look at her, his expression torn. "I can't leave you alone."

"I'm not alone. Edward's here." As if to confirm his presence, Edward's voice drifted in from outside. Hank gazed out the door where he could see Edward's back and the phone at his ear. "Hank, he's a child and I'm a grown-up. He needs you. You have to go."

"He made his choice. He has to handle the consequences."

"He doesn't have to handle them by himself. He has a family. He has you."

In the ensuing silence she took a breath. Ran her tongue over dry lips. "If it makes you feel better, I've . . . I've changed my mind."

"About what?"

She swallowed hard. "About Petrov." There, she said it out loud.

Hank gaped at her. She felt silly and false, but on the verge of another liberation. "I've been thinking about it all day. Letting Petrov go. Like Edward said. Letting him go and moving on with my life."

He stared at her, eyes narrowed in suspicion. "I don't believe I'm hearing this." He searched her face, his scrutiny as invasive as an X-ray.

"It's true. I . . . I'm backing off."

He snorted and jerked out of the chair. "Like hell you are." He paced the room, voice hard, finger stabbing the air. "You've been a damn pit bull about Petrov. And now, all of a sudden you get cold feet? Sorry, Countess, but I'm not falling for another lie."

She bristled, though she had no right. Lying was all she'd done from the first, no wonder he didn't believe her. But still, she raised her chin, feeling all prickly and defensive. "I'm not lying."

"And why should I believe you?"

"Maybe I found something more important than revenge."

"Yeah? Like what?"

"You."

The word was out before she knew she was going to say it, but once said she couldn't take it back. She didn't want to.

Their eyes met. Hers filled with sudden, unexpected tears. God, how like a stupid woman to cry.

"I love you. I don't want to risk the chance that you might love me back someday."

His face crumpled, softened. "Oh, Sasha Jane, you bring me to my knees." He eased into the chair with a massive slough of breath. "Come here. Sit." She sat on his lap, and he held her. "You know it's too late. That chance paid off a long time ago. You think I'm doing this for fun? You think I do this for every beautiful woman who gets in my way?"

She leaned against his chest, heard the strong, steady beat of his heart. A great warm contentment filled her veins.

"So go," she said. "Your family needs you. I'll be fine. Edward is here. We'll call Matt and Danny and tell them not to come. I'll let you handle Petrov; like you said, police business."

Hank hesitated, a tiny pause in which his options lay before him like a shell game. Tell the truth or dodge.

But if he told her that he wouldn't be handling the case much longer because he was leaving the force, she might not trust the next guy in charge. She might change her mind again and go through with her original plan for Petrov.

And that could be deadly.

So he kept the truth to himself, a tiny lie of omission. Anything to get her off that road leading to Petrov.

Instead, he took her hand, and his newfound right to

touch her, hold her, gave him strength and purpose. Carefully he chose his words. "What if we can't prove anything? What if Petrov walks again?"

He held his breath and waited, watching the play of their fingers. Despite his uneasiness, the feel of her skin sent a current of desire through him.

"I'll learn to grow apples," she said softly. "Fight hailstorms instead."

There was an edge of regret in her eyes, covered by a swell of determination.

"I've made my choice, Hank. I choose you."

His arms tightened around her. This was what he'd been angling for—both of them safe. Together. He hardly dared hope. "You think you'd like that? Apple House is a far cry from Moscow."

"If I don't like it, I can always run an oil company. Someone has to."

He rubbed his cheek against the top of her head, letting her words settle inside him. She was right, of course. She didn't have to abandon her career. If she called off her vendetta, if the fallout from Renaissance Oil wasn't toxic, if her reputation didn't suffer or her business collapse. If, if, if.

He hated hanging her future on such a slim word.

She kissed his cheek, her lips lingering on his skin and sending a new wave of electricity through him. "We can work everything out," she murmured, voice husky. "You'll see. As long as we're together."

Together. The word seemed to blink like a neon sign between them. Good. Bad. Life. Death.

"But right now, you should go. Trey must be terrified." She jumped off his lap and pulled him to his feet.

Trey. The boy's name sent a spasm of emotion through him. "He better be."

"Better be what?" Mason tramped into the kitchen and held out the phone to Alex. "It's Danny DiMarco. Tell him what you need."

She didn't move, and it seemed to Hank as though she were rethinking her decision not to pursue Petrov. In those few seconds worlds hung in the balance. Would her past outweigh their future?

She took the phone. "Danny? Yes, thank you for all your help. Actually, I don't need anything." Her gaze met Hank's. "In fact, I've . . . well, I've changed my mind. I've decided not to go through with this."

"What?" Mason looked from her to Hank and back again.

"I'm sorry to have put you to so much trouble." Alex was still talking to DiMarco. "No, absolutely. I'm sure. Look, can I call you back? I'll explain later. Thank you." She handed the phone to Mason. "He wants to talk to you."

"No, she's fine," Mason said. "I don't know. This is the first I've heard of it. Okay. Hang tight. I'll call you back." He disconnected and quirked his brows at Alex.

"I'll explain everything later," Alex said. "Right now, Hank has to leave."

"For a few hours," Hank said. "Family stuff." He checked his pockets for keys, phone, reseated his weapon. The firm shape of it reminded him of the man he should be, the one who knew his place in the world. "I'll be back as soon as I can. Tomorrow afternoon. Tomorrow night at the latest."

"Stay as long as you have to. Edward will be here."

She walked him to the door and slipped outside with him for a last private moment.

"You shouldn't be seen," he told her. "Go insi—" The last word was muffled by her kiss.

"I'm going," she whispered.

He captured her chin. "See you soon."

"Drive safe."

Alex watched him go, watched the car's headlights come from around the back to the front, turn left and disappear down the road. Their parting words—see you soon, drive safe—were so trivial. She imagined millions of people all over the world said them every day, casually, perfunctorily, never thinking twice about them. Yet to her they were talismans that resonated deep within. That she had someone to say such banal things to, who would say them back to her was extraordinary. Extraordinary, amazing, and wonderful, and it took her breath away.

She clung to the porch post, rooted to the spot. Tears at the back of her throat, she struggled for composure, crying and laughing at her mawkishness at the same time.

Mopping her eyes with the inside of her wrist, she closed the door and retreated inside, hoping that whatever Trey had done wasn't irreparable and that he and Hank would learn to forgive each other.

Was it possible?

She could never forgive Miki Petrov. But that didn't mean she would make him pay for what he'd done. Not if it meant losing Hank.

"What kind of games are you playing, Sasha?" Edward stood in the middle of the kitchen, arms crossed, a suspicious scowl on his face.

"I'm not playing games, Edward. I've changed my mind. I heard what you and Hank said. Using myself as bait is crazy and probably won't work anyway."

"I know you. You're plotting something."

"No. Hank had to leave because his nephew is in trouble. When he comes back we'll regroup. Talk about the next step."

Edward gave her a long, penetrating look. "So you're

giving up." Not a question but a summation of the situation. Unemotional and to the point.

She answered in kind. "I am."

"Bonner have anything to do with it?"

She raised her chin. "He does."

Another deep, thoughtful glance. "You care about him that much?"

"I do."

Slowly, Edward nodded. "Good. I like him. And I like the way your eyes soften when you look at him."

She felt her face heat. "They don't."

He grinned. "Oh yes, they do."

She smiled. "They do?" He nodded, and her smile widened. "They do."

He put his arms around her and gave her a hug. "Good for you, Sasha. It's about time. Good choice, good decision." He pulled away. "But more work for me." He pulled out his cell phone. "I'll call Danny back, then let Matt know. Why don't you get some sleep?"

She shook her head. "Too keyed up."

"All right, but don't go anywhere. I'm going to check the cabin perimeter, make sure everything is okay. I could use a few hours sleep myself."

"Are you hungry?" Suddenly she was starved. No wonder. She and Hank had been too busy for lunch or dinner. The thought sent love and a sense of belonging winging through her.

She hugged the feelings to herself, a private treasure.

"No, but you go ahead. There's soup, eggs, whatever you want." He pushed through the screen door and went outside. A few seconds later, she heard him talking to Matt.

Combing through the cabinets, she found a can of chicken soup. While she waited for it to heat, she gathered the weapons from the kitchen table and stowed them under the sink. She wasn't squeamish about them, but since she didn't need them anymore, why look at them?

When the soup was done, she took a cup to the recliner and snuggled in. Closing her eyes, she pictured the future. Apple House would be hers. She'd have a family, roots and branches.

Instinctively, she reached for her necklace, the last link to her old life. She set down her cup, undid the clasp, and removed the necklace. She tried to open the first little sister, but the latch hadn't been released in a long time, and it stuck.

Edward's tackle box still sat next to the chair. She unfastened it and found a long, pointed scaling knife, which she used to open the tiny clasp.

Inside—instead of the two other sisters the necklace had been designed to hold—lay the top half of a small gold lapel pin. Embossed with the seal of Mother Russia, its raised lines were marred by streaks of rust.

Her father's blood.

Through long years she'd been careful not to handle the pin overmuch; she'd wanted those streaks to remain, a visual reminder of his death and her purpose.

But now she took the pin out and studied it. The images she so often pushed away rose up, hard and strong. The last time she'd seen her father, his body broken, some final vestige of breath still left.

Luka had gotten her out of her father's office building, but as he was unlocking the car, she broke away, running around to the front where she'd thrown herself over her father's twisted body. Weak, barely alive, he'd pressed a hand against hers. That was all, that one feeble gesture. Then the light in his eyes went out, Luka wrapped a brawny arm around her middle, wrenching her away, and she never saw her father again.

But in those few precious seconds he'd given her a last cherished gift, and she was staring at it now. The top half of a lapel pin. Given to a select few by the head of the KGB for extreme meritorious service, each one was engraved with the bearer's initials. This one had two Cyrillic letters—M, which looked like its English counterpart, and "peh," which looked like a mathematical hieroglyph.

M. P.

Mikail Petrov.

She had long ago deciphered this mystery. Her father had struggled with Petrov, and in the end he must have clutched at him. Petrov had shoved her father away, and her father had fallen. But he'd taken the pin with him.

For thirteen years she had held it safe, discovered its secrets and kept them. The pin had been her goad and her burden.

And now she would let it go. The one secret she would never tell.

Forgive me, Papa.

She bowed her head, awed by the power of the words. Forgiveness ran like a river through the web of her life. Hank needing forgiveness from Trey, Trey from him, her from her father, Miki from her.

Forgiveness.

Possible for some, but not others.

Not Miki. Never Miki.

She fisted her fingers around the pin. She only hoped her father understood.

She replaced the pin inside the locket just as she heard Edward returning to the porch. She leaped up.

"I made some soup," she called. "Sure you won't have some?"

The door opened, slamming against the wall, and she froze.

Miki Petrov stood smiling in the doorway, arms outstretched to embrace her. "Hello, *dorogaya*."

19

Heading south, Hank negotiated a twist of the Taconic and ended his cell phone call. No answer from Apple House. He wondered if Lydia had called Rose anyway and she was already down at the police station. What would she have done with Mandy? Dropped her at Ben's probably. Then why hadn't he heard from his brother? They might disagree about the future of the farm, might argue about a lot of things, but Ben wouldn't have blown off Trey. Not when he was in trouble.

He sighed, punched in Ben's number. Lori answered the phone, sleepy and alarmed.

"It's Hank, Lori. Is Ben there? I've got some bad news."

"Hank? What's the matter? Is it Rose?"

For a moment, Hank was confused. "Rose? No, it's Trey."

From beyond his sister-in-law he heard Ben. "Let me talk to him." Then his brother's voice. "What's wrong, where are you?"

"On my way. I got a call about Trey. He's probably going to be arrested."

"What? What are you talking about? Why?"

"He broke into a bike shop and assaulted the owner."

"That's crazy. I know he's been a handful, but—"

"Look, I got a call from dispatch. They've already sent over a unit to bring him in."

"Wait a minute." Ben turned away from the phone. "Lori, go check on Trey. Hank says he's being arrested."

"Arrested? But—"

"Just go and see."

Hank said, "Ben, what's going on?"

"Just a minute. Lori's going to check on Trey."

"Check on him? What do you mean?"

"The kids are here. It was easier than driving over to the farm every morning to get them."

Hank paused, that news creating ripples of concern. "What about Mom, where is she?"

"At home. Why?"

"She didn't answer the phone."

"The kids were here. I told her to turn off the ringer and get a good's night's sleep." The simple explanation loosened the knot in Hank's chest, but didn't entirely dispel his un-easiness.

Lori came on the line, her voice subdued. "Hank, Trey is fine. Fast asleep."

What? "You're sure? I mean you checked to make sure it wasn't a bunch of blankets bundled up under the covers?"

"I'm positive. I'm looking right at him, and he's sleeping like an angel. I have to tell you, he's really been terrific. Helped Mandy with her homework and everything. Seems to have turned a corner."

Apprehension crawled up Hank's back.

From what must have been another extension, Ben said, "Why would someone say Trey was arrested?" He sounded worried.

The trickle of disquiet was fast turning into a river. "Must have been a misunderstanding. Look, I'm sorry I woke you. I'll be back in a few days. Give my love to Trey and Mandy. And thanks for helping out."

"We're family, Hank. That's what we do." Ben said it simply, a statement of fact. And of love. For the first time in a long time, Hank felt a burst of affection for his brother.

"Take care of yourself," Ben said quietly. "Come home soon." Hank heard the unsaid message. Don't take chances. Be careful. We've lost enough.

"You got it." The words were a promise between them. A promise Hank wasn't sure he could keep.

He disconnected and immediately the phone rang back.

"Hank, it's Jake Greenlaw. Dispatch got a call about your nephew, and I'm on graveyard this week. They sent me to check it out, but everything's fine."

"I know. I just talked to my brother. Trey's at his house. Asleep."

"That's good. Sorry about the false alarm."

Sirens were going off in his head. "Do me a favor. Run by the farm and make sure my mother is okay."

The Taconic didn't have much of an easement to pull off, so Hank took the next exit, turned into the first side road and braked. He waited, eyes on the inky road ahead. He'd already been given one reprieve tonight, two would be more than he hoped for.

He leaped for the cell phone when it rang.

"Hank, it's Jake Greenlaw. I—"

"Let me have this," his mother's voice said. "Henry? Are you there?"

"Yeah, Ma, I'm here."

"Are you all right? Where are you? Why did you send an officer here? He woke me up. Scared the wits out of me."

His mother's blunt voice, even rife with irritation, sent a

tide of relief through him. "Sorry. It's all been a misunderstanding. Go back to sleep."

"Are you coming back soon?" Again that unspoken message pulled at him. *We love you. Be careful. Come home.*

The air around him seemed to shimmer with warning. "Soon as I can. Let me talk to the officer."

"You're sure you're all right?"

Despite the anxiety, the corners of his lips tipped upward. If he had any doubts about his mother's well-being, her doggedness wiped them away. "I'm fine. Put Officer Greenlaw back on."

"Everything's okay here," Greenlaw said.

"Thanks for checking it out."

"No problem."

He disconnected and stared into the shadows. Trey was fine, his mother was fine. But Alex . . .

A terrible thought crashed into his head, and he struggled for breath, fear wrenching his chest. In an instant, he turned the car around, shot into the parkway like a demon and gunned the gas.

Alex stared at Petrov as though he were a ghost she wished would disappear. But he was solid and real and not going anywhere. He stepped into the cabin.

"You've been hiding from me, *dorogaya*."

She flashed a smile, hoped he bought it. "Just a small retreat. A rest."

How had he found her? Her mind kept beating out that question. How? How? And where was Edward?

"A rest? Here?" He looked around distastefully. "No, my dear, this is not a place where people like you and me go to rest. This is where we go to ground." He gave her a short, disappointed smile. "What are you hiding from?"

"Nothing. I don't know what you're talking about."

"Don't you?"

She shook her head. Where was her practiced calm? She could barely breathe, let alone think.

"I've had news about you," Petrov said.

"You shouldn't put stock in rumors."

"Ah, but this, I am afraid, is true." He stepped forward. She stepped back. "You've been less than candid with me, *dorogaya*. Or should I say Aleksandra Ivanovna?"

Her true name on his lips choked the air from her lungs. She tried to swallow, to bluff, her mouth barely able to form words. "I don't know what you're talking about."

"I'm talking about you, my dear. Daughter of Ivan Baklanov. The dear departed Baklanov. Thief and coward. Traitor to Russia."

The words scorched, a red-hot branding iron to her soul. "Don't speak of him. You aren't fit to say his name."

"And why is that?"

She didn't reply.

"Why am I not fit to say the name of a traitor, a man who stole from his own people and then killed himself when he couldn't face the consequences? Why?"

"Murderer."

A slow, arrogant smile crossed his face. She wanted to smash it away.

"Ah, is that what you think?"

"It's what I know."

"But not what you can prove." Confidence turned to indulgence. "You and Kholodov. Two little motors in an engine of conspiracy. He thought he could bring me down with the truth. You? What can you do?"

She thought of the secret hidden in her necklace. For

years she'd clung to it, knowing it was a start, but not the end of what she needed to bring Petrov to justice.

She needed more, and she'd spent what was left of her childhood and her whole adult life hunting for it.

But now, when she'd given up the search, her prey appeared out of nowhere. And her plan, so recently abandoned, was suddenly whole and in front of her. A gift from the universe.

Only a fool would refuse such a gift.

She edged toward the chair. "What are you talking about? What truth did Luka threaten you with?" Around the chair toward the wall.

He advanced farther into the cabin as she moved back, a panther certain of his prey. "Don't you know? Poor little Sashka. So innocent. So dependent on the adults around her. So doomed to disappointment."

"No one's disappointed me but you."

"Your friend Mason. I'm afraid he won't be helping you any longer."

A clutch of terror gripped her, a sick, familiar feeling. What had he done to Edward? But even as the answer stabbed into her, she eased toward the fishing rod, grasping it like a cudgel, as though she wanted to crush him with it. "What have you done?"

"Eliminated the weak to get to the strong. That is always the way, isn't it?" He spoke pleasantly, and she depressed the switch, praying his voice covered the sound.

"You're speaking riddles." Gliding away, she drew him toward her, toward the hidden microphone.

"Let me be plain then. I'm speaking about you and your *penchant*"—he gave the word its French pronunciation— "for leaning on the wrong people at the wrong time. Mason. That ridiculous detective. And, of course, your dear Luka.

He is the one to blame, you know. He told me where your father would be. He let me in."

She gasped and stopped short, outrage twisting her throat. "That's a lie."

"Is it?"

"My father had an appointment that night."

"With Bronsky, his aide."

"With you."

"No. I was quite unexpected. In fact, I wouldn't have known where your father was that night if Kholodov hadn't told me."

"I don't believe you."

"Kholodov is dead, so you'll never know, will you?"

That bit hard. "Why would Luka do that? He hated you."

"Well, to be fair, he didn't know what my plans were. He thought I was coming to talk. To confer. To see how I could help your father out of this . . . mess he'd gotten himself into."

Anger swelled again, but she held it back, a tidal wave surging and receding. "You tricked him."

He shrugged. "He allowed himself to be tricked. To be used. He was good for that. Most people are."

His condescension revolted her, and he wagged a finger in her direction, a pleasant expression on his face as though he enjoyed her discomfort.

"I wondered what had become of Luka Kholodov. He was a loose end I'd been seeking for years. And then"—he snapped his fingers—"like that he offered himself up to me."

"And you killed him, just like you killed my father."

"Yes, I'm afraid so. But it had to be done, you see. Your father was old Russia. A stodgy, stiff-necked bureaucrat who couldn't see that the world had changed. As for Luka, he threatened to tell the truth about my part in your father's sad demise. I couldn't let him do that, could I? Not with so much at stake." He spread his hands. "Our business arrangement, for one. The life of a county, a town. Our two countries. So many people to lift up. So many people to disappoint."

As if he cared. "You did it for yourself."

He shrugged as though that were an unimportant side benefit. "Oh, yes. That, too."

After so many years, why had Luka confronted Petrov? Guilt ran through her: the answer was obvious. He'd wanted to protect her, to save her from confronting Petrov herself. Tears thickened in the back of her throat, but she pushed them away.

"So you killed my father, and Dashevsky moved the money for you."

He bowed his head in acknowledgment. "Yes. A very clever man, young Dashevsky. Our oil deal would have been as dead as your father without him. Good thing I had something that would persuade him over to our side."

"His part in the theft, you mean."

"He is reluctant for that to be made public, yes. A few hints, a small threat. Antonin has been a valuable ally." He smiled, the expression without light or kindness.

"Yet your collaborator has been vocally opposed to the tax legislation we need."

"A smoke screen, my dear. I must let the man have some dignity. In the end, Dashevksy will do what is beneficial to himself. Doesn't everyone?" He reached into his coat and took out a gun. "And so we come to you, *dorogaya*. I am thinking you are not as headstrong nor as stupid as Kholodov. And that, I'm afraid, makes you far more dangerous."

*   *   *

Hank entered the shore drive with headlights off, proceeded slowly around the lake and parked far enough away from Mason's cabin to be out of sight. He got out, closing the car door with a soft click, and just in case he needed it, checked his weapon, grabbed extra ammo clips, and a pair of handcuffs from the trunk. For extra measure he stuffed a few flex-cuffs in his pocket, the plastic ties sitting light and easy there.

Then he crept toward the cabin, figuring to come around the bedroom where a window would give him a first glimpse of whatever was happening.

He never made it.

He hadn't come within ten yards of the cabin when he saw a form lurking outside. Too bulky to be Mason, it could have been either of his two bad boys. Except Mason had said he would call and tell them not to come. And he'd heard Alex tell one of them that she'd changed her mind.

He inched forward, and suddenly the man stepped out of the shadows beneath a tree to toss his cigarette and grind it beneath one heel. For a moment moonlight illuminated his face.

Yuri.

Recognition hit Hank like an electric shock.

Petrov was already there. *Jesus H. Christ.*

So someone *had* arranged the fake phone call. Someone who wanted him out of the way.

He scanned the area, assessing the situation. Where was Mason? In the dark, Hank could see no trace of him. Had Petrov already gotten to him? Hank's jaw tightened at the possibility, but he didn't have time to find out. He had to know what was going on inside that cabin and before he could get there he had to take out Yuri. Quietly. No shots to alert others to his presence.

He closed his eyes, closing his mind to the silent promise he'd given Ben, the unstated message he'd heard from Rose. With soundless steps he crawled forward, working his way around Yuri's flank to his back.

When he was close enough to smell the tobacco on Yuri's clothes, Hank took a breath, steadied himself and his footing, then smashed the butt of his gun as hard as he could on Yuri's head.

The big man went down like a falling tree. Ah, the advantages of surprise.

Or a lucky streak that still held.

Quickly, Hank searched and relieved Yuri of his weapon—a 9mm semi-automatic. If Yuri had killed Kholodov, he hadn't done it with this gun. Hank cuffed Yuri's hands behind his back, wrapped a plastic tie around his ankles, and removed Yuri's shoes, which he threw out of reach. Then he stripped off one of Yuri's socks and gagged him with it.

Busted and trussed.

That should hold him.

Relieved, Hank left Yuri on the ground and crept toward the cabin. No time for hedging bets; he needed to see exactly what was going on.

Crouching low, he inched toward the porch and almost tripped on the body at its foot.

Mason, dead eyes staring up at the night sky, a nasty smile sliced through his throat.

Outrage sparked into wild, untamed enmity. Hank tightened his hold on his weapon and stared up at the cabin, using ironclad control to constrain the unmanageable fury. With grim determination, he slipped up the porch. Keeping clear of the door, which was wide open, he peeked into one of the front windows.

Petrov was there all right. And he had a gun on Alex.

"Don't be stupid," she was saying, her voice strained but calm, "I have a policeman with me."

Christ, if only that were enough.

Petrov stroked the gun, caressing it like a treasured possession. "I don't think your Detective Bonner will be back anytime soon. Family troubles." The latter said dripping with false sympathy.

"How did you—"

"Oh, I know everything, *dorogaya*. I arranged it. A bit like God." He laughed, the sound smooth and filled with such conceit it foamed inside Hank like poison.

He ducked back down, hands shaking and slick with sweat. Adrenaline or fear?

"Tom!" His voice echoed inside his head as though in a tomb. *"Tom, I'm coming in."*

He closed his eyes, leaning against the cabin just below the window.

Not Tom, not the toolshed. Get a grip.

He was outside Mason's cabin.

Inside, Alex faced the door. Petrov had his back to it.

That was good. With luck Hank could get off a shot without Petrov knowing, and without his shooting Alex.

With luck.

But everyone's luck ran out eventually.

Instinctively, his hand pressed against his chest, fingers tracing the outline of the scar. His heart beat fast but steady. Whole. Alive.

He gazed blindly at the shadowed night, the harsh glow of lights on the lake, the mocking face of the moon.

Everybody had to die once.

Yeah, but he'd already had the privilege and lived.

Only on borrowed time, pal. Now the price was due.

He'd lost one woman he loved. He wasn't going to lose another.

He swallowed, took a breath, tightened his grip on his weapon, and launched himself at the door.

Sorry, Ma.

Like God. Alex saw the megalomania in Petrov's eyes and was staggered by it. But overconfidence was as much a flaw as anything if only she could find a way to use it.

"What a shame to waste our time together in violence." She spoke low, soft, hoping the heat in her voice would lull him while she edged toward the recliner.

He gazed at her with reptilian stillness, a snake about to strike. "Yes, I, too, would have preferred other ways to spend our time."

She threw him a seductive smile, eased against the arm of the chair. "We still can." One hand behind her, fingers creeping inch by inch, searching. She'd left the scaling knife there. Somewhere.

Petrov stepped toward her, a cool, calculating smile on his lips.

Movement behind him. A step. A shout.

"Petrov!"

Miki whirled around, gunshots exploded. Her fingers wrapped around the knife handle, and she ran, thoughtless, breathless. Seconds, she only had seconds. *Hurry, hurry.*

Her arm was up, her hand plunged down.

The knife went in.

Again. And again.

Miki staggered to face her, blood shooting everywhere. His gun went off three times into the floor.

He sank to his knees, astonishment crossing his face. He

raised the gun at her, arm shaky but straight. How did he have the strength?

She didn't. She couldn't move, couldn't breathe.

"Yebannaya suka." Fucking bitch. The words were a hoarse, dry whisper. Eyes open, staring, he toppled.

She watched him hit the floor, heard the thud, saw him still and unmoving, and was filled with revulsion and shock.

Her teeth chattered, her skin icy.

Over, her father's voice inside her head whispered.

It was over.

Not by Miki's own sword, not fine and elegant, but sharp enough.

Die enemy from my hand.

My hand.

Her fingers opened, and the knife dropped, hitting the ground with a metallic clink.

She moaned. Knees weak, she sank to the floor, sobbing.

And then she saw who had plunged through the door.

The bullet hit Hank hard, the impact strangely familiar, almost a relief.

He stumbled, went down on one knee, managed to keep hold of his gun. Sweat filmed his eyes. He squinted tight, aimed, but before he could depress the trigger she was there. A wild avenging Valkyrie, ice blond hair flying. Doing something to Petrov. Something . . .

His eyes refused to focus.

Jesus Christ, she was . . .

He tried to get to her, tried to crawl to her. Instead, he found himself on his back, looking up at the cabin ceiling. Pine beams. He saw pine beams above him.

He closed his eyes, concentrated on breathing.

Someone murmured something he couldn't understand.

Something fell hard.

All far away. Nothing to do with him.

Then hands touched him.

"Hank, oh my God. Hank!"

Her voice. Distant but there. Alive. She was alive.

He opened his eyes and smiled at her, or thought he did.

She was crying. Why were those tears on her cheeks? Didn't she know everything was all right now? The scales had been reset, the balance righted. She would be safe.

He tried to tell her, but she put a finger on his lips.

"Don't move. Don't talk."

That was fine with him. The words didn't seem to want to go from his head to his mouth anyway.

He closed his eyes. Fading. Happy to fade.

"Stay with me. Stay with me!"

He heard the 911 call. And then he heard nothing.

20

Alex watched the approach to Manhattan through the airplane window. The October day was clear and bright, a far cry from the gloom she'd left behind in Moscow. There, winter had hit early, and the city had been gripped in gray. The Moskva had already frozen into massive slabs of dingy ice, and the streets had been rimmed with soot-smudged snow.

It was a jolt to see the sun again. She stared through the lace of cloud at the New York cityscape far below. Framed against blue sky, the island's contours cut sharply into the water, the land a thick web of building and greenways vying for space.

The view pulled at her, the city chugging and pulsing, alive with imagined rhythm. Life tugging her back from all the deaths.

She was done with weeping now. She had cried her last over her father's grave. Visiting him had been her final stop before leaving Russia. Standing over the small, unkempt plot, she'd shed tears for all she'd lost and all she'd won. And in a voice thick with emotion she had read him the headlines. Headlines from all over Russia. Words that shouted his name again, this time in vindication and truth.

Except for one tiny omission. One more secret to keep.

A grim satisfaction tightened her chest as she recalled the look on Dashevksy's face when she'd played the relevant section of Miki Petrov's last moments. They'd met privately in a squat building that ironically had once housed the Soviet Ministry of Trade. She'd invited him to lunch and hinted that she'd brought some new and highly lucrative investment ideas with her.

But instead of a lavish spread, she fed him the truth and watched while he listened, stone-faced.

"So you killed my father and Dashevsky moved the money for you."

And Petrov's open acknowledgment. His assertion that he had the prime minister of Russia in his hip pocket.

Perhaps she shouldn't have used that information. By doing so, she was as much a blackmailer as Petrov. But Dashevsky deserved it. He should be in jail. Fortunately for him, she needed him. And his support for the oil bill.

She sat back in her seat. Yesterday at two-fifteen Moscow time, the bill had passed. With unqualified support from the prime minister.

All of Petrov's assets would be sold—including his huge stake in Petroneft—with two stipulations. First, a percentage of profits from the sale would go into a public trust in Russia so that the money stolen from the Russian people could be returned. Second, the deal to market Renaissance Oil to the United States would stand. Sokanan would have its chance at prosperity.

Thanks to Dashevsky.

And the secret about him that would now remain secret.

She only hoped her father understood.

She closed her eyes, seeking a whisper of his presence. Every nerve ending alert, she listened closely for some sign that he knew what she'd done and approved. But all she heard was the pilot's voice over the loudspeaker, telling the flight crew to prepare the cabin for landing.

The past was over, her future about to begin.

The drive from the airport north was a slow, unraveling journey. She'd splurged on a limo and then talked the driver into taking the long way via the parkway. The rolling vistas burned with color, trees a glory of golden fire and ageing green in the crisp autumn sunshine.

But soon the trees would be stripped bare as she had been. Her old life fallen away, her secrets released, her purpose fulfilled. She was naked. Ready to be reborn.

Into what?

So odd to have a dream come true. To see her goal reached, to have the reason for which she'd been living come to an end.

She felt free and light, but also adrift. As though tethered by nothing, she could vanish in the breeze.

The car took the first exit for Sokanan, and as they approached the outskirts of the city, she noted the contrast with the colorful parkway. The dreariness of the strip malls peppered with empty stores, the run-down gas stations. They passed the old GE plant, and it struck her how much work would be needed to turn the city into the showplace it was meant to be.

Hard work. Work someone had to undertake.

She recalled Ben Bonner's words.

"We need someone to bring jobs to Sokanan. Someone smart, an insider who can talk to business in their own language."

They'd been in the hospital, her clothes still stained with blood, Hank's and Petrov's mingling together.

Lori had scolded her husband. "Not now, Ben."

But Alex had understood and been strangely grateful. "It's all right. It's good to think about something else." Something besides the new loss she was bracing herself for.

A nurse came to bring them to the surgeon and Alex tensed, they all did, the short walk to privacy as grueling a moment as any she'd suffered.

Then the words that made her knees crumple.

"He made it through."

Tears burst out, and they were all smiling and hugging each other, she and Ben, she and Mandy, she and Trey and Rose.

A family holding each other up.

"He'll be okay then?" Rose had asked.

"Too early to tell. It looks good, but we'll just have to wait and see," the doctor had said.

Now the car headed out the other side of the city and she leaned forward in her seat, gaze glued on the road that would take her to Apple House.

They weren't expecting her. She was supposed to return tomorrow, but she couldn't wait and took an earlier flight. So when the limousine pulled into the dirt parking area beside the fruit stand, everyone stared.

Her own gaze was rocked by the vibrancy and the abundance, the heaps of orange pumpkins lined on the ground like plump ginger cats, the sheaves of purple Indian corn hanging from the sides of the stand, the mounds of crimson, green, and rose apples overflowing crates, boxes, and hay bales. She wanted to inhale the sight, take it in as nourishment. Food to live on for a lifetime.

Quickly she scanned the faces, picking out the familiar ones. Rose looked puzzled, one hand paused in the act of putting apples in a paper bag. Trey wore a covetous expression, as though he would have given anything to see inside the car or better yet get behind the wheel. Mandy's eyes were wide with astonishment, and her jaw gaped open. Alex giggled. Her Manya didn't hide much. There was another face, too, not as dear as the rest, but growing that way. Shatiqua Williams shifted the baby snuggled against her chest and shaded her eyes with a hand.

Alex couldn't hold the suspense much longer. She opened the door and got out.

"Alex!" Mandy raced up and threw arms around her waist. "You're back! You're back!"

"My God," Rose said, coming toward her. "We didn't expect you until tomorrow."

"Caught an earlier flight," Alex said, still gazing around expectantly.

"I got your postcard," Mandy said. "I took it to school."

Trey was already looking inside the limo, so it was left to Shatiqua to get right to the heart of things.

She thumbed over her shoulder. "He's in the orchard," she said simply.

"I'll take you." Mandy grabbed her hand and pulled her.

"You'll pull her arm off," Rose scolded.

"And I need help with little Mac," Shatiqua said, separating Mandy and holding her back while she gave Alex a conspiratorial wink.

Alex mouthed a thank-you, and Shatiqua grinned.

"Trey!" Alex called.

He popped his head out of the car.

"Would you mind showing the driver how to get to the house and help him unload the luggage?"

"Would I mind?" A stunned smile creased his face. "Do you mean it?"

Alex laughed. "Of course I mean it."

"Can I take Mandy?"

Her heart turned over that he wanted to share such a treat with his sister.

Mandy drew in a breath and looked up at Shatiqua. "Can I?"

Shatiqua rolled her eyes. "You are the laziest child. Always looking for a way out of work." She smiled. "Go on. Shoo. Don't see how no baby can beat a ride in that."

Mandy gave a whoop and leaped inside the car.

"Go on now," Rose said, nodding to her left. "He's in the north section."

Alex wrapped her coat around her and took off. It was a long walk, made longer by dry-mouthed anticipation. Hopped-up, nerves jangling like keys on a ring, she still couldn't help noticing the trees, some already bare of fruit, others not yet ready for harvesting. She tramped over the earth, breathing in the sun-cooked smell of dirt and leaves, staring up into the canopy of branches for holes of blue sky.

Fifteen minutes later, the men came into view. Mainly Jamaicans hired for the harvest, there were ten of them with picking sacks, most on ladders. Big Mac was there, too, the ghetto gear he'd first shown up in—hooded sweatshirt and do-rag—now replaced by a ball cap that still managed to look reprehensible.

Her lips tilted in a half grin. When it became clear Hank would take months to heal, they'd scrambled to hire a farmhand. Hank mentioned McTeer, and though Ben had been leery of his inner-city credentials, Rose had been intrigued by McTeer's loyalty to his family and his effort to keep his employer out of trouble, even at his own expense. She asked Mac, Shatiqua, and the baby to come out for a visit, then a two-week trial. The two weeks had turned into months. McTeer was smart and eager for the steady paycheck,

Shatiqua for a stable home. In the end, Rose gave them Maureen and Tom's old house, and the new family swept out the memories by making new ones. Shatiqua proved invaluable with the children—Mandy was half in love with little Mac—and having lived through hard times herself, she was wise to Trey. The arrangement had worked for everyone, and it freed up Hank to do nothing but get well.

From behind a clutch of trees, she spotted him by the flatbed attached to the tractor, shifting apple bins. Her breath caught. Should he be doing that kind of heavy lifting?

He looked strong and straight, moved without the sad, hunched-over shuffle of the early days. She took a moment to admire him. Tanned and healthy again, he was the same strapping figure who'd entered her life the eve of her party for Renaissance Oil, or almost the same.

Another scar rode his body now. Another death escaped.

A quiver ran through her as she remembered the blood, the grim ride following the ambulance, the despair that even at the last Petrov would take someone else from her.

But Hank had lived. She knew it for the miracle it was, but it had shaken him. She'd seen it in the depths of his green eyes, the bewilderment, the gratitude, the uncertainty.

She knew about his crazy decision to leave the police force. Bob Parnell had been a frequent visitor to the hospital, and he'd worked out a deal with Rose, keeping Hank nominally on the payroll until he was well enough to confirm the decision he claimed he wanted to make.

Had he made it yet?

Hank's heart jumped when he saw her outlined against the trees. Feeling the pulse, he set down the crate of apples and ran a hand over his chest. That much-bruised organ still pumped inside him.

He'd had plenty of time to accept that fact of life. Plenty of time to recognize the gift and decide to accept it. What else could he do? He'd offered himself to the universe, and the gods had thrown his gift back at him.

He'd taken the bullet, and she'd lived. They both had.

He'd be an ungrateful bastard not to say thank you.

He put a finger to his lips, nodded toward the trees. She backed up, and he murmured to McTeer.

"Be right back."

McTeer peered at him from under the rim of his ball cap. Apple House was scrawled across the top and dusted with leaves and dirt. It hung low over his forehead and looked like it had lived there for years instead of a few months. "Take yourself a vacation. I got it under control."

Hank had to admit he did. Bonner's job corps had worked out better than expected.

He strolled off with slow, casual steps, though that thing inside him, the thing that refused to give up and stop beating, was thumping away like a wild creature.

She was waiting behind a thick stand of Macouns that wouldn't be ready to pick for another few weeks.

"Sashka," he said softly, drinking her in. "You're home."

"Excellent deduction, Detective. You work fast."

He reached for her face, tucked a stray piece of hair back. It slid through his fingers, smooth and satiny as cornsilk. "You don't."

She huffed. "I don't think a month is too long to change the world."

"I do." He leaned in, inhaling her scent, cool and sharp as a fall morning, and skimmed her lips. She sank against him, wrapping arms around his neck, enveloping him with her energy, her life force. He held her close, letting it warm him.

She spoke low in his ear. "So, Detective, how have you

been? Stalked any other suspects, uncovered any more secrets?"

"Only my own."

"Ah. Those are the best kind."

He pulled away to look at her. "You think so?"

"I know so. Take my own, for example. I thought bringing down Miki Petrov would make me happy."

"And has it?"

"There's a certain satisfaction, yes."

"But?"

"But now I'm at loose ends. I don't know what to do with myself." She peered up at him. "Perhaps you have a few ideas."

"I might." He thumbed over his shoulder. "This place could use an overhaul."

"I understood you've already hired someone to do that. Rose e-mailed me that next year McTeer wants to bring out a crew from St. Martin's Square so we won't have to import harvest help."

He caught the phrasing, and it set off a little earthquake inside him. "We?"

She looked at him calmly. "I believe that's what I said. Is it true?"

"About McTeer? Yeah. He's a real go-getter."

"So he's aced me out of the picture." She gave him a small, regretful shrug. "I had something else in mind anyway."

"I'm all ears."

She held his gaze steadily, her expression composed, her words direct. "I thought you might like to make an honest woman of me."

Something tightened inside him, a spring waiting to uncoil. "Don't you think I should make an honest man out of myself first? Get a job so I could support you in style."

"Well, I didn't want to mention it earlier, but I do have rather a lot of money."

He saw a gleam in her smoky eyes. "Could have fooled me."

"It's true. I'm rich. And I remember you saying once that you'd prefer to marry a rich girl."

He nodded. "This is true."

"So what's the problem?"

"I don't think I'd like being a kept man."

Instantly, Alex sobered. "No. I don't think you'd like it either." She touched his face, the rough surface sweet to her fingertips. "So where does that leave us?"

"Back where we started."

"Maybe you could get a job."

"A job." He turned that thought over in his head, just as he'd been doing for weeks. "Doing what?"

"What you used to do."

She said it quietly, but the air seemed suddenly weighted, fate turning once again. "Ah, Sasha Jane, you know me too well."

"Been talking to Parnell?"

"Says he's ready when I'm ready."

"And are you?"

He leaned against the tree, letting it support him. He felt as though he'd passed an enormous test, and now it was over. Yuri was behind bars in Attica. Petrov was dead and his thugs were out of their lives. Alex was safe.

With McTeer and his family solidly in place, Apple House was taken care of, and Ben had backed off on his push to sell.

Trey and Mandy had spent an uneventful summer and were settling into a new school year.

Everyone seemed to have found their rightful places in the cosmos. Wasn't it time to take his?

He looked at Alex. She was watching him carefully, trying hard not to show her deep concern. But he saw right through her. "It's not a job that's conducive to long-term relationships. Call-outs in the middle of the night, days away, lots of stress. Puts pressure on a marriage."

"Bob's been married for thirty years."

"Bob?"

"Lieutenant Parnell."

He narrowed his eyes in mock suspicion. "On a first-name basis with the boss, are we?"

She stood her ground. "I'm a VIP, Detective. I call everyone by their first name."

"So you and 'Bob' have been talking."

"He thinks we suit."

"Does he?"

"I do, too."

He nodded, understanding perfectly. "You're ganging up on me."

"All we need is a little luck."

The word spiraled inside him. "That's what I'm afraid of."

"Why be afraid of what you can't control?"

"I can control whether or not I play."

"Well, my life has been one huge lucky streak since you walked into it."

"How do you figure that?"

"You saved my life twice. Once at the house and once at the cabin. You uncovered my secrets and helped me do the one thing I've wanted to do for thirteen years. You showed me that a family is possible, and I don't have to walk alone anymore. You make dreams come true, Detective."

He smiled to himself. She made him sound like Walt Disney and the Good Witch of the North rolled into one. "I don't know. It's risky."

"Life is risk, Hank. I love you. Be with me. Marry me. Take one more chance. I promise it will pay off."

"A million to one odds."

"The kind I like. How do you think I made all that money?" She took his hand, kissed it, and laid it along her cheek. "Stick with me, Detective. I've got all the luck you'll ever need."

Her words struck a chord deep within. Maybe it was her luck that had gotten them through.

Or maybe luck had nothing to do with it. Maybe it was just her. Alone, he stumbled through the universe in endless confusion. Things only worked in tandem. Together. With love.

Who knew? No one. It was all a big question, the answer a choice we make. She was right. Life was risk. But it was a risk worth taking. *She* was a risk worth taking.

He wrapped his arms around her and pulled her close. "Countess, you've got yourself a deal."

Author's Note

Tell Me No Lies was inspired by actual events. In 1991, the entire treasury of the Soviet Communist Party did indeed disappear, and two of its treasurers threw themselves out of windows within six weeks of each other. The Russian government hired the international private detective firm Kroll Associates to find the money, but after several months and a cost of nearly a million dollars they hadn't found a trace of the missing cash. The Russians then turned to the U.S. intelligence community for help. But a high-level White House group refused to let them intervene, calling the money's disappearance "capital flight," a normal part of any country's economic risk.

The money's whereabouts remain a mystery.

About the Author

A native New Yorker, Annie Solomon has been dreaming up stories since she was ten. After a twelve-year career in advertising, where she rose to Vice President and Head Writer at a midsize agency, she abandoned the air conditioners, furnaces, and heat pumps of her professional life for her first love—romance. An avid knitter, she now lives in Nashville with her husband and daughter. To learn more, visit her at www.anniesolomon.com.

More

Annie Solomon!

❧❧❧

Please turn this page

for a preview of

BLIND CURVE

available in mass market

in 2005.

1

The night was too damn cold to be out on the streets. The tall man with the knit cap draped low over his forehead hunched inside his green army jacket and stamped his feet to keep warm. A two-day growth of beard stubbled his face and dark, greasy hair hung beneath the cap. His name was Danny Sinofsky but on the street he was known as Turk, short for "turquoise," the color of his eyes.

He stood near a burned-out streetlight, just half a block from the west side projects. An abandoned grocery store hulked on the corner. Somewhere out there, hidden in the shadows, was the gun he planned to buy.

The seller was late, and Danny cursed silently. His neck bothered him. Two nights ago he'd been popped in the head during a routine drug sweep in the Dutchman's Tavern, and the cold was making it ache.

His cell phone vibrated against his hip.

"Yo," Danny said quietly.

"What's up, uncle?" the voice on the other end said.

"My date is late."

Footsteps approached.

"Catch you later, dude," Danny said.

The seller rounded the corner. Fifteen at best, he was scrawny, dressed in hip-hop mode with chains and a tracksuit hanging on his lanky form. The kid swaggered confidently toward Danny, who groaned under his breath. The young ones were the worst. You never knew what they'd do. And that was dangerous.

Danny didn't waste time. "You got it?"

The seller eyed him suspiciously. "Maybe. You got the dough?"

"Two hundred. Cash. That was the deal."

"Yeah, but I don't know you, bro. And I don't do business with peeps I don't know."

Christ. Danny tightened his jaw. First the guy was late, then he started giving attitude. Forcing himself to relax, he stuck out his hand. "My name's Turk. Ah, shit, no it ain't." He grinned sheepishly. "It's Danny. But don't you go telling no one."

Slowly, the seller shook his hand. "Danny, huh. Now that's about the whitest name I know."

"We friends now?"

The seller shrugged. In the dim moonlight his skin looked creamy and smooth, no trace of a beard. Danny tasted sadness. Kids with guns.

"Yeah, okay, Danny," the seller said.

"So where is it?"

"Not here. I got it stashed."

Silently, Danny cursed. Changing locations was not a good idea. It meant his ghosts would have to follow in the backup car. If they could, and sometimes they couldn't.

Or it could mean a setup: take the money and run. And he had a lot of money on him.

But an illegal gun was a gun, and he wanted it. He could already smell the steel. The town of Sokanan had had a rash of drive-bys and armed robberies, which meant too many weapons were bloodying the streets. And they had a tip from the Firearms Investigation Unit of the NYPD. Of course, New York City would have a whole unit devoted to getting illegal guns off the street. Here in Sokanan there was only the five of them in the Neighborhood Recovery Unit. And they recovered a whole lot more besides guns. Drug dealers. Users. Prostitutes. Johns.

"You bring it here, bro. That's the deal," Danny said.

The kid took a step back. "Fuck that shit. I ain't risking it. Cops all over the place."

"It's here or no place."

"Then it's no place, man." The kid started to turn around.

Christ. "Hold up!"

Going somewhere else sucked big time, but so was letting a gun loose on the street. You never knew what it would be used for and innocent bystanders could end up hurt or dead. The latest victim had been a three-year-old girl.

"Where we going?" Danny asked.

"I'll take you."

"I gotta know where first." If he could alert his ghosts they would have a better chance of keeping tabs. But the night was not going Danny's way.

"It's a sweet little secret spot. I got a car waiting."

The kid didn't look old enough to drive. Fuck. "Okay. I gotta have that piece."

"Yeah?" The seller led him around the corner to an old rusted Buick LeSabre. "You got a job in mind?"

Danny gave him a long look. Questions were never appreciated during these deals. "Never mind what I got in mind. I got the cash. That's all you need to know."

The seller nodded, fifteen going on fifty. "You got that right."

Danny got into the car, fingers tingling, adrenaline pumping. He imagined Parnell popping his cork when he found out. He almost grinned, picturing his lieutenant's face.

The car wheezed down Market Street toward the railroad tracks by the river. A century ago this was the commercial heart of Sokanan. Barges from Manhattan traveled up the Hudson and off-loaded at the dockside warehouses, filling up with light manufactured goods and produce from the Hudson Valley farms. Freight trains did the same, going west.

Now the place was deserted, though the upswing in business from the Renaissance Oil deal had started talk of renovating Warehouse Row into a shopping mall on the lines of Faneuil Hall in Boston.

But all that was down the line. Right now the place was dark and dusty.

"So where are we?" Danny asked, feeding clues to his ghosts. Finelli and Bayliss better be hearing every word coming through his hidden wire. "Down by Warehouse Row?"

"You got eyes, don't you?"

The seller pulled off the main drag onto a narrow path heading west toward the Hudson. The car bumped over old cobbles, then parked in a dirt yard fronting one derelict warehouse. Moonlight bounced off the river, creating shadows and gloom. Faded yellow letters at the top of the brick building spelled out its name. Danny could make out an "M" and a "C."

"McClanahan," Danny murmured.

"What you talking about?"

Danny nodded toward the warehouse. "The building. See the 'M' and the 'C'? I'll bet that was Mc-Clanahan's."

"Who gives a shit?"

Danny didn't tell him.

He got out, scanning the area. Murky and abandoned. No way backup could get there without being noticed.

His palms were sweating but he followed the seller toward the looming structure. He did not want to go into that warehouse.

"Where is it?" Danny asked.

"Inside."

Shit. "Go get it. I'll wait here. That place gives me the—"

The warehouse flickered in front of him. For a second he was in complete darkness. He stumbled, almost fell.

What the f—

A gunshot popped above him where his head would

have been. Someone grunted and his vision cleared. In that split second he saw the seller down on the ground.

Danny dove behind a Dumpster as a second shot chased after him.

"Rounds fired!" he shouted into the hidden wire. "I'm behind a Dumpster by the old McClanahan's warehouse."

His cell vibrated. He grabbed it. "You got the location?"

"We got you, uncle."

Danny looked around. It would take time for the ghosts to get there but less than that to die. The shot had come from the warehouse roof. An excellent position; it gave the shooter coverage of the entire grounds while Danny was pinned down, no vest, no weapon, just a fistful of cash.

Trapped, he banged the back of his head against the Dumpster in frustration. A shot pinged off the edge and instinctively he ducked.

The young seller lay unmoving on the ground beside the Dumpster, the soles of his Nikes to the sky. Was the kid carrying? It wouldn't surprise Danny. In any case, he couldn't leave him out there, wounded and exposed to the shooter.

He crawled to the edge of the Dumpster, reached out a hand, and got shot at for his trouble.

Shit.

He snatched back his hand, took a breath, tried again. This time he managed to latch on to one of the boy's feet. He dragged the body toward him. It jerked as another bullet hit.

When the boy was behind the Dumpster, Danny rolled him over. His eyes were wide open and a black circle decorated the middle of his forehead.

Fuck. Who the hell was out there?

No time to think about it. He patted down the body and found a fully loaded .38. It wouldn't do much good against the high-powered rifle the shooter had, but it was better than nothing.

He peered around the edge of the Dumpster, and once again his vision sputtered out. He blinked and cars squealed into the area, sirens screaming. Doors slammed, shots fired. Bayliss over the bullhorn, "This is the police! Throw the rifle down!"

Then another voice over that. "Sin! Where are you? Sin!"

Hands shook him. "Jesus Christ, what happened?" It was Finelli, his other ghost. "Sin? You all right?"

"Yeah, I'm fine. Except I can't see a fucking thing."

"It's called cortical blindness," the neurologist said, her voice so calm and matter-of-fact he wanted to deck her. He didn't know how long he'd been in the hospital, but it felt like years. He'd been shuffled between doctors and technicians who were a mush of voices with no faces. Now he sat in some kind of armchair; he could feel the shape and the fabric. And from the quiet and lack of movement around him, he sensed he was in a private office. And this doctor—Christ, he couldn't even remember her name—was telling him . . .

"You're kidding. One minute I'm fine and the next minute I'm fucking blind?"

"You had a stroke."

"I'm thirty-two and healthy as a horse. Guys like me don't have strokes."

"I understand you were hit in the head two days ago."

"In my line of work I get hit a lot. What the hell does that have to do with anything?"

"You injured your neck," she said gently. "Tore your vertebral artery. That's the one right at the top of your spine. The tear allowed blood to seep into the arterial wall. The blood formed an embolism. Clotted. The clot traveled to the top of the basilar artery, the main artery at the back of the head. It went from there to one of the posterior cerebral arteries and fragmented, plugging up your cortex."

"Yeah, but why can't I see?"

"Because the messages from your eyes can't get to the cortex, which is where they're interpreted. It's called a bilateral occipital stroke."

The words slid over him like fog. His heart was thudding wildly, his mouth was dry. He wondered if he'd been shot at the warehouse instead of his companion and this was a coma dream from which he would eventually wake.

"Detective Sinofsky?"

"Yeah."

"Do you have any other questions?"

He hesitated, feeling lost, adrift. "Am I . . ." He cleared his throat. "Am I dreaming?"

There was a short pause. "No." She spoke the word quietly, with compassion and complete certainty.

He nodded, dread gripping him. "Any chance this will go away?"

Another short pause. "It's possible. There have been cases of it clearing up on its own."

"But?"

"But the damage is extensive. I wouldn't count on it. I'm sorry." He heard the sound of her rising, the swish of clothing, the creak of a chair. "I'm going to set you up with a social worker. She'll get you into rehab. You'll need a mobility instructor."

He sat there, not taking any of this in. A gentle hand touched his shoulder. He flinched.

"How are you getting home?"

He had no idea.

"Are you married?"

He shook his head.

"A girlfriend? Parents, relatives?"

His parents were dead and he didn't want to dump this on his sister Beth.

"I'll, uh . . . I'll call a friend."

He'd been in and out of his clothes, his eyes and his head poked and prodded, his body X-rayed. But now he was back in his street wear—the ripped jeans and ancient army jacket that belonged to Turk. Fumbling in the huge pockets, he found his cell phone. His fingers searched the buttons for the correct ones, but his hand was shaking.

Gently, someone took the phone from him. "What's the number?" It was the doctor.

He swallowed. His brain had stopped and it took a minute to start it again. But he remembered the number at last and told her. A moment later she handed him the phone.

Mike Finelli's voice came on the line, an anchor of familiarity.

"It's me," Danny said, desperate to keep the tremor out of his voice.

"Sin, where are you? I've been at the hospital all day and they keep saying they're doing tests. What's going on? Are you okay?"

Not really. But he wasn't ready to get into that. "I need a ride home."

"Beth's here. I think she's got that covered."

A phone rang and he heard the doctor speaking softly into it.

"What about the kids?" he asked Finelli.

"I don't know. They're not with her."

"All right. I'll call Beth on her cell and tell her where to meet me."

"She's right here—"

A hand touched his arm. "Hold on," he said to Mike.

"Mr. Sinofsky?" A bright, cheery voice. "I'm Pat Embry. I'll be taking you to the waiting room where your mobility instructor will meet you."

"They're taking me somewhere," he told Mike. "I'll have them call Beth when I get there."

"If you'll just stand for a moment," the cheery voice said. He pictured a short, big-bosomed woman with tightly curled hair—an Aunt Bea type—but her hand, which she kept on him, was bony and smelled of disinfectant.

"Just a few steps," she said breezily as if he were three years old. "Here's your chair."

He felt the leather sides of a wheelchair and something tightened in his chest.

"That's right. Good boy. Comfy?"

His hands fisted.

"Okay, here we go."

They'd all warned her about him. Everyone from the supervising social worker to the nurse's aide had given her a sharp-eyed look, a cautionary word.

But she didn't need a warning because she remembered him.

Someone had wheeled him into the patients' lounge, and he'd managed to find his way out of the chair. One arm propped against the wall, he faced the window as though drinking in the night.

His jeans were outrageously worn, faded and ripped. After fourteen years she thought his wardrobe would have improved. His black T-shirt, at least, was in much better shape. The sleeves strained over well-defined biceps. A man's biceps, to match a man's body. Tall and rangy, he had wide shoulders that tapered down to a lean waist and a tight rear. A jungle cat. Strong, healthy. Young.

She stepped into the room and his shoulders stiffened. He had heard her.

"Detective Sinofsky?"

He turned and hit her with the full force of his face. Even prepared, she nearly gasped. Age had given him lines and hollows, hardened him into an adult. But he was still dark and intense, with a face born of movies and fashion spreads. Of dangerous dreams deep in the night.

Far away, deep in the recesses of her soul, something stirred. An echo of an echo, so thin and faint it was easy to pretend she hadn't heard it.

His eyes were deep-set and still piercingly turquoise. Clear and transparent as the Caribbean. And healthy-looking. No injury marred the lids or sockets. Nothing at all to signal they were useless.

"Danny Sinofsky?"

"Who wants to know?"

She swallowed, glad he couldn't see the shock and pity she couldn't hide fast enough. Would he have recognized her? Half hoping, half dreading, she steeled her voice into the safe rhythms of brisk objectivity. "Martha Coleman." She waited just the merest second to see if her name jarred memories, but he stared expressionlessly at her and she doused the flicker of disappointment. Why should he remember her? She'd been invisible to him then. "I'm a rehab teacher and an O and M instructor—Orientation and Mobility. I'd like to talk to you about your options."

"Options?"

"We can get started with a cane immediately. But there are other things to think about. A dog. Even some electronic devices."

His face—tough, impossibly handsome, shadowed by stubble—darkened even more. "Get lost." The expression was eerie because it looked as though he could really see her. "I'm fine."

Not one for false comfort, she opted for bluntness as a way to cut through the anger. "You're not fine. You're blind."

He tensed, coiled muscles waiting to spring. "It's temporary."

"Maybe."

"Definitely." His jaw set, his expression hardened.

She looked at his paperwork. Cortical blindness due to a stroke caused by a neck injury. A freak accident but not unheard of. The internal damage had been extensive; there wasn't much hope he'd see again.

"Look, detective—"

"Are you still here?" She remembered the rough-edged boy with the smile that could break hearts. The man he'd grown into scowled at her.

"I know this has been a shock but—"

"I told you to get lost. My eyes are fine. A few days and this will all be a bad dream."

"I hope so but—"

He took a threatening step in her direction. Despite his handicap, she instinctively moved back.

"Something wrong with your hearing? Get the fuck out of here!"

She inhaled a breath, let it out slowly. Sometimes shock therapy was the only way to get through a shock. "You want me to go? Why don't you come over here and make me."

A flash of panic crossed his face, quickly followed by fury.

"I'm right here," she said, using her voice to indicate her position in the room. "Throw me out."

He leaped at her like a caged tiger. But instead of bars, the darkness held him back. He ran into a row of chairs. Bolted to the floor, they didn't budge and he went flying backward, struck a low-lying coffee table, spilling the year-old magazines onto the floor. Cursing, he cleared the table and banged his head against a post holding a magazine stand. By this time he was completely turned around and would have headed off in the opposite direction, but she ran over, put a hand on his arm just above the elbow.

His arm was hard and powerful, intensely masculine. The feel of it beneath her fingers sent a jolt through her system, made her nervous and jittery. And yet he flinched. His whole body shuddered with rage.

Quietly, she said, "Even if you're blind for only a day, you should learn to get around without breaking your neck."

"Fuck you."

"Not likely, but if you'd like to try rehab, my number is 422-2222. Easy to remember. 422-2222."

He shook off her hold as a man hurried into the room. "Sin?"

Danny turned to the sound of the new voice.

"It's Parnell, Sin. How're you doing?" said a lean-faced man with silver hair.

"Terrific." The tone said otherwise.

"Look, can we sit somewhere and talk? I want to go over the investigation."

Panic surged into Danny's face again.

"To your left," Martha said quietly. "Nine o'clock. Three steps over."

Resentment tightened his mouth into a grim line, but he followed her instructions and found a seat without mishap.

Parnell looked from her to Danny and back again. "I interrupt something?"

She shook her head. "We're done for now." She turned to Danny, who sat stone-faced. "Again, 422-2222. All twos, detective. Except for that four in the front."

She left him. Half of her hoped he would call. The other half hoped he wouldn't.

THE EDITOR'S DIARY

Dear Reader,

They say blood is thicker than water. But what happens when love is thrown into the mix? Find a comfy chair because you're not going to want to put down **TELL ME NO LIES** and **ONCE A BRIDE**, our two Warner Forever titles this April.

Romantic Times calls **Annie Solomon** "a powerful new voice in romantic suspense" and it's easy to see why in Annie Solomon's latest book, **TELL ME NO LIES.** Alexandra Jane Baker has a secret. Thirteen years ago, her father jumped out of a window after being accused of embezzlement. Everyone called it suicide, but Alex knows the truth—it was murder. So she's set a trap to catch the man who murdered her father and she won't let anyone stand in her way—not even Hank, a homicide detective. To Hank, this is a textbook open-and-shut case . . . until he discovers a trail that leads directly to Alex. Beautiful and wealthy, she arouses his suspicions and stirs his desires. But as a new lead surfaces, uncovering a ruthless predator, Hank must break every rule and cross every line to protect Alex . . . before it's too late.

Moving from the skyscrapers and the hustle and bustle of New York to the rolling hills and the intrigue of 13th century England, we present **ONCE A BRIDE** by **Shari Anton.** *Rendezvous* raves that "Shari Anton creates a spell that keeps her readers captured" so prepared to be ensnared. Eloise Hamelin's life has been one nightmare after another. First her betrothed dies on the church steps. Then her father flees after being charged with treason. Worst of all, the king places her home in the hands of Roland St. Marten, the one knight she loathes and the one face burned into her memory. Roland is not exactly pleased with this assignment either. But his loyalty lies to the King and Roland must follow orders. Yet as sparks fly and their clashes become even more heated, Roland is drawn to her loyalty and fire. Any love between them would ruin him, but how can he turn his back on this irresistible woman who wants only to clear her father's name?

To find out more about Warner Forever, these April titles, and the authors, visit us at www.warnerforever.com.

With warmest wishes,

Karen Kosztolnyik, Senior Editor

P.S. Spring is here and that means love is in the air! So don't get left behind—grab our two Warner Forever titles this month. **Kathryn Caskie** pens a sexy and hilarious historical about a woman determined to avoid marriage and her two equally determined aunts who hatch schemes using an old military guidebook in **THE RULES OF ENGAGEMENT**; and **Melanie Craft** delivers a romantic screwball comedy about a woman who's helping her reporter friend get the inside scoop from a millionaire who's out to convince this respectable woman to pose as his fiancée in **MAN TROUBLE**.